The Necklace from harleem

The second book of Seeds of Balhok

By
Rick AW Smith

COPYRIGHT

The Necklace from Harleem, Book 2 of Seeds of Balhok, by Rick A.W. Smith

© 2018 by Rick A.W. Smith. All rights reserved.

No part of this book may be reproduced in any written, electronic, recording, or photocopying without written permission of the publisher or author. The exception would be in the case of brief quotations embodied in the critical articles or reviews and pages where the publisher or author specifically grants permission.

Although every precaution has been taken to verify the accuracy of the information contained herein, the author and publisher assume no responsibility for any errors or omissions. No liability is assumed for damages that may result from the use of information contained within.

Cover Design: Joel Ray Pellerin.
Map Design: Joel Ray Pellerin
Publisher: Kindle Direct Publishing Amazon.com Inc., CreateSpace, a DBA of On-Demand Publishing, LLC

Copyright registration number TXu 2-064-338
ISBN: 9781982984625

10 9 8 7 6 5 4 3 2 1

1. Fantasy, Science Fiction

First Edition, Printed in USA

Books written by Rick AW Smith

Seeds of Balhok

    Book 1 The Dream from Balhok

    Book 2 The Necklace from Harleem

    Book 3 The Caves of Balhok

The Gifts of Balhok

    Book 1 Balhok Departed

    Book 2 The Oracle of Pesh

Dedication

To my deceased mother ... a gentle soul ... ever concerned about her family ... even now.

Table of Contents

Books written by Rick AW Smith 4
Dedication 5
Table of Contents 6
Planets 8
Races 8
Cities and Villages of Storlenia (country north of the Southland Mountains) 9
Cities and Villages of Shaksbah (country south of the Southland Mountains) 9
The Guilds of Storlenia 10
Major Characters in "The Necklace from Harleem" 11
Preamble 13
Chapter   1 - Benekee's Dream 1
Chapter   2 - It isn't junk 4
Chapter   3 - The new Guild 8
Chapter   4 - We have a problem! 16
Chapter   5 - Bernado's gift 20
Chapter   6 - Can you see what I see 23
Chapter   7 - The proposal 31
Chapter   8 - Protas in Training 36
Chapter   9 - The Medallion 43
Chapter 10 - Going Home 50
Chapter 11 - The Test 58
Chapter 12 - The cabin rendezvous 63
Chapter 13 - The Mines of Tenleth 68
Chapter 14 - The village of death 77
Chapter 15 - Pass the wine 85
Chapter 16 - A delusional mind 94
Chapter 17 - Benekee's Hunting Device 103
Chapter 18 - A blinding flash of Light 111
Chapter 19 - A barn with a view 121
Chapter 20 - Jalek's funeral 128
Chapter 21 - The brother of Protas 136
Chapter 22 - Aram-Dentee 141
Chapter 23 - The Shard of conflict 149
Chapter 24 - Gaeten by any other name 156
Chapter 25 - Far-tel 161
Chapter 26 - The little green stone 168
Chapter 27 - The Waterless Well 174

Chapter 28	- A dark discovery	180
Chapter 29	- The fall of Mister Glickin	186
Chapter 30	- Tainted blood	190
Chapter 31	- The Future Emperor of Ankoletia	193
Chapter 32	- The Executive Command	200
Chapter 33	- The Future Queen of Ankoletia	202
Chapter 34	- Benekee in chains	208
Chapter 35	- Ranoof is missing	216
Chapter 36	- The Healers	221
Chapter 37	- The Black Wind	228
Chapter 38	- The Circle is severed	234
Chapter 39	- Biskin hunts Protas	240
Chapter 40	- Protas the Advisor	248
Chapter 41	- Sleepwalking in the enemy camp	256
Chapter 42	- The slaughterhouse dog	261
Chapter 43	- The bargain of a lifetime	269
Chapter 44	- The man from Harleem	275
Chapter 45	- Pheasant and conspiracy	283
Chapter 46	- The Regent of Shaksbah	288
Chapter 47	- Escape to the Crestal Mountains	296
Chapter 48	- The misfits	302
Chapter 49	- The gathering	309
Chapter 50	- The three-day death	315
Chapter 51	- The Stones meet	322
Chapter 52	- Benekee's plan	326
Chapter 53	- The apple of his eye	329
Chapter 54	- Where in the world is Chitouf ?	340
ABOUT THE AUTHOR		345

Planets

Ankoletia, a planet in the same Galaxy as Balhok and Harleem. Inhabited by two races, Storlenians in the north and Shaksbali in the south.

Balhok, a planet of Seers, located in the Middle of the Galaxy.

Harleem, a planet populated by a predatory race, located on the far side of the Galaxy.

Races

The Seers of Balhok

The Plunderers of Harleem

Storlenians, living in the northern hemisphere of Ankoletia (otherwise known as the country of Storlenia)

Shaksbali, living in the southern hemisphere of Ankoletia (otherwise known as the country of Shaksbah)

> The El-Bhat, living in the far southern reaches of Shaksbah, are a warrior group feared by the other Shaksbali. Their way of life is to plunder. They are known as Brothers of the Silk and are ruled by The Quorum.

> The Sherilin, an ancient and extinct Shaksbali tribe, lived on the eastern plains of Shaksbah before the Great War. They found the first Waterless well and the Dagger of Truth, which draws its power from the Green Necklace of Harleem.

Cities and Villages of Storlenia (country north of the Southland Mountains)

Arborville, home of the Tracking Guild that produces Olleti, north of Seven Oaks.
Border Pass, Tracker fortress in the Southland Mountains
Borit Betoon, Redemption Guild that contains ancient relics
Breckenden, home town of Benekee
Cradle Mountains, the location of the Cave. These mountains form the eastern edge of the Lithgate Wilderness, a large tract of forested area, north of Dead Rooster Junction
Crestal Mountains, area famous for its crystal. Along its borders lay the villages that spawned the Trackers.
Cross Rivers, town of Shu-len and his son Haybin, Blacksmiths
Lithgate Wilderness, location of Urshen's cabin
Mantel, Urshen's family town
Pechora, residence of Bernado (Guild Master of Pechora's Tracking Guild)
Pirtelin, Main headquarters of the Financial Guild
Qar-ana, Capital city of Storlenia
Seven Oaks Redemption Guild, Redemption Sanctuary, north of Border Pass
Tinker Village, established by Braddock, close to Arborville

Cities and Villages of Shaksbah (country south of the Southland Mountains)

Chitouf, El-Bhat village close to the Southland Mountains that contains the El-Bhat gold, in brick form.
District of Denlen, southern Shaksbah, where the El-Bhat Quorum live
Kel-eetan, capital of Shaksbah
Mines of Tenleth, Gold mines operated by the El-Bhat for the government of Shaksbah
Toobor, city populated by immigrant Storlenians

The Guilds of Storlenia

Accounting Guild
Astronomy Guild
Blacksmith Guild
Communication Guild
Financial Guild
Hospital Guild
Hunting Guild
Mechanical Guild
Medical Guild
Planning and Development Guild
Precious Metals Guild
Redemption Guild
Roads and River Management Guild
Sea Shipping Guild
Sporting Guild
Tinker Manufacturing Guild
Tracking Guild
Transportation Guild

Major Characters in "The Necklace from Harleem"

Aram-Dentee, an Assassin from the Butler Guild, hired by Craslin
Axion, Head Guild Master of the Planning and Development Guild at Qar-ana, the Capital city of Storlenia
Bellaroos, Guild Brother at the Redemption Guild of Borit Betoon that found the Waterless Well
Benekee, young Guild Brother at the Redemption Guild of Borit Betoon (repository of ancient relics)
Benton, Urshen's father; Assistant Guild Master for the Roads and River Management Guild
Bernado, Head Guild Master of the Tracking Guild of Pechora, he replaced Petin
Biskin, Tracker from Arborville with a Gift for smelling trouble, Assistant to Mitrock
Braddock, Leader of a Tinker Wagon Train and Zephra's father
Bru-ell, Braddock's Assistant
Craslin, Assistant Guild Master of the Planning and Development Guild at Qar-ana, the Capital city of Storlenia
Deema, one of the Circle who believes that Urshen is 'the One'
Ee-lath, Shepherd boy, rescued by Protas
Far fel, Special Assignment Tracker, assigned to hunt the Silent Reaper
Finn, Gatherer of the Special Assignment Trackers
Fre-steel, Tracker sent to Pechora by Pahkah of Border Pass, to work for Bernado
Glickin, Head Guild Master of the Financing Guild, town of Pirtelin
Haybin, Blacksmith at Cross Rivers, recruited by Urshen to help build the Tinker Guild
Jalek, Ferrier for the Tracking Guild at Pechora. Carries a knife he refers to as *Hunger*
Jokta, long-time Tracker friend of Axion
Kareen-hys-Tebeel-del-Harleem, goes by Kareen-del-Harleem; from the planet Harleem
Mitrock, Assistant Guild Master of the Tracking Guild at Arborville.
Ou-Leesen, El-Bhat Leader who escaped the devastation at Border Pass. He is assigned to take gold into Storlenia to buy Guild positions for the El-Bhat
Pechinin, Guild Master of Tracking Guild at Arborville, sent twelve Trackers to protect Urshen at Border Pass
Protas/Robe Man, Friend of Urshen and adopted brother to Ee-lath
Ranoof, Tracker who doesn't like wine, Tracker in Tal-nud's half-Circle

Shanteef, El-Bhat Quorum Leader, rules from The Keep in southern Shaksbah

Stek, Tracker hypnotized to believe he had joined the El-Bhat movement

Tal-nud, team Leader of the twelve Trackers who make up the Circle, whose mission is to protect Urshen

Toulee, woman Tracker with a Gift to hypnotize; one of the twelve Trackers who make up the Circle

Urshen, first Seer in a thousand years, carries an Amulet that is the Key to the knowledge and power of the Garden

Velinti, Urshen's mother

Wutherstop, Inventor, works at the Mechanical Guild at Breckenden, hires Benekee as his Assistant

Yaneek, sister to Benekee, doesn't believe in the power of Benekee's Shards

Zephra, a Tinker Wagon Mechanic, daughter of Braddock

Preamble

Previously ...

Urshen's simple life at the Sporting Guild was all he ever aspired to ... until the premonitions began. Just when he was sure they had stopped, he had "The Dream" which left him with an unquenchable desire to find the "Key".

Driven by this remarkable experience, he left the Sporting Guild, moved into a cabin in the Lithgate Wilderness, and waited for the Garden to speak to him. Instead he felt premonitions again, warning him of danger. But before that danger would reveal itself, five years past ... and Urshen discovered the Cave. With the Amulet in hand, he entered the doorway to the Crystal Garden he saw in his Dream. When he left, he knew that the Garden, and its tremendous power, were brought from a planet called Balhok.

Before he could receive further instruction, Protas showed up at his cabin. Terrified, Urshen returned to his family, intent on sharing his knowledge of the Crystal Garden and his concern regarding Protas.

Protas returned to the Lithgate Wilderness, with hired thieves, convinced that Urshen knew the whereabouts of the legendary Lithgate diamonds. Even though they were outnumbered, Urshen and his father battled successfully to protect the Amulet ... but their efforts left Urshen with an arrow through his chest and others dead.

Healed inside the Cave, Urshen continued his wilderness life, while Protas escaped to a remote Redemption Guild, where he hoped to search the Archives and find out more about the power of the Amulet. With the Assistance of Brother Ott, he succeeded.

Unknowingly Protas returned to Urshen's cabin with a disguised El-Bhat, who called himself Brother Retlin. Later as the three approached the Cave, a planned struggle broke out, leaving Protas near death's door, Urshen seriously wounded, and the disguised El-Bhat dead.

The healing experience of the Amulet took Protas back to his childhood where he remembered who he really was. Abandoning his recent life of greed and corruption, he stayed with Urshen until he made an incredible discovery! The Robes, worn by both Brother Retlin and Torken (another El-Bhat) were identical ... because they came from the same Redemption Guild ... the Seven Oaks Sanctuary ... just north of Border Pass.

Concerned that the Shaksbali infiltration into Storlenia involved more than two El-Bhat, Protas and Urshen travelled south hoping to find allies. Eventually they met up with a Train of Tinkers. Urshen agreed to share advanced wagon technology for a ride south. Over the next few weeks, Urshen fell in love with Zephra, built the new Tinker wagon with the help of a Blacksmith called Haybin, while Protas convinced Braddock the Wagon Master and Bru-ell his assistant, that their story had validity.
Prior to the celebration of the new 'Tinker Wagon', Urshen told Protas where other Caves were located and taught Zephra how to use her White Bauble.

Meanwhile, Jalek (the Ferrier working for the Tinkers) overheard the Tinker's plan to defeat the El-Bhat. He escaped south, anxious to share this information with the disguised enemies at Seven Oaks Redemption Guild.

Encouraged by the passionate assistance of the Tinkers, Urshen, along with Bru-ell, headed north to Arborville, hoping to add the Trackers to their short list of allies.
While there, Pechinin (the Head Guild Master) saw that his buried suspicions about inconsistencies among his men, were correct.
He launched a complete purge of his own Guild using Olleti, the Tracker truth serum. Satisfied that his own house was in order, he sent Urshen, disguised as Brother Retlin, to Border Pass with twelve of his most trusted Trackers. Tal-nud, the Leader of the group of twelve, became convinced that the Fates wanted him to preserve Urshen in this war against tyranny, at all cost. So he decided to tell Urshen about Toulee, a woman Tracker who had a Gift of hypnotism. She had been assigned by Pechinin to kill Urshen if his capture was at risk.

But things didn't go well for Tal-nud's group. All the Trackers were thrown into prison by Fre-steel, the Commanding Officer of the Trackers at Border Pass. He had joined the El-Bhat movement to purge Storlenia of its corruption and promised to kill the twelve if they did not switch loyalties.
Urshen was required to take the Olleti test, and failed on his pronunciation of Ehrlesk Vhrestisin, part of the oath to the Quorum. And as a result, he was also thrown into prison, soon to have his hands cut off for impersonating an El-Bhat.

Not far behind the twelve Trackers, the Tinkers, with horses drugged by Jalek, headed for Seven Oaks, to lure the El-Bhat into an ambush at Lundeen Forest. They would be assisted by Trackers, hiding in the forest at Bridge over the Narrows.

Successful against the El-Bhat War Wagons, they buried their dead at Lundeen Forest and then headed for Seven Oaks to find it empty of El-Bhat. But it wasn't completely empty ... an Assassin waited to kill Braddock. Instead, the deadly dart took Zephra through Death's door until her White Bauble snatched her from death's embrace. The next day, the contingent of Tinkers and Trackers headed for Border Pass, hoping the Gates had been left unlocked by Urshen and the twelve Trackers.

Meanwhile, Deema, an Assistant to Pahkah of Border Pass (the El-Bhat Leader) had been secretly waiting for 'The one' and was convinced that Urshen was the prophecy of his father's dream. He secretly helped Urshen and the other Trackers escape to the east Plateau, with plans to unlock the Back Gate. But by the time they realized that the El-Bhat trapped them on the abandoned Plateau, the forces from Seven Oaks had entered the Butcher Block.

Unable to leave the Plateau, Urshen and the Trackers formed a Circle of blood, allowing Urshen to expand the range of the Amulet's reach, to help the efforts of the Tinkers and Trackers, trapped in the Butcher Block, and failing under the barrage of the catapults.

However, because of Urshen's Circle and Zephra's White Bauble, a Wind was sent through the canyon, hurtling the enemy of darkness into the valley of death ... except for a small group of El-Bhat who escaped southward.

Chapter 1 - Benekee's Dream

Five years before Zephra met Urshen – Benekee, a young man, had a dream

Are we touched by the Fates ... ever?
Would they come to us if we are not ready?
Are we best prepared when we have descended into our dreams?

All good questions that Benekee had never considered. He was only fifteen and like his parents he was an unbeliever. But those comfortable thoughts were shattered by a dream in the middle of the night ... that spoke of his future!

He awoke, trembling and sweating. The dream was ... unexpected. He wondered if he should call his parents, but instead he searched for a pen and began to write. He wanted to capture his feelings before the dawn woke him to a world of forgetfulness.

I was wearing a Robe ...
When the sparkling Fragments called to me with their rush of Light!
Do they know my name? Do they tease me with their power?
Perhaps both.

Have they come to me because I was born belonging to them? Or were they sent that I might see clearly ... this wasteland to which I have surrendered?
Perhaps both.

In my Dream, the Fragments pulled me ... like the bottom of a hill as I tumbled downward.
But if I leave the comfort of my wasteland, will I know where to go?
Yet somehow, I do know, and the road is long ... but jubilant.

When I arrive, tears wet her face. She too has lived in a wasteland.
It has been four years since we parted.
If I tell her of my Fragments ... will she understand why I was born?
I tell her ... time passes, and she doesn't.

As I hold the Fragments, they promise to push back the wasteland that has come to my door.
Then on a different road ... a rush of Light
And she believes!

    He laid the pen down. He blew on the paper to dry the ink. It was the strangest experience he had ever had. It was like seeing one's future from high in the sky while you were spiralling to the earth ... trying to understand what you were seeing.

    He tried to capture the experience the best he could. Even the words seemed strange as he read what he had written. He shook his head, despairing at his confusion. He read it again. He was beginning to see some clarity. He could remember seeing his sister Yaneek in his future ... strange since they weren't particularly close. He read it again.

    Something about Fragments was floating at the edge of his mind. He read it again.

    Robe ... Light ... and Fragments. He seemed to understand that these words, would change his life in an immeasurable way. He read it again.

    And finally, he understood that something happened to create a four year gap. Something he wasn't supposed to know just yet.

Before he went back to bed, he hid away the record of his dream ... comfortable in the thought that he would never forget. But soon he would forget everything. The dream, and where he had hidden the written record.

But the Shards never forget.

Chapter 2 - It isn't junk

Four years later
Borit Betoon Redemption Guild
Country of Storlenia, World of Ankoletia

To one man it was all junk. To another, it was the finest collection of ancient relics under the Storlenian sky. After four years of toil, Benekee still hadn't changed his mind ... it was *all* junk. He had only come here at the insistence of his sister, following their parents' death. But today, an unsuspecting Benekee would have to re-evaluate what he thought.

He was assigned the dusting and preservation of relics on the third floor – west wing – and had decided to take a little rest, while standing in front of a collection of crystal shards. The tag in front of the display was barely readable.

These broken pieces are the remains of what used to be a powerful talisman from the Great Age.
Probably used by a Seer

"*Probably* ... written by the guy who sold them to our Guild," he grunted. He shook his head in misery as he considered his sad situation. A Brother of Redemption dedicated to preserve and investigate relics, that he was sure were utter nonsense.

He leaned against the rail, wondering why he couldn't seem to leave the Guild. "But what else can I do? I have never been trained to ..."

Startled by the sudden intense light, his hands flew up, as his dusting brush travelled through the air to someplace behind him. His bulging eyes stared in shock as the bright glow began to dim. As soon as the Shards returned to their lifeless state, he gingerly stepped forward and touched them. Cold and lifeless ... nothing to confirm his experience. But he had to grin at the irony.

"A thousand years of waiting, and the one to finally witness a relic's power, happens to be the *unbeliever*," he whispered to himself. As the significance of what just happened began to settle in, he felt compelled to carefully scoop up the Shards and raced down the corridors to the office of the Guild Master.

For a couple of weeks, Benekee and another Brother, were assigned to watch the Shards. After they excitedly reported another two occurrences of brilliant Light, the Head Guild Master was ready to take their discovery to the seat of power.

"Benekee, we leave Borit Betoon tomorrow for the Central Office of the Guild for Planning and Development. As we travel, I will advise you of what you can say."

"Qar-ana ... I have never been to Qar-ana!" he excitedly responded.

"Benekee ... you have never been anywhere. Make sure you have the shards. And pack for rain."

A few weeks of wagon travel found them at the enormous steps of the Central Office, the seat of ultimate power in Storlenia. They had come early in the morning to share their exciting discovery.

Benekee was staring at the massive columns that guarded the flight of stairs when the gold embellished doors at the top, suddenly opened to reveal a hallway, wider than two wagons. "Looks like they're open for business," he excitedly said to himself.

All visitors requesting audience with the Head Guild Master, were screened for suitability. A full day of filling out forms, waiting, and then interviews, finally granted them entrance into the office of the *Assistant* Head Guild Master.

"You have come a long way. It is appropriate that our screening staff have seen fit to give you an audience. So ... shall we begin?" With practiced ease, Craslin's eyes scanned the report, extracting the relevant information. "Your papers say that you wish to discuss a matter concerning an ancient relic. Not surprising, considering your Guild is the single repository, for *all* ancient relics." He closed the file and looked at the Guild Master, waiting for a response.

"Yes ... well, the distance is nothing if we can serve the people by what we bring to you this day." He cleared his throat. "As you said, we brood over thousands of relics from the Great Age and study them, hoping to glean valuable information that might serve society. Weeks ago, while Brother Benekee," he turned and extended his arm in the direction of Benekee who was standing politely by the door, "was performing his daily duties, one of the relics began to glow ... without any provocation," he added, hoping to stress the significance of what they were bringing to the Planning and Development Guild.

Now suddenly interested, Craslin waved for Benekee to come forward. "Are you ready to certify – on penalty of imprisonment – that this is indeed what you saw?"

While keeping one eye on the conversation, Benekee was using the other to study the magnificence of the Guild trappings, until he was interrupted and waved forward. Walking timidly he held the leather pouch tightly under his Robe. He paused for the right words. But the Assistant Head Guild Master was an impatient man.

"Well, did you see this relic glow, or didn't you?" He reached for their file, ready to discard it, if the answer was unsatisfactory.

Suddenly Benekee felt an unusual confidence. He took another step forward and said in a strong voice, "Actually, three times, and the last time, it glowed especially bright."

"Thank you Benekee," his Redemption Guild Master said with a nod, which indicated he could return to the position by the door.

"I assigned Benekee, with another, to continue to watch this Amulet. I wanted to see if we could confirm the first viewing by other viewings. We were successful and that is why we are here today. As you can see this phenomenon is very ..."

"Yes, yes," he cut him off impatiently, "you were right to report this. Did you bring the relic?"

The Guild Master looked over at Benekee again, with a questioning raise of his eyebrow.

From the time Benekee boldly spoke of the Shards, he was sure he could feel warmth coming from his pouch. 'Power ... I am feeling its power!' he contemplated, when the Assistant asked him the question. "They are stored safely back at the Guild," he lied.

The Guild Master was sure he had asked Benekee to bring them. Never mind, he would deal with Benekee later.

"They? There is more than one?" the Assistant asked.

"No. The original talisman was broken into many pieces, this is what Benekee means."

"So ... the relic is *broken*?" Craslin said with visible irritation. Relaxing back into his large leather chair, his demeanour changed to one of disinterest. "Why would you waste my time to talk about a *broken* relic, regardless of its ability to glow? Do you not know that certain fish glow, and the correct mix of powders will glow. So why ..." The Assistant closed his eyes and rubbed his forehead in exasperation.

"Good Master, it is not the shards themselves that we have come to report, it is what this incident could mean to your Guild," he said, as he nodded in humble submissiveness.

The Assistant Head Guild Master laid the papers down. 'True ... those glowing shards could hold a valuable secret ... if properly understood,' he considered, as his eyes went from Benekee to the visiting Guild Master. Craslin walked to the large windows to gaze out on the beautiful, manicured gardens as he considered his decision. Smiling, he turned around. He decided to grace his guests with his brilliant analysis. "What would make the old relic glow in the first place, if not the operation of another of its kind? A Talisman that is *not* broken!"

The Redemption Guild Master offered another submissive nod.

Craslin was satisfied that this was news he wanted to take to the Head Guild Master. Pleased with himself he rubbed his hands together, while returning to the chair that reminded everyone of his power. Craslin had skills ... it was why he sat in the Assistant's chair. 'But imagine having access to an Amulet of power,' he thought. He would make sure that the Head Guild Master placed the full responsibility of bringing this Amulet to the Head Office ... to him. "You have done well in bringing this to our attention. I will discuss this with the Head Guild Master as soon as he is free. You will be rewarded. How soon can you return with these glowing Shards?"

Chapter 3 - The new Guild

Previously. The Wind invoked by Urshen and the twelve Trackers, cleansed the darkness at the Butcher Block, killing most of the El-Bhat

Sometime later

Border Pass, Southland Mountains

Working their way from the eastern plateau, down to the bottom of the trail that opened onto the Butcher Block, Deema had listened carefully as Urshen explained what had happened on the plateau. The implications of Urshen's power were staggering. 'The Guilds must never know what he is capable of,' thought Deema. 'But that must be why he has been endowed with the *Circle*. Together, we will protect the Seer!'

Approaching the bottom of the trail, Tal-nud searched the narrow canyon for signs of Mitrock, the Tracker in charge. When he was sure he wasn't there, he looked for The Commander. Once spotted, he motioned the group to a halt as they positioned themselves protectively around Urshen.

Below them the Trackers and Tinkers were busy gathering the dead into two groups. "Must be at least two hundred dead El-Bhat," Tal-nud spoke to the group. "Add that to the Band at Seven Oaks, and the Shaksbali Trackers we discovered at Arborville, and we're looking at over three hundred. And my guess is that this number is not the only acorn that fell from the tree."

"Protas would agree," Urshen said, wondering about his friend.

"Protas?" Tal-nud asked, having never heard the name before.

"It was because of him that all of this started. He was the one who saw what no one else could see."

Encouraged, Tal-nud decided it was time to say what was really on his mind "If the Seer believes that our work is not finished ...

then we need a new plan," he said quietly, his eyes following The Commander as he escorted a woman across the canyon floor. The Commander stopped at a wounded Tinker, surrounded by other Tinkers. Tal-nud assumed this man was the Tinker's Leader. "Isn't that Zephra," he asked, recalling the name from their experience on the Plateau.

Urshen turned and caught sight of Zephra hurrying toward Braddock, her injured father. "Yes ... and I want all of you to meet her. Without Zephra, this success would have been impossible."

"We know," Deema said respectfully. "It would be an honour to meet her. But Tal-nud is right. Now that we have defeated *these* El-Bhat, we must carefully consider what we do next." He turned to Urshen and waited until he had his attention. "I suggest that we meet The Commander," Deema continued, "to discuss our next move ... and how we communicate *this*," his hand swept the canyon before them, "to the Planning and Development Group."

The group understood Deema's concern. The Governing Guild must always think that all power resided with them. This meant that certain things must be kept secret from *that* Guild. If knowledge of Urshen's power ever got out, the *Circle* would be hard pressed to keep him free ... never mind protecting him.

"What do Trackers normally do in a situation like this?" Urshen deferred to Tal-nud.

"*Normally*, we don't communicate much to the Planning and Development Guild. Only simple messages to keep them abreast of our activities. But *this* ... we will need to send a proper report to Qar-ana, and they will still have lots of questions ... it cannot be helped," he cautioned Urshen.

"They obviously cannot know about Urshen's power," Toulee emphasized, having spent years carefully guarding her own secret.

"Perhaps when we meet with The Commander, we can discuss what will be *in* this report ... and what will be left *out*," Deema suggested.

"It would be interesting to know what they think happened," Tal-nud added.

Suddenly the *Circle* went quiet as everyone turned to Urshen ... waiting for instructions.

Panning the group, Urshen remembered that they needed to do something about Toulee ... still wearing her black silk outfit. "Deema, until we can get Toulee back into a Tracker outfit, she will be your prisoner. Take half of the men and tell Zephra we wish to meet in private to discuss what happened in the Butcher Block. It will take her some time to finish taking care of the wounded, but when she is finished, bring her to the prison cell ... I will be waiting. Give us some time together before you enter." Urshen looked at Tal-nud. "Take the rest of the Trackers, inform Mitrock and Braddock that we were trapped on top of the east Plateau ... and invite them as well."

"I didn't see Mitrock," Tal-nud advised Urshen. "Perhaps he is among the dead. If I cannot find him, I will inform The Commander."

As soon as they left, Urshen headed for the prison cell.

Sitting against the cold stone, he could hear faint echoes of those who believed in him, as he rested chained to the wall, not many days ago.

It's only a guess but you might consider using your Amulet.

.. I felt in these circumstances they needed to know how our commitment to protect you has escalated

Urshen smiled. Without others, he would have failed long ago. He turned his thoughts to the future. It helped him endure the wait.

The rusty hinges told him she was coming. He stood as the door opened, the outside light outlining her perfect silhouette. For a moment, they both stood staring at each other in the darkened room. It was so quiet he could hear his heart beat as it hammered inside his chest. "Zephra," he whispered, and then rushed to hold her in his arms. He smothered her with kisses, holding her close, knowing that he never wanted to leave her again. Then he gently held her face in his hands as he stared into those golden flecked obsidian disks, his heart bursting with gratitude, knowing that she was still alive, and she was here with him!

"Urshen, we almost all died. I thought you might be dead. But it was you that saved us, wasn't it?" She said through trembling lips as she buried her face into his shoulder.

He stroked her black hair. "We were all saved by the power of the *Cave*, not me. And ... coaxing that power to destroy our enemies involved Toulee, myself, twelve Trackers ... and you."

"Me? ... Who's Toulee?" she added, as she pushed away to look into his eyes, wanting to know who this other woman was.

'Of course, the only thing that matters right now, is knowing about this other woman,' he smiled to himself. "Toulee? Zephra, I think it's time to introduce you to the entire team. And then we need to discuss our next move with your father. And whoever is commanding the Trackers." But he decided, that could wait another moment, as he pulled her close and smothered her with more kisses.

Then he heard a knock. "Let's continue this later," he smiled, as he headed for the outside door. "Thank you for coming," Urshen said, while holding open the heavy iron door. The twelve Trackers entered first, followed by The Commander and a blood-stained Braddock.

As everyone filed into the dark room, the Twelve Trackers were particularly interested in Zephra. One by one they all went to one knee as they introduced themselves, gently took her hand, kissed it, and said, "It's an honour to meet the Wielder of the Stone of Fire."

Braddock and The Commander exchanged looks, uncertain as to why the Trackers assigned to Urshen were behaving in such a manner.

Urshen stood back, just as surprised, and waited for the Circle to finish.

Zephra's first instinct was to reject the honour. But they were so … overcome to meet the person who held the Stone of Fire. She decided to humbly accept the attention. When the last of them retreated to Urshen, she sat against a wall, anxious to hear what the men had to say about their next move.

"How many of our people died?" Urshen started the conversation.

"Nineteen," The Commander volunteered. "A lot less than we thought … the way things were going."

Tal-nud wanted to know what the Commander thought had happened, so he said, "We saw scores of dead El-Bhat. Can you tell us what happened."

The Commander looked over at Braddock, hoping he could help him describe the strange event.

"Don't look at me," Braddock protested, "I was busy lying in my own blood." Braddock knew that Zephra was involved, and that was something he wasn't going to discuss with anyone!

"Alright. There was a Wind … hurricane force … that suddenly roared through the Canyon," The Commander offered. "It appears that we escaped because we were so low to the ground. But the El-Bhat were high up and felt the full force of the Wind. Except a small group … who escaped. About two hundred El-Bhat died, including nineteen of our force. The wounded have all recovered."

"Sounds like a report summary. Is that what you plan to send to Qar-ana?" Tal-nud questioned.

The Commander looked at the Trackers in the room as he prepared his response. "As you know, it's Tracker policy to never report what we do not understand ... or what we wish to keep secret." He looked over at Zephra. "The last two days I saw someone come back from the dead. And then she healed the wounded as fast as they were bloodied by the catapults. I only report what is easily understood ... and leave the other alone."

"What will the Trackers do next?" Urshen asked.

"My orders are to re-establish the force here at Border Pass, then return with the remainder of my men to Arborville."

"And then what?" Urshen was sure there would be more.

"Then we will begin our visits to every Tracking Guild across Storlenia. With a healthy supply of Olleti. We must first clean our own house." The Commander remembered something that Mitrock had said about Urshen. "And ... what will you do?"

"Spend some time with the lady who came back from the dead," he grinned, looking at Zephra, "and then find my friend Protas."

The Commander was disappointed that Urshen decided to tell him nothing. "Sounds like retirement."

Feeling the rebuke, Urshen looked at Braddock and The Commander. "First, I want to convince a Blacksmith that he needs to help the Tinkers establish their own Guild. Next, I am anxious to visit with Pechinin. I want to know what he thinks about Seven Oaks and Border Pass. And I will ask him for his counsel."

"Glad to hear you're still in the game," The Commander replied. Turning to Tal-nud, The Commander continued. "Now that your assignment is finished, I assume your task force will be coming back with me?"

"But our assignment *isn't* finished. There were special instructions regarding Urshen's safety. He must never fall into enemy hands."

"I see. Well ... it's time for me to take my leave." He walked towards the door but stopped and placed a hand on Braddock's shoulder. "Oh yes. There will be something else in my report. Honourable mention of the Tinkers who fought valiantly from Lundeen Forest to the Front Gate of Border Pass. Especially those who gave their lives."

The Commander then turned to Deema, "What is *your* name?"

Deema looked at Urshen who nodded encouragement. "Deema. I am from Toobor."

"It's good to have you back on our side," he said. And then he left.

"That worked out well." Tal-nud breathed a sigh of relief.

Zephra was playing with her Bauble as she watched The Commander leave. She remembered when it flared to life as the Wind howled towards her in the Canyon. And how Urshen included her in the list of those who helped invoke the terrible power that swept the enemy from the Ramparts. "Now that *that* part is taken care of," she began, "I need to know what actually happened. How you managed to use the power of *my* Stone." She was looking directly at Urshen, her mind swirling with recent memories of reminding her father that she was a Tinker's Boon. After all, she had experienced the power of the Stone as it twice turned her into a killing machine, strengthened their horses so that they could outrun the El-Bhat, and healed men as they writhed in agony, damaged from the catapults of the canyon. Her life had changed so fast since she met Urshen. But if the power wasn't hers, where did that leave her as a Tinker's Boon?

Urshen felt that the situation needed a measure of diplomacy he didn't possess. Leaning against the wall he said, "Deema, why don't you tell Zephra what really happened up on the Plateau."

Deema had been studying her Amulet noting how much smaller it was than Urshen's. He looked up at her and began. "I have never seen this kind of power before. And *never* imagined that I would have the privilege to touch it. And to think that with it, we were able to destroy the El-Bhat! The last time power like this was mentioned in our history, was ... over a thousand years ago. And even then, despite technological enlightenment, it was not understood and feared by many. How long have you had your Amulet?"

"Since I was a young girl. It has been passed down since the Great War. Tell me about the Plateau," she said with a hint of impatience.

Deema sighed. "My plan was to climb the trail under the cover of darkness and eliminate the El-Bhat on the Plateau. So the way to the Back Gate would be free from an overhead attack. Little did we know that it was a trap. They allowed us to climb but we found no El-Bhat. We couldn't come down, and we were too far away, for Urshen to use his power. That is, until he discovered that he could extend the range of his Amulet if he joined his blood to our Tracker blood. And it almost worked. We were so close but we were still powerless. Until we saw you in the Vision, calling out to Urshen. Because of this ... he was able to add the power of your Amulet and connect to the power. Because of you … we are all still alive." Deema knew he wasn't finished, she was still frowning. "I know it's good manners to ask before using someone else's property. But sometimes, it isn't possible." He looked at her with entreating eyes, and then added, "We are deeply sorry, if we have offended the Wielder of the Stone of Fire. We hope you will forgive us."

Deema's sincerity was overpowering. The anger that she felt a moment ago, disappeared. She was wrong to feel possessive about the White Bauble's power. She looked at the group. "The Wielder of the Stone of Fire is … humbled by your commitment. I have learned something today. And hope in the future, to be worthy of your praise."

Braddock was ready to bring up his question. "Urshen, what's this about the Tinkers setting up their own Guild?"

"When I was at Arborville, we were interrogating a spy. He was a Storlenian from Shaksbah. We asked if the other spies from Shaksbah had been given assignments of infiltration other than as Trackers? And the answer was *Yes*."

Braddock's eyebrows furrowed in concentration. "This expands the problem immeasurably! But what does this have to do with a Tinker Guild?"

"It means that we will need the help of Tinkers everywhere. But *not* as itinerant wanderers. But as another respected Guild. This will provide unity for all Tinkers. And respect from people everywhere. And power that will be recognized and accepted by the other Guilds. Only then will our efforts to fight these infiltrators be united."

Zephra, extremely curious and not wanting to miss a word, slipped closer towards her father.

"I see," said Braddock hesitantly. "I need to convince my people to 'settle down' after being on the move for a thousand years." He tugged at his gold earring as he looked over at his curious daughter. "But you're right. It's time we considered this change. And I think it can work. You mentioned a Blacksmith. Does this mean we are about to build wagons?"

"By the hundreds," Urshen responded.

"But … the wagon design you came up with, belongs to the Blacksmith shop that made them," Braddock protested

"I guess I will have to produce a *different* design. And that's where Haybin comes in. He has a unique talent for being able to take an idea and turn it into fashioned steel. Besides, we need someone to teach Blacksmithing to Tinkers. Of course, we need to find out if he agrees. So that's where I am heading next."

As Braddock contemplated the magnitude of those plans, his life experience reminded him that this was never going to happen unless ... "I need to catch The Commander," he said, as he bolted out of the prison.

"Commander," Braddock called, spotting him in conversation with another Tracker. The Commander heard him and turned.

"As you know, Urshen is proposing that the Tinkers start up their own Guild." Braddock hesitated. It was still hard for an old Tinker to ask a Storlenian for help. "Perhaps ... you could help us find some land to set up our own Guild," Braddock said hopefully.

The Commander's gaze drifted to the Tinker's blood-soaked tunic. "Of course. I know some people who can help. You know where to find me."

Chapter 4 - We have a problem!

Everyone emptied the prison, leaving Urshen and Zephra alone. She held his face in her hands, "You have made me a happy girl ... again! Imagine ... a Tinker Guild." She wanted to laugh aloud with excitement, but instead she pushed him against the wall and started kissing him furiously, as her lips began to burn with desire.

Urshen was a bit surprised at the sudden passion, but it felt wonderful as he surrendered to her love. Suddenly, he pushed her back, his hands firmly holding her shoulders. "Zephra ... I ..." he panted, lost for words.

"Yeah ... I know ... guess we uhh ..."

Gazing into the eyes that would always hold his heart, he stood there and held her until the fire had burnt itself out. "Let's go outside and discuss this new Tinker Guild."

Urshen invited Zephra to go with him to enlist Haybin. But the idea of being in on the planning stage of the Tinker Guild was too exciting to pass up. "You take your 'bodyguards' and bring Haybin back to Arborville. And I will go with my father to help him enlist whoever can assist us, in getting started." She gave him a quick kiss goodbye.

He smiled as he watched her scurry off to find Braddock. 'Strong like a rock,' he mused, knowing that he couldn't have walked away from her so easily.

"Our success began here," Urshen told Deema, as their wagon filled with Trackers rumbled into Cross Rivers. Then he thought of Zephra and smiled as he recalled how she had introduced herself to this bustling town.

They had just arrived at the Blacksmith shop and there she was, staring down the massive Haybin, with her hand resting on her lariat. Haybin never knew how close he came to a whipping!

He remembered his abduction and how she left two trouser-less ruffians by the river, as they pulled away, leaving them wagon-less!

Then there was the remarkable 'healing' between Haybin and his father Shu-len. He never would have guessed that Zephra could have so easily mended those two hearts.

And the wonderful memory of a gleeful Zephra, holding the reins of the 'improved' wagon as they left Cross Rivers.

Haybin was working the bellows when Urshen came through the door, followed by a dozen Trackers. At first sight, he left the bellows and excitedly walked towards Urshen, but halted as the room began to fill up with Trackers.

Urshen grinned and simply said, "Meet my new friends."

Tal-nud stepped forward with hand extended, "It's a privilege to meet the Blacksmith that rebuilt the Tinker wagons. Never thought it was possible that Tinkers could out-race a War Wagon. You helped us defeat an entire Band of El-Bhat!"

Soon the Trackers were swarming around Haybin, to shake his hand or pat him on the back. They had learned about Haybin from Braddock as they waited outside the prison for Urshen.

"Where is Shu-len?" Urshen asked Haybin as the Trackers began to disperse.

Haybin looked at the Trackers. "We need to talk. Urshen, won't you join me in the back room?" Once in the back he gave Urshen a blacksmith-style hug. He thought the Trackers might stay at the front of the shop, but it seemed that they needed to follow Urshen everywhere. "It's a wonderful surprise to see you again, but I have to confess. I wasn't expecting you to make an entrance like this," Haybin said, as he took a better look at the group that had invaded his shop. "Please, have a chair," Haybin insisted as he leaned against the drawing table, taking a moment to organize his thoughts. "My father is not here. He is off to visit the Blacksmith Guild Headquarters." Sharing this information was an obvious worry for Haybin. He looked down at the slat board floor before continuing. "Urshen, you were right about so many things. You tried to help us understand that we *needed* to share this new technology. But we saw the gold. As soon as you left, we fitted our own wagon with your changes and then father took that wagon to the Guild to secure the patent." His eyes stared at the floor again.

When they came up, he continued, "Blacksmith shops prosper when they have a closely guarded skill, or secret. But, the Guild only tolerates minor improvements. You can wander within those limits, improve things here and there, but if it's something big ... the Guild wants to retain complete control. My father was confident that he could secure the rights of your improvements. Because he believed the Guild would rather approve those changes than admit that they didn't understand this new technology. But as soon as he rolls into their yards with our wagon," Haybin sighed, "what a stir that will create! Who wouldn't want to own one of these new wagons. Faster, safer, and more comfortable! The potential royalties for the Guild are enormous. More Blacksmiths will be needed. The Blacksmith Guild could rise in power and importance. And my father thinks he can trick the Guild." Haybin grunted as he shook his head.

"Urshen ... I'm telling you this because I am concerned for you. It won't take them long to find out that it was not our talent that brought this new knowledge forward. Eventually my father will have to tell them. And then, you will be ... hunted down."

The Trackers glanced around the room at each other.

Urshen had been listening carefully to Haybin. He was impressed with how well the Blacksmith understood the challenges facing them. And how his attitude had changed since the last time this discussion had come up. "Well, thank you for your concern," Urshen said unperturbed.

Haybin nodded *you're welcome*, but he could see that Urshen had something else on his mind. "So ... what brings you here to my shop?" he asked.

"Haybin ... someday people will call this little shop the birthplace of the Age of Knowledge! I returned because I was curious to know how your work was progressing ... and to recruit. I am looking for a Blacksmith to help set up a new Guild." His eyes were locked on his friend.

Bushy eyebrows shot straight up. "A *new* Guild? But ... I only know Blacksmithing."

"That's exactly what we need. The Tinkers will start a new Guild based on building wagons that I will design ... new and improved."

"Better than your previous effort?" Haybin was already grinning.

"Yup, but I need you to convert these ideas into steel. Are you ready for a new career?"

Haybin laughed and shook his head, hardly believing what he was about to do.

Urshen turned to leave, then stopped. "Haybin, we will come by in the morning to help close up your shop. You focus on your goodbyes ... because you will be gone a long time." He smiled and walked outside. When Urshen began to pull himself into the wagon, he noticed the warmth of the Amulet and stood down. He looked around to spot anything obvious. It was Deema. He looked troubled. "Deema is something wrong?" Urshen said, as he walked in his direction.

Deema looked up and said, "I feel guilty. If you hadn't sent Stek away, he would be in this Circle of Brotherhood instead of me. If we ever find Stek ..." but Deema wasn't sure how to finish his thought.

The woman moved close to Urshen. Sure that she had heard something about Stek. She felt a chill go through her.

Urshen's imagination considered a multitude of possibilities. All bad. He turned towards Toulee. "You know, I don't remember seeing Stek as we gathered up and left."

"Oh, I thought you knew," Deema offered. "Stek was successful in delivering the message to Seven Oaks. And the El-Bhat chasing him were dispatched on arrival. But the next morning when they gathered to leave, Stek was gone."

"Was Mitrock among the dead?" Urshen needed confirmation.

"Apparently he headed north with Protas and others, after the battle at Lundeen," Tal-nud interjected.

Urshen turned back to the woman with one of those 'uh-oh' looks.

They nodded at each other, but it was the woman who said, "We ... have a problem!"

Chapter 5 - Bernado's gift

Previously. A hypnotized Stek asked to see Pahkah of Border Pass to deliver a message from Brother Retlin. After passing the Olleti test, Pahkah sent Stek to Pechora to find the location of the Cave

Running down the corridor, the man burst through the office door of Bernado, Guild Master of the Tracking Guild at Pechora. Breathing heavily, he said, "There is a Tracker at the gates ... he gave me this ... sealed by Pahkah himself."

Bernado examined the paper document. "Bring him in," he commanded, truly surprised.

The dust of several days travel shook itself loose into the streams of the office window sunlight as Stek walked confidently towards the desk of Bernado. The Guild Master was studying the man ... a first of his kind. All the El-Bhat-recruited Trackers, up to this moment, were pressed into service from the Storlenian community located in Toobor, south of Border Pass. They served the purpose of infiltration, but they weren't Trackers. So their usefulness was limited. He could count the authentic Trackers on one hand that had joined the El-Bhat movement. Petin his predecessor, Pahkah's pet dog Fre-steel, himself ... and now Stek. All assigned to find the Cave of Cradle Mountain!

'Pahkah always was clever. Appointing a genuine Tracker for work like this is perfect,' Bernado thought. The document had indicated that Stek was category three. Already subjected to Olleti. Impressive! But still, there was something different about this man. Was it his composure, his confidence ... or something else? Bernado was truly intrigued. "When you are finished with this assignment, we must talk," Bernado expressed with enthusiasm. "You come highly recommended by Pahkah. Not an easy accomplishment. Now, before you begin, we need to talk about what we know about the Cave of Cradle Mountain. There is a classified file that requires my signature so if you will excuse me; I need to go to the archives."

The Guild Master returned with a folder. "Unfortunately, the information we have about this Cave is somewhat incomplete." He opened the folder. "I have always wondered if it was more legend than fact," he said quietly to himself. "These papers begin with a report – filed by my predecessor Petin – of a small group that organized a search for a lost diamond bed. Petin had already formed a strategic alliance with a man by the name of Torken, an 'investor' from Shaksbah. The most interesting thing about this diamond bed, was that a previous hunt was attempted many years ago, reporting a brilliant light and strange deaths. This is why Torken was so agreeable to fund this group with Shaksbali money. The facts suggested that this diamond bed ... was actually a Cave." Bernado paused to see of Stek had any questions. He didn't, so he continued.

"It started well, but one day Torken and Petin were found dead in his home. Three of the group we funded, including a Tracker-for-hire, were also reported dead and buried in the forest. We needed to find the Leader, Protas. We believed he might possess knowledge about the Cave. But the first attempt by Trackers and a later effort by an El-Bhat to find Protas were unsuccessful. The two surviving team members were thrown into prison. Eventually, other Shaksbali 'investors' moved in to replace Torken and their first task was to question the two prisoners. But El-Bhat can be overzealous. The two men didn't survive."

Stek nodded, indicating that Bernado should continue his narrative.

"The final note in the file concerns Protas. He was convinced that a hermit – living in the forest – knew where the bed of diamonds was located. So the funded team searched for this hermit. But he had help, resulting in the deaths that I mentioned. I have the coordinates of the cabin where the hermit lived. A good place to start. Report back as soon as you have information regarding the Cave. And finally, you are instructed to find it. But don't enter the Cave! You may be excused."

But Stek didn't leave. He stood there as though he were trying to sort something out. "Why were the Shaksbali 'investors' invited to this Guild?" Stek finally asked.

"The Guild needed funding for expansion. And the Shaksbali provided the money because they hoped to establish better relations with their northern neighbours," Bernado added. "Stek, you have come a long way. You must be tired and hungry. My Assistant here will show you to the dining hall and help you settle in."

After the evening meal, Stek went to his room, but he was restless. He got up and wandered the halls, poking his head into open office doors until he was convinced that the person he was looking for wasn't there. In his room, he laid on his bed, staring out the window. He felt troubled … at war with himself.

What Stek couldn't know was that there was an unavoidable conflict between the mesmerizing instructions planted in his mind and the strength of his Tracker blood.

It was late. The candle was getting low as Bernado pulled out his journal. He wrote,

Today was an exceptional day. The El-Bhat have succeeded in recruiting a Tracker from the Tracking Guild at Arborville, the source of Olleti production. This has great future potential.

He walked into our Guild today, with an assignment to find the Cradle Mountain Cave. The El-Bhat are obsessed with these Caves. Finding one would bring me great fortune.

His name is Stek and he seems very confident. With the skills and immunity that the Trackers possess, I am sure he will succeed.

Chapter 6 - Can you see what I see

Previously. Prior to the battle at Lundeen forest, Mitrock gave Benton his Medallion. It was intended to open the door of Tracker's hospitality at the Arborville Guild. With the Medallion safely tucked under his shirt, Benton headed north, guided by the night-time lightning

The rain was heavy. Benton encouraged the horses towards the lights of Arborville. His thoughts were centered on his son. He was sure Urshen was involved in the state of affairs he had just left. Over a hundred Trackers meant that the situation was serious, and it could be weeks before they returned to their Guild, to take him south to find his son. Entering Arborville Benton decided to pass by the Guild and find an Inn at the next town. He was anxious to get home.

Over the next few days, the lonely traveller frequently found himself talking to his horses as he contemplated his situation. "You are probably wondering why we didn't stop at Arborville like I planned. You see, there are times when the current of life carries you along, and then there are times like now, when it's necessary to get out of the river and portage to a different river."

He flicked the reins for something to do. "In other words, sometimes you need to change your mind about something."

After a while he wanted to talk again. "What would you do if you were me? Would you be concerned? You see my problem ... is that I almost lost my son once. I saw first-hand, the danger his new life brings. And without me, he would have died."

"But ... he *is* a Seer and that means he has access to the power of the Cave. You know, I have been inside the Cave. The most remarkable experience of my life."

He paused, listening to the sound of horses hooves pounding the road. "Yes, I know. Why would I worry if he's actually a Seer. And I *have* seen the power of the Cave preserve his life once already."

He waved to a passer-by, and when he couldn't be heard, he resumed his monologue. "I suppose that one of my problems, is that I don't see what my son sees. Urshen has tried at times to get me to look 'further'. He has even suggested that this power was transported from another civilization. One living out in space. Unlike me, Urshen isn't handicapped with short-sightedness at all. Then there's the letter about Protas. And the mission that my son and his former enemy have embraced. You haven't met Protas but let me say ... he is very clever ... and very dangerous. And now," Benton waved his hand in the air showing his frustration, "apparently, he is Urshen's best friend! Would you be worried?"

He used the reins to flick the flies away from the horses. "Let me guess. You think I ought to consider the instinct of a Seer? I suppose you are right ... even though Urshen is still very young," he added emphatically.

He watched a large eagle soar overhead. "If you are right ... and I should stop worrying about my son ... I still have my family to be concerned about. What a terrifying day that was when they abducted Pateese, my youngest. Protas broke her arm. It could have been worse. And all because they wanted something from Urshen. As his power and influence increase, don't you think my family will only become more of a target?"

He sighed. "But what should I do? Should we start a new life? Change our names? I guess I could find a new Guild to work for ..."

Benton found it hard to imagine giving up the benefit of his experience, and quite frankly, he liked what he did. He thought back to Urshen's brave decision to leave the Sporting Guild.

"Unfortunately, his enemies are very powerful with many resources," he continued. "I wonder if we would ever be safe. And then there is the promise I made to Velinti that I would talk to our son. Come to think of it, how am I going to tell her that I haven't even *seen* Urshen?"

One of the horses whinnied. "Yes, I know. I worry too much. But then again, you don't know Velinti like I do!"

The Necklace from Harleem

Deema suggested they board the wagons and find a private place to finish their discussion about Stek. Outside of Cross Rivers, off the road, Deema, Tal-nud and the others gathered around Urshen and Toulee. "Tell us about Stek," Deema started, anxious to assist the Tracker whose place he had taken in the Circle of Brotherhood.

But before Urshen and Toulee could respond, Tal-nud explained. "Stek was unusually resourceful, perhaps he is taking care of something that came up."

Urshen looked at Toulee as he began their joint confession. "We needed to be sure Stek would make it to Seven Oaks ... and deliver the message that we would have the gates unlocked."

"So, I used my Gift," Toulee continued, "to convince his mind that he had made an oath to Retlin, to tell Pahkah that there was a Cave, which needed to be destroyed. Then to seek instruction from Pahkah. I presume that Pahkah gave him instructions to find the Cave and report back to him." She looked to Urshen to continue.

"This way, we were sure he would pass the Olleti test and complete his mission. And it worked except for one thing," Urshen paused waiting for Toulee to continue.

"I told him that when he met Mitrock, he would come out of his trance ... but Mitrock was already gone." The woman shook her head at the bad luck.

"If he has no idea where the Cave is, we can track him, find Mitrock and bring them together," Tal-nud reasoned.

"Except he probably *has* a fair idea," Deema added, having overheard enough from Pahkah to put the pieces together. "You see, years ago, gold was smuggled into Storlenia by El-Bhat, to fund an expedition of six Storlenians, searching for an old diamond bed. The El-Bhat cared little for diamonds, but the legend about a shining light and suspicious deaths, sounded too familiar. They thought it might be another Cave. They assigned an El-Bhat to work closely with a disloyal Guild Master in Pechora, to monitor the progress of the search. Unexpectedly, these two were found murdered in the home of the Guild Master right after the expedition was aborted. Of the original six, the reports claimed three dead, two in prison and the disappearance of the Leader. Those in prison knew nothing and Protas the expedition Leader was never captured. It is my belief that if the El-Bhat are resuming their hunt for the Cave, Pahkah would have sent Stek to Pechora," Deema concluded with confidence.

Urshen was slowly shaking his head, as though expressing an inner dread.

"You know something you need to share?" Deema probed.

"The first thing Stek will do, will be to search the records at the Pechora Tracking Guild. And he will find the report that my father filed ... including the attack on our cabin. Pechora is a long way from the Cave, but my cabin isn't!"

"Give us the location of your cabin," Deema suggested. "Our chances are best to find Stek there."

Deciding that they had the best possible plan, Urshen and Tal-nud watched the wagon leave with Deema, Toulee and four others, hoping to find Stek in the Lithgate Wilderness.

"I know of an Inn at the next village. It serves fresh bread, a fabulous stew, and the beds are clean," Toulee enthusiastically shared with the group.

"You were right about the meal," the Tracker said as he leaned back in his chair.

"Time to check out the beds," another said, pushing away from the table.

It was tradition for Trackers, to share a room, especially on dangerous missions. In the darkness, Deema could hear the soft breathing of Peloree who was fast asleep ... while he stayed awake. He felt troubled. Then he remembered a small meadow as they pulled into the village. Quietly he left the Inn and was soon staring at the stars on a carpet of thick grass. He thought of his father. He imagined that because of their success at Border Pass, he was free from his promise.

He also thought of his luck in becoming a member of the Circle. And their assignment to find Stek. Indeed, there wasn't much that could possibly trouble him, yet he felt it.

Suddenly he felt an intense pain in his shoulder, as though someone had stabbed him. Instinctively he grabbed his injured shoulder, shutting his eyes as he fought against the pain.

Although his body was still lying on the grassy meadow, somehow, he was immediately back in his room struggling against two intruders, his long knife finding flesh as he struggled to stay alive. He heard himself think 'Where is Deema? Is he already dead?'

Deema opened his eyes, jumped to his feet, and raced towards the Inn. It was now clear ... he was seeing through the eyes of Peloree! When he arrived, everyone was already staring at the three dead bodies on the floor. They looked at each other, waiting for someone to explain what had just happened. Deema was the first to speak.

"I couldn't sleep. I went for a walk, and then I felt a pain in my left shoulder." Deema went to examine the shoulder of Peloree and found a deep wound. "When I closed my eyes, I could see what Peloree could see. It was as if I were ... Peloree." He stared at the dead bodies, and then looked up at the others, remembering that they were in the room when he arrived.

"Did you hear the struggle?" He asked, as he studied their moonlit faces.

The silence was palpable but was finally broken by the Woman. "All of us were here at about the same time. We entered by the window or the door." She paused, as though she was trying to explain something to herself.

"I think I fought through many eyes," another Tracker volunteered, uncertain if he remembered correctly.

"Yes, you are right, so did I," the Woman readily agreed. "I could see ... through everyone's eyes," she said quietly, as if she was studying her words. "It appears that the power of the Bond has begun to reveal itself."

"It's unfortunate that the cost of learning was so high," Deema said, shaking his head in tragic dismay. "I should have never left the room. Maybe Peloree would still be alive. My fighting skills are no match. But I could have bought some time," he said, his words filled with grief.

Toulee knelt, to hold the hand of the dead Tracker. "Peloree was as fine a Tracker as there ever was. We will miss him. And he would've known that we were bonded in the struggle and came quickly to avenge his death." She stood, anxious to share another thought. "Urshen needed twelve to *create* the Circle. But obviously, twelve are not needed to use its powers!"

"And when we find Stek ..." Deema suggested.

"Yes, he will join the Circle," added another.

Toulee checked for the tattoo. "Definitely El-Bhat."

"And next time, it will not be so easy to kill one of us," a Tracker said, his words hard as stone. He looked at Toulee, "Perhaps it took the intensity of this experience to increase the power of the Circle."

A Tracker that had remained silent, joined in. "I would like to know more about how the Circle works ... starting tonight. As two of us sleep, let the remaining three search for El-Bhat. If I am right, those sleeping will see through the eyes of those who are seeking, while they who seek will feel your resting."

In the pre-dawn darkness, the Trackers gathered at the wagon with Peloree's dead body. A silent heaviness lingered as they commenced travelling. The sun had crawled above the horizon when they came to the first Tracking Guild, where they left his body to be taken home.

With every league travelled, the sun rose higher and higher, driving away the sorrow of their lost companion. Toulee was the first to speak. "While I slept, I saw a bell tower ... and a water pump beside stables ... where horses were sleeping."

Deema, the other person who slept, was nodding in agreement. "I saw essentially the same. But I also felt fragments of sorrow ... from someone."

"That was me ... as I searched for El-Bhat. But I also feel rested." His two search companions nodded in agreement.

For the rest of the day, they headed north as they tested their new ability. Some of the ideas could be tested in the wagon, but if not, they pulled over and slipped into a forest.

Back in the wagon, Deema returned to Peloree's death. "Urshen cautioned us that there would be more El-Bhat in Storlenia. But, why did they seek *us* out? Unless they know about our mission to find Stek. Which means that they know about his assignment to find the Cave ... and they want to keep us from him," Deema concluded.

"But how could they know about ... it's Fre-steel!" Another Tracker shared. "He wasn't among the dead and he would've known about Stek's assignment to find the Cave."

"When the two El-Bhat don't return, more will be sent," another added.

"Perhaps we should travel by night ... and train ourselves during the day," Deema suggested.

"And ... we must keep the Gift of the Circle secret," the Woman reminded them.

They continued their travels until they found a tavern for their evening meal.

When they were finished they slipped out the back and made their way to the wagon. The sky was clear and the moon bright. Perfect conditions to spot El-Bhat ... or be spotted.

Since bonding on the plateau, the eleven had coached Deema in the skills of a Tracker. He was a quick learner. Some of them said it was the blood. A while later he asked Toulee, "I'm still far from matching your skill or that of the others. What if the day comes when your life depends on me?"

"If that day comes before you are ready, then I assume that the power of the Circle will make up the difference," was her matter-of-fact answer.

"Perhaps," he responded. 'Or my role might always be different,' he thought to himself. Deema was seated beside Toulee as they drove the sleeping crew along the country road. "Toulee, I was thinking, since we trained so well in the forest, if El-Bhat attacked us again, we should head for ..." He was sure he had just heard the snapping of a branch. "... the forest!" he yelled. With the light of the moon, he could see three El-Bhat on horses galloping through the forest behind them.

Toulee drove the horses off the road at full gallop towards the trees. Three more El-Bhat riders were coming towards them from the road ahead. Jumping out of the wagon Toulee shouted, "Open the Circle."

Deema noticed an increase in the connection. The Circle seemed to respond to intense situations! He felt every move as the Trackers held their bows in an iron grip, slowly and steadily pulling the string and holding it close to their cheek, their keen eyes in search of the nearest target. Somehow this skill transferred to himself. His bow now felt a part of him, as if he had trained all his life to forge the skill, for this very moment. Deema watched the El-Bhat race from tree to tree, with the advantage of seeing what everyone else was seeing. Fighting as one, the Circle chose their targets ... two El-Bhat to their left.

Two of the Trackers drew their attention, while the other three sent arrows of death. With confidence, they moved towards the remaining four El-Bhat. The Circle constantly assessing the danger. Their arrows took down another El-Bhat before they were close enough to engage in hand combat. The three remaining El-Bhat drew deadly sabres and flew in frenzied fury towards the five Trackers. Soon overpowered, the El-Bhat lay dead.

    High in a tree, a man witnessed the impossible. Six El-Bhat ... five Trackers. The El-Bhat were all dead, and the Trackers were all alive. No wounded. He was assigned to climb a tree to help spot stray Trackers. But it never came to that, as he looked on from above. One by one, the six El-Bhat crumpled to the forest floor, never to rise again.

    He replayed the scene in his mind. He had never seen fighting like that before. 'Was it the training? Was their skill born of some dark power?'

    He would wait until he was sure they were far away. Then he would hurry back to Pechora, to inform Mishri. He would not suggest retaliation. They needed to capture these men and discover their secret!

    Three days later as the Trackers gathered supplies, one of them caught a brief glimpse of bright green eyes disappearing behind darkened windows. The Tracker immediately opened the Circle. Now alert, they quickly spotted another El-Bhat.

    'That's two. And there must be more!' Deema sounded the alarm to the Circle. 'We need to meet at the wagon ... Immediately!'

    Assembled, Toulee began, "Such lack of restraint. They must want something badly. I think it's us!"

    "They know about our Gift!" Deema was convinced.

    Toulee snapped the reins. "We cannot lead them to Stek and the Cave. For now, we head west!"

Chapter 7 - The proposal

Previously. Urshen took half of the Circle with him to recruit Haybin. Now the Tinkers could establish a Guild that built 'Urshen designed' wagons

Urshen was recognized as he walked through the front doors of the Arborville Tracking Guild. "I would like to see Pechinin. Please tell him I am here."

"No need. Follow me."

When the door opened, Urshen was surprised to see The Commander sitting behind Pechinin's desk. He hesitated so The Commander waved him in. "Hoping to find Pechinin," Urshen explained.

"He should already be back from Pechora," The Commander replied. "And … Mitrock headed north the same day we set off for Seven Oaks. Those two are definitely up to something. We just don't know what."

Urshen was hoping to draw upon Pechinin's experience and insight, to help him decide what to do next. "Thank you, Commander. While I'm waiting for him to return, I'll see how the Tinkers are settling in."

"Before you leave, there's been an incident that I think you ought to know about. Fre-steel has been here. He must have left Border Pass about the same time we left Seven Oaks. He claimed to have escaped the battle at Border Pass … as the only survivor. He immediately took control as the Commanding Officer, but when he insisted on having the formula for the Olleti, the Brew-Master threatened to contact his superior. He left a short time later. I have assigned a double Guard detail to watch the Brew-Master and his family."

"So many things could have gone wrong if the El-Bhat had defeated us at Border Pass," Urshen soberly commented. And then left.

When Urshen arrived at the new Tinker camp, he could see that The Commander was true to his word. Surveyors could be seen everywhere, assisted by a small army of Tinkers. Braddock was huddled over a large table as Urshen entered the tent that served as planning headquarters.

"We are busy building the largest Blacksmith shop I've ever seen. No more living in wagons." Braddock beamed with excitement, as his hand swept over the drawings. "Here is where the housing units will be located."

"So much progress in only a few days," Urshen exclaimed. "It's unbelievable. I didn't expect to see ..."

"It's because of Zephra. She pulled The Commander aside ... wanted to know if he knew of anyone who could benefit from her healing. She made it known that she wanted our Guild plans to succeed." Braddock glanced up at Urshen. The Seer looked troubled. The old Tinker thought he knew why. He thought for a moment then invited Urshen to step outside. They watched for a while, as Tinkers worked side-by-side with the Guild professionals. Then Braddock pointed to different areas, commenting on how bare land was turning into roads, while foundations sprouted upwards in other places. "Is not this a miracle?" He said softly, as his hand panned the scene before them.

Urshen nodded in response.

Then the Tinker added, "A miracle for a miracle. It seems fair and honourable to an old Tinker."

Urshen nodded again, seeing the wisdom in Zephra's approach. "Speaking of Zephra ..."

"With the children ... towards the river."

The reality of the miracle was not lost on the children who were noisily playing.

"This space will eventually be the play area," Zephra explained as he walked beside her. "Isn't it wonderful?" She studied him as he watched some of the children chase each other. "We gave you a ride, and you gave us this," she exclaimed, slipping her arm under his.

"Well I'm not so sure ..." he began, wishing she would give the credit to the Cave.

"Say what you want. But if I had chucked you out of my wagon, we wouldn't be here ... creating a Guild. How about a walk by the river?" They strolled quietly for a while by the water's edge. "Urshen tell me what happened back at the prison cell, when the twelve

Trackers kissed my hand. Why did they do that ... and why all of them?"

"Remember the healing experience," Urshen reminded her, "when you and I joined hands, while we held our Amulets? Up on the plateau we had a similar experience, except we were joined through their Tracker blood by cutting the skin on our hands. They saw what I saw, they felt the power, and they knew that it was because of you, that we succeeded. And that experience changed them in a way that they cannot explain. Other than it has bonded them ... like steel. So they wanted to honour the person who helped make that happen. As far as *why* they needed to do that ... perhaps the power helped them see a Tinker's Boon more completely ... as the Cave sees you."

"A Seer, a Tinker's Boon, Tracker blood, people bonded like steel ... it makes me wonder if there are other opportunities to access the power we know nothing about," she wistfully added.

"Perhaps. One thing I do know," Urshen responded, "is that there are many Caves and there can be more than one Seer. Protas has already been chosen to take my place ... if something were to happen to me. Maybe one day, there will be a Seer and a Tinker's Boon for every Cave." He smiled at the thought.

"So, if we had children," Zephra continued his thought, "they would be strong in the blood, great Seers and powerful Tinker's Boons."

Urshen stared, speechless as Zephra studied her White Bauble.

"Of course ... only one boy and one girl could inherit our Amulets," she clarified. When she looked up, Urshen's expression was frozen in shock.

She grinned at his reaction. "I see ... in your culture such things are never spoken before marriage."

She surprised him ... but he finally recovered. "Well ... such things *could* be discussed before ..." then he realized, 'did she just propose to me?'

"I see. It's not the subject," Zephra noted, "it's my boldness in bringing such matters to your attention." She kissed him. She found his shyness adorable. "Urshen, have you never thought of our children?"

"I uhh ... I have thought of *you* a lot," he reassured her.

With arms wrapped around his neck, she gave a small grunt.

"As my grandmother used to say, *love brings us together, but men and women will always live in different worlds.*"

"When did you ... start thinking about children ... *our* children?" Urshen timidly asked

"Since our first kiss."

"Oh!"

She laughed lightly, as she dropped her arms.

'Is ... this where I'm supposed to ask her to marry me?' he nervously thought, his heart racing while his lungs tried to keep pace. And the more uncomfortable he felt, the more she grinned with delight. Her expression told him that this walk by the river ... and the conversation ... was probably planned! 'I guess that's how Tinkers do it. Sure speeds things up,' he thought. It was always what he wanted, so why were the butterflies churning in his stomach like a hurricane. And he knew it would only get worse if he delayed this moment. "Zephra," he took a deep breath, "will you marry me?"

"So ... Mister Urshen, if you are asking me to marry you, you must own a wagon and a fine set of horses ... or, being a Stor, perhaps a nice house with a lovely flower garden?" She teased, fluttering her eyes.

"Well ... no," he stammered.

"Oh my, Mister Urshen, how can a lady like me ever say yes? Perhaps you have ... something else ... that would convince me to agree?"

"Well ... I'm the best kisser anywhere this side of the Southland Mountains."

"Oh, but that's not true ... I've kissed much better," she replied as she began to play with her long curls.

"Okay ... I'm very clever. Smart enough to know you are the only girl for me."

"Oh ... but Protas is far cleverer. Clever enough to save me on the battlefield. Perhaps I should check to see if he has a wagon. But first ... perhaps you have something else?"

Urshen was *very* curious as to how Protas saved Zephra? For now the answer would have to wait.

"Yes ... in fact I do," he solemnly said. He took her hands as he looked deep into her eyes.

"I have my heart ... say yes ... and it's yours. For now, and forever ... my devotion is only for you. Only *your* eyes will hold me prisoner. When I am away I will think only of *your* arms. So, Zephra, Queen of my heart ... will you marry me?"

The Necklace from Harleem

"Your heart? So, you *are* clever ... now let's see if I can teach you to be the best kisser in the world," she purred as she pulled him close.

Later that evening, alone under the clear starry skies, Urshen, studied the constellation of Purist, the ancient warrior who gave his life for his beloved Vilet. He thought about Zephra's question. She was right to ask him about the wagon. He would visit Braddock first thing in the morning.

People were beginning to stir when Urshen pushed back the flap to the Planning Tent, knowing Braddock would already be there.
"Good morning Urshen," he said without turning around.
'He knows about the proposal,' he thought, 'might as well get right to it,' he decided. "A married man needs a place to live, and I thought maybe ..."
"Come over here, I have just the location, overlooking the river. And high enough that you never have to be concerned about flooding."
Urshen examined the drawings for a while, then he whispered to himself, "Zephra will love the location."
"She ought to ... she picked it," Braddock chuckled.
"And I was worried about ..." he started as he shook his head.
"Lad, do you know who you're marrying?" Braddock asked.
Urshen wiped the thin film of perspiration with his sleeve. "I know my heart is settled ... I guess it's the rest of me that's still trying to catch up."
Braddock laughed heartily. "Welcome to the family. May I suggest the wedding be in six months ... when the house is finished?"
"Zephra's idea?"
"Uh-huh." Braddock thought a moment then laid a hand on Urshen's shoulder. "Would you like to be married in a wagon ... Tinker fashion?"
"So, I can retain a bit of pride, and tell Zephra it's my idea?"
"Uh-huh."

Chapter 8 - Protas in Training

Previously. After leaving Lundeen Forest, Mitrock headed north with Protas, Bru-ell and other Trackers to move Urshen's family to a secure location

A week earlier

The single wagon pulled away from the camp, heading north to Arborville, in anticipation of finding Benton. Biskin and two other Trackers rested in the back of the wagon while Mitrock, Bru-ell and Protas sat up front. Protas leaned to Bru-ell and muttered, "Just like old times, squeezed between two old men, sitting on the hardest bench in the world."

As the sun came up, Bru-ell turned to Mitrock, "What does Urshen's father do?"

"Benton is the Assistant Guild Master for the Roads and River Management Guild at Mantel."

"Isn't that quite far north from Arborville?" Bru-ell hesitantly asked.

"That's correct,"

"So, why would he come that far to work on a road?"

"I needed to hide one hundred and fifty Trackers at Bridge over the Narrows. Easiest way to do that was to invent a road-works project. And the easiest way to maintain secrecy was to bring in support from far away."

"Why is he still at your Guild in Arborville, instead of returning to Mantel?"

"He wanted to see a friend further south before heading back. We discussed the danger and suggested he stay at our Guild until things were sorted and then I would send men back to escort him south."

"And that friend was Urshen," Bru-ell whispered as the improbability of the whole affair sunk in. 'Of course the father of a Seer might find himself walking down roads he never expected to,' Bru-ell considered silently.

"Once we pick up Benton at your Guild," Protas joined in, "will we just keep travelling to Mantel and pick up the rest of the family?"

"Yes. My promise to escort Benton to see Urshen, will have to be deferred."

Bru-ell detected a hint of anxiety in Protas's question. Surprised, he probed with a question of his own.

"Protas ... you being a good friend with Urshen, you must know his family quite well?"

"I know *some* things. Like ... his dad is very good with a bow. Did he bring his bow with him?" he asked Mitrock.

"Yes, he even brought it into my command tent. Strange ... but some men are very *attached* to their weapons."

"So ... he has his bow with him." Protas said quietly.

"You know anybody else in the family?" Bru-ell continued.

"Well ... I have met his little sister Pateese."

"The family knows you quite well then?" Bru-ell suggested.

"Oh yeah," Protas was nodding. "You might say I'm a household name."

When they pulled into the Arborville wagon yard, Mitrock glanced around and with worry in his voice, said, "I expected Benton's wagon to be sitting here. I'm going to check inside."

A moment later Mitrock hurried down the front entrance. "He's not here. He never arrived. We are leaving for Mantel as soon as we supply up. Biskin, you three grab supplies while I fill in a quick report."

As the three Trackers leapt out of the wagon, Protas hollered, "Biskin, would you mind throwing in a cushion?"

The early dawn shuddered to life, as the crack reverberated across the Meadow. Bru-ell always started with an aggressive strike and swiftly retreated, allowing Protas to pick up the offensive.

If not for Biskin, Protas and Zephra would have died in Lundeen Forest. Protas had vowed that he would never feel so helpless again. Before leaving to find Urshen's family - while Zephra headed south towards Seven Oaks - he had struck a deal with Bru-ell. To teach him how to use his staff.

It didn't take Bru-ell long to tailor his training. It was all in the Robe. Protas's problem was that he fought it, like it was in the way. But anything could be turned to one's advantage if you had the eye ... and that was Bru-ell's specialty. "You know you fight like a woman," he quipped as he retreated from Protas's attack.

"Trying to distract me? You'll have to do better than that," Protas said as he rushed into an overhead swing ... and landed on his backside when Bru-ell casually deflected the strike and hooked his leg upwards.

"No ... really. You treat that Robe like it's a dress. I'm surprised you don't lift it when you cross a stream," he chuckled.

"You think it's easy, learning to fight in this Robe?" Protas protested.

"That's what I mean. It's your secret weapon and you keep ignoring it."

Protas stopped and glared at Bru-ell until he realized he was serious. "Okay, I'm listening."

Bru-ell pulled off his tunic and Tinker trousers and threw them at Protas. "Let me have your Robe." Once dressed, Bru-ell practiced a few moves until he could feel the balance of the Robe. "Alright ... watch and learn."

The threat sounded comical to Protas, as he danced around Bru-ell, who looked ridiculous in the Robe. "Perhaps I will give *you* a whipping ... then what would I do ... believing that I'd do better ... without my Robe," he spat out the words while pressing Bru-ell with a relentless attack. "It will feel ... like betrayal," he grunted, while blocking a blow.

Ten minutes later, his scepticism had left. Bru-ell used the Robe like he did a lariat. The large folds of coarse wool were used to trap his staff or to deflate the energy of a well-placed swing. The harder he tried, the more Bru-ell demonstrated the effectiveness of the Robe.

Finally, Protas collapsed, exhausted in his effort to get an effective blow past the Robe. He began to chuckle. "I bet you could stop arrows with my Robe," he said, thinking about the blankets they used in Lundeen forest.

"The wagons leave soon. This evening I hope you will whine less and fight more." He grunted as he threw the Robe back to Protas.

Several days later, they pulled up in front of Benton's picket fence. Bru-ell and Mitrock jumped off the wagon. "You coming in?" They asked Protas.

"You go on ... I'll just wait here while you make sure someone's home."

"Strange ... must be more to the story," Bru-ell muttered as he looked back to see Protas pull up his hood.

Out of the corner of his eye, Protas watched them bang on the door and gain entrance inside.

"Mitrock!" Benton exclaimed as he swung open the door.

For a moment, Mitrock's mouth hung open. It had never occurred to him that Benton had simply gone straight home. "Uh ... Mister Benton ... it's good to find you here."

Benton, looking past Mitrock's massive frame, saw several Trackers sitting in the wagon. "Yes, I decided it was best to head home. So ... what brings you all the way to Mantel? It can't be good news." By now he was aware of the Tinker, almost hidden by the wide shouldered Tracker.

"We prefer to talk inside," Mitrock replied.

Once inside, Velinti appeared. She was surprised to see that the visitors included a medium built Tinker and the largest Tracker she had ever met. "Is it about Urshen," she asked, nervously wringing her hands.

"This is my wife ... Velinti ... and our daughter Pateese is somewhere upstairs."

Staring into the concern of her soft blue eyes, he nodded, "Yes ... it's about Urshen ... and your family," Mitrock replied. "As far as we know, Urshen is safe and well. But first ... may I introduce Bru-ell, a travelling companion of your son. And outside in the wagon are a couple more Trackers, and a young fellow by the name of Protas ... apparently he knows your family."

Velinti looked at Benton with a 'here we go,' expression. "Yes, some of us in the family actually know Protas very well," Velinti acknowledged. "We understand that he has become quite *friendly* with our son Urshen." The irony in her voice was obvious.

'So, there is uncomfortable history between Protas and the family,' Mitrock realized, remembering a promise he made to Protas after Lundeen forest. *May I also say, if there is ever anything an old Tracker can do, please get word to me.* Here was his chance. "I have heard they are good friends. What I can tell you, is that in this conflict with the El-Bhat, they have *both* become legends." He turned to Bru-ell, expecting him to support his claims.

Bru-ell cleared his voice. "We will always remember the day that we picked up Urshen and Protas to give them a ride. Tinkers are suspicious of everyone ... but these two young men are like our own sons."

Satisfied, Velinti glanced at Benton with a 'let's get down to business' look.

"Sounds like there's a lot to catch up on," Benton suggested. "Won't you come sit and tell us why you're here."

They were barely seated when Velinti began, "Who are El-Bhat and what is this about a conflict? And tell me something about Urshen."

Mitrock spoke first, "The El-Bhat are warriors that belong to a tribe who live in the deep south of Shaksbah. Traditionally they plundered anyone outside their tribe, until the government of Shaksbah employed them as peacekeepers, much like Trackers here in Storlenia. But plundering is in their blood so they cross the Southland Mountains to take what is ours. History proves that the Trackers Guard the passes so well that most people don't even know who the El-Bhat are. Unfortunately, that has changed. But thanks to Urshen and Protas, we know that the El-Bhat ... are among us. They first shared this information with the Tinkers, so I'll ask Bru-ell to fill you in on the rest."

Bru-ell covered the two weeks that the two young men had spent in their Tinker camp. He explained how Protas had convinced them, that El-Bhat were inside Storlenia, and of his plan to lure them out of their stronghold at Seven Oaks. He continued with how Urshen had produced a new wagon design, helping the Tinkers escape the El-Bhat War Wagons, as they chased them all the way up to Bridge over the Narrows.

"And that's where your husband joined our Tracker 'road crew'," Mitrock said to Velinti, wondering how much she knew.

"Yes, I've heard," she replied.

Mitrock nodded, then turned back to Benton. "After you left, we waited, hidden from view, for the Tinker wagons that were racing from Seven Oaks, with El-Bhat War Wagons in full pursuit. Those Tinker wagons charged into Lundeen forest where other Tinkers were waiting. Many died that day, but with Trackers and Tinkers fighting side by side, we managed to defeat the El-Bhat."

"You would've been proud of Protas," Bru-ell boasted, "his quick thinking saved an entire wagon of Tinkers, as well as Braddock's daughter. He's our Leader."

"Was Urshen involved in that same battle?" Velinti was quick to ask.

"No," Mitrock answered, "but his assignment was just as dangerous. Shortly after Urshen suggested that El-Bhat had taken over Seven Oaks Redemption Guild, we discovered Shaksbali spies in our own Tracking Guild. This meant that our Border Pass contingent had probably fallen to the El-Bhat. It was your son's suggestion that he take a small group of Trackers with him to Border Pass, pretending to be supporters of the El-Bhat. After the battle in Lundeen forest, the joint team of Tinkers and Trackers headed for Seven Oaks. That's when we left them. After retaking Seven Oaks, their plan was to head for Border Pass, hoping that Urshen and the Trackers had successfully sabotaged the locked gates."

"Do you know if our son is still alive?" Benton spoke for the two of them.

"Is Urshen in some kind of trouble?" Pateese interrupted as she entered the room.

"To both of your questions ... we don't know. We have heard nothing since they headed south to Seven Oaks," Mitrock replied.

"And now you're going to tell us why you're here?" Benton reminded him.

Mitrock was nodding slowly in the affirmative. "By the time your son left Arborville, it was obvious to us, that he was a very gifted young man. When I say gifted I mean ... we have never seen anything like it before." They all offered blank stares so he continued. "Unfortunately, someone like that is *very* valuable to both sides of the conflict. To protect Urshen, we need to protect his family. It's why we are here."

"How ... do you plan to protect us?" Benton asked.

"Not in this house ... not in this town. We need to take you somewhere else."

"Inside a Tracking Guild I presume?" Benton proposed.

"The closest Guild is at Pechora. I suggest we leave as soon as we can."

Benton stood, "I think we've left our visitors waiting outside long enough. Pateese, let's go bring them in. There's someone out there that you already know."

The following morning, after a quick breakfast, Benton pulled Mitrock aside. He reached for the chain around his neck. "Here, let me give you your Medallion back."

At first Mitrock accepted the glittering artefact. Then he said, "You need to keep it ... at least for a little while longer."

Benton was puzzled. The big Tracker had given him the Medallion as a way to freely enter his Guild. But now...

Mitrock lifted the chain and lowered his voice. "The Medallion has been in our family for centuries. It is now yours. If you need to make an important decision, to know if something is right or wrong, hold it in your hand while asking if your question is true. You will know."

Mitrock relaxed his hold on the chain and let the Medallion rest on Benton's chest.

To Velinti, Mitrock's passing of the Medallion sounded *formal*. Almost ritualistic.

Benton took a moment to think about what Mitrock had just done. And the power of this artefact. It begged a question. "Mitrock, when we first met, and you asked me all those questions ... why didn't you just use the Medallion to get your answers?"

Mitrock nodded in agreement. "You're right. It would have been easy. But I've learned long ago to use the Medallion sparingly. Otherwise you lose a part of yourself."

"I see," said Benton. He slipped the Medallion under his shirt, trusting that somehow Mitrock knew what he was doing. "Thanks."

Every morning, Jalek entered the stables of the Pechora Tracking Guild. Today, like every other day, it reminded him of the time he saw himself wearing Protas's Robe. An image that spoke to his heart. He had put it off long enough. It was time to get that Robe. His wagon was already hidden away from the Guild and his possessions were meagre. There was only one thing he had to leave behind ... for now.

"I cannot take you now, but don't worry, Destiny will bring us together again ... I just know it!" He looked deeply into the horse's eyes as a tear slid down Jalek's cheek.

Chapter 9 - The Medallion

Early in the morning, Mitrock took Biskin aside. "Best if you and the boys head back to Arborville. With Pechinin gone, and no news about Border Pass, The Commander in charge could use you. Now that we have Urshen's family, a smaller group will attract less attention. You will see me as soon as I finish settling them at Pechora. If you see Urshen, let him know his family is safe."

As their wagon headed east, Velinti looked back, wondering if she would ever see her home again.

A couple of days later the dusty wagons rolled up in front of the Tracking Guild in the late afternoon. "I'll go inside and let them know we're here," Mitrock explained as he jumped down from the wagon. A short time later he returned and informed them that they needed to leave their weapons in the wagon. "A new security rule. Pechinin must have told them about our problem at Arborville. The good news is that Pechinin is still here."

'A new security rule for Trackers?' Protas thought to himself. 'A bit odd and I don't like it,' he thought as he reached down, grabbed a stone, and plopped it into one of his boots. "Hope they understand that I cannot get along without my walking staff," he warned, limping along, thanks to the stone.

Once inside, Bernado welcomed them and turned them over to his Assistant, to show them their rooms.

"Mitrock," Bernado addressed the large Tracker, "I will be by a little later, to take you to see Pechinin, and then we will finish the discussion about the family."

Mitrock and Protas had just settled into their room when there was a knock on the door.

"Time to meet Pechinin ... and find out why he insisted on coming here in the first place," Mitrock declared, heading for the door.

"When did he leave Arborville?" Protas was suddenly curious.

Mitrock paused, with his hand on the door handle, "Same time we headed south to the bridge."

"It must have been awfully important," Protas responded as he considered the odd timing. "I look forward to hearing all about it."

As soon as Mitrock left, Protas hid his El-Bhat garments under his mattress. "No sense in giving them the wrong idea," he muttered to himself. But there was still something that didn't feel right. He began to pace the floor. 'I need to talk to Benton,' he realized.

"Tried the Medallion yet?" were the first words out of Protas's mouth, as he shut the door. Benton realized he must have overheard Mitrock when he refused to take the Medallion back. The old memories of Protas made him hesitate ... he looked over at Velinti.

"You always said he was clever," Velinti reminded him.

Benton gave a little nod to his wife and turned to Protas with a response. "Simple answer ... no. Not even sure how it works. Why?" he challenged Protas with penetrating eyes.

"I want you to use the Medallion to ask if you should stay ... or leave immediately."

There was something in Protas's words that made him reach under his shirt without hesitation.

"But we just ..." Velinti started.

Protas looked at Velinti. "Something bothers me about this place. Please hurry and use the Medallion," he pressed.

Pateese wandered closer to her father, while he held the bronze disk.

"Should we stay here?" he said firmly ... then waited as the others looked on. "Nothing. I feel nothing," he shared with the others.

"Try again," his wife encouraged.

Returning his attention to the disk, he tried again. "Should we leave immediately?" A surprised Benton confessed to Protas, "It's not working. I still feel nothing."

A frowning Protas responded. "I think you need to be more specific. Just like if you were asking me the question. In other words, whether we leave or not depends on why we are asking the question."

Encouraged, Benton nodded and started again. "If we want to be free and safe, should we leave immediately?"

The response from the Medallion was so strong, he almost dropped it.

"We should leave while we still can!" Protas urged, opening the door to check the hallway. "Leave your things here, walk out the front door, and take the wagon. If anyone asks, you're going for a ride. I'll let Bru-ell know to follow you. Then I'll try to find Mitrock and Pechinin. Let's meet at Urshen's cabin." Protas quickly opened the door. He waited until they had enough time to get safely out the front entrance, then he went to Bru-ell's room. He quickly explained their experience with the Medallion, and the plan. "You catch up with the wagon," Protas added, "I'll see if I can find Mitrock and Pechinin."

"What you want to do ... sounds like Tinker work to me," Bruell protested.

Protas paused. "Unless it's already too late for Mitrock and Pechinin. Then it would be a waste of a good Tinker. But *I* still have my El-Bhat garment to help me sneak out the back door ... if they are already dead."

Mitrock followed Bernado down the hallway.

"Pechinin has already left his room," Bernado advised. "He must be interviewing prisoners. We'll check there first." They passed the security Guards and made their way down the cellar stairs to the underground prison. While passing prison cells Bernado remarked, "Did you know that Pechora has the largest underground prison cell complex of any Tracking Guild?"

"Yeah I think Pechinin might've mentioned it ..." Mitrock's words trailed off as he caught a glimpse of a prisoner's bright green eyes. He stopped and moved to the bars. The man inside turned. His deep set *green* eyes did not share the desperate look of a prisoner.

Bernado had stopped to watch Mitrock.

"Why weren't we told that you have an El-Bhat prisoner?" Mitrock asked. His suspicions about looking for Pechinin, down in the prison area, were growing!

"No need for concern. If you wait a moment, Pechinin will fill you in on everything."

Halfway down the corridor Bernado stopped and entered a prison cell. Pechinin was sitting on a cot ... with two El-Bhat in the room. Mitrock could see that he didn't look so good. He needed to buy some time while he figured out how he was going to get Pechinin out of there.

"I see that the place is *full* of El-Bhat," Mitrock said with contempt. "Where are all the prisoners? I mean the regular prisoners." Mitrock's eyes were smouldering, but his mind was busy finalizing the details of their escape.

"We gave the prisoners a choice," Bernado said smugly, "and most of them now serve us in other places. As you can see, the cells are bursting with El-Bhat. And they are anxious to serve me, alongside the Trackers ... once the Shaksbali control the Guilds. Mitrock ... no one needs to die ... you only need to cooperate," Bernado said encouragingly.

Mitrock was already sure about two things. Pechinin came here because he was suspicious of an old friend. And second, Bernado couldn't have heard about the losses at Lundeen forest, or he wouldn't be talking about control of the Guilds ... and asking them to cooperate. 'Nope, if he knew, we would already be dead!' Mitrock thought to himself. Mitrock allowed his shoulders to relax, as if he had already acquiesced to Bernado's suggestion. "And if we cooperate," Mitrock began slowly, "what will ..." Suddenly Mitrock's thick arms threw the closest El-Bhat against the wall, while he smashed into the second one, breaking his neck. Grabbing the dead El-Bhat's weapon, he turned and thrust the sword through the other El-Bhat before he could get to his feet. Snatching up the second weapon, he threw it at Pechinin, "We must be quick."

The moment the struggle erupted, Bernado rushed out of the cell. He had no desire to fight the massive Mitrock, especially without his prized Long Knives. His destination was the bottom of the stairs, confident that the pair of Trackers would never make it that far.

As soon as the two Trackers rushed out of the prison cell, doors on either side began to fly open, but Mitrock's foot slammed them shut, throwing many anxious El-Bhat back into their rooms. Behind them El-Bhat began pouring out of their unlocked prison cells, forcing Pechinin to turn and fight those that were rushing from behind. Fortunately, they only had knives, and Pechinin was deadly with the sword.

While Pechinin guarded his back, Mitrock, as thick as an oak tree and as quick as a snake, cut down the black silk warriors crowding the corridor. Eventually, the sheer numbers of the enemy brought their rapid retreat to a crawl. "Watch the doors," Mitrock yelled, noticing that some of the El-Bhat had stayed in their cells. But he knew that wasn't his biggest worry. He could hear Pechinin's sword begin to slow. He wasn't surprised. The Head Guild Master was half dead when he found him.

Suddenly several El-Bhat threw themselves at Pechinin, determined to crush the defence to Mitrock's rear. "Run," was the last thing Pechinin said, as he crumbled under the weight of several El-Bhat.

Knowing his rear would soon be exposed, Mitrock pushed forward with abandon, slashing with his sword while using his body as a ram. Another six warriors fell dead before the El-Bhat in the rear tackled him by the stairs. Their angry knives bringing a quick death to the Tracker called Mitrock.

Bru-ell was already out the front door when the alarm sounded. He spotted Benton and his family as they made their way to the gate. The single Guard responded to the alarm and was rapidly shutting the large doors trapping them inside. Bru-ell snatched his lariat from the wagon, and with a quick release, dropped the Guard. Benton jump down to help Bru-ell open the Gates.

"You're going to need a distraction," Bru-ell shouted. "Hide in the first wooded area you come to ... I'll find you."

While the wagon headed east out of town, Bru-ell picked up a large rock, waited for the next Tracker to emerge and then threw it, hitting the man square in the chest. He rushed down the street that led north. Racing along the boardwalk, Bru-ell noticed that everyone turned their head to stare at the Tinker ... in his colourful attire. He realized that he may as well be running through the streets with his clothes on fire. Definitely more of a distraction than he had planned! 'I need a place to hide,' he decided, taking as many side streets as possible in search of something suitable.

Eventually, at the outskirts of town, he came across a small farm with a few cows ... and a manure pile. He skidded to a stop. 'Perfect to hide in ... and great camouflage for my clothes,' he decided quickly. Bru-ell squirmed into the pile feet first, with only moments to spare, as the Shaksbali Trackers raced past.

The womb he chose to enter, was warmer than he had imagined. After a while, he could no longer smell anything. 'Perhaps I will never smell again,' he thought gloomily.

Eventually darkness descended. 'Time for my birth,' he thought as he gladly left the farm behind.

Protas waited a few moments to allow Bru-ell to make it past the front door. Then he headed towards the administrative offices, his best guess as to where Bernado would've taken Mitrock. Before he got there, the sound of combat echoed from the underground chambers. He had guessed wrong, and now he knew for sure ... it was already too late. He hurried back to his sleeping quarters where he quickly changed into the El-Bhat garment, grabbed his staff, his bag and headed out the back door.

Once outside he saw the stables and immediately knew that was his best option. Quickly closing the door behind him, he found the horses feeding in their stalls. A quick glance and he decided on the big, tall black one. "Wow aren't you a beauty," he said softly as he stroked the neck of the stallion, "so tall, built for speed and ... legs with distinctive white stockings!" He had seen this horse before. "I need just a minute. Then you and I will be off like the wind," he whispered as he rushed to the end of the stables searching for Jalek. Rounding a corner, he knew immediately, that it wasn't the Ferrier he was expecting. The new Ferrier turned towards the sound, but all he saw was a blur of black silk, so he went back to his work.

Protas hurriedly rode the black horse out of town heading east. Leaving the road, he slipped into the forest where he changed into his Robe. He had passed up a chance once before to bring the infamous Jalek to justice. The rendezvous at Urshen's cabin would have to wait another couple of days. He had someone to find!

Benton spotted a forest up ahead, not far off the road. Driving the wagon into high bushes, they jumped down and drifted further into the trees. It was a cold and damp night. Velinti and Pateese huddled together for warmth as drizzling rain tormented them. Benton stood Guard, his bow loosely strung and fitted with an arrow, waiting for Bru-ell.

Several hours had passed when he heard movement deeper in the forest. He crept closer to investigate. Very quickly he knew it wasn't an animal. The sound continued to move forward, but cautiously. Eventually he could see movement between the trees. He pulled back his bowstring.

Bru-ell heard the sound, swiftly placing himself behind a tree, as he whispered, "Benton?"

The bowstring relaxed. The men approached each other. Benton could smell Bru-ell before he could see him in the growing darkness. "You smell terrible! Where have you been?" he asked.

"You should have smelled me before the rain washed me down."

"Follow me," Benton directed as he turned and led Bru-ell towards Velinti.

"I'll find a creek first thing in the morning," Bru-ell promised Benton's wife.

"Guild Master, we have checked the entire compound. All the visitors are gone ... with the wagon. The Shaksbali Trackers have already been sent in pursuit and as soon as it is dark enough, El-Bhat will join them."

"It's too bad Mitrock is dead," Bernado complained, "I would've preferred to know why he was so anxious to bring these visitors under our protection. Keep me informed of the search. We must bring them back!"

"Yes, Guild Master," he bowed and turned to leave.

"One last thing. There is a good chance they know our secret." With eyes full of fire, he whispered to his Assistant, "Don't ... fail me."

His Jerkin fluttering in the wind, Stek sat and watched the cabin. Occasionally his gaze would drift to the trails that fed into the Lithgate Valley. He saw a few hikers and hunters, but the one he was waiting for, would head for the cabin.

When he first arrived, he visited the cabin, but it proved fruitless in helping him find the Cave. It appeared that no one had been there for months, and a careful search revealed nothing new. He spent a couple of days hunting, to stockpile some food. Now he only had to wait. Eventually someone would come to that cabin, and then they would tell him about the Cave!

A dripping Bru-ell returned from the creek and stood before Benton. "I'll bet that smells better?"

Benton smiled. "How soon do you suggest we begin our trek to Urshen's cabin?" he asked.

"The search will continue for at least another week in this area, and then they will move further out. That's when it will be safe to begin our travels by night. Today, we need to disassemble the wagon and move the parts further into the woods. By afternoon we will hunt for food and find better shelter."

Chapter 10 - Going Home

Previously. Benekee accompanied his Redemption Guild Master to Qar-ana where they discussed the remarkable glowing Shards with Craslin. During their discussion, Benekee felt the warmth of the Shards in his hidden pouch and decided he wanted to keep them for himself

Benekee was standing outside the Qar-ana Planning and Development Guild, waiting for his Guild Master. His hand, safely inside his Robe, played with the broken fragments of the ancient Amulet. He had told them that the Shards were still back at the Redemption Guild. Surprisingly, in spite of the lie, he felt strangely euphoric. He was never a *devoted* Guild member of ancient artifacts, but neither was he a thief. And yet ... he felt like the contents of this leather bag belonged to him. Feeling its warmth and power while he bore witness to Craslin of the recent signs of *life* shown by the fragments, was something he never expected. 'How long has it been since I felt so alive ... and so confident,' he thought. 'It's so strange that my Guild Master didn't seem to notice.'

As the wagons on the street passed by, Benekee's thoughts travelled back a thousand years to the original owner of this Amulet and wondered if he was pleased that his Talisman was once again *speaking* to the people of Ankoletia. 'But really ... it's only speaking to me,' he corrected himself. 'Which could mean that ... perhaps ... this is destiny directed at ... me.' His fingers continued to trace the shape of each shard. His mind went back to the exhibit table, where he first saw the Shards come to life. He felt embarrassed that he had mocked the inscription.

'Odd, that an unbeliever like me should be ... *adopted* by this Amulet,' he mused. That thought made him realize that the bond between the Amulet and himself, was becoming more important than he had originally considered. He turned around, stared at the large oak doors of the Planning Guild, and immediately comprehended another truth.

When his Guild Master came down those stairs, Benekee wouldn't be waiting. He was not going back to the Redemption Guild at Borit Betoon. The Fates were calling him to a different direction. He was going *home.*

Benekee started walking, arm raised while looking for a Transport Wagon for hire. He jingled the coins in his other pouch. Before leaving the Guild a few weeks ago, he had felt pressed to take it, although he shouldn't have need of it. His Guild Master would cover all expenses. But now that he had turned his face to another life, he was glad to have it. He gave a small squeeze to both pouches as he hurried towards the Transport Officer waving him to his wagon.

"Please take me as far as you can towards Breckenden. I am off to visit my sister Yaneek," he said with great satisfaction. He had barely settled onto the padded bench when he knew he had been wrong about *him.* He couldn't help himself ... the discovery about the true owner of the Amulet erupted from his lips. "I was wrong! *He* wasn't a *he*; he was a *she.*"

The Transport Officer was busy pulling into traffic as Benekee pronounced his discovery. Confused about his excited passenger, he turned with a slightly amused smile. "Sorry, did you say your sister isn't a he, she is a she?"

Benekee laughed, "No, the person who owned the Shards was not a man, it was a woman. For some reason, I am supposed to know that."

The driver was politely trying to understand the thread of Benekee's conversation. "So, this woman, not a man, owned shards, as in broken pieces of glass?"

"Yes! Exactly! And now they're mine!"

He would have normally dropped the insane conversation at this point, but the boy's enthusiasm intrigued him, so he continued. "So ... it's about worthless pieces of glass ... and it's important that you know that it wasn't a man who owned these, it was a woman. And, it gets better. Through some twist of fortune, *you* ended up with these worthless pieces of glass. Did I get the story right?"

Benekee just smiled at the driver, not caring how silly it sounded.

The driver was beginning to see why this young man was wearing a Robe. Probably fresh out of the Redemption Guild for

Lunatics. He decided he would have him pay in advance as soon as they left town.

When Yaneek opened the door to her small cottage, she immediately sensed that things were out of order. 'Of course ... it's too clean,' she thought. But who ...' and then he poked his head around the corner busy cleaning a plate. "Hi, sis, the lady next door let me in. She recognized me right away." He was grinning from ear to ear.

"Benekee, I ..." her hand came up to shield her trembling lips. But her tears could not be hidden so easily. "What a surprise," she squeaked out. Seeing Benekee dressed in the same clothes that he wore, when their parents died, opened the prison of her suppressed emotions.

He remembered his older sister being cheerier than this. So he quickly laid down his plate and towel and rushed over to give her a big hug. "I have some great news, but that can wait until tomorrow. For tonight, I have prepared a nice dinner and I want to hear everything that's happened since we separated four years ago."

Yaneek was too tired to talk. So she encouraged Benekee to tell her about life at the Redemption Guild and his training in the Guild kitchen.

Sometime later, he made the comment, "I'll bet you were surprised at how tasty this ..."

Unexpectedly, Yaneek cut him off. "Work comes early for me. So if you will clean up, I need to go to bed."

"Of course, Yaneek. Goodnight," he said as she shuffled off towards her bedroom.

As soon as the early dawn coaxed Benekee's eyelids open, he bounded out of his warm bed, anxious to continue his discussion with Yaneek. And tell her about the Shards! But a quick search told him she was already gone to work. Last night's discussion had left him troubled. He was expecting more warmth and enthusiasm after being apart for four years. Then when he found the note detailing his chores for the day, he grinned. 'Glad to see nothing has changed,' he thought as he headed for the food pantry.

He decided it was probably better that she had left early. "This way," he said to himself, "it will give me all day to decide exactly how I am going to tell her why I left the Guild." It should have been simple, but he found himself frequently pausing to re-work his speech. "Yaneek, I possess glowing Shards and ... they've adopted me."

It all seemed so simple when he was on the road heading home. But now that he was back with Yaneek, those words seemed unbelievable! "She will think I'm completely crazy."

Benekee rambled about the cottage, completing one chore after another. He was gratified to feel a level of comfort that he didn't expect. Four years ago, he never wanted to return to his parents' home. But now, to his surprise, there was a pleasant feeling reminding him of happier times.

By mid-day this unexpected comfort seemed too much of a coincidence. He slipped into his bedroom to pull out the Shards. He spread them on top of his bed and arranged them in order of size and asked, "Are you responsible for the good fortune I feel right now? Of course you are," he cheerily concluded. The bright sunlight coming through his window released brilliant rainbows from the center of the Shards. He grinned. "If the power of a *broken* Amulet can be felt ... imagine if these pieces could be fit together into their original shape?" With excitement, he headed for the kitchen.

Eventually he held a small cage-like box made of bread dough that housed all the assembled Shards ... except one. There was a missing piece! "Interesting," he muttered to himself. "But maybe ... I could have the Gemstone Guild create a crystal replacement, and have the reassembled Shards set in a silver setting!"

His excitement was interrupted by steps on the front cobblestone path. He hurriedly hid the Shards. Yesterday, he had expected to discuss all of this with his sister. But he was beginning to see that he would have to wait. Something was not quite right.

"Starting to make dinner?" she inquired as she looked in the kitchen.

"Yes ... just starting. But give me another hour and a tasty meal will be ready."

She dropped her bag in the big chair, and with a frown she turned to him. "Benekee, I am only a second-level seamstress. We will have to eat simple meals most of the time. In fact, the thought that has been on my mind all day, is that you will have to find work. I hope you understand."

"Yes ... of course," he said, trying to hide his fear. It had never occurred to him as he headed home, that his sister would be so poor.

Then he thought of his *other* leather pouch. Enthusiastically he shouted, "Wait till you see the surprise that I have brought with me." He scurried to his bedroom to retrieve his coins. With eagerness, he emptied his four years' worth of treasure onto the kitchen table beside the bread dough box. "My Guild earnings," he declared, his face beaming as he watched his sister's reaction. Yaneek spread them out to get a better estimate of the value. For the second time in two days, her hand came up to hide trembling lips. "This will save our house," she whispered, as tears tumbled down her tattered blouse.

Now he was beginning to understand her despondent state. "Oh my goodness Yaneek. What would you have done if I hadn't come home?" She walked around the table and hugged him while she sobbed on his shoulder.

"Sorry sis, that wasn't such a good question." He was busy patting her on the back. "There, there. The point is, I *am* here," he said softly, "and you are right. I will find a job. A good job. And everything will be fine." His eyes drifted to the lump of bread dough on the table. His plans to tell her about the Shards, would have to wait.

As the need to seek comfort ran its course, Yaneek pushed herself away from Benekee. "You mentioned yesterday that you had some great news to tell me," she said grabbing a kitchen towel to wipe away her tears.

He hesitated ... but only briefly. "Oh yes, that. Well ... I have decided to leave the Redemption Guild for good. I guess you could say that I have sorted myself out and I am ready to fit back in with society."

"That *is* good news," his sister said as she placed a gentle hand to his cheek.

That night propped up in bed, Benekee spilled the contents of the leather pouch in front of him. "You've waited a thousand years to come to life. I guess you can wait a little longer until I find a job and can put you back together." He imagined the woman who used to own this Amulet and wondered about her history, until he was interrupted by a knock on his door.

"Breakfast will be early Benekee ... lights out," he heard his sister through the door. Yesterday was the only day he had slept in for the last four years, and it appeared, from the tone of her voice, that it might just be another four years before it happened again. He gathered the Shards, but instead of placing them back in the pouch, he held them tightly in his hand. He extinguished the candle and bringing his hands close to his chest, he let the darkness of the room carry his tired body to a place of dreams and quiet slumber.

Behind their cottage, was a trail Benekee often used in his youth, to explore the surrounding fields. Summer days found Benekee skipping down this path, pulling a little red wagon filled with his treasures.

Benekee burst out of the back door anxious to start exploring, but the wagon was not where he usually put it. Undiscouraged, he ran down the trail confident that his wagon and treasures would not be far.

Eventually he did find the wagon but to his dismay, the red box was broken into several pieces and his treasures were scattered about. He examined the broken pieces of the box. They looked a lot like pieces of a puzzle. He quickly assembled those pieces until he had rebuilt his red box. "Like new," he proudly said.

Placing one foot in the wagon and the other outside, he began pushing himself down the gentle hill. As the speed increased, he jumped into his wagon and steered it down the familiar path.

With the wind to his back, the bushes on either side flew by faster and faster. He suddenly remembered a large bump in the trail ahead. But before he could think about it, the wagon was airborne.

He braced for a hard landing, but to his surprise, his wagon began to rise upwards, high above the rooftops. To his delight it responded as *he steered his flying wagon on a tour above his town. He looked around hoping to spot some of his friends ... what fun if they could see him flying in his wagon.*

Not seeing them, he headed for the town square and circled it. He was surprised to see the fountain gone. In its place was a large statue ringed with benches. 'I must tell Yaneek,' he thought. 'She won't believe that the fountain is gone.' He returned home, ran up to the back door and yelled, "Yaneek, Yaneek, I have something to tell you."

But before he could grab the handle, someone was knocking on the other side of the door!

"Benekee, time to be up."

He stirred to the sound of her voice and groggily sat up in bed. He opened his hand and remembered the dream. He had a question he needed to ask his sister. Hurriedly he dropped the Shards into the leather pouch, dressed and bounded down the stairs to the kitchen. The porridge was already in the bowls, sprinkled with sugar and a bit of cream, just like his mother used to serve. He suddenly felt very hungry.

"Do you have any idea where you want to look for work?" His sister queried.

"I guess I will start on Guild Street and check the Guilds one by one." He looked up at Yaneek, "The porridge is the best. Should keep me going most of the day."

"Benekee, I don't want you to work at just anything. Just because we need the money. Isn't there something that you think you would like to do?"

He thought for a moment, but his mind was a blank. "Apparently dusting artefacts for four years has stripped me of creative thinking. Any suggestions?"

"What fascinated you as a child?"

"Metal. Things made from metal. But not stuff a Blacksmith would work with. Smaller things, like watches and ... doorknobs."

"Doorknobs?" She queried, not following his logic. "I really don't see the connection between watches and doorknobs."

That brought a smile. "Well sis, it's not the shell that fascinates me, it's what's inside the doorknob, the gears and levers that make it work."

"Then why don't you check the Mechanical Guild. Apparently, they pay well if you have natural talent." She winked and then took the dishes to the sink. "Can you clean up before you leave?"

"Sure thing." He watched her as she grabbed her day bag and slipped into her boots. He wondered, 'Why is it that whenever I want to talk to Yaneek about the strange side of my life, I can't.'

She opened the door and looked back to leave a word of encouragement. But his look told her there was something unspoken. She stepped back into the house and closed the door. "What is it you haven't said Benekee? You know you can talk to me about anything. Don't you?"

"I ... had a very odd dream last night. I saw ..." He sighed as he looked away. "Is the large fountain still in the middle of the town square?" he finally blurted out.

"No, a large statue has replaced it."

Benekee was nodding slowly as he waited for her to say more.

"They put nice benches around it," Yaneek continued. "We should go there some weekend and have a picnic lunch." She thought it strange that he would know to ask about the town square. She would have to finish this conversation over dinner. But for now, she needed to be on her way, or she would be late. "Good luck with that new job. We will talk about your dream over dinner ... okay?" she proposed as she closed the door.

Now he was sure. The dream was about the Shards, and the importance of assembling them back into their original form. An Amulet of power. His emotions danced inside as he returned to his room and removed the leather pouch from its hiding place. "Just one last look before I leave to find that job." He took out the largest Shard and held it up to the early morning light. Then he slipped it into his pocket.

Chapter 11 - The Test

Benekee watched the Transportation Wagon pull away until it rounded a corner and was lost to sight. Turning to stare at the front doors of the Mechanical Guild, he couldn't make himself walk up those steps. Putting his hands in his pockets he walked up and down the street, contemplating what he might say. Four years of seclusion had spun a web of indecision that he was finding hard to unravel. On impulse, before he left the house, he had grabbed the largest Shard for good luck. He traced the edges of it, as he considered ascending the steps. 'Yaneek will not be pleased if all I have to tell her tonight, is how I stood outside all day.' With that reminder, he bounded up the steps two at a time and once inside, went straight to the front desk, where a young woman was busy with papers. "Hi, I am here to apply for a position of Apprentice."

As she pulled herself away from her papers to look up at him, he gave her a polite nod and then quickly gazed around the room. A sensation of familiarity washed over him, as though he had worked here before ... or was about to.

"Welcome," she responded, and then retrieved a form, and with pen in hand began to question Benekee. "Your name, your age, and who you've apprenticed with previously."

"Benekee. Twenty. Until I was sixteen, I apprenticed with my father at the Accounting Guild. My parents died, and I just spent the last four years at ... a Redemption Guild."

His last three words almost didn't make it out. He gave her a weak smile as he waited for her next question.

"You look young for twenty," she said as she placed the form and her pen to the side.

"Am I too old?" he quietly asked, staring at the partially filled form and the abandoned pen.

"I am sorry. We have an age restriction of eighteen for junior apprentices."

He hadn't anticipated that he might not get past the front desk. He let his eyes wander around the room again. Trying to recall the feeling he had, only moments before. 'Wait a minute,' he realized, 'she said *junior!*' He enthusiastically placed his hands on her desk and leaned forward. "What is the age limit for senior apprentice?"

"Twenty-four. But you would have to pass a qualification test, demonstrating previous training or natural talent."

He pushed himself away from her desk, satisfied that somehow, he was going to be accepted here today. "In that case ... I am here to apply for the position of *senior* apprentice. How soon can I take this test?" He grinned at her.

She stood to escort him to the testing room. "Someone with your enthusiasm should be given a chance. But I warn you," she declared while he followed her down the hall, "most applicants fail the test."

She approached a grizzled old man with droopy eyes, sitting behind a small desk. "Good morning Wutherstop. Mister Benekee is here to take your test."

"Thank you," Benekee said as she passed him on her way back to her work.

"Don't thank her yet, young man," Wutherstop said gruffly. He slowly pulled himself out of his chair, trying his best to stand erect. "Follow me." Inside the testing room, on top of a table sat a mechanical Device, with a few items lying at the side. "You have ten minutes to decide what this Device is used for and how to operate it. When the time is up, I will be back to receive your report," he explained.

Benekee thought he heard him say 'Good Luck', as he shut the door. But the words of encouragement were empty. He knew he didn't expect him to pass. Benekee quickly turned to the task, anxious to prove them both wrong. He had a natural aptitude for this kind of thing. But seven minutes later, Benekee was no further ahead trying to understand the complicated assembly, which consisted of gears, springs, sliding sleeves and a drum. And he was certain that he wasn't going to figure it out in the next three minutes. He was going to fail.

Yet he *knew* he was supposed to get this job. The feeling back in the front entrance, it was so ... so much like a message. 'Of course ... the Shard!' he happily thought.

He reached into his pocket and quickly pulled out the crystal piece. He reasoned that if the Shard had directed him this far, surely it could help him see what the mechanical Device was used for. He held it tightly, closed his eyes and thought, 'I need to know what this Device is used for ... please help me.'

When Benekee opened his eyes, he was standing in a room filled with swirling smoke. He struggled to remember why he should be in this room. He had no idea how he had gotten there. The smoke ... why was there so much smoke? He waited but when nothing changed, he cautiously moved his feet forward, until he hit a wall.

'This is progress,' he thought. With his hands on the wall he moved until he came to a door. He pulled it open and walked into a smokeless room.

'More progress,' he happily thought as he looked around. The room was completely empty except for a small object resting on the floor a few paces away. He approached it but discovered that it was much further away than it appeared. The closer he walked to it, the larger it grew, until it reached the height of his chest.

He walked around this amusing contraption, essentially a large drum with a door, and around the back, there were levers and springs, much like a clock. Curious, he opened the door. The inside revealed metal vanes and clothes sitting in soapy water. He thought a moment and concluded that if the drum turned, those vanes would tumble the clothes.

'It's for washing clothes!' he laughed aloud. He had never seen anything like it, but now he needed to know how it worked. "Of course," he exclaimed as he looked closer. "The gears are designed to turn the drum, and the large springs store energy to keep it turning and ... this lever is meant to compress the springs, just like winding a clock. But it's missing the handle.'

He searched the floor around the Device until he found a rod about the size of his arm among several objects. He slid it into the sleeve on the crank and using all his strength, he pushed down.

The gear went click-click-click and a small metal catch held it, allowing him to lift the handle and push down again. By pumping the lever, the drum began to turn, and the springs kept the drum turning smoothly. Within a short time, he stopped pumping.

"That ... is hard work. It would be easier to wash by hand," he laughed to himself. Then he walked around the back to get a better look. "It's a thing of beauty," he remarked, listening to the sloshing sound of the turning drum. "But unfortunately ... too difficult to use. I wish I knew how to improve this remarkable Device ..."

Immediately, a swirl of smoke temporarily covered the machine, but when it dispersed a moment later, the improvements were in place. He had just finished memorizing the new design, when he heard a creaking door opening.

Benekee was opening his eyes when he heard shuffling feet approach him from behind. Wutherstop laid a hand on his shoulder. "Well lad, what do you think?"

Staring at the model, Benekee responded with, "It's a washing drum ... for clothes. Changing it to a miniature model was clever ... made it difficult to see the true purpose of the Device." Benekee turned to the old man. "If you will allow, I would like to suggest a change or two, to make this Device easier to use and more practical."

Those droopy eyes suddenly went wide, as Wutherstop took a closer look at the boy. He removed his hand from his shoulder and walked around the table to the small mechanical Device. The tiny rod that pumped the main gear, was surprisingly still lying with the other items. He absently picked it up, slid it into the sleeve, and began to pump the gear, watching the drum turn. Wutherstop looked across the table at Benekee, impressed but bewildered.

Benekee broke the silence. "Is this your design?"

The question brought Wutherstop out of his trance. "Huh? Oh ... yes, many years ago. But the full-scale model was too difficult to operate. Our testing group concluded that women would rather ... but then you already know that ... don't you?" He suggested, his mind suddenly alert as he remembered the boy's comment. Wutherstop shuffled back to Benekee, grabbed his arm, and smiled. "You will start tomorrow, and you will be *my* Apprentice. How does that sound?"

"Wonderful," Benekee replied, smiling at the sparkle he now saw in the old man's eyes.

The man offered a handshake to confirm their agreement.

Benekee quickly slipped the Shard into his pocket before clasping the feeble hand. "Tomorrow then. I'll see myself out."

Chapter 12 - The cabin rendezvous

Previously. Pechinin and Mitrock were killed in the Pechora prison cells. Bru-ell and Benton's family escaped into the wilderness, while Protas rode east determined to find Jalek

With the wagon reassembled, Benton led the group of four from their hiding place in the trees, to Urshen's cabin under the light of a large and brilliant moon. Once there, Benton's first priority was to line up Urshen's telescope towards the valley below. Pateese and Velinti agreed to take turns watching for movement along the trails while Benton and Bru-ell scouted the area for signs of Bernado's Trackers. Or El-Bhat.

Stek had been away hunting for food while the party of four hurried towards the cabin. Returning to his observation point he was surprised to see a girl on the cabin's balcony searching the valley below. It's not what he was expecting. Checking later, he grew more confused. A woman now sat at the telescope.

'Strange,' he thought, as he considered the new occupants of the cabin. The old reports that Bernado had provided, talked about a man who lived in the cabin. That might know about the Cave. But this looked more like a family concerned with being followed. He wondered from whom they were hiding. Regardless, they couldn't stay. They might scare off the visitor he was waiting for. It was time to pay them a visit.

Now that they were familiar with the main trails, Velinti and Pateese extended their search to all trails that led to the cabin. It was why Pateese spotted the Tracker coming up the eastern trail. She ran inside to bolt the front door. Breathless she grabbed her mother, "A Tracker is coming up the eastern trail. What should we do?"

"Quick, up on the balcony," she said as they hurried upstairs.

"Good afternoon, may I help you?" She shouted from the railing above.

The Tracker stopped and wiped his brow. "Hello, are you the owner of this cabin?"

"Normally our son lives here, but he is off on other business. So we came here for a rest period."

"I couldn't help notice that you are using a telescope to search the trails. If you have a problem, perhaps I can help?"

"Thank you for the offer, but we are expecting a friend to join us and are concerned that he may be lost. He was never good with wilderness trails," she smiled.

"I understand," Stek smiled back. "I will be in the area for a while on Tracker business, so I will keep an eye out for anyone who looks lost. I will check back to let you know." He turned to leave but stopped and looked back. "My name is Stek ... see you soon." Then he vanished into the forest.

Later that day Benton and Bru-ell returned with a good catch of fish.

Running down the trail, Pateese couldn't wait to tell her father the news. "Dad, we had a visitor, a Tracker by the name of Stek."

The two men looked at each other. "Was he by himself?" Benton queried.

"Yes. If he finds Protas, he said he will come back and let us know."

Benton immediately hurried to the cabin and upon entering asked, "Velinti, you told the Tracker about Protas?"

She saw the bundle of fish, "Nice catch ... and no, of course not. He saw Pateese using the telescope, so I told him we were expecting a friend, and thought he might be lost." Suddenly Velinti's expression registered fear as she looked over Benton's shoulder.

He turned around to see a Tracker standing in the doorway with bow drawn.

"Lay down your weapons and move into the other room," Stek commanded.

Benton was cautiously lowering his bow, when a surprised Bru-ell asked, "Aren't you one of the Trackers that followed Urshen to Border Pass?"

Recognizing Bru-ell, Stek remembered where he had met him, and Urshen. He needed to explain himself, without giving away his plan. "So, this is Urshen's cabin?" He murmured, lowering his bow. Then he turned to Velinti and addressed her with an apologetic look. "The son you mentioned ... it's Urshen isn't it?"

She nodded.

Then he added, "And Urshen's Cave ... must be close by?" The reaction he witnessed, told him what he wanted to know.

"Why are you here?" Bru-ell asked.

"I was given a special assignment to deliver a message to Seven Oaks, *that the Back Gate would be open.*" Then he paused considering his assigned task to find the location of the Cave. It was gut-wrenching. But he needed to deal with this conflict the best he could. He had to make up something that produced the least amount of problems. "And ... I was asked to continue north to help secure Urshen's Cave. It is very fortunate that I found you. Can you show me how to get to the Cave?"

"Of course ... we can go tomorrow," Benton replied, glad that a Tracker had joined their little group.

Over dinner, they shared with Stek their experience at the Pechora Guild.

He listened intently until they were finished. "It is hard to believe that the infiltration has spread as far north as Pechora," Stek commented, shaking his head in pretended amazement. For now he would have to ignore his commitment to Pahkah and focus on his commitment to Urshen. "My assignment to come here and help secure the entrance to the Cave is timely. Sounds like we have no time to waste."

"I'll lead the way," Stek suggested as the small group entered the misty forest. He wanted to see if he could spot the secret entrance. After checking the trail well past Urshen's entrance, the Tracker turned to face Bru-ell and Benton. "I've been checking for something better ... but it appears that Urshen chose the best possible place."

By the time they made it to the top, the sun's rays had filled the valley. As Benton and Bru-el stood on the Ledge in front of the quartz door, Stek was busy searching the area around the small plateau. "The bramble bushes, the loose rock and a very steep incline on all sides of this ledge, guarantees that to find the Cave entrance, one would have to come up Urshen's trail." Finished with his brief survey, Stek turned his attention to the quartz face. He began to study it, searching for clues to the entrance.

Bru-ell was content to stand and watch. For him, just being in front of a Cave was the most exciting event of his lifetime.

Eventually Stek's searching brought him to a small hole on the left side of the quartz face, about the size of his finger. On his knees and studying the shape of the hole, he turned to Benton and asked, "You ever see Urshen open this door?"

"Yes," Benton replied.

"Our work is done here, "Stek declared, as he surveyed the view one last time. "It's time to return to the cabin and bring back some tools."

"Why did Urshen follow twelve Trackers to Border Pass?" Benton asked Stek, while working on the trail the first day.

"Actually, it was the other way around," Stek corrected. "He claimed he knew that El-Bhat were at Border Pass and Pechinin believed him. The plan was to send twelve relief Trackers, to get inside the Pass. Urshen was wearing the Robe that was worn by Retlin, an El-Bhat he had killed. He was pretending to be this man."

Benton stopped and asked, "And how did that work out?"

"At first, not well at all. They intended on killing us unless we joined the El-Bhat. And they were going to cut off Urshen's hands. The punishment for pretending to be an El-Bhat."

"How did you get them to change their mind?" an anxious Benton asked.

"We didn't. When four El-Bhat came to inflict Urshen's punishment, he had already used his Amulet to 'prepare' himself, and with amazing skill … he killed them," Stek explained.

Benton slowly nodded his head with an 'I see' expression, and then added, "But wouldn't that have simply brought immediate death to everyone, once they found out?"

"It would have, except that one of the Shaksbali Leaders, called Deema, joined us after he saw Urshen fight. He believed Urshen to be 'The One'. Someone who was to come and save the Storlenians in Shaksbah."

"Was Border Pass retaken?" Benton was anxious to get a response to the question that Mitrock couldn't answer.

"Don't know. I was sent to Seven Oaks with the message that the Gates would be unlocked. After I left the message, I continued north to find the Cave."

"Tell me more about this tale of 'The One' and the Storlenians who live in Shaksbah," Benton urged.

"A few hundred years ago, Storlenians migrated across the Southland Mountains into fertile areas of Shaksbah. Initially there were conflicts but eventually the Storlenians were accepted. But now, the El-Bhat are recruiting these men to assist in their infiltration efforts and sending the women and children to the Mines to secure their loyalty. Deema's father had a dream that 'The One' would appear to save their people and Deema was to watch for this person."

"Do *you* think Urshen could be 'The One'?" Benton asked, trying to grasp the growing influence of his son's Gift.

"More so than anyone else I know."

Chapter 13 - The Mines of Tenleth

Previously. Although the Wind that rushed through the Butcher Block killed over two hundred El-Bhat, a small group managed to escape

Barely three dozen El-Bhat survived the devastation at Border Pass. They managed to escape with their horses, but nothing else. Fortunately, Shaksbali hospitality would supply them with food and water along their weary journey southward, to the District of Denlen, deep in the far south of Shaksbah where the El-Bhat lived. The dishonour of fleeing the enemy demanded a journey of silence.

But on the morning of the fifth day while they prepared their horses, Ou-Leesen turned to address the group. "There is no dishonour in fleeing an enemy that you cannot see," he declared. "It is better to save our lives for the day when we can defeat this enemy. For we *shall* find the man who wields this power." Ou-Leesen saluted his Brothers and mounted his horse. They would rest little until they could report to the Quorum.

As they approached the borders of Denlen, they pulled straws. They needed a messenger who would report the incident at Border Pass. The task would bring the wrath of the Quorum and 'death with dishonour' to the messenger. The worst punishment that could be inflicted on an El-Bhat warrior. The straws were passed around until it was Ou-Leesen's turn. He stared at the hand holding the remaining straws and simply said, "I will do it." He walked over to his horse, leapt into the saddle, and waited for the others. With eyes fixed on the road ahead, he urged his horse forward.

The flap of the large tent was pulled back and a head poked through with a message. "Shanteef, a messenger from Border Pass has just arrived. It is most urgent."

"Have him wait until we have gathered the Quorum. Then bring him in."

Waiting under the hot sun, Ou-Leesen used his anger to finish forging his resolve. He would find the man who unleashed the power of the Cave on his comrades!

The Guard finally gave him the signal to enter. "Remove your sword," he ordered as he pulled back the tent flap.

Ou-Leesen ignored the request, approached the Quorum Leader, and kissed the emerald pommel of his knife.

"Were you not instructed to leave your sword outside the tent?" queried an irritated Quorum member.

Ou-Leesen turned slowly to the speaker. "I am El-Bhat. My sword burns to protect the Quorum."

Shanteef's eyes narrowed. Here was a man he would have to pay special attention to. But the other Quorum members disagreed as they drew their knives and laid them on the carpet for Ou-Leesen to see.

"You have a message?" Shanteef asked, ignoring the vote of offense.

"The El-Bhat at Border Pass have been defeated by the power of the Cave. Everyone was killed except a small group that escaped. I fear that those at Seven Oaks have suffered a similar ..."

Angry murmurs ignited instantly at the unbelievable pronouncement. Ou-Leesen noted that no one wanted to discuss the Cave. Rather, their frustration was directed at the messenger.

"This is impossible! We had the advantage of Border Pass! And now you tell us that you have fled the enemy. Losing the 'golden gate' into Storlenia?" The mounting hostility was no surprise to Ou-Leesen. He had expected it. The insult weighed heavily on him, but he was determined to remain silent.

When there was no reply, a Quorum member cried, "For this you will die a death of dishonour!"

"That is impossible," Ou-Leesen calmly replied.

"You disrespect the Quorum," another member spit out.

"I tell the truth," he simply stated turning to address the challenger. "I *chose* to be here, this can only bring honour. I am ready to die."

Shanteef raised his hand to speak. He wanted this warrior alive not dead. "Our ancestors believed that the only way to purge the stain of dishonour is through death ... chosen by the short straw. Why did you disrespect this tradition ... and yet you speak of honour?"

Ou-Leesen turned to Shanteef. His hard, unflinching eyes could not have spoken more clearly than the words that followed. "There is *always* a way to find honour in death."

'It's time to rescue him,' Shanteef decided. He arose and walked towards Ou-Leesen as he withdrew his knife. "Give me your hand," Shanteef demanded, grabbing it quickly. The sharp blade drew blood easily. Then quickly cutting his own hand, he clasped Ou-Leesen's before anyone could object.

"This day, the mingling of our blood binds us in life and death," Shanteef declared. Then he returned to his position in the Quorum circle. Either they would both live to see another day, or they would both die ... but Shanteef knew the Quorum. Shanteef had not saved Ou-Leesen's life for any honour. He had saved it because here was a warrior that he could send back into Storlenia, to regain what they had lost ... and more. For the remainder of the meeting, Shanteef would do all the speaking while the others listened. "What is your name?"

"Ou-Leesen."

"Ou-Leesen, now that we have lost Border Pass, what do you propose we do?"

"Some would say there are other passes, but I say, let us find one of our own. Let us take as many men as it takes and carve a suitable Pass. If we can bury the dark power, we can create a Pass."

"But how will we fight a power such as this? We cannot always ... run away."

Ou-Leesen shifted his feet at the subtle rebuke. "Pahkah sent a trusted man to find this Cave. Perhaps he will succeed, perhaps not. What I do know is that at one point, we had the Trackers and Tinkers trapped ... victory was certain. Then the *power* came. Somehow the Storlenians were able to use this power. Someone can turn the Cave's power against us. We need to find this man."

"Ou-Leesen, Storlenia is a large place ... and the Storlenians all look alike." Disdainful chuckles fluttered around the circle.

"I will not look everywhere. I will look for the *scent* of this power. This will lead us to him. Then, once we destroy the person, we destroy access to the power."

Shanteef allowed himself a weak grin of approval. "Ou-Leesen, with so many answers, it is obvious that your mind has wrestled with these problems during your long trip home. You bring honour to me this day, as one bonded by the blood. Quorum members, I propose that we give Ou-Leesen the authority to move forward with his plans. Do we have an agreement?" The knives were raised and then pommels pounded the carpet to signal agreement.

Ou-Leesen watched the men as they slipped their knives back into their scabbards. He waited. Perhaps the Quorum thought they were done with him, but he was not finished with them.

"There is something else?" Shanteef asked.

"How will others know I have the authority? I will need some signet of power ... for the task is large."

Shanteef looked at the Quorum members as he thought of the request. 'Perhaps it's time to replace the oldest member?' he considered. 'But I think not. I have a better plan.' "Very well." Shanteef arose from his kneeling position and removed his knife and sheath. He stepped forward and handed the bejewelled knife in its polished leather scabbard to Ou-Leesen. "This will get you what you want. Return it to me when the dark power has been silenced – not before." He placed a hand on his shoulder. "Before you leave, come see me. I have instructions that you will find helpful."

As the Quorum looked on in amazement, Ou-Leesen kissed the green jewelled pommel, tied the scabbard to his waist, and bowed to the Quorum. Then he left to find his men.

He knew there was something significant about the group of men that had followed him back to the tent of the Quorum. They had not died when others had. He would organize them into a Band and together they would find the man with the power. They were busy tending to the needs of their horses when Ou-Leesen strode into the corral.

The men uttered murmurs of surprise. They never expected to see Ou-Leesen again.

Ou-Leesen pulled the knife from the sheath and held it high. The large emerald pommel gleamed in the strong sun of southern Shaksbah. "We have been preserved by the spirits of our ancestors. The ancient evil can have no power over us," Ou-Leesen declared to the small Band that had survived the dark power. "Instead of dishonour ... honour. Instead of death, we have been given the charge to *bring* death to the power of the Dark Cave." He replaced the knife.

A few hours later, satisfied that everything was ready, he headed for Shanteef's tent.

Entering, Shanteef offered a thin smile, directing Ou-Leesen to sit down. "Are you ready to leave?"

"Yes ... I have recruited the men who survived Border Pass. We leave at first light."

"A wise choice. To take men who have no fear of the ancient dark power. How will you choose the location of the mountain pass?"

"Our ancestors will guide us."

"Your ancestors will guide you through the efforts of our skilled surveyors," he corrected and handed Ou-Leesen a sealed scroll. "Follow these instructions and you will have your surveyors."

Ou-Leesen tucked the scroll into his belt.

"Now ... another matter. The Quorum has decided to expand your commission. Once the Pass is finished, you will help move our gold into Storlenia."

"Gold?"

"Yes. Storlenians crave it like the air they breathe. We will exchange gold for influence among the Guilds. Once we control the Guilds, we will be close to controlling Ankoletia. So, you see ... our future depends on the quick and successful completion of this new Pass."

"Have the gold shipments already been arranged with our Government?"

Shanteef stood. "Ou-Leesen, we will finish this discussion at the Mines of Tenleth. I will leave tomorrow. Wait for me there."

At the mines, Ou-Leesen was surprised to see many Storlenian women and children working alongside the men. He learned from a foreman that they were the family members of the Storlenians recruited from Toobor to assist the infiltration effort into Storlenia.

"Helps keep gold production up and the Storlenian recruits focused," the foreman offered.

Ou-Leesen studied the miserable working conditions for a while. Then turned his horse back to the camp.

The next day, Ou-Leesen and his Band rode out to meet Shanteef and his escort. They rode together into the town of Tenleth. At the visitor's camp, Shanteef turned to Ou-Leesen, "Have your men stay here. We will ride to the Quorum's Keep."

Within a few leagues of the dusty camp, Canopy Trees circled well-kept grounds surrounding a large fortress. The contrast of the Keep to the conditions at the camp irritated Ou-Leesen. But he remained silent as he followed Shanteef along marble corridors to an elegant room.

"Have you seen the El-Bhat wealth before?" the Quorum Leader asked as he motioned for Ou-Leesen to join him on an array of soft pillows. A servant brought food and drink.

The question was unexpected. And the words troubled him. "Yes ... but the Mines of Tenleth do not belong to us." Ou-Leesen said the words ... but they sounded false. He was beginning to understand why he was asked to come here. He needed to be educated.

Shanteef poured himself some tea. "Officially yes ... but for decades we have been falsifying reports, manipulating inspections, and stockpiling a portion of the gold. The Government at Kel-eetan has always squandered their share. It is what inspired us to keep some for ourselves. This gold will place our recruits on the Guild seats of power within Storlenia. Once we have that control, our Brethren will move to overthrow our own weak government. Then the El-Bhat will take their rightful place as Rulers of the World!"

Ou-Leesen stared blankly while listening to the flood of information Shanteef was sharing with him. El-Bhat were trained to submit to the Quorum. But some things still required answers. "How do you plan on moving all of this gold from Tenleth to the pass?"

Shanteef smiled at the ignorance. "There is too much gold to hide here at the mines. It has been re-located to Chitouf, a village close to the Southland Mountains. The homes are made of gold bars ... covered with clay. Build me *Ou-Leesen Pass* ... and you will see that the gold will accomplish what ten thousand El-Bhat cannot."

Ou-Leesen fell to his knees. "We have lost Border Pass but the El-Bhat sword is still strong ..."

Shanteef silenced him with a motion of his hand. "Ou-Leesen, you have not failed us. We never expected to keep Border Pass. The Quorum needed an entrance into Storlenia to seed the Guilds. We have achieved more than we ever expected. The Storlenians regaining Border Pass, will be seen as a great victory. They will assume they have driven the enemy back into the wilderness." He laughed. "They will sleep while we are busy transporting our gold."

Ou-Leesen's eyes studied the luxurious carpet. "We have shamed the Quorum."

"Given a choice, the Quorum prefers to send gold to the battlefield ... than our sons."

"We are not afraid to die," Ou-Leesen answered.

Shanteef decided it was time to tell him about the Dagger of Truth.

"You think we value our gold more than El-Bhat?" Shanteef's eyes narrowed. "I will *not* squander El-Bhat when I can save them with my gold. Remove the Knife."

Ou-Leesen unsheathed it and held it out for Shanteef to take.

Shanteef didn't move. "Once passed, it can never be taken back. The power of the Knife is yours."

"Power?"

"It is the Dagger of Truth."

Ou-Leesen stared at the blade. "This cannot be … the legend teaches …"

"The legend protects the secret. The Dagger has always been in our tribe."

Ou-Leesen examined the large Emerald encased in the pommel while reflecting on Shanteef's words. "Tell me about the power."

"In a time before the Great War, the Sherilin – a tribe who lived on the eastern plains of Shaksbah – found a stone box at the bottom of a Waterless Well. It was handed to their Leader. Inside that box was found a Necklace, which cradled a green stone of enormous power … and this Dagger."

Ou-Leesen had never heard the thread of history that revealed the connection between the Sherilin and the El-Bhat. "Our ancestors are … the Sherilin?" He couldn't believe what he had just heard. But suddenly understood a mystery that had haunted him for years. "It is why we are the only tribe who possess eyes of brilliant green?" Ou-Leesen probed.

"Yes … using this power transforms the eyes. The effect is so powerful; it is passed on to the children."

Ou-Leesen remembered that Shanteef had just mentioned 'enormous power'. "Can this Necklace crush the dark power of the Cave?" Ou-Leesen asked.

"The legend suggests that it can … but after the Leader's death, the Necklace and the stone box were never seen again. The Dagger, stained with his blood, was found where he had fallen dead."

"Why … would a Sherilin Leader kill himself?" Ou-Leesen wanted to know.

"Great power is not so easily harvested. The Dagger must not be used too often … otherwise the mind of the user is lost."

"Does the power of the Necklace continue to flow to the Dagger of Truth?"

"Yes ... but the purpose of the Knife is different from the Necklace. First ... it can cut anything." Shanteef nodded towards the brass water pot.

Hesitantly, Ou-Leesen placed the Knife against the brass edge. As soon as he applied pressure, the Emerald glowed, and the blade slid through the brass like butter. Water flowed onto the marble floor. Ou-Leesen withdrew the Dagger. The Green Light immediately winked out. He took a deep breath ... fighting for release from the power of the Knife. He stared at Shanteef, seeking an answer.

"Be wise in its use and you will live to pass on the Dagger ... as I have."

Ou-Leesen slipped the Dagger into the scabbard as he considered its title and how it could cut through anything. "Nothing can be hidden from this blade. Truly it is a Dagger of Truth!"

"Well said. But there is another reason for its name. The truth of anything can be extracted, by placing the blade against the forehead of a victim. Ask your question and the victim will answer. All truth can be revealed."

Once Ou-Leesen found the man who used the power of the Cave, he would ask where it is located. Then forty thousand El-Bhat would bury it! "How will the Quorum supply us with enough men to prepare the Pass and move the gold?"

"The people of Chitouf have kissed your Knife, felt its power, and made an oath. These five thousand men will be enough. Our time here is finished. May the Dagger of Truth give you what you need," Shanteef concluded.

Ou-Leesen rose, bowed, and left the Keep. As he walked to his horse, an image flickered across his mind – of kissing the Dagger's emerald stone when he first entered Shanteef's tent. It was an ageless tradition that honoured the prophecy. One day this knife – and the man who held it – would be the hope of every El-Bhat.

Everyone kissed it ... except the man who possessed the Knife! Shanteef should have kissed the Dagger before *Ou-Leesen* left the elegant room. Ou-Leesen turned to look back at the Keep. "Now I am sure that I know your heart. When I return, we will discuss this matter!"

Shanteef waited in the room for his next visitor. The man entered ... troubled that Shanteef had given the Dagger to Ou-Leesen.

"You place too much confidence in this dog ... who claims to be a warrior."

"My confidence ... is placed in both of you!" Shanteef's words were hard.

"You will be my eyes *and* my leash. He is a warrior of passion. His mind is strong. Use this to your advantage. My instructions direct him to look for you at Chitouf. He is to use you as an Advisor. When the Pass is finished, Ou-Leesen must return to me ... alive! Then we will see about the Dagger of Truth."

Chapter 14 - The village of death

Previously. After Peloree was killed by El-Bhat, the remaining five Trackers discovered the power of the Circle and used it to kill six El-Bhat who had tracked them. Other El-Bhat were spotted, confirming that the enemy knew of their mission to find Stek and the Cave. Changing plans to protect Stek, they headed west

For the next two weeks, the Circle led by Deema, never stopped, except for fresh horses and food. They avoided main roads and eventually abandoned the wagon as they travelled on horse though a large forest.

As forest became flat prairie they stopped and kept watch for a full day. They saw no El-Bhat. Satisfied, they headed north into the hill country.

The area was remote but populated with enough villages to allow them to replenish their stock. From time to time, they climbed to a high spot looking for crops, the best indicator that a village was close by.

Striklin hurried down the hill with the news, "Head north, with a small lean to the east, for about ten leagues and you'll find the next village."

On their approach, it became obvious that something had gone terribly wrong. On the outskirts of town, a single man was busy digging graves. Stretched out along the border of the graveyard were multiple bodies covered with white lime dust. They cast a glance but kept walking.

Inside the village were so few men that it looked deserted. Then a bold boy stepped out of the shadows and ran up to Toulee.

"Do you have any food?" he asked with hopeful eyes.

"Sure," Toulee answered with a smile. "What's your name?"

"Kitcan."

"What happened here Kitcan?" She asked as she opened her bag.

He went silent. He could only stare at her hands as they dug into the bag for food. As soon as she handed him the supplies, he was gone.

They stood there for a while looking at each other, wondering what could have happened. "Perhaps we ought to go back to the Grave Digger," one of the Trackers suggested. As they contemplated that suggestion, a man exited one of the buildings down the street and headed towards them.

"Welcome to our village," he said flatly. "I see you gave some food to the boy. I thank you for that. You're welcome to stay before you move on. There's no need to worry. I'm sure you saw the dead men before you entered here. But it's not pestilence. It was the well water used by the men in the fields. It got contaminated. Maybe an animal fell in and died. But before we figured things out, we lost around forty men. There are only ten of us left. There's an Inn where you can find a place to sleep before moving on. But you will have to supply your own food."

"That's very kind. Can you point us in the direction of the Inn?" Deema asked the old man.

At the other end of town the small Inn served as a stopover point for Merchants and Guild travellers. They went straight to their room. They needed to talk.

"We can't move on," said one of the Trackers. "There must be more hungry kids out there, besides the one that found us."

"I agree," replied Striklin, "but I'm also concerned about Stek. We've already had a major delay and we're looking at another couple of weeks before we find him."

"I have to believe that if we take care of these people," Toulee suggested, thinking about the eyes of that hungry boy, "the Fates will take care of Stek."

Everyone knew that Deema was short on faith when it came to the Fates. All eyes turned to him.

He responded. "Perhaps. But even if the Fates are sleeping, we cannot leave this place without doing what we can to avoid the inevitable starvation of these people. Let's find the old man and have him show us what needs to be done."

It was surprisingly straightforward. The crops were mature and hanging heavy. The harvesting had begun but with too few men. Graves needed to be dug before pestilence set in, and firewood gathered from the nearby forest for the winter. More cheerful than before, the old man asked, "How long do you plan on staying?"

"Until it's done," was Deema's terse reply. Then he decided he needed to say more. "When we're finished here, we will advise the villagers along the way of what has happened. I am sure they will want to help during the months and years ahead."

Three weeks later, a tired, but satisfied group of Trackers headed north again.

As promised, they gathered the villagers together at the next town, to explain the situation. Once they were finished, a large man with a large mouth protested, "I don't see how that's any of our business. People get what they deserve. It's that simple."

"Well then I guess I wasn't talking to you," Striklin responded. "Didn't figure you had the brains to understand what I was saying anyway," he declared, as he turned and walked away.

Toulee opened the Circle to let Striklin see the man charge from behind. Without turning around, he blocked the blows with feet and hands. Then with a back kick, he sent him sprawling. The Tracker kept walking.

With fire in his eyes, the man got up and attacked again, determined to pummel the Tracker to the ground.

The Tracker moved like lightning to avoid the blow, allowing the man to crash into him from behind and just as quick, he brought his heel up into his groin. The man collapsed. Striklin knelt beside him and spoke to a face tortured with pain.

"I'm going to say this real slow ... so you can understand. I never forget a face. Remember this. You have a choice to help or not. But if I hear that you have interfered with those who want to help ... I *will* be back!"

As the villagers watched them leave, one of them remarked, "He must have eyes in the back of his head!"

As they continued through northern Storlenia, Toulee wrestled with the conflicting need to use their Gift or keep it a secret. While resting in the late afternoon sun, she opened the discussion. "Striklin, I don't say I was wrong to want to protect you when you were attacked from behind, but I'm convinced that we need to be more careful when it comes to using our Gift. I overheard one of the men comment about *eyes in the back of your head*. And in villages like we are passing through, where nothing of significance happens, it doesn't take much imagination to consider that these kind of tales would spread like prairie fire, and unwittingly lead the El-Bhat right to us."

The men glanced at each other considering Toulee's counsel.

"I think what Toulee is saying," Deema began, "is that we don't need to stop using our Gift … but we need to be more guarded and elegant in how we use it."

"I prefer that we even keep this secret from other Trackers," Toulee added.

While heads were nodding in agreement, Striklin decided it was time to voice a question he had been considering for some time. "Does anyone else wonder why we didn't connect to the rest of the Circle the night Peloree died?" The blank stares encouraged him to continue. "I mean … it's obvious that they are not connected, or we would know … right? But why not? Are we not all linked through the blood?"

The Trackers exchanged glances. It was clear that everyone had considered the puzzling question.

"What we do know," another Tracker suggested, "is that the Circle *knows* things. For instance … we were the only ones who *could* respond to Peloree's need … and therefore the Circle … *decided* … to include only us when it expanded the capabilities of the Circle."

"That makes sense," Deema said approvingly. "And consider this. It suggests that as soon as our half joins up with Tal-nud's Circle …"

"And there is a need to protect someone …" another Tracker added.

"Then everyone will be linked as we are," Toulee finished.

"So the sooner we find Stek, the sooner …" Striklin concluded, ready to move on.

"There is one other thing," Toulee addressed the group. "It has occurred to me … that the El-Bhat have seen that this 'gifted group' includes a *woman*. Once we are back among civilization, it won't be hard for them to spot us."

"They won't see anything if we stay north and only head south when we arrive in the Lithgate Valley," a Tracker suggested.

"Agreed," Deema said.

The Necklace from Harleem

A week later the trek across northern Storlenia ended, and the group of five headed down the Lithgate Wilderness. They spread out, stopping to ask if the occupants knew the whereabouts of Urshen's cabin.

Velinti had just started to prepare lunch when she heard a knock. She opened the door to find a Tracker standing there.

"Hello ma'am, name's Striklin. I'm looking for a cabin owned by Urshen. Wonder if you might know where it is?" He smiled to let her know his intentions were friendly.

"Urshen is my son ... please come in."

Striklin connected to the Circle, advising the other Trackers that he had found Urshen's mother. It was an exciting moment for the weary Trackers to meet Urshen's family. And a relief for the family to feel secure in the presence of five Trackers.

While Velinti finished preparing a quick meal, Benton started the conversation. "Perhaps you have heard about our experience at Pechora? Is that why you have come?"

"No ... we're here because we need to find a Tracker who used to be part of our group," Deema offered.

"Was his name Stek?" Benton asked.

The entire group went quiet as Deema asked the hopeful question. "Have you seen him?"

"Worked with him for three weeks ... and then he left, heading south. Said he needed to find someone," Benton shared.

One by one, all the Trackers started laughing at the irony, and how close they came to catching him.

"With our luck," Striklin remarked, "he's heading for Border Pass!"

"I take it you've been trying to find him for some time," Benton suggested.

"It's important that we do," Deema volunteered," but I'm starting to think we never will."

"You said you worked with him ... what on?" Striklin was curious.

Benton looked at Velinti, unsure what to reveal. But the answer didn't come from his wife.

"These are the men who followed Urshen to Border Pass," Bru-ell offered, standing at the entrance to the cabin. He had heard

81

most of the conversation as he cautiously stood outside listening. Entering, the Trackers gave a wave of the hand towards the Tinker they met in Pechinin's office. "Five Trackers on a mission to find one ... must be quite a story," Bru-ell added, inviting comment.

But the Trackers, still waiting to hear the answer to Striklin's question, remained silent as they waited for Benton to respond.

"The secret entrance to the Cave," he divulged, without hesitation.

"So Stek knows the location of the Cave," Toulee concluded.

The rest of the Trackers exchanged glances suggesting concern.

Bru-ell couldn't imagine why that would be a problem, but he knew it was. "Want to tell us the story behind Stek?" Bru-ell asked.

"I'll handle this," Toulee quickly volunteered. "Bru-ell, you will remember that twelve of us were assigned to follow Urshen into Border Pass where we would be responsible to make sure the Gates were unlocked. Unfortunately, after we arrived we found ourselves in prison ... condemned to die if we didn't defect. Our situation was quite grim until we met Deema," she added nodding in his direction. "However, we still needed to send someone to Seven Oaks to advise our forces that the Gates would be open. Urshen and I decided that the best option was to have one of us pretend to defect and then ..."

"But they have Olleti," Bru-ell protested.

"Correct ... but I have a Gift that allows me to plant an idea in someone's mind that he will believe is his own. I used it on Stek to convince him, that he had a message to deliver to Pahkah ... about the location of a Cave, and he was to accept any orders that Pahkah might give him. This of course would get him past the Olleti, but we needed to have a way to cancel the directives given to him by the El-Bhat Leader. I did it with the instruction that as soon as he saw Mitrock, he would forget everything regarding Pahkah, and believe that he had received my instructions ... from Tal-nud. Unfortunately, Mitrock had plans of his own and he wasn't there! Stek, unable to find Mitrock, left without telling anyone, probably because Pahkah asked him to find the location of ... Bru-ell, why are *you* here?" Toulee suddenly saw the irregularity.

"To protect Urshen's family. Mitrock already understood how important Urshen was going to be in this conflict. But what would Urshen do if the enemy captured his family?"

"Does Urshen know this?"

"Biskin was sent back ... so yes, he would know."

Bru-ell thought of the probability that Mitrock was dead. Perhaps he would say something later.

Toulee and Deema exchanged glances. "Well ... looks like our mission is finished," Deema sighed looking around the cabin.

"Why don't you stay here awhile and assist in guarding Urshen's family?" Bru-ell suggested, turning towards Benton and Velinti for agreement.

Benton nodded, and Velinti followed with, "Lunch is ready," settling the matter for everyone.

Sometime earlier

From Urshen's balcony, the three men looked across the valley towards their finished work. "Benton ... Bru-ell ... it's been a pleasure working with you but now I must move on. I need to find someone that I have ignored for too long." Stek didn't mention that he absolutely had no idea who it was.

"Urshen will be pleased to see what we have done with the trail," Benton added.

"About that," Stek responded, "I would feel better if you took your family further up the Lithgate Valley. The El-Bhat will be back. They will not give up so easily and they are obsessed with finding the Cave. The last time the El-Bhat had Storlenians in this valley looking for the Cave, they spent some time at this cabin."

"You mean Protas ... and the misdirected search for diamonds?" Benton queried.

Stek nodded. "Before you arrived, while hunting small game, I came across an abandoned cabin about five leagues north of here. That's where I think you should go. And you should leave tomorrow."

'There it was again,' thought Stek, 'the feeling of being divided.' He knew he must take the location of the Cave to Pahkah, but he also knew he wanted to protect these people from the El-Bhat, who would soon arrive. He never remembered being such a complicated person before. 'But I am sure,' he thought as he moved down the wilderness trail, 'once I find this *other* person, my confusion will be a thing of the past.'

At dead rooster junction, he headed southwest to Pechora, where he would report to Bernado before leaving for Border Pass.

"Bernado ... Stek's back!" A surprised Assistant Guild Master blurted out, as he entered his office.

"Bring him in." Bernado knew he was bringing news about the Cave. Someone like Stek wouldn't come back unless he had the requested information. "Did you find the Cave?" Bernado asked excitedly.

"Yes. I will leave tomorrow for Border Pass."

"Good ... but your orders have changed. Pahkah died during the conflict and the Trackers have resumed control of Border Pass. From now on, your orders will come from me. Considering the importance of the message you carry, you will have to use a pass that is far to the east of Border Pass. Five thousand Shaksbali are busy widening this mountain trail, under the leadership of Ou-Leesen."

Bernado passed him a package. "I am returning the original orders from Pahkah as well as a letter of introduction from me. Give these to Shanteef, the Head of the Quorum. Ou-Leesen will tell you how to find him. By morning, a wagon with supplies, and an escort, will be ready."

"There is no need. I will leave now ... because I prefer to walk ... alone." Stek left as he arrived. Confident and determined.

Bernado stood on the front steps as Stek left. He was still amazed that Pahkah managed to recruit him. "Perhaps we will meet again," A hopeful Bernado whispered to the retreating figure.

Chapter 15 - Pass the wine

Previously. Pechinin headed for Pechora to talk to Bernado, an old friend about inconsistent reports. Mitrock also headed for Pechora, determined to find out why Pechinin was delayed and also to find a safe haven for Urshen's family

The Commanding Officer sent for Biskin. "I received a letter from Bernado, Guild Master at Pechora. Thought you should read it before you heard the news from someone else."

Biskin hesitated, reluctant to take the letter.

Surprised by Biskin's reaction, the Commanding Officer asked, "Do you already know about the letter?"

Pechinin's instruction was that only Trackers in authority should know about his Gift. He assumed this included The Commander. "I need to tell you what only Mitrock and Pechinin know. I have a Gift. I can 'smell' trouble, and this letter … smells of trouble."

The Officer looked down at the terrible news he was still holding. "Yes, you are right. You will not like what you are about to read." He tried again as he extended the letter.

Biskin took the letter and began to read.

To the Commanding Officer of Arborville Tracking Guild:

As you know, Pechinin recently visited our Guild. He had concerns that El-Bhat had managed to slip through the passes and had moved as far north as Pechora and wished to discuss the matter. Then Mitrock joined Pechinin, to conclude some other business between the two Guilds.

> While they were here, we received a tip that El-Bhat were spotted north of Pechora, supporting Pechinin's suspicions. Both Pechinin and Mitrock insisted on joining the group of Trackers sent out to investigate. We left immediately, hoping to catch the El-Bhat by surprise.
>
> Unfortunately, our arrival was anticipated. The El-Bhat knew we were coming. Our losses were high, including Pechinin and Mitrock. All fifteen El-Bhat are dead.
>
> I have sent a report to Qar-ana. The Arborville Guild has lost two great men. We wish their families our sincere regrets and sympathies.
>
> Regards, Bernado, Head Guild Master, Pechora Tracking Guild

Biskin stared at the letter, wanting to understand what his Gift was trying to tell him. But it was no use. His Gift was buried under an avalanche of emotion, from the loss of his two good friends. Perhaps The Commander was right, perhaps it was the heart-rending news that his Gift identified. Biskin tucked the letter into his leather pouch and left to find Urshen.

"I have withheld news about your family," Biskin started, "only because I thought it more appropriate that Mitrock tell you himself. He would've preferred that, but now he's dead."

"Mitrock?" Urshen was in shock.

"Pechinin too. Trackers at Pechora went out to investigate a report of El-Bhat in the area. Pechinin and Mitrock joined them."

"I heard you were close to Mitrock ... I am sorry," Urshen said quietly. After a pause he continued, "He would have preferred to tell me ... what?"

"After the battle in Lundeen forest, Mitrock found out that Benton, the surveyor from Mantel, was your father. He became anxious to protect the family of the 'first Seer in a thousand years'. Braddock agreed and asked us to take Protas and Bru-ell with us. We explained our concerns to your family and they agreed to let us relocate them to a safer place. When I left them at Mantel, they were heading for the Tracking Guild at Pechora."

'And now Pechinin and Mitrock are dead,' Urshen thought as he considered his family. 'At least Protas and Bru-ell are still with them,' he reassured himself. "Thanks for your concern about the safety of my family."

As he watched Biskin leave the construction site of the new Tinker Guild, his heart was reminded of the grief that would continue to flow through his life as a Seer. Life in the Sporting Guild would certainly have been different.

When the Commanding Officer asked him at Border Pass what he was going to do next, Urshen already knew that he wanted to discuss this with Pechinin. He sighed, feeling the terrible loss. He turned and headed for the Planning Tent. Braddock should know about the recent development.

"This is terrible news," Braddock said as he motioned Urshen to a chair, "but it's obvious that something else is bothering you."

"I was hoping to lean on his counsel. I believe Pechinin understood the El-Bhat crisis better than anyone. But now he's gone."

As those wise eyes stared back, Urshen realized the solution was right in front of him. "What do *you* think I should do?"

With hardly a hesitation, Braddock suggested, "First, let the Trackers clean up their own shop. And let the Tinkers finish building their Guild. Second, at Border Pass you talked about wanting to find Protas. He might still be at Pechora, but with Bru-ell in the mix, I doubt it. If you find Protas, you will probably find your family. And tell them about your wedding! And if that isn't enough to do ... visit your Cave. And don't worry about Zephra. She will stay busy helping me here."

Urshen placed a hand on Braddock's shoulder and grinned, "Thanks. I'll be back in time for the wedding."

Braddock's expression sent the unspoken message of what would happen if he weren't.

"We will travel as Arborville Trackers to Pechora, on assignment to follow up on the Benton family." Urshen informed Tal-nud.

"I'll find you a Tracker outfit," Tal-nud offered. "Do you expect to find Protas there?"

"Maybe ... apparently he's with Bru-ell."

"This will be good news for the men. They've been restless to do something."

Tired and hungry they pulled into the Pechora Guild wagon yard. Urshen looked around but didn't see any sign of his father's wagon. But on second thought, he realized it would be hidden ... just like his family.

As agreed, Tal-nud took the lead. Everyone following him to the front desk. "Hello, we are Trackers from Arborville, here to follow up on a security matter. Some time ago, Mitrock, the Assistant Guild Master from Arborville, brought a family here for safekeeping. The father's name was Benton. We have come to see them."

The man at the desk immediately stood, excused himself, and said he would bring back the Assistant Guild Master.

As they returned, Tal-nud watched while they discussed something in hushed tones.

"Gentlemen, welcome," the Assistant greeted. "I am told you are from Arborville and have come seeking information regarding the family that Mitrock brought to us?" Tal-nud nodded so he continued. "Unfortunately, I have some bad news. This family that you speak of simply disappeared one night.

Tal-nud frowned, "Disappeared ... under the protection of the Tracking Guild?"

"Perhaps they became unsatisfied with the 'protected' lifestyle that we imposed upon them, or maybe they became nervous when they found out Mitrock and Pechinin had been killed. Mitrock brought them here to be safe ... and then he was killed. It would be unsettling for anyone. Perhaps they decided they had a better plan. Regardless, we searched the area for quite some time ... but we never found them."

Bernado was returning to his office when he noticed a group of Trackers gathered at the front desk talking to his Assistant. He stopped and as soon as he heard the word 'searched' he slowly walked towards the group. His Assistant was just finishing when he said, "Perhaps I can be of some additional service. My name is Bernado. I am the Guild Master."

Tal-nud asked when the family had departed and was told they had been gone about two weeks.

"I had half my men out looking, but they seem to have disappeared."

Tal-nud noticed Urshen at his elbow. "The man likes to hunt up in the Lithgate Wilderness," Urshen interjected, "perhaps we should look there."

Tal-nud offered his thanks to Bernado and everyone turned to leave.

The words, *Lithgate Wilderness*, rang bells for Bernado. Suddenly he knew why the family was brought to him for protection. *The man* was the father of the two-man team, that Protas ran up against. 'So, he probably knows where the Cave is, and he probably knows about my secret. These Trackers must not find him!' he anxiously thought.

"Before you leave ..." he cheerily called after them, "please, won't you stay and have some food with us. I am sure your journey has been long and hard. By the time you clean up, it will be ready. I promise you, the food is great. Our kitchen staff were trained in Qar-ana."

The self-imposed exclusivity of Trackers was counter-balanced by their overt hospitality to one another. It was natural to offer and just as natural to accept. But Tal-nud was hesitant. It was important that they push on.

Bernado was quick to react. He knew how to deal with hesitation. "Please follow me, I will show you to our guest rooms where you can relax."

After Bernado left, and while they waited for the meal, Tal-nud gathered everyone in the privacy of one of the guest rooms. "Were you surprised that your family wasn't here?" Tal-nud asked Urshen.

"Well ... I was half expecting Protas and Bru-ell to be gone. It wouldn't take much for Protas to feel he was needed elsewhere. And it's possible that the news of Mitrock and Pechinin's death spooked my father."

"Perhaps they went looking for Protas and Bru-ell," suggested Ranoof.

"Maybe. Whatever the reason, Lithgate would be a natural choice for my father, and an easy place to hide."

Satisfied, Tal-nud encouraged his men to get some rest.

Sometime later, they heard a knock at the door.

"Your meal is ready," The Assistant Guild Master announced, holding the door ajar.

The food and drink were already on the table when they entered the room. The display before them was impressive.

"It's as good as promised!" Ranoof said with enthusiasm.

"Bernado will be detained for a short while and he insists you not wait for him. He will join you as soon as he can," the Assistant Guild Master reassured them. Then left the room and closed the door.

Tal-nud grinned as he swallowed his first mouthful. "I'm considering a transfer."

"Wait till you try the wine, you won't ever want to leave," another Tracker teased.

The men were in good spirits when the Assistant Guild Master entered with more wine and to check on the food. "I bring you more wine as an apology for Bernado's tardiness, but he is almost finished with his duties." He made a mental note of which dishes needed refilling. "I will send more food shortly," he promised as he left.

Bernado entered the room with a flourish, "It seems I am not a free man. Anyone has access to my time." He saw the half-empty wine glasses and smiled. "The wine is brought by merchants from far away. It's truly remarkable, isn't it?"

Tal-nud shook his head to dismiss the images that swam in front of his eyes. "The wine is also strong ... I drank too much," he confessed to Urshen who sat across the table. But Urshen was too busy rubbing the sleep from his eyes to notice Tal-nud.

"Yes ... I fear all of you drank too much. And it wouldn't be right to send you on your way in your present condition. For now, you must rest. We will help you to your rooms," Bernado offered and opened the door wide.

'Present condition?' Ranoof thought to himself, while watching others around the table try to stand.

"It's the wine ... we've been drugged." Tal-nud struggled to push his chair away. But it was too late.

Seven El-Bhat walked into the room and each slung a Tracker over his shoulder.

"Take them to the prison cells. Leave one empty cell between each of them," Bernado instructed.

He panned the table, congratulating himself on his quick thinking and expert use of drugs. That he had acquired over the years. He stepped out of the room and heading towards his office ... he paused. Something had caught his eye. One of the glasses was *full*. 'Perhaps the Tracker had only just re-filled it,' he thought as he quickly returned, to examine the glass. But unfortunately, it was never used! He dashed out the door and shouted, "One of them never drank the wine!"

Ranoof never did like wine. And when their situation turned for the worst only moments ago, he was quick to adapt and pretended to be drugged. For now, he would stay with the men and figure things out the best he could.

But that was before Bernado shouted down the hall. Ranoof wasn't going to give them time to figure out who was sober. In the blink of an eye, he reached down, pulled out his hidden boot knife, and plunged it into the heart of the El-Bhat who was carrying him. Before the El-Bhat hit the floor, he was running towards an exit.

By the time the El-Bhat shed their burdens, Bernado had caught up. "You must catch him before he leaves the building! Spread out and block all exits." The last thing Bernado wanted was for the El-Bhat to be seen in the Guild yard!

All Ranoof had to do, was make it out one of the exits, and he knew which one that was going to be. He was familiar with the layout of the Pechora Tracking Guild. He worked there when Petin was still the Guild Master. He dashed down the hallway that led to the Kitchen and Service Entrance. The Kitchen door was always barred with a thick oak beam at night. He grabbed and lifted it, and once inside the Kitchen, he braced it against the door and the floor. They wouldn't be coming through that door anytime soon!

This used to be his favourite room, so everyone knew him. He walked briskly to the Service door. He paused and pointing towards the staff, he warned, "Don't open the door, he's stomping mad ... the meat in the stew ... I'm on my way to the butcher." In a blink, he was out the Service Entrance.

Miles from Urshen and the others, Ranoof sat in the upper loft window, of an abandoned barn, watching the fields below for signs of Shaksbali Trackers or El-Bhat. It was already too late to try to make it to another Tracking Guild. The messenger pigeons would be there before him, carrying a notice for his arrest.

Urshen stirred from the clank of a large metal door. His head hurt, and his body felt like a bag of sand. He laid there for a while, trying to understand why he felt like he did, but his mind was caught in a fog. He tried to remember something that happened in the past, so he could work forward.

He remembered Zephra by the river ... telling Braddock he needed to find Protas ... arriving at Pechora and finding everyone gone ... a table full of wonderful food. And that's where clarity stopped, and the fog began. He was lying on his side when he opened his eyes. At first, he saw only fuzzy black lines. But soon, those lines became iron bars ... framing a face staring back from the cell beside him. Someone with brilliant green eyes!

His trembling hand immediately went for his hidden Amulet. It was gone. It had finally happened, the thing he had dreaded the most. Being separated from the power of the Cave.

The Amulet was taken to Bernado for further discussion. "We found it on the one with blond hair. It might be important."

"Well ... soon we will know," he said in response. "If your interrogation isn't successful, bring him to my office. I will have the Olleti ready."

Six Trackers watched as three Guards headed towards Urshen's cell. The worse part was having to sit helplessly, feigning indifference regarding the ongoing interrogation. Urshen was supposed to be just another Tracker.

Eventually the unsuccessful Guards removed Urshen from his cell and dragged him, beaten and bloody, down the hall. Everyone knew that Olleti was next.

Urshen had already thought carefully about this day, and knew exactly what he would say, after he drank the Olleti. "My father encouraged me to wear it. I'm less tired and never sick when I wear it," he said flatly. And they were words that he knew were absolutely true.

A disappointed Bernado was about to leave the interrogation room, but decided he had one more question. "What is your name?"

"Gaeten." It was a name he had always liked ... so he decided it belonged to him.

Back in his office, Bernado reflected on the talisman. "Not what I had hoped for. But nevertheless, it appears to be an Amulet of *some* power ... and perhaps more than the Tracker realized," he concluded.

"Only one sure way to know," he declared as he slipped it around his neck. Bernado expected to at least enjoy the spoken benefits of feeling better. But within moments it seemed to do the opposite. He quickly removed it and with contempt threw the sparkling talisman on his desk. "You are unpredictable. Or maybe you dislike me. And I'm concerned that one day, someone will coax you to share your greatest powers with *them*. For all these reasons I am going to place you in the storage room, locked and guarded."

"Besides," Bernado said to himself, "men who rely on 'devices' to achieve greatness ... are always at risk of losing everything."

He picked the Amulet up by the chain. "I prefer to trust in my own skills and mental prowess. May I never become seduced by one of your kind." Within moments it was safely locked away.

Chapter 16 - A delusional mind

Previously: Benekee had passed Wutherstop's test and was hired as his new Assistant at the Mechanical Guild

Securing employment early in the day allowed Benekee to return home and prepare a wonderful dinner, fitting for the news he was anxious to share. The meal would be hard to keep secret, the smells already filled the entire house. He was excited. She would never guess what he was about to tell her. With everything ready, he looked for a book to read. He had hoped that the book would help him relax, but he couldn't concentrate enough to read. He kept putting it down and picking it up. He occasionally got up to look out the window to check if she was coming down the road.

Finally, he heard her boots on the outside walk, so he quickly picked up the book. When Yaneek entered, the aroma of freshly baked lamb, spicy beans and bread wafted into the front entrance. She was surprised and should have been delighted, but they had already had that conversation about watching expenses. 'Perhaps I need to say it again,' she thought irritably. She took her time hanging up her coat and removing her boots. She didn't want anger to ruin the evening. 'I need to remember that Benekee has just spent four years never having to worry about money,' she realized. 'It might take some time to get the message through his thick head.' She wandered into the hearth room. "Good book?" she tried to sound calm.

"Yes … well … not really. Just putting in time waiting for you to get home." He smiled at her.

It was hard to scold him when he was so sweet about everything. But someone had to be the responsible one. She cleared her throat, "Benekee, it smells wonderful, but I need to ask, where did the money come from to prepare such a meal?"

"Uhh … I dipped into the savings because I wanted to celebrate." He smiled again.

How could she be serious with him when he kept disarming her with those dimpled smiles? "I'm sorry Benekee but I need to say it again …" she began, as she placed a hand on the back of his chair. Instead of continuing her rebuke, she stopped mid-sentence. "Celebrate what?" Suddenly very curious, she looked over at the table and sure enough, there were even flowers sitting among the steaming dishes. 'Of course!' she thought. 'It's about the job.' "Did you find a job today?" she exclaimed with amazement, not daring to believe it was true.

"Yes. How about that. But I must confess, I had help." He was anxious to tell her about the Shards and his remarkable experience at the Guild … but that could wait. Instead, he leapt out of the chair, grabbed her arm, and gently pulled her towards the table. "Let's eat while it's still piping hot."

"I have to admit," she teased, "the best thing I ever did was to send you away to the Redemption Guild. They really know how to teach their people how to cook. This is absolutely delicious!" She grinned at Benekee while tearing into the chewy bread rolls. "So, tell me about your job."

For the next ten minutes they chatted about the test, Wutherstop, and his new position. But Benekee never mentioned the Shard. Then he went silent, hoping that she would remember to ask about his dream. Unfortunately, his sister was enjoying the meal too much, so he decided she needed a reminder. "So, when did they replace the fountain with a statue?"

"The same time they added the benches."

'Aha,' he thought. So, she didn't forget. She was purposely avoiding the topic. He wasn't surprised. It would be difficult for her to reconcile his comment this morning about his dream, the fountain, and how that just couldn't fit in with her logical world. Regardless, he needed to discuss it. "You don't think that's a little remarkable, that I learned through my dream about the fountain being replaced with the statue and benches?"

"Maybe you drove past it as you came into town, and you just forgot."

He was tempted to remind her that the road from Qar-ana came from the opposite direction. Instead, Benekee sighed and stared at his empty plate. He remembered being just like Yaneek before he saw the Shards glow. After all, their parents raised them as unbelievers. If it seemed irrational, it probably was. He looked at

Yaneek and gave her another smile. If she was this stubborn, even with the advantage of his dream ... well he knew it wasn't going to be easy. "Yaneek, I know how you feel, and I know why you feel the way you do. We have always been a family of unbelievers." He let her think about that for a moment. "But it doesn't have to be that way. And it isn't necessarily right. Just because you have been trained that way. *Experience* can teach us something different. In fact, experience *has* taught me something different." He paused, waiting for her to respond.

"Something happened at the Guild, didn't it? That's the real reason you came home, isn't it?"

He was nodding slowly but waited for her to continue.

"And ... this dream you had last night, somehow it's tied to what happened at the Guild?"

He nodded again, but barely.

A suspicion was forming in her mind. It left her feeling concerned and a bit distraught. She laid her fork down, suddenly disinterested in the meal. She wondered about how hard it must have been for the last four years, living alone, away from friends and his sister, carrying out meaningless tasks day after day. It would be enough to drive anyone ...

"Benekee have you ever considered that ... whatever it is you wish to talk about, might be the result of, uhh ... too much isolation and emotional scars from losing our parents?"

His eyebrows furrowed, not quite sure what she was suggesting.

"Benekee, there are people that can help with this kind of *thing*," she said, her voice trailing off.

Now his eyebrows shot straight up. He understood. "Yaneek," he chuckled, "you think I'm crazy." He leaned back into his chair with arms crossed, gazing across the table at her uneaten food. She looked awkward, as though he wasn't really supposed to understand what she was implying. "Please, eat your food, it's getting cold," Benekee encouraged.

But she just sat there, wrestling with her concerns, knowing how people with problems were quick to deny that anything was wrong.

He sighed. "Okay, let me back up four years ago. But first you have to eat. You start eating and I will start explaining."

She decided it would be good to get him to talk about his problems. She picked up her fork.

The Necklace from Harleem

"Of course it was hard losing mom and dad. But what I found out after living inside the Guild for that first year, was that there were lots of people in there with worse problems than mine. Being separated from you and my friends was hard at first, but I eventually found my own bit of happiness, through my association with the Brothers of the Guild. Our Guild Master was sometimes a bit too preoccupied with our Redemption, but he was fair. So, in many ways, your idea of sending me off to the Redemption Guild, was probably the best thing for me. So ... by the way, thanks for that." He noticed that she was eating heartily now that she was into his lamb stew. "Isn't that the best stew you ever had?"

Without commenting on the food, she gave him a weak smile. Now he was changing the subject, another strategy used by people in denial. She kept eating without taking her eyes off him, sending the message that she wanted him to continue.

"Now, here is the strange part. The Guild you sent me to, housed ancient relics of power and knowledge ... or so we were told. And for four years, I spent my time dusting, polishing, and preserving these relics, while others examined them, hoping to discover their ancient secrets. Imagine me, an unbeliever, hovering over these old pieces of junk, devoting my life to something I had no interest in ... at all!"

"Must have been difficult, all those years of mindless tasks?" She suggested carefully.

"Not really." He had to smile at the thought of Redemption life being difficult. "I had no ambition. The work was easy, and the food was good, and I slept well. I really could have left after the first year. I was over my grief. But the sad part of my life was that I was *content* doing very little."

That last comment helped her see something she hadn't considered. "Perhaps all this ... *lack*, was more of a strain than you realized. And eventually ... you found yourself *imagining* that something important had come into your life?"

Now it was his turn to stare into her soft green eyes ... with unbelief! "Sis, has it ever occurred to you, that when an unexplainable experience presents itself ... your explanation is always a frenzied mind."

She couldn't believe he had just put *her* on the defensive. She was going to have to be more patient, clever, and more subtle than she had initially thought. But that shouldn't surprise her, she realized. 'Who likes being told they're crazy.'

When his sister didn't respond, he took it as a sign he could continue. "Listen Yaneek, you need to know that in the future, I will have more of these experiences. I am convinced. And you cannot start worrying every time I have a remarkable story to tell, thinking that I am delusional and losing my mind."

'He desperately wants me to believe in him,' she thought. 'I wonder which is worse, temporarily accepting his fantasy in hopes that he will turn himself around ... or risk pushing him further into his delusional world, by trying to convince him that he is a bit crazy.' She was finished eating. She curled up in her kitchen chair, ready to try another angle. "Benekee, I hope that my disbelief has not upset you. You need to know that I will always be there for you ... you know that right?"

He couldn't help smiling at her concern. "No, I am not upset at all about your disbelief ... in my belief. You remind me so much of myself ... before I found the Shards."

"Shards, what shards? You mean shards as in broken pieces of ...?"

"Wait a minute, you need to see something," Benekee interrupted, heading for his bedroom. He returned with a leather pouch and dumped the contents into his sister's hand.

Yaneek stared at the shards. 'It's incredible,' she thought, 'they really are just pieces of broken glass!' She had to ask. "This is what it's all about ... these worthless pieces of broken glass?"

Benekee laughed aloud. "That's exactly what the Transport Driver said."

Yaneek examined them. She had expected more to fall out of that leather pouch. Perhaps something that looked like an ancient relic. Something that could twist Benekee's fragile mind into believing that he really had something of significance. 'It's worse than I thought.' She wanted to cry. Her little brother was really mixed up. And she was the one who had sent him away for four years.

He saw the disappointment on her face. "I guess they don't seem like much, but these broken Shards used to be a powerful Amulet in the days before the Great War."

Another concern wiggled its way into her consciousness. "So, these used to be part of the Guild's collection that you dusted every day?"

"Yes." He decided a direct answer was best.

"How did they come to be in your possession Benekee?"

He sighed. He always knew that *how* he got them would have to be discussed. "They, meaning the Shards, have ... adopted me. Otherwise I wouldn't have taken them. You need to believe me on this." He watched her closely, expecting an emotional outburst. Honesty was always an important thing in their family. But she just sat there observing Benekee, her eyes betraying her sadness. He was prepared for a tongue lashing, but this was worse. He couldn't bear to see her looking at him like that. He needed to say something more. "Yaneek, I guess you must be disappointed. But hear me out." He adjusted his chair and took a deep breath. "My life as an unbeliever wasn't much of a life. I didn't believe in the relics, but I was content to spend the rest of my life dusting them. But since I have become a believer, my life has taken on meaning. I have greater confidence. I seem to have a future. Before my experience with the Shards, I really didn't care about anything. I guess because I didn't believe anything. And more importantly, I didn't believe in myself. But now that I believe in the Shards, I find it easy to believe in myself. I've gone from being content, to feeling a fire inside that ... Yaneek, you do understand, don't you?"

Yaneek wasn't sure if she understood anything Benekee was saying. She found herself wishing her parents were there to help her pull her brother back from his delusion. But of course, if her parents were there, Benekee would never have been sent away. It was all *her* fault. There was only one way forward.

"Benekee ... I really want to understand, but it's going to take some time. And no, I'm not disappointed. You have been nothing but good news since you arrived. As for the shards, I doubt the Guild will miss a broken relic." She forced herself to smile, a suitable mask for the concerns she needed to set aside.

Benekee felt relieved. "You'll see sis. Everything is going to work out just fine."

Lying under the comfort of his feather blanket, Benekee compared his hopes with how the evening turned out. He so much wanted Yaneek to believe ... 'well at least to begin to believe,' he corrected himself. As he considered the accomplishment of the evening, he had to smile. She was beginning to believe all right ... believe that he was nuts!

He sighed and turned over on his side. He couldn't expect more from his sister than he would of himself. And *he* had only started to believe because he had the remarkable experience of seeing the

Shards glow. Would she need something like that, to break her doubts? He had hoped that she would begin to believe based on his witness. But it only seemed to push her further away.

He turned to face the other wall. He wondered what she would think if he told her about his experience with Wutherstop. 'Probably deny it ... like the Shards,' he admitted. 'Good thing I didn't tell her!'

He got up on one elbow to fluff his pillow. If he wasn't careful, he might eventually lose his sister. And all because of his commitment to the Shards. He decided that he would have to keep things to himself from now on. It had never occurred to him, that the cost of being adopted into this ancient power, would be so high. He thought of the woman who previously possessed the Amulet and wondered what advice she could give him.

He pulled his pillow tight under his neck and with eyes closed, he began his descent into the world of dreams.

She was shuffling around her kitchen, preparing some tea for Benekee. She wore a simple long Robe with billowy sleeves, her long white hair almost touched the floor. Turning to bring him his tea, he saw eyes clouded with age. She gave him a wispy smile as he thanked her for the tea. She settled herself into a wooden chair, pulled out a Shard, larger than any of the ones he had, and laid it on the table.

'It's the missing Shard,' he thought excitedly. He looked up. She was eager. She was waiting for his questions!

"What do you think about my experiences with the Shards?" he found himself asking.

"I think it's amazing that you have managed to coax so much power out of them." Her voice was raspy, occasionally a word would crack. "After all, they are only broken pieces meant to fit together. And ... you are missing one piece."

Their eyes went to the Shard in front of her. 'Someday,' he thought, 'I will have that piece, and the Talisman will be restored to its former usefulness.'

She must have read his thoughts, because she reached towards the Shard and it disappeared under the swish of her sleeve. Startled, he considered what she had just done. 'She is sending me a message. Or have I misunderstood.'

As his eyes drifted from her sleeve back to her questioning look, he remembered how she was surprised in his ability, and she had reminded him that after all, the Talisman was broken. She wanted him to see something.

He thought back to his experience in the smoky room. "Is it ... the smoke?"

She offered a smile of encouragement.

"The smoke represents the brokenness of the Talisman," he began, "and ... making an effort to get past the smoke ... I was forging a connection between two Shards," he suggested.

"Benekee, you are indeed a clever one. The Amulet has chosen ... well."

But there was more she wanted to say. He could tell by how her words trailed off at the end. "There is a reason isn't there? I mean why I am able to coax the power from the Shards."

"Yes. Your bloodline gives you a significant advantage." That made him think about his sister ... the same bloodline.

"But what about my sister. I cannot seem to get past her wall of unbelief?"

She reached across the table and placed her withered hand on his. "Benekee, the Garden of Belief is not a crowded place. Pleasant, but lonely."

He looked down at her hand on his. He had expected to hear words of greater encouragement.

She continued, "Just inside the entrance of this Garden, there is a chair, where all who are patient wait."

He wanted to thank her, but suddenly swirling smoke took her away from him.

Opening his eyes he realized he was still holding the Shards. Dropping them into the pouch, he placed the bag on his night table, blew out the candle, and contemplated his dream-visitor for a while. And then he fell asleep.

Chapter 17 - Benekee's Hunting Device

The next morning, standing in front of the bottom steps, Benekee looked up at large oak doors, carved with the symbol of the Mechanical Guild. He couldn't believe how different he felt today about those doors. Inside, the same receptionist was busy with her papers.

"Hi, I'm back."

She looked up. "I've been expecting you," she said as she rummaged for some papers. "Here we go. You will need to fill these out."

He hated forms. He glanced around and whispered, "Is this really necessary?"

"Actually, this will avoid administrative hassle later. Courtesy of Wutherstop. If I were you, I would fill them out."

Eventually he returned to her desk. She quickly checked the completed forms. "Follow me, he's waiting."

As they walked through his door, Wutherstop arose quickly, anxious to take the forms from the receptionist. Benekee could hardly believe his eyes. The old man was shaved, wearing clean and pressed clothes and radiated enthusiasm.

"Well done lad, well done," he exclaimed as he finished reviewing the forms. "Does you-know-who know anything about this?" He glanced at the receptionist.

She winked, telling him that their secret was secure.

"Wonderful, you may go." He turned to Benekee who was trying to hide his surprise. "I'll explain the paperwork later. Let's just say for now that I still have a few friends in high places ... and this will protect your work."

"Still have ... protect?" Benekee asked Wutherstop while he filed away the papers.

"Your ears are as keen as your mind," Wutherstop smiled at Benekee. "Don't worry lad, I was getting to that. Yesterday when I signed you up, I should have told you a few things to help you make a proper decision. So, I'm going to do that now. Fifteen years ago, I headed the design team, which produced the model you saw yesterday. But just as we had finished testing it, another Guild announced it was beginning production of a similar unit. All of our hard work was lost."

"But ... your design was flawed," interrupted Benekee, "how could your team lose anything?"

"You are correct in your objection," Wutherstop affirmed. "But ... we were confident we could redesign to correct those flaws. However, we learned that the other Guild already held the patent of the flawed model. And that killed the project."

Benekee was shaking his head, "But obviously history tells us the other Guild never built their machine either."

"Precisely. Because they stole our flawed design. And we had the genius to correct it, they didn't!" Wutherstop paused in his narrative, fighting emotions that reminded him of a difficult time.

"There is more isn't there," Benekee prodded.

Wutherstop grunted and continued. "I was convinced that we had a problem from within, but others said, it was simply coincidence that these two identical designs emerged at the same time. It can happen, I agree," Wutherstop waved his gnarled hands to emphasize his agreement.

"But ..." Wutherstop raised a bony finger to his nose, "I could smell a rat ... and I was determined to push the Guild Council to find the rat." The finger dropped and Wutherstop looked over at Benekee with sadness in his eyes.

"And that's when you were reassigned ... to testing." Benekee guessed.

"Yes, I pushed too hard. I could have been smarter about it. I should have never traded my position to keep my pride," he admitted, scolding himself. "So, there you have it. The history I should have shared ... before asking you to apprentice under me. Now ... you decide if you still want to work with me. And if not, I will find you the best position I can. I promise."

Without hesitation, Benekee responded enthusiastically. "Yesterday I said yes because I like you and ... I want to improve your model." Benekee grinned. "So, let's get started."

Wutherstop walked to the door, opened it, and waved Benekee to join him. "I want to show you the lab," he declared, as they walked down the hall.

Behind them, a door went ajar, as eyes peered out of a darkened room.

A week later, the new design was finished and tested. They both watched the rotating drum come to a stop. Wutherstop turned to Benekee, "Thanks to your brilliant modifications, we are ready to go to market!" he said triumphantly.

"Except for one last thing," Benekee added, looking in the direction of the reception area. "Someone other than the Inventors, needs to crank that handle … wouldn't you agree?"

After Benekee had finished explaining the purpose and function of the Device, the Receptionist peered inside the drum. "This holds a lot of clothes!" she remarked.

"There is some effort involved," Benekee explained and handed her the brass pipe. "Slide it into that sleeve and pump the handle for a minute or so. Like winding a clock. The pumping will keep the drum going for a while. If you repeat the process about every ten minutes … about two more times … well then you're done!" They chatted until the washing was finished.

"What do you think?" Wutherstop asked anxiously.

She handed the pipe to him and said with a smile, "For my services … I want the first one produced … and I expect a big discount!"

When they left the lab, Benekee reminded Wutherstop to lock the door.

"Don't need to. The papers were filed on the day we started the modifications. I received the patent this morning."

"But you can't file without a working model," Benekee protested quietly.

"Confidence my boy … I can tell when something is going to work. Besides," he looked around suspiciously before continuing, "I wasn't going to be trumped like last time. Now, let's go celebrate."

Leaving the Guild together, Benekee thought of how different Wutherstop presented himself compared to the first time he met him. "What will you do next?"

Wutherstop looked around for a minute, and then offered, "*We* … will begin work on a new Hunting Device. Ever been hunting?"

"My father loved hunting … very skilled in tracking and archery. He tried to teach me, but my skinny limbs were hardly a match for the stiff unyielding bow."

"Perfect idea … we will craft a weapon that *anyone* can use!"

The man behind the darkened window watched the two men leave in a spirit of celebration. "You will not be so lucky next time …

old man." He had crafted a plan to cheat him out of his success, just like before. But the old man had submitted the papers before the working model was finished. "Illegal for sure ... but I'll let it go. Such easy success will make him careless next time." He turned his attention to the boy, somehow the cause of Wutherstop's re-birth. "He is a surprise. But I doubt he will last long." He breathed against the window pane and drew the outline of a dagger on his condensed breath.

The work began on the new design. Benekee mostly listened while he watched Wutherstop work possible concepts. He had no choice ... the Shards were silent. This was a change that he found hard to accept, but he wasn't totally surprised. It had always been his intent to place the Shards in a silver cage, restoring them to their original shape ... and power. But he allowed the demands of his new life to let that goal fade into a distant memory. Feeling the chastisement of silence, he decided that as soon as he had sufficient funds from their first success, he would approach a Jeweller to encase the Shards.

"It was broken years ago, and I always said that one day I would have these broken pieces put together in a silver case." Benekee spilled the broken fragments onto the counter and began to show the Jeweller how they fit together. "As you can see, there is a missing piece which needs to be made." The Jeweller brought some silver designs from the back of his shop to choose from. Once they agreed on a price, Benekee left.

Four days later, he re-entered the shop, anxious to retrieve his Shards. "It's beautiful," Benekee praised. The words came easy as he held the chain, the Amulet twirling in the sunlight, sending its refracted rainbows dancing on the walls of the shop.
"Best quality crystal I ever worked with," the Jeweller responded. "I'll have to charge you more for the missing piece. Didn't seem right putting in anything but the best," he declared seeking confirmation.
"Yes. Of course. You did the right thing." Benekee stared at the piece the Jeweller had added, knowing that someday, the missing Shard would be there instead.
Benekee left the shop pleased that the workmanship turned out so well. All the way home his hand never left the comfort of the silver cage, tucked safely out of sight in his pocket. He thought about

the recent silence of the Shards, hoping that now, the power would return. He had just considered that thought, when he felt a familiar warmth in his pocket. He grinned ... the power had answered.

He spent the evening in his room, pouring over Wutherstop's sketches with the Amulet hanging against his chest. Insights and images guided him in the finishing features of the design. By the time a weary Benekee laid his head to the pillow, he knew Wutherstop would be pleased.

The next day, Benekee laid his sketches across Wutherstop's desk and carefully reviewed the details of the new Hunting Machine. At one point, Benekee grabbed the sketch that showed how the gears and levers fit together, and after a detailed discussion he concluded, "... right here is where the many gears and levers compress the air, inside this cylinder. As you can see, the levers are activated by this turning handle on the outside. The Machine can compress a lot or a little, depending on how far the brass ball needs to travel as it leaves this tube." He pointed to the tube included in a different sketch. To his surprise, the old man was very quiet, no questions, no excitement. When he was finished, a concerned Benekee asked, "So what do you think? Can we start building a test model?"

Wutherstop wore a grave expression, and eventually he explained. "As an Inventor I have spent some time studying what little history we have of the time before the Great War. They had amazingly advanced machines. But there was little detail to guide us, only brief references to what they could do. Your proposed design ... goes far beyond a new Hunting Device. It reminds me of a time when machines had great power. This," he pointed at the revised sketches, "could change our society!"

"Do you think we should scrap the project?" Benekee asked, fearful of what the response might be.

"Benekee ... these old bones feel something. Progress is coming at us whether we are ready or not. If you could produce this design, it means someone else can. No, we will not scrap it. It is better to stay on course. At least we will have some control on its development and distribution."

Stepping closer to Benekee and laying a hand on his shoulder, Wutherstop whispered a concern. "We must keep this *very* quiet. If our 'Device' were to fall into the wrong hands ... it could be catastrophic!"

After the excitement of crafting the various parts of the machine, Benekee suggested that they call it either the *Brass Bow* or the *Brass Sling*.

Wutherstop preferred the *Brass Sling*. "The name is an understatement. But I believe that will work in our favour. Until we get this thing patented, it's best to have a name that attracts less attention, not more," Wutherstop suggested. And so it was settled. "We can improve the accuracy if we account for the drop of the ball," he explained to Benekee. "I have added two more thin wires in front of the scope lens. The bottom wire makes a correction for one hundred and fifty paces, the next wire up, for one hundred paces."

There were essentially three parts to the Brass Sling. The rectangular box, that compressed the air inside the cylinder and fired the brass ball. Next there was the scope that mounted on top of the rectangular box, and finally the tripod that the Brass Sling was attached to. It was relatively easy to smuggle these items outside the Guild into the waiting wagon. Today was the day that they decided to test the machine, at their chosen spot in the forest outside of town.

Assured that they weren't followed, they carried the Device to a clearing among the trees. Testing in the lab was confined to very short distances. Now Benekee had a chance to see how it performed at one hundred paces, the second setting on the scope.

Wutherstop used his pocket knife to cut a small target on a tree. "Ready," he shouted back to Benekee.

Benekee cranked the pressure to the maximum. Back in the lab they had reinforced the chamber until it could withstand the pressures of the original design. With excitement he adjusted the position of the Brass Sling until the scope lined up perfectly with the one hundred pace marker. With his eye on the scope, he held his breath and squeezed the release trigger. The image through the scope suddenly exploded into a thunderstorm of splinters and wood dust as the brass ball sank deep into its target. He grinned when he saw Wutherstop extract the ball with his knife.

While patting the top of the Device, Benekee displayed a smile of triumph. "I have to confess, I cranked it up all the way!"

"Well done lad!" Wutherstop replied enthusiastically. He scanned the trees as he absent-mindedly passed the brass ball to Benekee. "However ... we will soon find out that this was the easy part. Someone tried to break into the storage bin last night and failed

... luckily for us. I had reinforced the door when we first started, something they weren't expecting. But tonight, they will come ready to tackle anything. Benekee bring me your bag, I want to see if it's big enough."

Every day Benekee brought his canvas bag to work, carrying his sketches, his lunch, and a cape plus boots, in case it rained. He quickly retrieved it, passed it to Wutherstop who immediately began to empty its contents. Then carefully slid the rectangular box into the bag.

"Yes, it will do. Starting today, you will carry the Hunting Device home every evening, and return it every morning. Find a secure hiding place in your house. Now that the Device is finished, we are at great risk of losing everything. I have already contacted the Hunting Guild. They are very interested in our model!"

"That's wonderful," Benekee whispered.

Wutherstop nodded. "Yes, you are right, even out here we need to be alert," Wutherstop whispered back. "We will have to exercise great secrecy until we show this Device and sign the contracts," Wutherstop warned. Laying a hand on Benekee's shoulder, he added, "Remember to act natural whenever you carry the Hunting Device. No one must suspect that you have it in your bag!"

Benekee and Wutherstop spent the rest of the afternoon refining the adjustment of the scope for the longer distance of one hundred and fifty paces. The distance they intended on using at the Hunting Guild. With practice, Benekee could hit a target the size of Wutherstop's hand three times in a row.

A day earlier

The hole in the wall wasn't much bigger than the size of a nail, but it was large enough to spy on Wutherstop and his apprentice. Unfortunately, he couldn't hear their conversations. Only the loud bang every time they fired off the new invention. The first time he heard it, he knew they were making significant progress. Soon it would be time to steal their Device.

The previous evening, when everyone was gone, he entered the lab, and went straight to the storage bin, where Wutherstop's machine was stored. Unfortunately his meagre tools failed to break through the door.

"Never mind, tomorrow will be different," he smugly said to himself.

At mid-day, he watched them leave with the wagon. The 'device' was hid from view but he was sure it was ready for field testing. He was about to leave the window, when he spotted three men who stopped at the Guild front doors. They looked around before entering, as though they had something to hide. 'I must speak to them first,' he thought. He turned and ran down the stairs.

When he burst into the entrance way, they turned and ran. Now he was sure that he was right about their intentions. "Wait ... please wait," he shouted after them.

He quickly learned that they only wanted the lad. Perfect! He gave them what they needed ... the information where he lived. And before they left, he was promised that as soon as they had what they had come for, the machine would be his!

Chapter 18 - A blinding flash of Light

When Benekee and Wutherstop left the forest, the sun had already set. They stopped briefly at the Guild to give the impression that they left the machine locked in the lab. Benekee bid Wutherstop a good night and began his long walk home.

He had been thinking about their success in the forest when he turned into Yaneek's yard. At the front door, he laid his hand on the doorknob but his happy thoughts fled. Something was terribly wrong ... the latch was broken! He dropped his bag and rushed inside to find Yaneek in the large chair, eyes red and fearful. Looking around their small house, he saw that everything was in disarray. Someone had been desperate to find something. Instinctively his hand went to his chest ... and then he quickly returned to the front door to retrieve the machine ... hidden in his bag.

'Were they looking for the Shards ... or the Machine,' he wondered. Either way, they didn't find what they were looking for. The Machine didn't make sense. Except for today it had always been locked up at the Guild. But the Shards – always worn under his shirt – was truly the greater prize.

So the question was ... who? He didn't think it was the Redemption Guild. They would just confront him and demand that he return it. No ... this was someone who knew about the power of the Shards. Wutherstop was concerned about the Machine falling into the wrong hands. But Benekee knew that the Shards made the Machine possible. Wutherstop didn't understand that the Machine was nothing, compared to the Shards. His hand drifted to the chain that held the silver cage, as he looked back at Yaneek. He wished he could tell her what was happening, and why they needed to leave their home immediately.

Instead, he walked across the room, encouraging her to bury herself in his arms. The fearful sobbing returned as Benekee gently stroked her hair, while his eyes scanned the room again. Whoever they were, they were very ambitious about finding something valuable ... that was hidden. But luckily there was nothing that was ...

His head suddenly looked towards his bedroom, as a memory returned from the place that forgotten memories go. A *letter* ... that he wrote to himself, about four years ago, before his parents died. There was a dream one night ... a very special dream. He wrote it all down to never forget it. And he hid the letter in a special place, a place where no one would find it. When his parents died, he didn't care about anything anymore ... and he forgot about his hidden treasure. As soon as the sobbing stopped, he whispered to his sister, "Yaneek, I need to check on something," and gently pulled himself away.

Inside his room, with door closed, he removed the secret floor board and retrieved the small wooden box. Inside he found his letter. He read the forgotten lines.

I was wearing a Robe ...
When the sparkling Fragments called to me with their rush of Light!
Do they know my name? Do they tease me with their power?
Perhaps both.

Have they come to me because I was born belonging to them? Or were they sent that I might see clearly ... this wasteland to which I have surrendered?
Perhaps both.

In my Dream, the Fragments pulled me ... like the bottom of a hill as I tumbled downward.
But if I leave the comfort of my wasteland, will I know where to go?
Yet somehow, I do know, and the road is long ... but jubilant.

When I arrive, tears wet her face. She too has lived in a wasteland.
It has been four years since we parted.

If I tell her of my Fragments ... will she understand why I was born?
I tell her ... time passes, and she doesn't.

As I hold the Fragments, they promise to push back the wasteland that has come to my door.
Then on a different road ... a rush of Light
And she believes!

    He tucked the letter into his pouch and looked at his bedroom door. Yaneek was on the other side. She was the reason for the dream. The dream told him of his future ... of joining the Guild, which became his wasteland until he found the Shards. Then he came home, to find that Yaneek had been living in a wasteland of her own. But ... the dream was clear about the most important thing of all. Soon she would believe! He took a deep breath and opened the door. "Yaneek, we can't stay here any longer, it isn't safe," Benekee announced.
    "Why would anyone do this to us?" She asked with trembling lips. Then she remembered how secretive Benekee had been about his work. "Does this have something to do with your new project?" She asked, wanting to know the truth.
    "Maybe," he suggested, knowing this was the only story she would believe.
    After hastily packing, they ate a simple meal.
    "We should leave as soon as it's dark," Benekee suggested.
    "Where will we go?" Yaneek asked fearfully.
    He stared back at her red eyes. "Wutherstop. He'll know what to do."

    He didn't get much company, so he was surprised at the knock. There standing in his doorway was Benekee with his arm around a frightened woman. The late night visit told Wutherstop two things. He was meeting Benekee's sister Yaneek, and the Machine was in danger of being stolen.
    "Please come in," he pressed, opening the door wide. That was when he noticed they had brought bags with them. Before he closed the door, he took a quick look up and down the darkened street. It appeared that they had not been followed. "You must be Yaneek,"

Wutherstop said warmly. "Why don't you make yourselves comfortable while I make us some tea."

"Now, what desperate situation has brought you to my door?" Wutherstop asked, as he poured her drink.

Benekee looked at his sister and replied, "Today, someone ransacked our house ... looking for something. They were *very* thorough," he emphasized.

Wutherstop blew across his tea cup for a while considering the news. He took a sip, then began to share his thoughts. "They should have known the machine wasn't there. Perhaps they were after sketches, to help secure the patent."

"Does this change our plan?" Benekee asked.

"It most certainly does. We need to speed things up."

"Whatever the new plan is, we can't go back to our house," Benekee warned.

"If the Hunting Guild likes what they see, you won't ever have to go back. We will both be rich!"

Benekee's eyebrows went up in surprise.

"I put you on the patent ... but first we have to get there."

"Why don't we leave tonight?" Yaneek asked, surprising both men with her boldness.

"We could be in White Boulder by morning," Wutherstop admitted, trying not to think about his old bones making the long trip.

"We weren't expecting you for days," the Head Guild Master exclaimed, standing behind his large walnut desk.

"Ahead of schedule ... long hours. Couldn't wait to show you the most important invention of this century." Wutherstop gave him a toothy smile.

Soon everyone was at the Archery Targets where the Machine would be tested against the skill of the Hunting Guild at one hundred paces.

"Your letter indicated that your new Hunting Device would easily match the performance of our best Archer." The Head Guild Master waved the bowman to come forward.

Benekee's father was pretty good with a bow, so he knew what to expect from the competition. But he also knew *they* were in for a surprise. Especially at one hundred and fifty paces where his machine would truly shine. Benekee nodded to Wutherstop that he was ready.

"Gentlemen," Wutherstop started, "if you will allow a suggestion. To truly demonstrate the ability of our Hunting Device, it would be best if you moved the target further down the field. Say ... to one hundred and fifty paces."

The man supervising the review of Benekee's demonstration, raised an eyebrow, but Benekee was already nodding his support. The man waved to his two Assistants who went running to the target to move it to its new location.

"We would be pleased if the Archer went first," Wutherstop suggested.

When the marksman was finished, all three arrows had hit the target. The two Assistants were sent to report the details.

Returning, they gave the brief report. "One in the bullseye and the other two arrows in the middle ring." Benekee heard the hushed murmurs of praise.

As the marksman unstrung his bow, Benekee caught his eye and said, "Well done." Benekee cranked the winding lever to maximum and checked the scope one last time. He rested his thumb on the firing latch and pulled down as a loud bang followed the brass ball to the target. Benekee looked through the scope. Satisfied, he proceeded to fire the second and third ball. Benekee started putting the Device away while occasionally looking up, noting that there was some delay at the target.

When the men returned, one of them went straight to Benekee with an extended hand. "Sir ... your three brass balls." He then turned to the Guild Master and reported, "All three were deeply imbedded ... in the bullseye."

Yaneek found a large tree where she could relax. She divided her attention between the men setting up the demonstration and the beauty of the forest around her. On one occasion she noticed three men, in plain clothes, walking through the trees towards the testing area. 'If they aren't Archers, I wonder why ...' and then she heard a loud 'pop'!

'Did something go wrong,' she worried as her head jerked towards Benekee. But there was Benekee calmly loading the Hunting

Device for the second time. Now, more curious, she watched him fire the next two brass balls. She was amazed that such a loud sound could come out of such a small machine. 'If sound counted for anything, the Hunting Guild must be truly impressed,' she thought and leaned back against the tree. Then she saw the three men leaving, the same way they came. 'Must have been invited,' she decided.

Later, Yaneek waited in their wagon while her brother and Wutherstop signed the papers. She wondered if the Hunting Device would be as successful as Wutherstop boasted. She wouldn't mind that. She was tired of working as a second-level seamstress.

A soft rumble told her a wagon was approaching from behind. Mildly curious, she glanced as it passed by, and watched the three men until they were out of sight. She recognized them to be the same men she had seen in the forest.

A short time later, Wutherstop and Benekee arrived. As Wutherstop took the reins, they grinned at each other. "Nicely done lad, nicely done. When we get back to Breckenden we will start looking for your new house ... a bigger one, with two House Guards," he added, grinning at Yaneek.

It was late afternoon on the road home when they came across a broken-down wagon with three passengers. One of the men walked to the middle of the road and raised his arms, a sign for them to stop.

Wutherstop reined in the horses. Yaneek recognized him as one of the three men from the forest. She thought it might be important. "Wutherstop," she quickly whispered in his ear, "I saw these men back at the firing range."

But it was too late. One of them had already secured Wutherstop's horses while the other two searched the back of the wagon for the Machine.

"Steady lad," Wutherstop said softly, seeing Benekee's obvious agitation. But Benekee wasn't worried about the Machine.

After moving the Hunting Device to their wagon, the two men joined their Leader. Menacing eyes stared directly at Benekee. "Our business here is not yet finished. Now we will take the Shards."

Yaneek fully expected her brother to put up a fight, knowing the great value he placed on the worthless pieces of glass. "Benekee ... let them have them," she encouraged him. To her surprise he quietly climbed down the wagon.

The Necklace from Harleem

As he walked to the front, hidden by the horses, he undid a few buttons on his shirt, preparing for his encounter with the three men. Two of the men had already drawn their knives when Benekee came into view. He knew he must be careful if they were to get out of this alive. Standing in front of them, he reached into his trouser pocket and pulled out the shards. He opened his hand for them to see ... and then flung them at their feet.

The Leader extended both arms to hold back his men. He didn't care about the insult. First, he would collect the shards. Then they would kill everyone.

Benekee watched the Leader, carefully gathering every shard. When he was almost done, Benekee slipped his hand inside his shirt and pulled out the Amulet. "You forgot this!" he said loudly. Everyone looked at the raised Amulet, not noticing that Benekee had covered his eyes with his other hand. The flash of Light was so brilliant that Benekee could see it ... even through his hand ... with his eyes closed! He waited a moment then opened his eyes. The after-effects of the flash affected his vision, but at least he could see. "Drop your knives," Benekee said angrily. The men had no choice, they were blind. "Turn around and crawl to your wagon." The three of them meekly obeyed.

The last thing Yaneek remembered before she lost her sight, was that her brother held something up to the bandits. Then she heard his voice commanding them to crawl to their wagon. 'They're blind like me,' she realized. "Benekee ... are you alright?" she shouted.

"I'm fine."

She felt the wagon shift as he climbed aboard.

"Mister Wutherstop ...?" she asked turning in his direction.

"Apparently everyone is blind except Benekee. Not a strategy I would have used," the old man muttered glumly.

Benekee had already taken the reins from Wutherstop and hurried the horses forward. He was fairly sure the three men acted alone, but he didn't want to take that chance.

A while later, he looked over at his companions. Both were staring straight ahead, with eyes wide open. "You should close your eyes," he said matter-of-factly. Without a word, they both obeyed, assuming they looked quite morbid with them open.

Eventually the voice of Wutherstop was heard above the creaks and rattles of the wagon. "Benekee, I changed my mind. Your strategy was both reasonable and effective. Not sure how you did it, but one thing is for sure. We were all as good as dead."

Yaneek agreed, but she was still young and facing a lifetime of blindness was a hard pill to swallow.

"I 'did it' by using the Amulet. Sorry, but there wasn't time to warn you and Yaneek," he said, knowing he could no longer keep the secret of the Shards from Wutherstop. His mentor would soon know that he was not as gifted as he had assumed.

This was the first time Wutherstop heard of Benekee's Amulet. And being a man of science, he always thought the old legends about these things, were more tale than fact. But all that was changing very fast, and Benekee's secret explained a lot of things about his Assistant. "How long have you had this Talisman?"

"Since before we met." He would have said more if it was only him and Wutherstop ... but talking about it in front of Yaneek ... knowing she didn't believe ... was too hard.

Wutherstop decided that the lad would discuss it when he was ready, so he changed the subject. "I am curious as to why you left the Machine behind. You could have easily taken it."

"Yes ... but as soon as they got their sight back, they would hunt for us in earnest."

"So, we're not blind," Yaneek exclaimed, touching her eyes.

"It's temporary," Benekee responded, "it's why I asked you not to stare into the sun with your eyes wide open ... or you *would be* permanently blind."

"Benekee, that's wonderful news!" She said with a smile.

It was good to see her smile. She had been through a lot lately. Yesterday, she had lost the only home she had ever known. And today, they lost the Machine that could have changed their future, and almost their lives. And of course she had thought she was permanently blind.

"Yaneek this must be very difficult for you," Benekee said, wanting to comfort her. "I wished it could have been different. I never intended all this trouble to fall upon your head."

"Are you sure this blindness is temporary?" His sister asked.

"Positive."

"Because the Amulet speaks to you?"

Benekee sighed, "I suppose that you've always known this, but I'm really not very clever. This *new Benekee* that knows things and can design things from a different age ... it's only because I possess the Amulet." He looked at his sister wondering if she would refuse to believe this too.

The Necklace from Harleem

"You mustn't talk like that Benekee," she scolded him. "I've always thought you were clever, and very good with mechanical things. But *now* ... I want you to tell me about the Amulet. Tell me everything."

Then on a different road ... a rush of Light and she believes, he thought, smiling to himself. She said *everything* so Benekee started at the Redemption Guild, on the day he turned into a believer. He talked about the trip to the Head Office of the Planning and Development Guild, and how he could feel the warmth of the glowing Shards under his Robe. The way he felt accepted, perhaps even adopted, by the Shards. He mentioned the trip home and his dream about his little red wagon, high above the town of Breckenden that taught him that the Shards needed to be put back together. About the day he went to the Mechanical Guild looking for a job, and the test he had to pass, designed by Wutherstop. How a single Shard helped him understand what the Device was for, and how to improve it. He mentioned his fear when the Shards went silent, letting him know that he had forgotten his promise ... to put them back together.

He talked about his trip to the Jeweller, and how all the Shards – including a copy of the missing one, made by the Jeweller – were all placed inside a beautiful Silver Cage which now hung around his neck. And how keeping that promise brought the power of the Shards back, allowing him to help design the Hunting Machine. And then, after Wutherstop warned him that others would want the Machine, he decided it was time to ask the same Jeweller to make a second set of Shards. He laughed aloud as he thought about the conversation. "He thought I was absolutely insane, asking for a copy of something broken! "Anyway, good thing I had them. It bought me the time I needed to think of a solution. And lucky for all of us, the Amulet agreed with my request."

"It ... obeys you?" A surprised sister asked.

"I forgot to tell you about the dream I had about the Old Woman. She told me about the missing Shard. And why I can draw upon the power of the Amulet even though it's broken. It's because of our bloodline. Yaneek I'm sure this all sounds so ... unbelievable!" He added quietly.

"Benekee ... maybe I'm stubborn, but I'm not stupid. How could I not believe? I'm blind. And I'm happy for you. Like you said before, now you have a wonderful purpose in life. And if I can ... I want to be part of it."

He was grinning again. He always knew it would take a miracle to help Yaneek become a believer. He looked over at Wutherstop, wondering what *he* thought about everything. "Wutherstop, I'm sorry I had to hide all this from you. I'm sorry I pretended to be something I wasn't. But I hope you will understand that the power of the Shards was a secret that I felt I could share with no one ... until now."

"Benekee my boy, my life was over when you came into the Guild that day. Because of you, I have my life back." He chuckled. "I can't imagine what's next! Imagine ... a Talisman with power ... in our time! However, I have a question ... that *you* need to answer. Those men who stole our Machine will want us dead. We know we cannot go back to Breckenden ... and yet a man with your power needs to know where he is going," Wutherstop concluded.

But Benekee was not the least familiar with Storlenia. He had spent all his life either in his hometown or the Redemption Guild. He had no idea where to go to hide. And with his work at the Mechanical Guild finished, it felt like his life with the Shards had ended. 'Correction ... there is *one* thing left undone,' he thought to himself. He still needed to find the missing Shard! He grinned as he reached under his shirt, pulled out the Amulet, and asked the question. "*Now* I know where we're going," a jubilant Benekee announced to his passengers.

Chapter 19 - A barn with a view

Previously. After their successful escape from Bernado's men, Bru-ell and Benton's family met Stek, who helped them improve the security of the path to the Cave entrance. They also continued to search the Lithgate Wilderness trails for Protas who was still missing.

Protas escaped from the Tracking Guild on the back of the beautiful black horse with white stockings. Unfortunately the animal was easily spotted and surely they would be looking not only for him, but for the horse. He found a stable where he could leave him until he was ready to go to the cabin.

Now it was time to find Jalek. Here in Pechora, they probably sent him out on short missions. To kill, and then like a hunting hound, return to the Master. With that in mind, Protas watched the Guild every day, from an empty bell tower. Far enough away to be safe and high enough to have a reasonable view of the Front Gate. He was beginning to wonder if he was wasting his time when he heard shouting. A moment later, his eye caught movement at the Service Entrance when a Tracker bolted out of the building. This Tracker was moving fast. 'I need to hear his story,' thought Protas as he moved around the bell tower, trying to follow the Tracker's movements. He lost him a couple of times but the last time he saw him, he was leaving town. "Could be tricky tracking a Tracker," he muttered under his breath, as he made his way down the bell tower. But a Tracker dashing out of the Guild, just like he did, was worth talking to.

After a few days of searching he came to an abandoned barn. 'A possibility,' he thought. He had gotten a good look at the Tracker, so he was sure he would recognize him if he got close enough. But would he be welcome? 'What am I going to tell him to convince him I can be trusted?' It certainly wasn't that he had an El-Bhat garment in his bag! Cautiously, he approached the barn from the front, to give the Tracker lots of warning. He opened the large door and walked in. It appeared that no one was there so he began talking. "My name is Protas ... I saw you leave the Guild in a hurry ... from the abandoned Bell Tower. I barely escaped the Guild myself, some time ago."

He paused, waiting for a reply. When none came he continued, "We share the common knowledge that this Guild secretly shelters an entire Band of El-Bhat." He listened carefully for any sound of movement. "They killed Pechinin and Mitrock. But Urshen's family, as well as Bru-ell and myself, made it out alive. Well, as far as I know. I haven't seen them since I escaped." Without warning he heard someone land behind him. He turned, and there was the Tracker he was looking for ... holding a knife.

"How do I know you're Protas ... instead of someone I should kill?"

The Tracker didn't move any closer, but Protas had no delusion about outrunning him or defeating him with his staff. "What do you want to know?" Protas asked quietly.

"Tell me how Urshen discovered that El-Bhat were in Storlenia. I mean from the very beginning ... what gave him the idea?"

Protas grinned. "Not what ... but *who*. And 'the who' ... was me. And that's when the two of us wandered south and met the Tinkers."

The Tracker put his knife away. "My name is Ranoof."

"How do you know Urshen?" Protas asked.

"We have lots to talk about, but I prefer to do it up in the loft, with *that* door closed," he nodded towards the open door.

"Perhaps we could eat while we talk," Protas suggested. "I brought some food with me," he said, as he grabbed his bag. Sitting up in the loft, beside the Tracker, Protas placed his hand on the bag, waiting to open it. "Inside this bag I have enough food to last us about three days ... and a black, silk, El-Bhat garment."

The Tracker didn't bat an eye, and without looking at Protas he simply said, "Probably come in handy."

"I think we're gonna get along just fine," Protas said with a smile.

They hardly said a word while they ate. They both knew they weren't going anywhere, so there was no rush. Finally, Protas broke the silence, "So tell me what happened at the Guild and how did you manage to escape?"

"I am one of the Trackers that protects Urshen. We were on our way to find his family and stopped in at the Guild to get information. It had been a long trip and we were hungry, so when they extended hospitality of good food and wine, we accepted. But the wine was drugged."

Protas chuckled, "Let me guess, you don't like wine?"

"Never have. But when I could see what was happening, I played along. Until Bernado noticed the unused wineglass. And so here I am talking to someone who has had a similar experience." Ranoof's sudden silence was invitation for Protas to tell his story.

"Well ... at some point, Mitrock realized that it was just as important to protect Urshen's family as it was to protect Urshen. So, he decided to take a few Trackers and head up to Mantel to find the family. Braddock, Leader of the Tinkers that fought at Lundeen forest, insisted that Bru-ell and I go along. Simple enough. We picked up the family and then took them to the Pechora Tracking Guild where they would be secure and safe. And if it weren't for the Medallion that Mitrock gave Benton – Urshen's father – we would all still be there."

"Medallion?" Ranoof was curious.

"Apparently the Medallion has the power to answer questions. Sounds unbelievable ... unless you've met Urshen. Anyway, when we first arrived, we were sent to our guest rooms, but something didn't feel right. So, I went and asked Benton to use his Medallion to ask the question if we ought to leave. With the positive response from the Medallion, we immediately escorted ourselves out of the Guild. And not a moment too soon, as an uproar broke loose in the prison below where Pechinin and Mitrock were fighting for their lives. I'm afraid they're dead."

Jalek turned his head. On the other side of the road, another Brother was running towards him. Having joined a Redemption Guild, he now paid more attention to Robed Brothers ... especially one that was running. They were *never* in a hurry! Suspicious, he brought his hood up while he carefully watched the man fly by. 'Protas! Again!'

He was sure that Destiny lurked in the shadows of this coincidence. But what was it? There was no time to think, he must act! As soon as Protas was past him, he turned and hastened to follow.

Some time ago, Jalek had abandoned the Tracking Guild – crowded with El-Bhat – for a Redemption Guild that would suit his purposes more completely. The day he had arrived at the sprawling Redemption Guild, tucked away in the opening to a forest, he knew he must find a resting place for his beloved *Hunger*. He chose a large tree with surface roots the size of a man's leg. He removed the moist forest dirt. Under those roots he laid *Hunger*, wrapped in oilcloth. "We must be apart for a while," he told his knife. "Our new home will not allow you to enter. But I will return soon. Rest my beloved ... until I find our next victim."

Following Protas reminded Jalek that he hadn't returned to *Hunger* since arriving at the Redemption Guild. He would have to be careful. He was on his own, without his friend to protect him. He paused as he realized something else. He was losing his desire to go back to his friend. He found something at the Redemption Guild that he couldn't explain. Like horses, the place calmed him. 'But never mind,' he thought, '*Hunger* will always be there ... waiting.'

A few weeks earlier

Stepping inside the Redemption Guild for the first time, Jalek felt nausea sweep through him like a hot dry wind. He was about to turn and abandon his idea. Willing to acknowledge that his decision was a miss-step, a flaw on the path of his destiny, when he heard a voice from behind.

"You must be Brother Jalek ... I'm pleased you have decided to join us. I am Brother Pull-Tuck, the Head Guild Master here."

The sweat was already running down Jalek's temples. His eyes darted anxiously to the exit. But before he could get his legs in motion, Brother Pull-Tuck slipped an arm under his and pulled him towards the dining area.

A chuckle suddenly erupted from the determined Guild Master. "Your timing must be guided by the Fates. Our last Ferrier left two days ago without any notice. Said it was a matter of life and death. Have you seen the horses yet?"

Jalek managed a nod indicating 'yes'.

"Beautiful animals ... even to someone who doesn't know horses. Only fitting to have a Ferrier as experienced as yourself." Close to the Dining Hall, Brother Pull-Tuck stopped. "I want you to meet all of our Guild members ... and here they come ... ready to eat."

"I can't do this," Jalek whimpered, tugging against the grip of the larger man.

"*Everyone* dislikes their first day. That's why I'm here ... to make sure I get you through it. Don't worry ... you will like your second day." He gave Jalek a big smile. "Just do what I do." With his free hand, he shook hands with the first Brother as he introduced Jalek, their new Ferrier. When the last Brother hurried to his place, the Guild Master pulled Jalek to the smells that made his mouth water. "And now ... you will discover for yourself, the real reason we are all here ... redemption being a close second."

After Jalek found himself seated across from the Head Guild Master, with a remarkable spread of fresh bread, wine and savory dishes, Brother Pull-Tuck explained. "Every day you will sit at that chair ... until you tire of my jokes. And then you are welcome to sit at the table where the Ferrier usually sits. And now this is when we bow our heads while I express thanks to the Fates for this wonderful food."

Jalek bowed his head for the first time of his tempestuous life, as an unexpected calmness settled over him.

Back to the present

After trailing Protas until he entered the barn, Jalek was ready to tell Bernado where he was located. But he hesitated ... because he was very curious to know *who* Protas was tracking. Being able to deliver both the Fox *and* the Hen might prove very valuable. He wanted his horse back more than anything, and this would surely be enough for Bernado to send him away with his blessing ... and his horse.

"You have come with information?" Bernado was surprised. He never expected to see Jalek again.

"I have returned because I have *very* useful information," Jalek announced. Meanwhile his hand kept drifting to his side where *Hunger* used to sit.

Bernado was glad that Jalek had disappeared. True, he had his uses. But he was so *unstable*. Someone like him could bring a lot of unwanted attention to his carefully kept secret. No one suspected there was a Band of El-Bhat in the Guild and he wanted to keep it that way. "What information?" he asked, his lack of interest showing as he returned to scanning some papers.

"His name is Protas. He is an enemy of the El-Bhat ... and I know where he is hiding."

Bernado set aside his papers. "Yes, I've heard of him. You're sure it's him?" he queried, surprised that Jalek had found someone the El-Bhat and Shaksbali Trackers could not.

"Yes ... and he is with someone. I heard them talking. I think the second man is a Tracker."

'Could Jalek have found the missing Tracker as well as Protas?' he thought, stunned at the possible good fortune. Reports of the successful routing of the El-Bhat at Seven Oaks and Border Pass had been delivered. And the names of Protas and Urshen were given honourable mention. It suddenly felt like gold was raining from the sky. The El-Bhat would reward him handsomely if he sent them Protas. Too bad he couldn't deliver Urshen as well. But still, they would be impressed! "How did you come to know Protas in the first place?" The Guild Master asked, needing further confirmation before he acted.

"I was Ferrier with the Tinker Train that took in Protas and his friend Urshen."

He scribbled a note and passed it to Jalek. "You will show my men where they are. Then when you return, choose any horse you want." A thin smile crossed Bernado's face as Jalek took the note. Bernado had never given so little and received so much. His prosperity was certainly on the rise.

The following day, the conversation between Protas and Ranoof turned to planning. "Like I said, I am a marked man in any Tracking Guild across Storlenia. I will have to think of something else," Ranoof said dryly.

"I'm probably not very popular myself right now," Protas countered. "But who says you have to go to a Tracking Guild. If I were you, I would take my story to the Planning and Development Guild."

"I could," Ranoof replied. "But who's to say, I am not going to walk into *another* nasty surprise."

"Oh, I didn't mean just any Planning and Development Guild," Protas clarified. "I would go to the Head Office of the Planning and Development Guild at Qar-ana."

Ranoof turned and looked at Protas, wondering if he was having a little fun with him. But he wasn't. He got up, walked towards the loft window, and looked out across the golden fields caressed by the late afternoon sunlight. He thought about Protas's idea, and decided it made sense. "I guess if I walk into that office and it's a sand trap, then obviously it doesn't matter where I go. I'll leave tomorrow before the sun comes up. Thanks for the company," Ranoof added. "You got any plans for yourself?"

"Before I saw you running out of the Tracking Guild, I was searching for a fellow by the name of Jalek. But then again, that was a diversion. I was supposed to meet up with Bru-ell. So, I'm trying to make up my mind. Whether to resume my search for the man with the lethal knife ... or find my Tinker friend."

"You seem pretty lucky," Ranoof said with a grin. "Maybe it doesn't matter what you decide."

Protas was slowly nodding his head, as he considered Ranoof's words. "Yeah, maybe."

Watching the sun slip beneath the horizon, the two of them sat in silence pondering what tomorrow might bring.

In the early hours before the dawn, Protas heard Ranoof prepare to leave. He rolled over and said, "You have a long way to go ... you will need a horse. On the south-eastern edge of town, there is a stable not far from a small bridge. My horse is the tall black one with white stockings."

"Thanks, I'll take good care of him. I will return him if I make it out of this alive."

"No need. Set him free. He'll find his way back on his own." Protas rolled over and went back to sleep. It was much too early to be starting his day.

Chapter 20 - Jalek's funeral

The crowing rooster brought Protas out of his fitful sleep. With Ranoof gone he felt uncomfortable staying in the barn. He knew from experience, it was never a good idea to stay in the same spot for more than a few days. His thoughts wandered back to a time several years ago, when Trackers pursued him all the way to Hilltop Redemption Guild. He gathered his things and packed his bag. He would eat later. He paused to take one last look out of the loft window. He truly enjoyed the peaceful ...

He quickly stepped backwards, wondering if he was seen. He didn't think so. They were still far away. He just might have a chance to make it to the woods. He hastened down the ladder and quietly slipped out the large front doors of the barn. Taking advantage of the tall crop of grain, he crouched low while hastening toward the trees and away from his pursuers. He was within fifty paces of the forest when he took a last desperate look, wanting to know if he was being pursued. They were still moving slowly towards the barn. They hadn't seen him.

He wasn't far into the forest when he tripped and tumbled into a roll that brought him onto his feet again. He resumed his sprint, but he knew his luck had taken a turn for the worse. He remembered hearing little bells as he fell! Whoever strung out that tripwire wouldn't be far behind.

A Tracker came at him from his left. Protas used his Robe and his staff to send him flying. Then a second one came at him from a different direction. Again he left the Tracker on the forest floor.

'Must be Shaksbali Trackers,' he thought, confident that he would yet escape. Bru-ell had taught him well. But a short time later brought him face to face with two men with brilliant green eyes. The struggle was over quickly, and now Protas was the one lying on the forest floor.

Searching his bag, one of the El-Bhat found the black silk garment. Angrily he drew his long knife and attacked Protas who was already on his feet.

Protas used his Robe to stop the first and second knife thrusts.

Then fortunately, Mishri barked the order, "Stop! Orders are to deliver him *alive*," the EL-Bhat Leader bellowed. The warrior held out the black garment towards Mishri, in his defence.

"We are here to *obey*," he responded sharply.

The bright green eyes of the warrior reluctantly turned away.

A lone man in a Robe watched the procession as Protas was led back to the Tracking Guild. Now Bernado would have Protas ... and soon he would have his horse. But better to wait a day. Let Bernado enjoy his prize.

Protas and Urshen locked eyes for only a heartbeat, while Protas was led towards his cell. He noticed that Urshen wore Tracker attire. It probably meant they didn't know who he was.

Protas sat in the cell for only a few hours when Guards came to take him to Bernado's office.

"Welcome back. I would have been more careful the first time, if I had known who you really were."

"Whoever you think I am, you are mistaken. I am a Brother of the Robe from Hilltop Redemption Guild. I have my Certificate."

"Well then ... you will be pleased to hear, that within the hour, you will be leaving these premises," Bernado replied mockingly. "I have decided to send you as a 'gift' to the El-Bhat Quorum. Perhaps *they* will be interested to see your Certificate."

Jalek strode through the front gates of the Tracking Guild, and immediately headed for the stables. He decided he couldn't wait to see his horse. He paused at the stable entrance. Surprised to feel such strong emotion towards the black horse. He had heard people talk about love. 'Maybe this is it,' he thought to himself. Then he went in. The black horse was not in his usual stall, nor the next, or the next. After a frantic search, Jalek asked the Ferrier where he was.

"Some days back, someone wearing black poked his head around that corner," the Ferrier said, pointing to the spot. "Later that day, I noticed the horse was gone."

Bernado was called to the front desk. A visibly upset Jalek was waiting for him there.

"I see you've come to collect your horse. What is the problem?" A slightly irritated Bernado asked Jalek. He knew the importance of rewarding those who pleased him, but Jalek had always been demanding in the strangest ways.

"Where ... is ... my horse?" Jalek shouted.

Bernado was ready to suggest that Jalek could take any two from the stable, but it was obvious that he was set on *his* horse.

"It must be Protas. I remember a missing horse being reported on the day our 'guests' departed. Since the Tinker was on foot, and the family took their own wagon ... that leaves only Protas. He must've taken him. My men left yesterday to escort him to Shaksbah."

Jalek was shaking, biting his lip in frustration.

To appease him Bernado added, "Take another horse for now. Return him when you find *your* horse."

After searching all the stables in town, Jalek headed South, on his borrowed horse, determined to find Protas.

Riding a horse was a new experience for Jalek. In all the years of caring for them, he had never owned one ... never rode one. He had driven Kahleet's wagon up to Pechora. But that did not prepare him for the experience of sitting high on the back of a horse, feeling its rhythm league after league. It was simply more wonderful than he had ever imagined.

For years he had taken care of them. Expecting nothing in return. He was simply overjoyed to find peace whenever he was with these magnificent animals. Now, here he was, being carried by one. He laughed aloud imagining himself on the black horse! He knew that anticipation would stay with him while he tracked Protas's captors.

The black horse had introduced him to the concept of love. And now he was learning something else from a horse. How a relationship was supposed to work. He cared for the horse ... and in return the horse cared for him. He leaned forward and stroked the neck of the animal. In a strange sort of way, it appeared to Jalek that horses were above human beings. They accepted you without judgement, and they served you with no complaint.

When they stopped at the end of the day, Jalek fussed over the horse more than usual. He couldn't help it. He was profoundly touched by the animal's willingness to serve him.

When he tucked *Hunger* under his bedroll he realized that his relationship with the blade was changing as well. His eyes were opening to who *Hunger* really was. Before, he saw *Hunger* as his only friend, someone who shared in his lust for blood. But now, he was beginning to see things more clearly. Especially as he considered the sickness and the trembling he always felt after the killing. "Of course," he whispered into the night, "I hate killing, *Hunger* is the one who loves it!"

He had brought *Hunger* on this trip. A needed companion. Someone he could trust. Someone with skills to assist him in getting the information he needed. Jalek propped himself up on one elbow and stared at the horse tied to the tree. A silhouette framed by the light of the rising moon. So beautiful. Why did *Hunger* have to be so jealous of the horse. It was time to change that! He would rename the knife. He would never again call him *Hunger*. From now on, it would be ... *Submission*.

Jalek approached the wagon from behind until he could see the Robe. Certain it was Protas, he slowed and followed at a safe distance. In a few hours they would arrive at the last town on the southern road. The Southland mountains rose high in the sky as Jalek watched the wagon enter the town. It was a place to purchase supplies for those that hunted the wildlife among the many valleys framed by the mountain chain.

Soon he would know where to find the black horse. "I shall call him ... *White Stockings*, he said triumphantly. And with *Submission's* assistance, he would be on his way north before he saw the sun again. Jalek waited until an hour after dark. Then he crept into the stable where everyone lodged the horses. He knew he would find Protas there. "I am here to free you," Jalek whispered to Protas.

Protas watched a Brother of the Robe cut him free from the wall. He was surprised that he left his hands tied as he led him away. As though he could read his mind, the Brother said, "It's better this way ... in case we're spotted." They came to a horse, mounted it, and rode outside of town a couple of leagues. Then his rescuer suddenly pushed him off the horse.

A bit bruised, he struggled to his feet, Protas saw the knife that reflected the bright moonlight. "Jalek?" He queried, astonished. 'How could he be here?' An unbelieving Protas thought.

"Where ... is my horse?" Jalek responded, ignoring the question.

As Jalek waved the knife in his face, Protas remembered what the Tracker Shabalin had said about the lethal blade, *The edge has been laced ... with a deadly poison*. Protas decided it was best to cooperate.

"The horse is somewhere in Qar-ana ... borrowed by a friend of mine. However, he promised to return it to Pechora, to the stable on the south-eastern edge of town, not far from a small bridge. Or if he couldn't, he was going to set the animal free, to make his own way back. He might even be in the stable, by the time you return. He is truly a beautiful animal," Protas said in admiration. Then a very strange notion crept into Protas's mind. "Brothers of the Robe ... ought not to take from one another," Protas apologized.

Surprisingly, Jalek had gone silent. He had even stopped waiving his knife around, which prompted Protas to continue.

"I see that you now belong to a Redemption Guild, like myself. It's the *best* place for people like you and me." Protas was half guessing when he made the comparison, but when Jalek slowly lowered the knife, he knew he had the truth of it. "You see, as a young boy ... my father killed the only thing I ever loved. I couldn't endure it. It changed me. I didn't want anything to do with love anymore. And that's when hate became such a big part of my life. But at the time ... it was all I had ... until I entered a Redemption Guild out of desperation. I was being hunted by Trackers for murdering two people in Pechora."

Protas slowly shook his head and continued, "Then I met Brother Ott, the Guild Master." Protas let out a small grunt before he went on. "For some strange reason, Brother Ott liked me, believed in me ... so I stayed. And I started to change. Although I fought it and denied it for a long time. Three years later, after Brother Ott was murdered, I finally realized what he meant to me. That's when I began to push away my dark side." Protas paused for a moment before he continued. "I hope the Guild has been as good for you ... as it was for me," he finished. Protas knew he had said enough. And strangely, he now saw Jalek in a way he had never thought possible. His own words had taught him that Jalek was not so different from himself.

But this was still Jalek, and if he came at him with the knife, he would use his Robe the best he could, with his tied hands. He was hoping he wouldn't have to. He hoped for Jalek's sake, that he would go back to the Redemption Guild and find himself as Protas did.

Jalek raised his knife again, and with a steady voice, he began.

"For a long time, *Hunger* was my only friend. So, I fed him. Things you do for a friend. But the black stallion taught me that someone that only takes, should be regarded with suspicion. So, I renamed him *Submission* ... to help him understand that things need to change."

In the darkness Protas heard the knife hit the ground

"But ... you were never really my friend ... how could you be with a name like *Hunger*?" Jalek whispered to the knife. He turned around, mounted his horse, and rode off.

Protas listened to the diminishing sound of Jalek riding away in the distance, until the silence of the night returned. He thought of the knife, the poisoned edge, and his bonds. One slip in the dark and he would be a dead man. 'Perhaps I can find water somewhere to wash the blade.' He carefully picked up the knife and headed south. He gave wide berth to the town where his abductors lay asleep. In the morning, they would head north, the obvious direction for his escape. But that couldn't be his choice. The arid landscape would allow them to spot him from leagues away.

By morning, Protas had found a creek cascading from the foothills. He washed the blade, freed himself, dug up edible roots, and gathered a good supply of mountain berries. Climbing higher into the mountain range, he found some relief from the daytime heat, and the Robe offered protection from the cold nights.

It didn't take long for the Guards to realize that Protas might have gone south, so they split up.

By the third day, the El-Bhat who headed south – while the Shaksbali Trackers headed north – found Ou-Leesen, and a wide search was immediately organized for the man in the Robe.

Protas spotted the search party the following morning when he carefully poked his head above the dense brush where he had been sleeping. It appeared they had already searched the general area around him, because everyone was heading away from him. He waited an hour until they were completely out of sight, then continued to head south while keeping an eye on the narrow valleys that wound their way through the massive mountains. It felt ironic that while he was making his best effort to escape the enemy, circumstances were pushing him deeper and deeper into their territory. Staying high up on the ridges he expected to see more Shaksbali, so it was no surprise when he came across several thousand men, busy working to expand the narrow trail of the valley below.

Successfully making it through the Southland Mountain trails, he headed west, hoping to find Border Pass. Unfortunately, it didn't take long to run out of food, forcing him to head south again in search of a village or town. He wondered what response he would get, wearing his Robe and speaking with an obvious Storlenian accent. He wished he still had his staff and decided that at the first opportunity he would use his knife, hidden carefully in the folds of his robe, to make one.

The following morning, while Protas continued his search for a village, he spotted a Mountain Cat searching for prey. 'My chances are better following you,' he thought, hoping to share the spoils of the kill. He was getting closer when the Cat stopped, crouching low. 'He has spotted his prey,' Protas excitedly thought. Curious, Protas kept moving as quickly as he dared, until he could see what had caught the attention of the Cat.

A boy herding three sheep and a few lambs. The boy looked about twelve and held a shepherd's staff, meant for a man. 'Normally Mountain Cats stay clear of humans,' thought Protas. 'But a boy? This might get serious real fast.'

While the Cat remained still, studying his prey, Protas began moving towards the boy, as fast as he dared, without alerting the Cat. He knew the boy's only chance of survival was if he could get to him before the Cat did. Then the Cat began to make his move.

Terrified, Protas sprinted towards the boy. "Throw me your staff ... throw me your staff," Protas shouted, but the boy had seen the Cat and was standing his ground ... these were his sheep!

With only his knife, Protas was no match for the Cat. He needed the boy to toss him the shepherd's staff. "I can fight the Cat ... throw me the staff!" His desperate shouting managed to extract a brief glance from the boy ... but that was all. Protas began looking for a large rock. It was his only chance. 'There it is,' he thought, seeing one five paces ahead. His FieldBall training served him well as he scooped it up and in one fluid motion, threw the large rock as the Cat leapt for the boy. The rock hit the Cat so hard, Protas heard the cracking of ribs.

The boy tried to strike the Cat when it hit the ground. But the agile animal swiped away the staff with an angry blow and lunged at the boy, fangs determined to rip away his flesh.

In the same instant, Protas threw himself at the Cat, plunging his knife into the animal's side.

With a snarl, the Cat let go of the boy and turned on Protas with claws ripping at his Robe. Protas could no longer think fast enough to fight the Cat. Instinctively the primal part of Protas kept plunging the knife into the Cat, as they rolled together in their death struggle. The nightmare of searing pain from claws and teeth and the growls of an enraged Cat suddenly stopped. Protas let go of the knife. His limp body slipped away from the animal while his mind tumbled into a welcome oblivion.

Eventually his consciousness returned. He could hear the boy shouting something. He fought against his exhaustion until he was standing. But his body was spent from the loss of blood that covered the ground around him. He teetered and then collapsed to the ground.

Chapter 21 - The brother of Protas

When he awoke, Protas was in a sea of pain. With eyes still shut, he cried out for Urshen, knowing that he could take away the suffering. Eventually, his shouting brought him out of his half-conscious state and to the horrible realization that Urshen wasn't there. Immediately a boy came running into his tent, quickly followed by several women. They spoke with a heavy accent, but he understood that he wasn't to move. But he couldn't stop thrashing against the pain. So they pinned him as they slowly poured a thick drink down his throat. Within minutes he lost consciousness again.

They continued the process for days and eventually insisted he drink water before taking the potion. And by the end of the week he started to eat ... but he rarely finished his food before he reached for the potion. The doorway to another world where there was no pain.

By the fourth week, the pain had subsided. They continued to change the dressing on his wounds. One day, while a woman fussed over him, he noticed his bed cover. They had tanned the skin of the Mountain Cat he had killed and used it to keep him warm. "Is it mine?" he asked. She gave him a big smile and said, "Yes."

It took many more weeks, but eventually he was hobbling around the town of Chitouf, escorted by his guide. The boy he had saved. They had also carefully patched up his Robe and washed out the blood. He was sure that without the iron-tough material of the Robe, the Cat would have killed him.

Slowly, Protas regained his strength, and often accompanied the boy as he tended his small flock of sheep in the hills. One day while they sat eating their lunch, Protas saw another wagon train pull into Chitouf. It happened every week and they always made sure he was off helping Ee-lath with the sheep. "Ee-lath, I see the supply wagons arrive every week loaded with food and the needs of your village. But how do your people pay for it?"

Protas had come to understand that this village was like none other. Their flocks were meagre, they produced little, and even the location was a mystery. The place was in the middle of nowhere, in a barren landscape. Its only redeeming feature was good access to the mountain passes he had recently travelled through. That advantage could have turned into a good profit if they provided supplies and lodging to travellers ... but they didn't.

"We are favoured by our Great Leaders. It is they who bring us our supplies," Ee-lath said proudly.

"Leaders?"

"We call them the Quorum," the boy volunteered.

"How long have they been sending the wagons to Chitouf?"

"Since my grandfather was a boy."

Surprisingly, the wagons containing supplies and bricks, were heavily guarded as they rolled into town. After the supplies were removed, everyone joined to escort the wagons to the edge of the village, where new bricks were unloaded. Three days later, those bricks became part of a new dwelling place for the villagers.

'What could these people give in exchange for a perpetual supply of daily necessities,' he wondered, sitting on the hilltop finishing his lunch. 'AND ... supplies to build more brick houses ... even though some of them are currently empty.' Wiping the crumbs from his robe, Protas looked at Ee-lath considering the correctness of pressing this innocent young man for more information. As the strong mid-day sunlight sparkled off the boy's earring, he realized he didn't have to. He grinned at how easily he had overlooked the obvious! Everyone in the village wore at least one gold earring. His first impulse was to conclude that these village people supplied gold, and in return ... but there was no activity that suggested this was a reasonable conclusion. So, if the gold wasn't leaving ... it was coming! "The empty houses," Protas quietly said to himself, "they probably explain *everything*."

"What's that, Robe-Man?" The boy asked.

"Just thinking how lucky your people are to have a surplus of houses. It means that when you grow up and get married, you will be able to move right in," Protas teased a blushing Ee-lath.

'But why bring the gold here?' He continued his silent questions. He turned around and looked east, back towards the trails he had travelled through. He reflected back on the several thousand men busy widening the trails. When he first saw the activity, he was more concerned with Shaksbali War Wagons eventually making their way through that Pass. But he was beginning to see things differently. Someone wanted to move gold from Chitouf into Storlenia! That was as far as his reasoning could take him. Because moving gold meant trade between the governments of the two lands. 'But then again, this couldn't be government gold. That would be stored in government vaults at Kel-eetan, capital of Shaksbah. Not in some remote village. And the other strange thing is the amount of gold. It must be massive, if this has been going on since Ee-lath's grandfather was a boy!'

He suddenly realized how lucky he was that he saw the boy on the day he spotted the Cat. Wandering this close to Chitouf – if he hadn't seen Ee-lath – he would have been killed as soon as he was spotted. If they suspected he knew about the gold ... then even saving the boy wouldn't protect him. He needed a plan!

A few days later he was awoken by loud voices. He hurriedly put on his Robe, but before he could get his boots on, two villagers came into his room and rushed him outside to the village square. Protas felt like an execution was about to take place ... his!

Over thirty El-Bhat, plus villagers, formed a large circle around the El-Bhat Leader, who was vigorously challenging the Mayor of the town.

The threesome entered the circle and then waited. The shouting ceased and all eyes turned to Protas. As he suspected, there was normally no such thing as a breathing visitor in Chitouf. The Leader of the village beckoned the two Assistants to bring their visitor forward.

"Remove your Robe!" the Mayor commanded.

Protas was quick to oblige.

"See for yourself!" The villager shouted as he pointed to the terrible fresh wounds. "Show him your back."

Protas turned obediently.

"He gave his life for the boy. His life is bonded to Ee-lath as long as the boy lives. Would you kill the boy too?"

There was a pause. Ou-Leesen asked the visitor his name.

"Robe-Man ... it is the name given me by Ee-lath. This is now my name," Protas answered.

The villagers nodded in agreement.

"What brought you to this land?" Ou-Leesen asked, remembering that not long ago, his men assisted in a hunt, for a man wearing a Robe.

"First, I have a question of my own. Are you going to kill the boy or not?"

Ou-Leesen understood the implication of Robe-Man's question. Skilfully he had avoided any further questioning. "Alright ... bring me the boy."

Ee-lath was placed beside Protas. "It would not be fair to Robe-Man if we failed to explain the nature of the bond," Ou-Leesen scowled. His eyes scanning the circle. "The *bond*," he continued, but now with eyes fixed on Protas, "is more than the obligation that Ee-lath has to protect you for the remainder of your life. It also means that you now *share* each other's values."

Cleverly he turned to the boy. "Ee-lath, would you ever consider killing another Shaksbali ... just because he was Shaksbali?" he added, turning to Protas. The boy shook his head 'no'.

Returning his gaze to the boy, he continued, "And if you were asked to fight to preserve the freedoms of your people, would you refuse?"

"No," the boy said softly.

Ou-Leesen, addressing Protas, added, "Your life has been rescued by these honourable villagers. Do you think you understand the cost to them ... and to you?"

"Yes," Protas simply said, as he looked deeply into the brilliant green eyes of the Leader. "And what is *your* name?"

"Ou-Leesen ... and when we depart tomorrow, you and the boy will be coming with us."

"The *boy?* You mean my brother Ee-Lath?"

Ou-Leesen paused. "Yes." Then he turned and walked away.

Before leaving the village, Protas threw his fur blanket into the wagon, his only possession other than Jalek's knife and his Robe.

When they stopped to eat, Protas motioned Ee-lath to follow him. He went straight to Ou-Leesen. "I have a request." Protas placed a hand on the boy's shoulder.

"Speak." Normally Ou-Leesen wouldn't extend the courtesy to a Storlenian, but he had seen the multiple fresh wounds. Symbol of Protas's willingness to protect an unknown village boy ... inside Shaksbah.

"I want you to teach me how to fight with a shepherd staff ... and my knife," he patted his robe where the knife lay hidden. "And then I will teach the skills to my brother Ee-lath."

Ou-Leesen kept eating. "You're not ready. Your wounds need more time to heal. But in the meantime, you and your brother will carry water for my people. When we eat, we need water, when we work, we need water. Do not slacken your duty," he said firmly and waved them away.

The Advisor had watched the conversation with great interest. As promised by Shanteef, Ou-Leesen sought him out at Chitouf. It was his responsibility to advise the El-Bhat Leader. And of course there was something else he wanted to do. And now, the young man from Storlenia, had provided him with the perfect opportunity to blame the murder ... on someone else!

Once they were out of range of hearing, Ee-lath asked, "Do you think Ou-Leesen will teach you?"

"Of course, Ee-lath. When a man in his position does not say no ... it means yes."

Chapter 22 - Aram-Dentee

Previously. The three men Craslin had hired to find Benekee and bring back the shards, sat in their wagon for hours. Fearing they were permanently blind. Luckily for them, before the sun set, their sight came back, and the Hunting Device was still sitting in the back of their wagon

They spilled the shards onto Craslin's desk. He picked up one of them and held it to the light. "You will be rewarded as agreed," he said, gathering them into a fine leather bag. He scribbled a note and then handed it to the Leader of the three men. "Give this to the Clerk outside my office and he will pay you. Good day."

"You pay well," the Leader remarked as he examined the note. "But I wonder what you would pay for something more valuable than the shards ... many times more valuable!"

"Close the door ... and tell me what you have," Craslin said softly, his keen mind already speculating what could be of more use to him, than a tool to find an Amulet with power.

"Assistant Guild Master, It's a killing machine." The slight lift of the eyebrows told him Craslin was pleasantly surprised ... and he should continue. "The lad was working with an Inventor from the Mechanical Guild. We followed them up to White Boulder where they demonstrated the Device to the Hunting Guild. Very impressive. It fires a brass ball with enough force to kill a deer ... or a man. And more accurately at a hundred and fifty paces than an Archer."

"I want to see this for myself," Craslin said firmly. "Find a suitable place for the test and let me know by tomorrow. If I am pleased, I will pay you accordingly."

The next day, after the hired Archer sent his three arrows into the target, he was excused.

The Assistant Guild Master stepped up to the machine, "Show me how to operate it. If I can use it, anyone can."

The results convinced Craslin that with this new Device, he was ready to move forward with his plan. His ambition had always exceeded his authority. But now, that was all going to change.

※ ※ ※

"Why did it take so long for us to receive the report?" Axion demanded, furious that something as significant as the war with the El-Bhat, was not reported immediately.

"The Tracking Guild took three weeks just to finish all of the interviews. Then, due to the sensitive nature of their findings, they decided to hand deliver their report, rather than use the Communication Guild," Craslin answered submissively.

"These Trackers ... can be so infuriating!" The Head Guild Master shouted, pounding the massive oak table.

His Assistant took a step closer and suggested, "Perhaps it's time we sent them ... a message."

"What kind of message?" Axion asked, angry enough to consider a suggestion from his silver-tongued Assistant.

"Pass a law that gives the Head Office of the Planning and Development Guild the right to form their own Militia Guard."

Ignoring the suggestion, Axion walked around his desk to stand in front of Craslin. "El-Bhat as far north as Lundeen Forest?" He asked.

"Yes," Craslin answered quietly. "Perhaps *another* reason to consider the Militia Guard. We have never had security issues of this magnitude before ... this close to Qar-ana," he added, determined that his suggestion would not be ignored.

Axion looked Craslin in the eyes, "This is very touchy ground, and you know it. The Tracking Guild has been our security for over a thousand years. Why would you mention this now?"

"It is not my intention to challenge the right of the Trackers. But you know that if we suggested that fifty Trackers move permanently into *our* Head Office to ensure sufficient security, they would refuse."

"Of course they would ... the idea is ridiculous."

"But ... after they refused our request, if we asked them if they would train fifty men of our choosing, then how could they say no?"

Axion knew a crack when he saw one. Fifty could turn into five hundred and Axion would go down in history, being the only Guild Master to challenge the undisputed right of the Tracking Guild.

"So, you think we should send a message ... perhaps we should. But listen carefully. The law allowing the formation of the Militia Guard, will be *temporary and provisional.* The Tracking Guild will have the right to demand its dissolution once the security issues have been resolved. Hopefully, this will motivate the Tracking Guild to get this El-Bhat situation under control!"

Craslin nodded. "I will begin work immediately on drafting the legal documents for your signature."

He turned, allowing himself a smile once he had left the room. His plans were moving along even quicker than he had hoped. Axion was in for a great surprise.

A few days later, Craslin entered the office of the Guild Master.

"What is it?" Axion said without lifting his head.

"My time to oversee the formation of our new Militia Guard is becoming more demanding than I expected. I would like to suggest that I search for a temporary Special Assistant ... for you. I assure you, he would have the necessary skills and I would personally supervise his duties. Do I have your permission?"

"Yes." He raised his head. "How temporary?"

"Three months, probably less."

"That would be fine," Axion replied, returning to his work.

'Probably a *lot* less,' Craslin thought as he left his office. His ambitious plan to replace the Head Guild Master with himself, without pointing the finger of suspicion, would require someone special. And Axion had just given him permission to hire this someone special. The reckless speed with which his plans were progressing, almost made him dizzy. Now he needed to find his Assassin.

The Assistant Guild Master approached one of his Aides. "The responsibility of our Guild continues to grow. I wish to create a new position, a Special Assistant to the Head Guild Master. He needs to be someone with significant training, someone who understands the complications of leadership, but does not aspire to it. Someone who will not be burdened to stand at the side of the Head Guild Master, because he is discrete and knows when to speak and when to be silent. Your task is to help me find this man."

A week later the Aide stood before Craslin, "The man you wanted is on his way."

Craslin felt pleasantly surprised and irritated at the same time.

"You have done well ... but I would have preferred to examine a short list of candidates. Surely you understood this."

"Yes, I did. But the Butler Guild doesn't work that way."

Not surprisingly, Craslin's raised eyebrow confirmed the astonishment the Aide expected.

"Before this assignment," the Aide explained, "I had never heard of this Guild. In my search, someone suggested that I ought to contact the Butler Guild. However ... very few people know of this Guild, and no one knows where it is located. But here in the Capital, the Communication Guild is the home to messenger pigeons that are trained to take messages to the Butler Guild."

Craslin was still annoyed, "Did you really expect to find our man from an unrecognized Guild?"

Without apology, the Aide simply said, "My careful research tells me that he will be exactly the man you seek. Butlers are trained in such a way, that they can fulfil any assignment. However delicate or dangerous the task. They claim their skills exceed the training of Trackers."

"Very well. As usual, if what you have done pleases me, you will be rewarded. Now leave me."

Several days later, in the middle of a busy day, Craslin hurried into his private office, sat down, and began to review his daily reports. After a few minutes, someone in the room cleared his throat. A surprised Craslin looked up to see a man standing in the corner by the heavy drapes. Sitting back in his large leather chair, Craslin thought 'this must be the man.' He was already impressed that he had drawn no attention to their meeting, and no one knew he was in the building. But he was surprised with the man's appearance. His white-gloved hand held an elaborately carved cane with a beautiful gold handle. His clothes were antiquated yet dignified. His bearing reflected a life of culture and education. "You must be the man I've been expecting ... from the Butler Guild?"

"I am. And you are Craslin, the Assistant Guild Master. Ambitious and in need of my services and extensive training."

Craslin ignored the Butler's personal assessment and simply said, "Do you have a name?"

"Aram-Dentee."

"Your name, the clothes ... one would think you were born a thousand years ago."

"Our Guild has studied the ancient records carefully. They were a people of significant power and study. We seek to emulate their patterns, for they achieved greatness in all things."

So far, everything about the man, cast doubts on his abilities. It seemed to Craslin that the 'Butler' was just another person trying too hard to be different. "You suggested you have extensive training, and apparently, your Guild claims skills superior to Trackers. I find this hard to believe."

"It is time I introduced myself properly," Aram-Dentee announced. Stepping forward, his white-gloved hand pulled a silver engraved card from his embroidered linen vest. He placed it on the desk.

"My credentials. If you accept this card, you accept my services." Then he pulled out a red velvet bag and laid it beside his card. "My payment will be this pouch, filled with gold coins."

Craslin touched neither item, but instead glared at Aram-Dentee, still unwilling to accept his claims.

"And as for my skills ..." With the speed and grace of a Mountain Cat, he grabbed Craslin's hand and lifted it high as he slammed his shoulder into the desk. Craslin's face, firmly pressed against the polished oak, grimaced in pain. He felt like his hand was on fire. Through clenched teeth, he sputtered the words, "I believe you."

With similar grace, Aram-Dentee pulled Craslin back into his original position, as though nothing had happened. "I detest these exhibitions," Aram-Dentee said softly. "They are barbaric. But often the only way to convince my client." He picked up his cane from where it leaned against Craslin's desk.

After rubbing the pain out of his hand, Craslin picked up the silver card, signifying his acceptance. "Come by early in the morning, and I will explain your assignment."

The Butler left the Guild as he had entered ... silent and unnoticed.

Aram-Dentee was as perfect as his Aide said he would be. If he wasn't a Butler, Craslin might be concerned about being replaced. When the man walked in the corridors of the Guild, the women flustered about like chickens. And other Aides treated him like the Guild Master himself, holding doors and always using his title of

Special Assistant with a slight bow of the head. He was charming to a fault. Craslin was beginning to believe he could charm fish right out of a river.

The three men who brought Craslin the Machine, had finished recruiting the fifty men he had requested. The new law legalizing his Militia was drafted, waiting for the Guild Master's signature.

It was on the day that Bernado was busy composing the letter to the Tracking Guild at Pechora – to invite them to train his fledgling Militia – when an Aide walked in, informing him that a Tracker had arrived. He insisted on seeing either the Guild Master or his Assistant.

"Bring him into my office," Craslin enthusiastically said. He was not a believer. But the way events were unfolding in his favour, he was almost convinced that the Fates were smiling down upon him!

"My name is Ranoof. I am here representing myself. But my message is grave. It is why I have travelled to Qar-ana and sought out the seat of power."

Craslin laid aside his documents. "You have my full attention."

Having gained the ear of the Assistant Guild Master, Ranoof carefully related the story of his experience in Pechora. He left out the fact that Urshen was there, and the part about meeting Protas. He wanted to keep his message focused on the problem of corrupt leadership within the Guild.

"I will look into this immediately," Craslin said with great sobriety. "Ranoof, what will you do now?"

"I'm not sure," he answered honestly.

Craslin was nodding, "Yes … It would give anyone pause. Your word against the Head Guild Master … of a Tracking Guild!"

Ranoof simply folded his arms and looked at the floor. He hadn't really thought much past delivering his message at Qar-ana.

"Perhaps our two needs can fit hand in glove," Craslin offered. "With all these reports about El-Bhat, we have decided to increase security within the walls of this Guild. Preferably with Trackers. But we know *that* invitation would not be acceptable to the Tracking Guild. So, I have already recruited fifty men, and I need someone to train them. I will pay you handsomely. You will have full authority to train them as you see fit, and until this matter with Pechora is sorted, you will be under my protective custody."

What Craslin wanted to do was certainly unusual. But Ranoof couldn't deny that these were unusual times. "When can I start?"

A whispered message brought the Aide directly into Axion's office. "How can I be of service Head Guild Master?"

Axion was by the window watching the Militia Guard work through training exercises. "Who is the Tracker training our new Militia?"

"His name is Ranoof. He arrived a week ago."

'The ink is barely dry and already Craslin is hiring men into the Guild's Militia,' he thought, not totally surprised. Craslin's efficiency was only exceeded by his ambition. For that reason, Axion had been careful to restrain the new Executive Order to three months. "Have Ranoof come up to my office after he is finished."

"Thank you for coming. We appreciate the Tracking Guild's assisting us on our Militia experiment. I want to emphasize that it is temporary at best. It is only meant to increase security at our Guild, while the Trackers clean up their shop."

"I must tell you," Ranoof began, "that my acceptance of this assignment is personal. And has no endorsement from the Guild."

"Personal?" Axion's brows furrowed.

"Yes sir. I have recently escaped from the Tracking Guild at Pechora where the rest of my unit remain in prison."

"Escaped?"

"Yes sir, I don't drink wine."

By now, Axion knew the conversation wouldn't be a short one. "Ranoof, why don't you sit down, and tell me why you are here helping us."

When the picture became clear, he excused Ranoof and brought in Craslin. "I don't know what to make of it. Ranoof claims that El-Bhat are living in the prison cells at Pechora. Normally I would have dismissed him as a lunatic. But with everything else going on ... Craslin, I want you to investigate, and report back."

Axion was surprised that Craslin would hire Ranoof if he knew he was a wanted man. Perhaps the report would help to clarify this question as well.

Craslin left the office with a slight bow. Since Ranoof told him about El-Bhat hiding in the prison cells, at the Tracking Guild at

Pechora, he knew that one day, this information would prove *very* useful! And once Axion was murdered, he fully intended to honour the Head Guild Master's request to follow up.

Chapter 23 - The Shard of conflict

Previously. While assisting Braddock to build the Tinker Guild at Arborville, Zephra had not used her White Bauble since her offer to The Commander to heal someone in his family. But soon her Talisman would flare to life again. But not by her bidding

Zephra was in the Planning Tent with Braddock, leaning over the maps. Suddenly a brilliant flash scorched her eyes. She was immediately blind. "I can't see. Father can you see?"

"No. What just happened?" he asked frantically.

Instinctively she reached for her White Bauble, and grasped it, with a question that needed an answer. "We need to stay in the tent, until the blindness leaves," she answered.

"Do you know what happened?"

She sank to her knees, confused. "The flash of light came from my Amulet."

"This must be the place." Benekee pulled the wagon to a stop and watched the hive of activity before them.

"Maybe the strangest sight I have seen in my entire life," Wutherstop muttered. "Imagine ... Tinkers working to create a village." He shook his head. "Must be an interesting story behind all this. And one that I am anxious to hear."

"You must be excited to be this close to the missing Shard?" Yaneek said, turning to her brother.

He nodded, feeling at once eager and anxious. Eventually they were directed to Braddock's tent.

With all the various services required to build the Tinkers Manufacturing Guild, it was not uncommon for non-Tinkers to visit their site. Braddock heard the wagon approaching through his open tent door and was already outside when the horses stopped.

"I was told you're the man in charge," Benekee said.

"That's correct, my name is Braddock. What can I do for you?"

While travelling the plains of Storlenia, Benekee had imagined a grand introductory speech about the Shards and the missing piece he had come to find. But now that he was finally here, he simply said, "I was told that someone in your camp owns a Crystal Shard. I have come a long way to talk to that person."

"I know who you want to talk to," Braddock offered, "but she's off on an errand right now, and won't be back till this evening. Why don't I fetch a Tinker to show you around till then? I would be pleased if you could join us for supper. Then you'll have a chance to meet Zephra, my daughter. She's the one with the Crystal Shard."

As they gathered for the evening meal, Wutherstop joined Braddock while Yaneek and Benekee sat close to Zephra.

"How long have you owned the Crystal Shard?" Yaneek inquired, nodding towards the necklace Zephra wore.

"Got it from my grandmother, and she got it from hers," she explained.

"Sounds like it's been in the family for a long time," Yaneek added, taking a spoonful of stew.

"Yes ... it has," Zephra stated proudly. "Father tells me that you have come a long way to talk to me about ... the White Bauble."

"Longest trip I've ever taken," Yaneek replied. "And I hope it's a while before I have to climb into a wagon again. But it's really my brother who wants to talk to you about your Shard," Yaneek added, as she looked towards Benekee.

Benekee had only been half listening to his sister. He was studying Zephra's captivating features. Suddenly Zephra looked directly at him. "How did you hear about my White Bauble?"

"I ... uhh ... used to clean relics at the Borit Betoon Redemption Guild. And then one day," he continued, "while I was examining this pile of crystal Shards, they suddenly started to glow." His eyes dropped to the White Bauble necklace. It felt strange to be finally this close to the Crystal Shard, which started everything ... including his new life.

Zephra was considering his interest in her White Bauble, when she suddenly saw the connection. "When did this happen to you?" She asked Benekee, sure that she knew what he would say.

"Oh, it was a couple of months ago."

"Did the Shards ... ever glow again?" Zephra asked hesitantly.

"Yes, in fact I believe they glowed ... every time you used your White Bauble."

The threesome stopped eating and stared at each other. Zephra thought about the blinding flash of light that had come unbidden from her White Bauble a week ago.

"These Shards ... that you used to clean ... at the Redemption Guild ... are they still there?"

Benekee was starting to feel that retrieving the Single Shard was not going to be as easy as he thought. He answered, "No."

His abbreviated answer suggested that he knew more than he was saying. Zephra pressed him, "Do you have the Shards?"

Benekee looked at his sister, and she nodded as if to say, "tell her."

"Yes."

"Do you have them with you?"

"Yes."

He might be reticent, but at least he was willing to answer her questions, so she continued. The eagerness was building within her. She already suspected where this conversation was headed. "May I see them?" She excitedly asked.

Without a word, he reached inside his shirt and pulled out the silver cage.

Zephra had expected him to show her a handful of Crystal Shards. Her eyes went wide when she saw a complete Amulet, identical to Urshen's, framed inside a beautifully intricate silver cage, hanging from a silver chain. She was instantly *jealous*. Suddenly suspicious she asked, "You said that you came here to talk to me about the White Bauble. Exactly what did you want to talk about?"

Benekee laid down his half-eaten bowl of stew and looked squarely at Zephra. "I don't know why ... but my experience with the Shards suggest ... that they have adopted me. And more than this, I have known from the day I tried to reassemble them, that there was one Shard missing. From that moment, a desire was placed within me to find the missing piece ... that I might make the Amulet complete again."

"So, you have come here to ask me ... to give you my White Bauble?" she asked in amazement.

Benekee cleared his throat. "It's clear to me now, that I hadn't really thought this through very carefully. I just figured that, whoever had it, would want to give it to me so that the Amulet might be complete. It never occurred to me that it might be a family heirloom." Benekee looked at Zephra expectantly, hoping beyond hope, that she would grasp the importance of completing the Amulet, and want to give the Shard to him.

The whole idea of giving up her White Bauble seemed ridiculous and irritated her *immensely*. She changed the subject. "Do you know anything about a blinding flash of light?"

"Yes, we do," Yaneek answered excitedly. "It happened about a week ago when we were being robbed by three men. They would've killed us, but a blinding flash of light from Benekee's Shards, saved us. Wutherstop and I couldn't see for hours. Why do you ask?" Yaneek was curious.

"My Shard gave off a brilliant flash of light, about the time that you mentioned, blinding both me and my father … for a couple of hours." She returned her gaze to Benekee, "Do you know what caused the Shards to explode with light?"

"Yes … I asked them to do it."

Of all the things he had said so far, this humble reply disturbed her the most. It suggested that, more than anything else, the Amulet *certainly* belonged to him. She had *never* had access to such power. 'Perhaps I should give him the White Bauble,' she contemplated. But then she remembered how irritating he was and said, "Maybe you were supposed to come here, to give *me* the Shards … to complete the White Bauble."

"But … I met this old woman with long white hair, in a dream, who originally owned the Amulet, and she confirmed that it has chosen me," Benekee replied in desperation.

The more he talked, the more irritated Zephra felt. "Yes … and I have met my dead grandmother who passed the White Bauble on to me. And she showed me how to use the power to heal."

"But … don't you agree that the Shards need to come together, to experience the full power of the Amulet?" Benekee protested.

"Of course, and I am grateful that you have made such a sacrifice, to bring the Shards to me. You see, it was the old woman with long white hair, who first gave this Shard," Zephra declared as she held it in her hand, "to my ancestor. That makes *me* the rightful owner of the Amulet."

"Stop!" Yaneek suddenly shouted. Braddock and Wutherstop cast a glance their way. "This isn't right!" she boomed, as Zephra glowered and Benekee shrank, at her rebuke.

"Not too long ago I didn't believe any of this!" she continued. "I thought my brother was going crazy ... from the disappointment of losing our parents," she explained to Zephra, her voice now quieter. "I thought he was delusional. That he wanted so badly, to believe in something ... that he ... But now *I* believe!" she whispered. She paused and considered her next words. "And ... you are *both* wrong. The power isn't a possession ... it's a *privilege*. You don't own it."

Benekee was so touched by his sister's words, that he immediately pulled the chain from off his neck and handed it to Zephra.

"I'm, I'm sorry. It's, it's yours," he stammered.

Yaneek's little speech reminded Zephra so much of what Urshen might have said. And imagining his voice say those words, cut her to the heart. She didn't take Benekee's Shards. She could only stare at the ground. The silence persisted until Zephra had an idea. "We need to find Urshen. He will know what to do."

"Who's Urshen," Yaneek asked.

"He is a Seer, and he ... has an Amulet, just like the one Benekee has." She glanced at the beautiful Silver Cage. Zephra threw a few more logs onto the fire as she prepared to tell her visitors about Urshen. Anyone with so strong a connection to an Amulet – and a broken one at that – ought to know about Urshen. By the time she was finished, the wide-eyed Benekee was anxious to meet the legend. They agreed to leave as soon as Zephra could make arrangements to have others carry out her duties. "And we will take *my* wagon. Yaneek you will love it!"

But Braddock was insistent that Urshen should be back soon, and that they ought to wait at least another week. He thought he had lost her once to the Assassin's dart and was reluctant to have her leave Tinker Village unless necessary. Especially without a Tinker Guard. Something she would insist on.

"Okay, but when the week is up ..." she said firmly.

Braddock was pleased. He figured he had won a concession that he normally wouldn't have realized.

Zephra was pleased. She thought of a great way to use her week. She would spend some 'girl time' with Yaneek! Despite their short time together, she had come to realize that she really liked her. Perhaps it was the display of her strength and wisdom, so obvious when she challenged Benekee and herself to stretch for a higher ideal. Instead of squabbling over the rights to the Amulet. 'In fact,' Zephra said to herself, 'I am going to show her a perfect building site ... not far from where *our* house will be. As fugitives, they need a new place, and why not here in Tinker Village.'

When the week had passed, a reluctant Braddock said goodbye to the young group as they climbed aboard one of their newly constructed 'Tinker Wagons'. It was his idea ... another concession to his agreeing to the long trip. "Tell people about our wagon in your travels and bring back orders!"

He wanted to suggest that Coustin go with them, but he knew that wouldn't settle well with a Tinker's Boon. So, he watched them leave, hoping that all would go well.

As the silhouettes disappeared over the hill, Braddock returned to continue his conversations with Wutherstop. He had convinced the brilliant Inventor to stay behind and work with him. He promised to tell him all about Urshen's 'twice-improved wagon'.

While on the road to find Urshen, Yaneek and Zephra chatted away. But Benekee couldn't stop thinking about how the White Bauble was always in full view. His Amulet was always hidden. Then one day, he just had to say something. "Zephra, I know it's the Tinker way to wear your possessions with pride, but as more people begin to learn about the power of our Amulets, don't you think it might be better to keep it hidden."

The words were like sparks to a box of dry kindling. But for Yaneek's sake, she suppressed her anger and replied without hesitation, "A Tinker without Jewellery, would look very suspicious ... don't you agree?"

Benekee nodded in reluctant agreement. He was beginning to see that getting through to Zephra was no easy task. Now he was even more curious to meet Urshen.

"We have more visitors," Bernado's Assistant began. "It does not appear to be anyone of consequence ... and no Trackers."

"Send them in," Bernado ordered, intrigued by the Tinker wagon that now sat in the wagon yard. "Welcome to our Guild," Bernado offered a welcoming smile to his three visitors. "How may I be of assistance?"

Zephra, the most familiar with the details, took the lead. "A few weeks back, several Trackers left Arborville, heading for Pechora. Wonder if they might've stopped here."

Bernado saw an opportunity to gather intelligence. "Because we are a large Guild, we deal with a lot of business. The size of the group and a name or two would help."

"Seven Trackers. The youngest is called Urshen," she offered, hoping to see a flicker of recognition. The image of Urshen wearing his Tracker outfit was still fresh in her mind.

"Never heard the name mentioned ... but there was a group of *seven* Trackers ... searching for information. I was convinced that what they wanted, could probably be found at the Planning and Development Guild at Qar-ana. They left in a hurry. I assume they went there."

As he watched them leave, the rage within him grew. Urshen, one of the two young heroes mentioned in the reports, had been down in the prison cells all along! He quickly returned to his office and slammed the door.

"Well ... *Gaeten!*" He snarled in contempt. He picked up the nearest thing he could grab. "This will be you when I'm finished!" he yelled in anger and threw it against the wall. The reward the Quorum offered for Protas *and* Urshen was enormous. And it had slipped through his fingers!

A head peeked through a partially opened door. "Everything okay in here?"

"Accident. Send someone later to clean it up." By the time the door closed, his anger had abated. With returned clarity, his thoughts considered the staggering fact, that Urshen could lie to the Olleti! Bernado had always wondered if there was a way to lie to oneself ... *so* successfully ... that your mind would believe it. "To think that you have accomplished it!" he muttered, "is still hard to believe!" "But *now*," his anger rising again within him, "I know you've done it. And next time, there will be no Olleti, only pain ... a lot of pain. And then you will tell me why you and the others came here. With a wicked grin he continued his soliloquy. "And eventually, I will send you to the Quorum. After Protas they will be ready for someone new. In the meantime, I must think carefully about your Amulet."

Chapter 24 - Gaeten by any other name

Previously. Bernado had Urshen beaten by his Guards and then subjected to Olleti, to extract the secrets of the Crystal Amulet. Disappointed, he sent a bloodied Urshen back to his cell

Two weeks after the interrogation, Urshen turned on his cot, trying to find a position that didn't hurt so much. Then his thoughts drifted to his new name ... Gaeten. 'I wonder if Zephra will like it ... perhaps even prefer it!' He thought in amusement.

Zephra. It was where his thoughts drifted to every day. He imagined her frenetic activity at Tinker Village. Mothering the younger children. He remembered the river where he proposed. He imagined going for a stroll, hand in hand as he watched the sun dancing on her long black hair. He wondered what he would say. 'I would say ...' he thoughtfully considered. "You are *here!*" he suddenly exclaimed.

He bolted upright and wondered why he should know that. But then quickly realized that what he felt, was not Zephra ... it was her White Bauble. His mind reached out for the location of her power. He wanted to know how close she was ... fearful that she might be inside the Tracking Guild! She was!

His heart began to pound as he paced like a Mountain Cat within his cage, trying to find a way to warn Zephra. He stopped, closed his eyes, and looked upwards, past the ceiling. Something remarkable was happening. The power of the White Bauble started to flow to him! As the Light filled his mind, he could sense the Circle of Trackers dispersed among the cells facing his direction.

'Can you hear me?' His mind cried out to the statues of flesh.

'We can,' the chorus came back.

Urshen sent another message. 'Zephra is here. Her Amulet is connecting us. Sit down as though nothing has happened. Let your minds try to understand it,' Urshen instructed the Trackers. Together, they felt the power weave a web that stretched through the space between them.

'Our bond is increasing,' one of the Trackers enthusiastically observed. Then suddenly it stopped.

'What happened?' was the common chorus.

'The Amulet has moved,' Urshen responded, 'Maybe it's too far away?'

'Considering our experience at Border Pass, that doesn't sound right,' Tal-nud offered.

There was a pause. 'You're right. It stopped because the power was *finished.*' Urshen followed Zephra's movement until she was safely out of the Guild. 'Now we have something we didn't have before,' Urshen acknowledged.

In response to Urshen's encouraging words, Tal-nud volunteered, 'I can feel some of your pain.' The others agreed that they experienced the same thing.

Urshen considered Tal-nud's comment and then explained, 'Everyone ... I have just made a remarkable discovery. My pain is almost completely gone. Brothers of the Circle think about what has just happened to me. If the group can share the burden of pain ... then I ask, what is the true nature of this bond!'

'It teaches us,' Tal-nud offered, 'that the power of the Circle extends beyond communication. It means that any one of us is as strong as the combined strength of the Circle! We can endure what no other mortal can. We can defeat an enemy that seems undefeatable. This is truly a gift of immeasurable value,' he eagerly exclaimed. Everyone was silent as they contemplated Tal-nud's words.

Urshen smiled. 'Bernado is in for a surprise next time he straps me to a chair.' But a sobering thought intruded his eager pride ... the other side of a Gift ... the necessity to keep it secret or reap the inevitable consequences. 'Actually,' he amended, 'it's very important that Bernado *not* be surprised. We must keep the discovery of this Gift a secret, or it will be used against us.'

'Urshen, why do you think you couldn't accomplish this bonding with your own Amulet?' Tal-nud asked.

'I don't know ... I really don't know,' Urshen replied. Then as though everyone understood that he needed to be alone, they all closed their minds to the Circle.

The Tracking Guild prison cells were small, hardly room to do anything other than rest on the bed or pace back and forth. But today he needed to do something other than just pace. He thought back to another cell, when he bonded with an ancient ancestor of tremendous physical skill and endurance. 'Warriors must do things to keep themselves fit,' he realized. He immediately sat on his bed, closed his eyes, and drifted back a thousand years. When he opened his eyes, he was ready to train.

Thirty minutes later, he was so tired, he practically crawled to his bed and within a moment his head sunk into the thin pillow ... as his mind filled with images of the Garden.

Urshen looked up again at the Tree sitting on a raised hill, surrounded by a hedge. The canopy of crystal branches shimmered like a thousand rainbows dancing among the leaves. The beauty that represented its power was unmistakable. But he could see no way to get to it ... he had lost the Key.

He sat in agony for some time, staring at the unapproachable Tree. It was so majestic, casting a soft white light on the extraordinary array of flowers and plants that surrounded it. More than ever he felt like it was calling to him ... but he had lost the Key.

"I should have been more careful!" he mourned as he gazed helplessly at the shimmering rainbows. Eventually, he stood up and exclaimed, "I am forgetting something ... or someone ..." That's when he caught sight of a man observing him, wearing an exquisite White Robe,.

"The Guide," he said softly, and without hesitation, he walked purposefully towards him. "I ... have lost the Key," he confessed, his heart near to breaking. He looked back at the Tree, "And without it, I will never again obtain entrance to the Tree."

His gaze returned to the Guide, his eyes begging for an escape from his dilemma.

"The Key will be given to another. This is not a punishment. It is the way of the Garden. The power of the Key is needed elsewhere. Be patient in your affliction and remember that the Garden has already touched you with the power of another Key. Now, you have your friends who add to your power."

'Yes,' Urshen thought, 'I remember being touched with power.' "How is it possible?" Urshen wanted to know.

"At Border Pass, when you reached out to Zephra, your Amulets became as one," explained the Guide. "This allowed you to reach out to her from your prison cell and connect to her Amulet's power." Before Urshen could ask his next question, the Guide continued, "She couldn't feel your connection because you had been stripped of your Amulet."

Urshen nodded in gratitude for the enlightenment.

"But know this, a great evil has entered the world." The Guide turned towards the forest that bordered the Garden, "And it will continue to grow. If not checked, it will envelop the entire world. Look," the Guide directed Urshen as he pointed to the forest.

Standing just inside the mighty black oaks, a man was wearing a Golden Necklace. Green Light poured from it and swirled around the man like a cocoon of power. The man's eyes were filled with envy and hatred as he stared at the Garden only a few paces away.

"The power of the Black Ghosts," Urshen realized, remembering the fearful experience when he had run for his life, while the fiendish shades pursued him, hoping to keep him from entering the Garden.

The man with the Necklace turned around and walked deeper into the forest as the Green Light whirled ahead like a hurricane. Soon he was hidden from view, surrounded by dark wraiths that gathered around him by the hundreds.

"Is there no hope for the world," an anxious Urshen asked the Guide.

"The Necklace cannot enter the Garden. It has no power here. If the world is to survive, it will have to do what you did. Its people will need to leave the forest with haste and come to the Garden."

"What can I do to help?" Urshen begged.

"Remember my instructions ... to be patient," the Guide replied, placing a hand on his shoulder. Then he disappeared.

Chapter 25 - Far-fel

Far-fel could hear the creak of the Bow when the string was pulled back, followed by the high-pitched whistle as the arrow took flight. It was more instinct than thought, but he turned and dropped, just enough to grab the arrow in mid-flight. Just as quickly, and holding the arrow perfectly still, Far-fel brought his eye to the tip of the arrowhead, then looked back down the shaft in the direction it had come. He caught a glimmer of movement seventy paces away. 'There you are.' The Tracker had no time to waste. He knew there must be others!

He darted behind a large oak ... just in time to avoid another arrow, which caught the edge of the tree trunk instead of his flesh. He quickly examined the second arrow. This time, his eye traced a path upwards, into the trees. Now he had the location of a second pursuer.

'A good choice and a bad choice,' he thought. Someone up in a tree was very dangerous, but once spotted ...

Far-fel sprinted away from the oak, towards the Mercenary above. But not directly towards him. He didn't want him to know that he knew where he was. Then abruptly, he turned towards his prey, keeping large trees between himself and the man above. Soon the forest echoed the sound of a body crashing onto its cushioned floor.

Shifting his target back to the first Mercenary, Far-fel sprinted like a deer through the trees. If he were to stay alive, he needed to become invisible to their arrows. But a moment later, he felt the wind of feathers as a shaft whistled past his neck and hit the tree in front of him. With lightning reflexes, he looked down the arrow and traced its origin. But he didn't need to ... his third pursuer was sprinting towards him like an enraged bear. Soon they would have him dodging arrows from both directions if he didn't do something fast!

Quickly scanning the forest, Far-fel bolted to the place where the trees thickened towards the first Mercenary. Spinning to a stop, behind three large oaks, Far-fel stretched his bow into position. The sound of the Mercenary behind told him he was further away. Right now he needed to focus on the Mercenary in front. He trained his arrow on the narrow space between the trees where the Mercenary in front, would be, in a heartbeat. The sounds of his rapid approach triggered his release. The arrow was still in flight as Far-fel turned towards the third Mercenary.

A cry of death followed by a muffled crash to the forest floor, had brought the third Mercenary to an abrupt stop. With his associates dead, the last Mercenary listened for the sound that could only be the Tracker.

Far-fel began circling the last man, trading bursts of speed with moments of careful listening. Eventually he had positioned himself with the sun at his back. Without further delay, he rushed towards his foe. As soon as they spotted each other, they sprinted while trading arrows.

Moments later, the Mercenary caught a glimpse of Far-fel's quiver as he slipped behind the cover of a tree. 'Only one arrow left,' he grinned, knowing how he would trick the Tracker into wasting it. He suddenly dashed towards a large Oak, listening for the sound of a released arrow. His signal to dive towards the forest floor. His timing was perfect. The arrow caught a piece of his vest ... instead of his flesh. By the time he threw away the damaged vest, Far-fel had vanished, stealing away the advantage the Mercenary had hoped for. Undaunted, he pulled out his throwing knives and dashed towards thinly spaced trees, where he would re-establish his advantage. He was expert at throwing knives and wanted to have a clear view of Far-fel approaching. He heard a movement to his left and like a streak of lightning, Far-fel was careening towards him without an observable weapon. With blinding speed, the Mercenary threw his two knives, but Far-fel caught them with the heavy leather applets he wore on each hand. With a deft movement he discarded them, pulling his long knife from its sheath, as his opponent did the same.

Colliding, the Mercenary drew first blood. He expected to. He had never met his equal when it came to knives. He was anxious to finish this Tracker and claim the largest reward of which he had ever heard. But as the encounter continued, the dance of death changed. The Mercenary barely avoided a thrust from the Tracker that would have left him dead. He withdrew a step and began circling as he tried to understand what was happening. He concluded that the Tracker was just lucky and re-engaged. But things continued to change. That was when he realized that the Tracker was adapting to his style of fighting! Unwittingly he was tutoring the greatest student with whom he had ever fought. He wanted to run, but the fury of the fight escalated, giving him no opportunity to withdraw. Moments later the Mercenary grunted, his knife slipped from his hand. He dropped to his knees, wavering as the trees around him became blurry. And then he fell lifeless to the forest floor.

Far-fel scouted an expanded area until he was sure there were no other Mercenaries. He returned to the bodies and gathered them together for the search. Using his long knife, he cut away their clothes, looking for secret pockets. The Tracker knew they were professionals, hired by someone rich or powerful ... and probably both. Somewhere he would find the document that protected them from the law. And that document would take him directly to the Reaper.

With shredded clothes surrounding him, he sat in dismay, uncomfortable with his failure. It didn't make sense. "They must have left it behind. It would be unusual, but not unheard of," he reluctantly said to himself. He stood up and walked away.

A hundred paces out, he stopped and turned slowly as he considered a small insignificant detail. "The left sole of the second Mercenary's boots is slightly thicker than the others," he muttered, annoyed that he almost missed it. Carefully peeling back the first layer of leather, he exposed the cavity and the hidden waxed parchment he was expecting to find. At the bottom were the seal and signature. With a smirk of satisfaction he read aloud, *"Glickin, Head Guild Master, Financing Guild, town of Pirtelin."* Thinking of the other Specialist Trackers that had died, he promised, "Guild Master Glickin, I'm bringing you down!"

A month earlier

Racing along the foothills of the Crestal Mountains, Far-fel spotted the sign, easily missed by someone unfamiliar with what to look for. He immediately headed north, entered the forest and after a while climbed a tree and waited. Comfortable he wasn't being followed, he came down and continued his trek.

Far-fel was a 'Special Assignments' Tracker. One in one thousand Trackers who demonstrated exceptional skill, were recruited to a Special Tracker force. These Trackers were assigned to sensitive and dangerous tasks. But there was a cost. Special Assignment Trackers rarely married and didn't live a long life. The sound of an arrow sinking deeply into a large hemlock just ahead, told him Finn was close by. Like a phantom, the man came out of nowhere.

"Far-fel, good to see you're still alive." It was the common greeting among their kind. "I have good news. We finally have useful intelligence on the Silent Reaper."

Far-fel took out his long knife and started to sharpen it. The sound helped him remember every detail.

"He has access to an ancient artefact," Finn began.

"Explains a lot," Far-fel returned. "Do we know anything about it ... other than making our target extremely dangerous?"

"Probably very old ... most likely from before the Great War."

Far-fel thought for a moment, "A comment like that usually means we don't know what it does. Am I right?"

"Or, it performs multiple functions which confuses everyone," Finn offered.

Far-fel paused his knife sharpening. "Artefact or not, it would be nice to know who the Silent Reaper is. If I did, I might even complete the mission."

Finn continued. "I have leaked reports that we know who the Silent Reaper is and that you've been assigned to bring him in. If he takes the bait, he will hire Mercenaries. If you survive the Mercenaries, look for the signature on the protection agreement. With that positive identification, you should know where to find him. If you locate the artefact, bring it to Qar-ana. Stay at the usual place and send me word. Stay alive," he said, as he slipped into the forest.

Back to the present

Far-fel tucked the parchment into his pouch. The scheme had worked, and now he was the only man alive that knew Glickin was the Silent Reaper. But the Reaper also knew who *he* was, and that disadvantage would make the next part of his assignment very difficult. Especially since he would be facing *the Artefact* that he knew nothing about. Other than it had killed many men, including three Special Assignment Trackers! And that had never happened before.

He took the time to bury the men, hoping to hide the fact that they had failed and that he knew who the Reaper was. As he finished throwing deadfall over the shallow grave, he couldn't help admiring their skill. Two weeks ago, he spotted them and several times they had come close to achieving their goal. But he was still alive ... and he hoped to keep it that way!

Entering the town of Pirtelin, Far-fel made inquiries regarding the location of the Financing Guild. The answer was always the same, there was only one way to enter the Guild. Finance Road. Single entry, single exit. Like a fortress. And he wasn't just walking in there to arrest someone. He was going in to kill the Head Guild Master. As he observed the people on the street, he wondered who else the Silent Reaper had hired besides the Mercenaries.

The Reaper shuffled to the window, pulled back the curtain and looked outside. The men were still there, playing a pretended game of Gambit. The Mercenaries had sent a message several days ago, that they had found Far-fel and were closing in for the kill. Perhaps Far-fel was already dead ... perhaps. Experience had taught the Reaper that the only sure way to kill someone was with the Necklace. But he preferred that the Specialist Tracker never enter his Guild, so he hired Assassins to intercept and dispose of Far-fel before he got that far.

The man across the street turned away, when he spotted the Tracker moving rapidly along the crowded boardwalk. Luckily Far-fel didn't notice him. As Far-fel passed by, the Assassin signalled a man waiting in the tall building across the street, who used a mirror to alert someone else further down the road.

'Things are going just fine,' the man further down the road thought. With a wicked grin he stepped away from the doorstep and hurried across the street, joining the traffic behind the Tracker. When he was first hired, he never expected to be this close to the Tracker that everyone feared. He didn't look all that *Special* to him. 'In fact,' he mused to himself, 'I think I'm going to change the plan.' The plan was to involve the other men waiting ahead, but it was double money for whoever could claim the death stroke. 'And that will be me,' he assured himself. He reached inside his cloak to grip the handle of his Assassin's knife and increased his pace. He was now ten paces behind the overconfident Tracker. His heart was beating strong, feeding his lust for murder. He reached into his pocket to pull out a small rock. The 'distraction' that was going to ensure a quick and easy kill. Hurrying along, he manoeuvred carefully among the flow of people. Within moments he was only three paces behind the Tracker! Trembling with excitement, he played out his plan in his mind. He would throw the rock, clattering to the boardwalk, barely in front of his victim. For only a split second, the Tracker's attention would be diverted by the sound. And that would be enough time to swiftly come up behind him and pull his knife across his throat.

For some time now, Far-fel had been aware of the anomaly. The traffic behind him suggested that someone was hurrying forward. He estimated that the 'someone' was now five paces behind and closing quickly. He scanned the scene in front for potential accomplices but nothing stood out. He listened carefully to the man behind. The sway of his knife-hand matched the rhythm of the man's walk. He was ready. The clatter of the rock sent Far-fel into a swirling crouch. He turned, long knife in hand and planted the blade into the man's heart. The Assassin crumpled to the boardwalk. Far-fel stood and with sleight of hand, tucked his knife away, while exclaiming to the onlookers, "This man needs medical help." Far-fel knew this man didn't act alone. Now that he was dead, several possible accomplices appeared. He decided he would take a different path to Glickin and hurried back the way he came. He raced down the first alley he came to.

The Reaper knew it wouldn't be as easy as his hired men thought. His previous experience with Special Assignment Trackers taught him that. So, he had several 'spotters' placed inside three-story buildings to assist in following the movements of this Tracker. In addition, skilled Archers were strategically placed, if the others failed.

❦ ❦ ❦

Half way down the alley, three men came running out of a back door and began the chase. Far-fel was being hunted and he needed to find a temporary burrow to hide in. In the blink of an eye, he turned with an arrow ready, and dropped one of the three. The other two hesitated but when he raced on, he heard their boots when they resumed the chase. He rounded the corner, dashed down a side alley, and stole a quick glance to check out his pursuers, as he forced open the door of an abandoned shop. Two pursuers had turned into four. 'Never mind,' he thought. He grabbed a sturdy piece of lumber that lay among the refuse and jammed it between the door and the floor. 'They aren't getting through that door any time soon.' The pursuers were blocked but flowed up the outside steps to the second level. Once inside, they followed the Tracker to the front street.

Sprinting a hundred paces, Far-fel spotted a shop that was closed for the morning. He forced the lock, but a quick look over his shoulder told him they had already recovered from the barricaded door. He up-ended a heavy desk across the entrance and headed for the back of the building. The alley to the right was a dead end. They wouldn't expect him to head this direction. So that was the direction he would go. If he could just get to the building window on the second floor without being seen! Ten paces into his sprint, he knew how he would scale the wall ... but then he caught the glint of steel.

Chapter 26 - The little green stone

At the end of Driven Road Alley, the Archer gave his shaft one final polish, and preened the feathers. He secured the string on his hardwood bow and pulled it back a couple of times to awaken his trained muscles. Then he rested against the upper story window frame waiting for his accomplices to drive the Tracker toward him. He thought he could already hear the chase from several streets away.

'Here he comes.' He placed his arrow into position. His eye followed the shaft to the end where the fine steel head reflected a small amount of light, heralding his position.

'Better pull back a bit' he decided, moving further into the darkness of the room, just as the Tracker burst through a back door and raced towards him. He was coming at him with incredible speed.

He knew he couldn't afford the luxury of staying hidden if he wanted to hit this Tracker. He stepped right up to the open window, drew, and released the arrow, then quickly reached for a second.

Far-fel's eyes never left the glint of sunlight that came from the upper story window. He rushed forward, swift as the wind, with hands ready. A heartbeat later, the sound of a released arrow activated his instincts. His body twisting just enough for his hand to catch the arrow. Only one in a thousand Trackers could do that.

When the second arrow was released, he was much closer, but his weaving sprint made him a more difficult target … and it simply missed him.

The skill of the Tracker was unnerving and hard to ignore. After missing twice, he stepped back into the room and hesitated. Should he run while he could or lean out the window and try a third time. The money was too good. So he rushed to the open window where a hand thrust a knife into his world.

The Necklace from Harleem

🌱 🌱 🌱

Far-fel pushed the dead Archer into the room. A heartbeat later, he was wearing the Archer's hat and holding his bow. He knelt in front of the window. The others knew the Archer was there and would see what their eyes expected to see. The six men cast a hasty glance towards the window with the Archer, then turned and headed the other direction.

Under cover of darkness, Far-fel slipped through the back door, making his way swiftly towards the front of the Guild building where he knew his victim was waiting. Silently he moved down the short hall through a door into the next room. It was empty, except for a large candle on top of a small table, placed to the side. Moving quickly through the room, he grabbed the doorknob ... when he felt it.

He turned to the unpretentious table. Somehow it ... felt important to his quest. But there was nothing on it and it looked rather un-special. His focus was to find Glickin, so he pushed the image of the table out of his mind. He turned again to the door, but as he replaced his hand on the doorknob, the feeling grew stronger ... compelling. 'Okay, let's get this over with,' he agreed, willing to concede that there could be something behind the strange influence. He walked briskly to the table and immediately began searching for hidden cavities. 'Well-made,' he thought, as he pushed the metal button, releasing the latch. He pulled out the small drawer revealing a dark green stone. 'Not much to look at,' he considered. In fact, he decided that if it had not been hidden, he might have walked right by it. But it *was* carefully hidden. Which meant only one thing. 'I have found the Talisman,' he excitedly concluded.

Hesitantly he moved his hand toward the stone, wanting to take it. But his instincts demanded respect of a power, poorly understood. He allowed his hand to hover over the stone but felt nothing. He decided it was safe to remove it. He grabbed it and stood, considering his next move. The rest should be easy ... now that he had the ominous Stone of Power. He continued, confident he would complete his mission.

In front of him was a large stately room, with an open door to his right. 'An invitation?' he wondered. Or maybe simply a door that someone had not closed. As he considered his options, he looked at the Stone. True ... he had the Stone, but it was not his way to be careless. He placed the Talisman inside his shirt. He could feel the cold stone against his skin. Carefully he checked the other doors around the room. Satisfied that he was alone, he moved carefully towards the opened door. On the other side of that doorway was a dimly lit room with a man sitting in a chair. He appeared to be waiting. Far-fel didn't like the look of the situation. But he was sure he had found the Silent Reaper.

"I am alone. What do you want?" The voice was hoarse.

Far-fel moved through the doorway, surprised to find an *old* man. Certainly not an obvious threat. Now he *really* didn't like the situation. Unexplainable things always meant trouble. He thought of the other Special Assignment Trackers who had died at the hand of this *old* man. He decided to end it quickly! He reached for an arrow ... but the man touched the Necklace he was wearing and Far-fel crumpled to one knee, unable to continue holding the bow. He could see a Green Light glowing through his shirt.

"I'm not sure what I would have done, if you hadn't found the Green Stone," the old man mocked Far-fel. "But the call of the Talisman is ... irresistible, wouldn't you agree?"

Far-fel felt life and energy flow *out* of him and *into* the Green Stone. He quickly closed his eyes, searching for the strength to resist the insidious power.

"Surprised to find an old man?" the Guild Master laughed wickedly. "Your timing couldn't have been better. You have saved me the trouble of finding another victim ... to give *me* life and strength." He moaned with pleasure, in anticipation of retrieving the Stone from the Tracker. "But I am curious beyond belief, to know how you made it this far ... right into my lair!" He said, shifting his touch to a different Medallion on the Necklace. "And especially, I want to know what your people know about me."

As the Reaper let go of the first Medallion, the Tracker felt the flux of the Green Light retreat. His head snapped up, eyes open, towards the Reaper, who was about to touch a different Medallion on the Necklace. Quickly closing his eyes again, Far-fel focused on the spot where the Green Light had left his body, knowing *there* is where it would re-enter. Perhaps this damnable Talisman had the power to read his mind. And discover the secrets of the Special Assignment force! Or maybe, the power to make him talk. Either way, he braced his will against the next flash of Green Light. Many lives depended on him.

Far-fel felt its return. But this time he was ready. The Stone glowed fiercely as the fight for dominion raged within the Tracker. Like a far-away echo, he heard a raspy voice. The Reaper was asking questions. He must give misleading answers if he were to save the others.

"What Unit do you work for and who is your Leader?" the old man began.

Far-fel's false words were spoken through clenched teeth as he grunted against the thrashing power of the Green Light, as it tried to re-enter his body. When the interrogation was over, he was dripping with sweat, kneeling, and exhausted beyond belief.

Satisfied that he had enough information to hunt and destroy the only threat that he had ever come across, the Silent Reaper quickly released the Second Medallion. He was feeling very weak and much older ... the unfortunate side effect of using the Medallions. However, thanks to the First Medallion, once he dropped the green stone into the Necklace's cradle, the 'life' of the victim would be transferred to him ... giving him youth and vitality! The green glow of the stone slowly faded. He considered using the first Medallion again, to finish extracting the remaining 'life' from his victim. Always safest to extract until the victim was dead. But in this case, would it be prudent, considering how weak he already felt. 'Probably not much life left in the Tracker anyway,' the Reaper reasoned. Besides, if he continued, the Necklace might push him to an age that would prevent him from getting out of his chair! 'I asked too many questions,' he scolded himself.

Using his cane, he hobbled towards the Tracker, where he would retrieve the green stone. Soon it would sit in the cradle of his Necklace and the Green Light would envelope him in a baptism of youth and vitality! He approached the Tracker ... and hesitated. 'What if he is pretending?' He asked himself. He didn't think it possible, but he struck him with his cane anyway, checking for a response. His hand ready to touch the Necklace. There was no response. Still suspicious, he jabbed his ribs with his cane. The unconscious Tracker fell over. Satisfied, the Reaper reached down to remove the Stone from inside his shirt.

When he felt the hand, Far-fel grabbed it, pulled the man to the floor, and slit his throat. Having brought an end to the Silent Reaper, Far-fel collapsed … with a *very* faint heartbeat.

Eventually the light of the early morning sun found its way down the hallway and into the room. Eyelids fluttered, responding to the brightness. Far-fel turned his head, needing to know that the old man's body was still lying beside him. Then he reached for the Stone under his shirt. The rest of his life resided inside that Talisman … and he needed to get it back.

Far-fel remembered the old man's words, *to give me life and strength.* He reasoned that whatever life was in that Talisman would flow into the body of the person wearing the Necklace. He propped himself up and crawled to the blood-covered Necklace. It felt *so* heavy as he removed it from the Reaper. He rested again. He didn't have enough strength to fasten the chain, so he just let it rest on his chest.

He was so weak, it took him several tries to get the dark green stone into the cradle. But once accomplished, it flared to life. The room was suddenly filled with swirling mists of green. Enveloped by this Green Light, life and strength flowed back into Far-fel like water into a barrel, while a Voice filled his mind with a story of the generous gift of the Golden Necklace and the dark green stone. It was a feminine voice, a desirable voice … like a lover he yearned for. It spoke to him of the six gold Medallions strung out along the Necklace. Each one had a purpose. But they relied on the power of the green stone. That must be held by its prey.

The first Medallion could transfer the life and strength of another to him. The second Medallion could get his victim to share his secrets … and so it went, as long as his prey was holding the green stone. Her education of the Medallions was finished as the last of Far-fel's lost life, re-entered his body. She wished him to embrace this power. Instead, he had a question for the Voice. "How was I able to keep the Green Light from entering my body when the old man wore the Necklace?" But there was silence. Apparently, She would tell him what She wanted him to know … not the other way around. He jumped to his feet, flinging the Necklace to the floor.

He walked around it for some time, like a Mountain Cat studying its prey. The power was dark and unclean. And the Necklace was intelligent! It understood that its new host was not the Reaper.

The Necklace from Harleem

But was eager to please its new Master. And ... anxious for Far-fel to embrace its power!

Chapter 27 - The Waterless Well

One hundred years earlier

Bellaroos nodded politely, pulled his hood up and turned to leave the humble stone hut. Although he was good at it, he wasn't always successful in redemption. His talent was discovered years ago, when he accompanied the Assistant Guild Master, on an assignment to a family in a desperate situation.

Trackers were called out for anything that disturbed the peace, but if they discovered it was a family dispute, it was immediately turned over to the Redemption Guilds who were far better equipped to help in these circumstances. Brothers of the Guild went to these families and offered a refuge. Sometimes it was to protect the innocent, but sometimes they offered a path of redemption for the guilty.

The Assistant Guild Master had risen, ready to leave the stubborn, recalcitrant father, when the words 'Can I say something?' blurted out of Bellaroos's mouth. The Assistant was pleased at his youthful courage, but he responded, "No, it's time to leave."

Bellaroos couldn't leave … in fact he couldn't move. Instead, he just said what flowed into his mind. "Mister, how did you feel when your oldest son was born?" And for the next ten minutes, the Assistant watched with amazement as Bellaroos convinced the father that the path of Redemption was exactly what he wanted! But today, was one of those times when Bellaroos wasn't successful. With heavy heart, he made his way back through the valley of the Stone Mountain, northeast of Borit Betoon. It was another two weeks travel past the Dark Lakes, before he made the most incredible discovery of his life.

He was travelling through rugged terrain, and hoped to get further, before camping for the night. The sun was rapidly plunging towards the skyline to his right. Bellaroos knew he would have to walk many hours before he found himself in a comfortable meadow. Sometime later, darkness had already settled and he was still far from that meadow. So he stopped for a brief rest.

Gazing at the black canopy that rose from the horizon upwards, he watched as the first stars were coaxed from their hiding place. Within an hour the sky would be littered with thousands of bright shining lights. While staring upwards, he said aloud, "I wonder how far away you really are?" Seemingly in answer to his heavenward question, a pulsating green glow was immediately visible, coming from a heavily wooded valley not far to his left.

It lasted for about a minute ... long enough to convince him that it wasn't something born of a travel-weary mind. Bellaroos was dumfounded. It was real, and he had to investigate ... but not until morning! He never liked the darkness of night and whatever was creating this eerie light, would still be there when he awoke. He laid his travelling staff on the ground pointing towards the location of the light. Then he unpacked his bedroll and fell asleep.

The next morning, Bellaroos fought his way through the overgrown forest for about two hundred paces. His best estimate of the distance to the pulsating light. Supposedly at the correct spot, but still surrounded by thick forest, he began to circle the area ... until he heard a low hum. "Green Light by night, strange noises by day," he softly whispered. He paused. And questioned his curiosity. He started to quietly re-trace his steps when the humming stopped. This *thing* was taking steps not to scare him away! Which made him wonder if he was stalking something more dangerous than a Mountain Cat.

He turned to leave. But then he thought of the long journey back to his Brothers. Where a strange tale would be welcome conversation at dinner. Bellaroos took a deep breath and walked in the direction of the noise until he found ... a well. "Not exactly what I was expecting!" he exclaimed. He walked up to the edge, placed his hands on the short wall, and peered into the depths below. It was deep.

When he pushed himself away, he noticed how smooth the rocks were. They looked like granite but felt like glass. He crouched down to examine the workmanship and saw there was no mortar. The stones fit so tightly together, it was only the colour that made it possible to see where one stone ended, and the other began. "The workmanship is certainly from another time," he admiringly said, as he slipped his fingers across the stones one more time. "I wonder how far down it is to find water," he questioned. He left to find a couple of small rocks. Rushing back to the well's edge, he dropped his first rock.

'*Crack,*' was the unexpected sound. Like a rock hitting another very hard surface. Bellaroos walked around the well and released the other rock from a different location. 'Thump' was the next sound, suggesting it hit dirt. He estimated the well was about thirty feet deep, based on the time to hit bottom. "So ... a Waterless Well that glows and hums, with something below that is very hard," he summarized. Satisfied, he made his way back out of the dense forest. He was only half way to the perimeter of the thick foliage when he heard another humming sound. He turned. The eerie Green Light could be seen above the tree tops for a moment. It felt like an invitation to return. "Don't worry, I'm coming back ... with a rope ladder and a lantern."

Continuing his travels, he shook his head, wondering what the Brothers would say about having a conversation with a Waterless Well. Perhaps he wouldn't tell anyone. "Yes ... best to keep this secret to myself," he decided, as he began planning his return visit.

Several months later his chance came when another assignment required him to travel a long distance to the east. The Tracking Guild suggested that the need was great, but unfortunately the family was very uncertain about whether they really wanted help or not. It was perfect. Instead of fulfilling the assignment, he would visit the well and claim that the family sent him away, preferring that he visit another time. With his rope ladder and lantern stuffed among his bedding and food, he headed east for half a day. Then satisfied it was safe to abandon his assignment, he headed back to the Waterless Well.

Securing the rope ladder to a large tree, he unrolled it into the mouth of the well. Once at the bottom he lit the lantern. In the centre, sunken into the dirt, was a highly polished black stone box. He began to dig it out with his knife. It was heavy like granite. Excitedly he hefted it onto his thick shoulder, and slowly carried it to the surface.

Inside, sitting on a velvet-looking cloth, was a Necklace that shone like gold. It was arrayed with Medallions, three to a side, and in the middle there was an empty cradle. Bellaroos removed the Necklace and cloth, searching for the missing item. He retrieved a dark green stone, the size of the cradle. But there was also a dagger of unusual workmanship, with intricate carvings along the blade. Another stone, similar in size and colour to the dark green one, was imbedded in the pommel of the knife. But it was polished and reflected light like an emerald. The longer he held the knife, the more he was fascinated by its beauty.

'I wonder,' Bellaroos thought walking to the closest tree. He swung the knife at a thick branch. His eyes popped wide open, when the branch fell to the forest floor. There wasn't *any* resistance! It was like cutting air. The power of the knife frightened him. He was a man of the Robe, not accustomed to weapons. He quickly returned it to the stone box.

And there lay the green stone, obviously meant to be placed in the cradle. He considered it for quite a while and then decided to take a chance. Crouching, he propped the Necklace against the well and dropped the stone into the cradle. The sudden flare of Green Light startled him, causing him to fall backwards. To his amazement, he watched as the Light swirled around the Necklace, accompanied by the previous humming sound and the pulsating Green Light that shone upwards from out of the well!

Within moments the miraculous display was over. Puzzled, he retreated to a large Oak tree. He sat there staring at the Necklace for a long time as it shone in the afternoon sun. What was he to do? Bellaroos had certainly made a wonderful discovery. The Necklace had probably been here for thousands of years, based on the strange design of the well. It was like nothing he had ever seen before. He whispered to himself, "If the Dagger can cut hardwood like it's air ... well then ... what can the Necklace do?" He was terrified at the power that was revealed to him, but he also felt like he was invited.

Bellaroos wondered if the Stone Box was placed in the well to be discovered ... or was it meant to be hidden away from the weakness of mankind, forever? In his line of work, he saw much of the dark side of human living. There were days when it seemed that the work of Redemption was like clawing at an avalanche of mud that threatened to bury the Guild itself.

With a sigh, he arose, disappointed that his adventure had come to this. "But ... I think it's best if I place you back at the bottom of the well," he said, convinced by his concerns. As soon as he lifted the Necklace to place it back onto the velvet cloth, he heard a voice,

I can assist you in your duties. To help those who need redemption.

It was a whisper, a lovely voice, soft, feminine, and alluring. And she knew about his work! Could she read his mind. Because he touched the Necklace. As Bellaroos stood there holding it, he wondered who would be using who.

I am only a tool, I can do nothing without your permission, the reassuring voice responded. *You are the master.*

'Perhaps today is not the best time to make this decision,' he thought. Besides, he could always return it to the Well. With that comforting thought, he wrapped the Necklace and the green stone in the velvet cloth and placed them in his bag. Then he returned the Black Box to the bottom of the well, where he wanted the knife to remain. Walking away from the Waterless Well, he stopped occasionally and looked back. There was no humming or Green Light pulsing heavenward. Was this power content to let him make his own choice, or did it know that he would never be free to decide? He considered what he knew and decided that the Necklace couldn't read his mind if he didn't touch it.

Once Bellaroos was leagues away and out of sight, a single burst of Green Light shot heavenward, from the well.

On the way home to the Guild, he carefully considered where he might hide his new artefact. He wasn't comfortable bringing it into the Redemption Guild. After all, he hadn't decided yet whether the Necklace was a threat or a gift. After some thought, he remembered a forest, with lots of deadfall, about twenty leagues from the Guild. Far enough ... and yet close enough.

A few months later, the Guild Master approached him with a particularly important assignment. "Bellaroos, please come in." The Head Guild Master rose to close the door. "I have received word that a wealthy family has need of our assistance. It's regarding a problem with their twenty-year-old son. The situation is ... delicate and ... I am convinced that you are the only one that has a chance to help them. They will pay very well, and our funds are low right now, so ... will you accept?"

He accepted but also heard the unspoken suggestion that he could not fail. They needed the money! He thought of the Necklace and its promises of assistance. He remembered that the Necklace knew about his work with only a touch. Surely this kind of power would be very useful in assuring success in his line of work.

But there was still part of him that regarded the Necklace like he regarded the knife. Such power terrified him. He had decided against using it, but on the day of departure, the Guild Master visited him in the privacy of his room.

"Bellaroos, I want to thank you for your willingness to accept this assignment. It is *very* important to the future of our Guild. I haven't told anyone. I have been borrowing funds for some time, to keep food on the table and pay the bills. I was considering closing the Guild until this opportunity came our way." He placed a hand on his shoulder. "Thank you Bellaroos." Then he left him.

With a heavy sigh, Bellaroos grabbed his travel bag and headed for the forest where the Necklace lay hidden.

At the edge of the forest he stopped and examined his decision one more time. He felt trapped. He wanted to abandon the strange talisman, but he was also concerned about his Brothers at the Guild. He wished there was another way. Perhaps he should just turn away from the Necklace and have confidence in his native ability. It had been a source of comfort for many people. But ... there were always the few that he didn't get quite right. And they had slipped through the net of redemption.

What if this one didn't respond. Then all would be lost and eventually everyone would find out about their troubles and how he had failed them. He probably should have talked to someone about the Necklace weeks ago, but he didn't and now there was no time. Standing in front of the hiding place, he thought to himself, 'I wonder how the Necklace will react to a *reluctant* host.' Surely it would know how he felt about using a power he didn't trust, as soon as he placed the Necklace on himself. But ... once it was fastened under his Robe, he was surprised at how silent the artefact was.

As he left the forest he heard the words, *Don't worry, you are the Master. If I can be of any service, all you need do is ask ... and the Necklace will help you get what you want.*

She was back! He wished he knew if he had done the right thing!

Chapter 28 - A dark discovery

The family was very gracious and pleased that Bellaroos had come. The Guild Master had sent a message ahead and had reassured them, that he was sending them their very best. They showed him his room, then explained briefly that their worry was their son.

"Please allow me a few moments to unpack and I will join you as soon as I can." In his room, he removed the Necklace and stone, and stared at the second Medallion. The Voice had told him that if he touched it, at the same time the son was holding the small green stone, *She* could reveal the son's secrets to Bellaroos.

He slipped the stone into his Robe pocket, still unsure of what to do. Then, like a lover he was about to leave, he touched the second Medallion. He immediately regretted his impulsive behaviour and put the Necklace back in his bag.

"He is lost to us," the father began. "For over a year, he has been acting very strange. Once he was filled with ambition and happiness. But now he is interested in nothing and rarely talks. Do you think ...?"

"These things can happen," Bellaroos comforted them. "The important thing is that we find out the *cause*. That is often the key to turn something like this around. Now, if you introduce me to the young man, I will get started."

"Of course. His name is Hensten," the hopeful mother informed Bellaroos, as she led him to her son's room.

The young man scowled at Bellaroos as he entered his room. Bellaroos was not welcome.

"I know this is difficult for you. I am an unwelcome intruder into your private world. But your parents insist that we meet. I will be as quick as I can, then I will be gone, and you will have your privacy back." Bellaroos looked expectantly towards the young man. He didn't protest but he was restless, and his eyes wandered around the room. Bellaroos knew the meeting wasn't going to go well unless he could get Hensten to relax. "I usually ask my clients to hold something familiar while we chat. Is there something in your room ...?" Hensten didn't respond. Then Bellaroos remembered he still had the rock in his

Robe. "I have a small green rock that I want you to hold. Roll it between your hands if you prefer. It will help you to feel ... peaceful, while I talk." He passed it to the young man, confident that without the Necklace, it was just another stone. "Now ... I will ask a series of questions. You don't have to answer any of them today. Perhaps never. But it will at least give you an idea of some of the things that I would like to discuss with you, once you are willing." Bellaroos began reviewing the questions.

"Hensten, do you have any secrets that you wished you could share with someone?

"Do you have any regrets?

"If you had unlimited courage, what do you think you would do, to make your life better?

"If you had no regrets, what would you do with your life?"

Bellaroos continued for a while, but when he felt he had asked enough questions, he took the rock back.

As Hensten gave him the stone, he commented, "You're right. I wouldn't call it peaceful, but it was relaxing." Bellaroos took care to notice the distinction as he thought of the sleeping Necklace ... and wondered how asleep it truly was.

After Bellaroos had retired to the guest room of the family's mansion, he decided to return the small green rock to the cradle, the place where he should have left it. With a sigh of relief, he removed it from his pocket and dropped it into the awaiting golden bed. He jerked backwards in surprise, as green mist erupted, swirling until it touched him. With that brief touch he understood that the Medallion could give him the answers to the questions he had asked. He was surprised. He hadn't worn the Necklace and yet the second Medallion was activated! It was tempting.

He had made no progress with Hensten and expected future visits to be the same. Without those answers, he would fail in his assignment and the Guild doors would have to close. With a reluctant sigh, he reached for the Golden Necklace. At once Bellaroos found himself wrapped in Green Light, as he reviewed the history of why the young man was disturbed.

Hensten had a good friend, and they did many things together. One day they went hiking up a mountain, which presented a significant

181

challenge. Often, they teased each other and on one such occasion, he playfully shoved his friend, but the shove turned into a slip which turned into a tumble. Then he watched in horror as his friend fell over the edge of a cliff to his death below.

He had told everyone his friend slipped but mentioned nothing about the playful shove that caused the fall. They misinterpreted his deep melancholy as sorrow ... but it was guilt. He should've told them.

Although he now knew Hensten's secret, Bellaroos wished he had never opened the black box. He felt the sorrow of being unclean. He was usually not this bewildered about temptation. He sighed. The only thing left to do was to return the Necklace to the bottom of the Waterless Well. And then fill it with rocks!

The next day he gathered the family together, armed with a sure knowledge of what had really happened to cause Hensten to reject himself. "I am sure that your son's condition is because he feels severe guilt. I have seen this before," he said, pretending to draw on his experience. "Am I right Hensten?"

The young man, not really paying any attention, suddenly lifted his head and stared at Bellaroos. He should have been impressed that a Counsellor of Redemption was so insightful. But Hensten was used to hearing sympathetic words like *grief* and *sorrow*, not the word *guilt*. The word threatened to expose Hensten's secret. It was his parents who wanted the truth. But they had no idea how painful the truth would be! So, he had always said nothing.

"Guilt can paralyze anyone's ambitions," the Counsellor continued, "especially when the incident involved ... was unintended. Like a careless accident." He looked at Hensten, hoping that he would respond, and begin the healing process.

Instead, Hensten was feeling the fear of the convicted, as he reviewed Bellaroos's words. *Guilt ... unintended, a careless accident.*

'But then again,' Hensten thought as he fought to keep his secret, 'how could those words be so true ... so accurate? And how could this man know so much!' Now his fear had turned to anger. Because he remembered the green stone. The one he wanted him to

The Necklace from Harleem

hold. "What dark arts do you practice, Man of the Robe? And what was that green stone you had me hold?"

"Hensten, what are you saying," his mother objected.

"No need for worry," Bellaroos jumped in. "I obviously hit on a sensitive nerve. May I suggest that after I am gone, you discuss this further as a family." Bellaroos gladly retreated to his room to gather his things. He threw the Necklace and green stone in his bag and departed.

"How could I have been so foolish! I should have known that any talisman that would enter the sanctity of one's private history was using a dark power!" he angrily muttered. And yet he had faltered and assumed that he could safely take what it offered ... this once, and all would be well. He was so angry with himself that he walked all day without stopping to eat or rest.

Days later, twenty leagues from the Guild, he stood at the hiding place in the forest. He would hide it again, until he could bury it at the Waterless Well. For now, he needed to return quickly to the Guild Master to report on the session with the wealthy family. And answer any questions that would most assuredly come. Perhaps with his help, they could still convince the parents that at least a partial payment would be in order.

He moved the log and opened his bag. As soon as he lifted the Necklace to bury it, Green Light swirled into the form of a woman. Startled by the image, he dropped the Necklace and fell backwards. He looked up at her eyes as she smiled and said, *Bellaroos, where do you get these ideas? Is it fair that because you failed, you choose to call my power ... dark? The young man didn't want help and you know from your experience that if someone doesn't want to be helped ... well ... they cannot be helped.*

He crawled backwards to get as far away from the green witch as possible, while muttering, "You lie! You lie!"

Her smile never wavered as she added, *If you fail to see what is so evident, then let me leave you with something that will soon be evident ... to even you. My gifts are not free. The green stone was able to search the young man's history because you touched the second Medallion ... while still in your room. The green stone and the Medallions work together. That is how I am able to bestow my gifts.* She offered another smile.

183

But the power of the Necklace must be fed ... by the energy of a living being. It is the only thing it wants and really the only thing of value that you can give. So, by tomorrow, you will begin to feel ... less, than you have in the past. And every time you use the Medallions, it will cost you.

"Keep your gifts," he said as he glared at the green image. "I would rather die from this affliction that you talk about, than use the Necklace again!" His voice was hard.

Before you depart, I must tell you about the first Medallion. It restores life to the user of the Necklace. It is simple. Have someone hold the green stone – perhaps someone who is a plague on the rest of the community – then touch the first Medallion. The green stone will drain him of his life and when you place the stone into the cradle, this energy of life will be transferred to you. You will look and feel young again! She paused.

Now, my impetuous Bellaroos, before you run off, you must return the Necklace to your hiding place. It would not do for someone else to find this ... dark power, she said as she teased him with a playful grin. *I look forward to seeing you again.* Then the Green Light disappeared.

Bellaroos buried the Necklace, being careful not to touch it. Walking towards the Guild he trembled to think of the power he had unleashed upon the world. Who would not be attracted by the power of this evil artefact? Imagine, power to search the personal history of others ... and immortality! And there were still four other Medallions! He didn't want to think about it, lest the seed of temptation be watered. At least he knew that soon, the Waterless Well would become its grave.

The Guild was in sight when he became aware of a disturbing thought. Before visiting Hensten, he believed he needed to touch the Medallion to invite Her power. That was what *She* taught him. But his visit demonstrated that the green stone could search Hensten's history and yet he wasn't wearing the Necklace ... but he had longingly touched it *before* his meeting. He tried to remember if he had touched any of the other Medallions. He didn't think so. And ... what if there were other payments required, for using that power. After all, it wasn't free! His fear of the Necklace's power continued to grow since he left the family. He wondered where it would end, if he couldn't hide it, where no one would find it. But he thought he already knew. *The power to rule the world!*

He was now on the doorstep of the Guild, twenty leagues away. He turned and looked back towards the forest, determined to hide the Necklace in a place where no one would ever find it. 'But ... will *She* know what I am about to do! And try to stop me. Maybe *She* can even read my mind?' Discouraged, he turned to enter the Guild. But with the door still unopened, he realized he had overlooked an important possibility. 'Maybe ... there's a limit on how close I have to be to the Necklace, before the Green Lady can read my mind!' He tried to think back to an occasion where she might have said something. Anything that would reveal that she ...

Then he remembered a small detail that was exactly what he was looking for! When he had reluctantly decided to re-visit the forest to retrieve the Necklace, to help him in his session with Hensten, he was back at the Guild. And yet, later that day at the forest, as he picked up the bag that contained the Necklace and stone, *She* had said,

Don't worry, you are the Master. If I can be of any service, all you need do is ask ... and the Necklace will help you get what you want.

She didn't know what he wanted the Necklace for! 'There *is* a limit!' He rejoiced. 'Or ... maybe *She* cannot read minds at all!'

He turned the doorknob and walked through the front door, allowing a thin smile to celebrate his victory. Now he knew there was a way to defeat the Necklace. First, he would come up with a plan ... at the Guild. Far away from the forest. Just to be sure. Next, he needed someone who had never touched the Necklace, to carry out his plan.

Chapter 29 - The fall of Mister Glickin

Inside the Guild Bellaroos's weary body tumbled into his bed. He had travelled far with little food or rest. But soon a knock awakened him from his deep sleep. It was the Guild Master.

"I heard that you had arrived. I came right away because I have received a message from the family. They were most appreciative of what you helped them see. They apologized for Hensten's behaviour and sent the full payment! And just in time, because tomorrow the Assistant Guild Master of the Finance Guild is arriving to discuss my overdue payments. Bellaroos, you have saved all of us. Thank you!"

Bellaroos offered a weary smile in return.

"Tomorrow we will be hosting a dinner for our guest. His name is Glickin. From the town of Pirtelin." The Guild Master apologized for his interruption and then left.

Bellaroos spent the following day going over the roster of the Brothers in the Guild, trying to find someone that he could trust to take the Necklace to the Waterless Well. But everyone was there to be redeemed ... from past mistakes. What if the Necklace was too much of a temptation? 'I am no further ahead,' he shook his head, 'and it's almost time to go for dinner. With Mister Glickin,' he added, seeing a possibility he hadn't considered. 'Perhaps ...'

When dinner commenced, the Guild Master noticed that Bellaroos looked worse for wear. "Starting tomorrow, I want you to take some time off and relax. Perhaps it's only travel fatigue, but best to play it safe," he suggested.

Bellaroos nodded, remembering the words *by tomorrow, you will begin to feel ... less*. But that only made him more determined to follow through with his plan to involve Glickin. All through dinner he studied the visitor and his responses. He knew he was looking for someone who was ethical, reliable, and devoted to the better good of those around him. By the time dinner was over, he was sure he had found someone he could trust. And because Pirtelin was located in the opposite direction of the Waterless Well, he modified his plan. He would ask him to drop it into the middle of Lake Win-rik. 'Much better' he thought. 'In fact, to take it back to the Waterless Well was careless thinking ... the Necklace probably got its power from the Well.'

When they arose from dinner, Bellaroos approached Glickin with a suggestion, "Perhaps before you retire, you would like a brief tour of our Guild and gardens. Our wines are famous ... perhaps we can find a bottle or two that you would like to purchase for your journey home?" he suggested.

"A splendid idea," Glickin agreed. "Getting to know our clients is always important to the Finance Guild."

After the tour, Bellaroos thanked him for his interest. Then, still confident that he was the man he was looking for, he added, "Mister Glickin, do you have a moment?"

"Of course, how can I be of assistance?" Glickin offered. It was common for individuals to approach him on matters of investment, when he visited Guilds.

"Some time ago," Bellaroos began, "on one of my journeys I discovered an ancient artefact of curious workmanship. The gold-like material is truly beautiful. At first, I was very excited and anxious to discover what powers the Necklace might yield, for the benefit of our Guild. But unfortunately ... it has proven to be malicious in its design. Because you see Mister Glickin, when you first touch it, its power is manifested by a brilliant Green Light that will fascinate you. Then you will hear a voice that will promise you gifts. But this is deceitful. Because this talisman needs the energy that our bodies contain. We become payment for using the gift. If you use it, like I did, you will quickly regret having ever laid eyes on this deadly artefact." Bellaroos sighed. "When our Guild Master made mention at dinner of my condition, he thought it was because of my recent travels. But I know different. I have *aged* ten years ... from touching this Talisman *only once!*"

Mister Glickin's expression was intense and showed serious concern, so Bellaroos continued.

"I hid the Necklace in a forest twenty leagues from here, but it needs to be dropped into Lake Win-rik, which is convenient to your travels back to Pirtelin. I am desperate to hide this wicked talisman away from unsuspecting travellers. But I don't dare go near it again. I need someone who shares my concern and is willing to do as I suggest. Do you think ...?"

Glickin was not expecting such a tale, and yet he could see the terror in the eyes of Bellaroos. "What you have told me is certainly unusual. But your story and your request, deserves *careful* consideration. Please allow me to think about this tonight, and I will give you my answer in the morning before I leave."

Bellaroos was satisfied and grateful that the man was not too quick to agree. It spoke of responsible commitment. Exactly what he was looking for.

Glickin had dismounted from his horse and walked to the edge of the forest with a sack and a map. Soon he was moving the fallen log to expose the bag containing the golden talisman. Bellaroos had given him gloves to ensure there would be no error in handling the object. *You must not touch it!* were his last words.

Within moments he had the cloth covered Necklace in the carrying sack. It was almost too simple. 'So much precaution for this!' he thought. He stood and gazed down upon the infamous artefact. *Of curious workmanship*, the Brother of Redemption had said, Glickin reminded himself. Then he realized how foolish he would feel if he went through the entire exercise, of dispatching the talisman, without even having seen it. Bellaroos had said, *don't touch it*, and he fully intended to do that. But he needed to convince himself that it existed. He carefully pulled it partially out of the bag and folded back the heavy cloth covering. He let out a small gasp. It was truly beautiful. Golden-like in appearance, with intricately carved Medallions strung along the front of the chain. His curiosity should have been satisfied, but now he felt an insatiable desire to touch it. He began to tremble with fear as he remembered the warning and the consequence that Bellaroos had endured. He quickly rewrapped the artefact and pushed it back into the sack. With everything in place, he headed south where he would complete his task.

Glickin paused at the top of the hill overlooking the valley that cradled Win-rik Lake, soon to become the new home of the evil talisman. It was a calm day with no clouds in the sky. He felt confident there would be no difficulty in hiring a boat. He snapped the reins and encouraged his horse downward to the water's edge. He dismounted, grabbed the bag, and slung it over his shoulder. From the top of the hill he had seen a dock with a few boats, approximately a league from where he stood. In less than an hour, this evil object would rest on the bottom of a very deep lake.

The Necklace from Harleem

As he made his way to the boats, his thoughts went back to the beauty of the object he was carrying. It seemed like such a contradiction. So evil. So beautiful. But he vividly remembered the surprise and concern the Head Guild Master had expressed for Bellaroos's deteriorated condition.

"It *has* to be done ... and quickly!" Glickin reminded himself. "Besides, anyone would consider it an honour to dispose of this menace." With renewed determination, he continued his trek to the water's edge.

Eventually his thoughts turned to the excitement of having a wonderful tale to tell his children and his grandchildren. 'But how much better, the tale would be,' he thought, 'if I had actually seen the Green Light that Bellaroos had talked about. But surely that would be too risky,' he reflected.

Once the dock was in sight, he could hear voices from the fishermen. His thoughts returned to the Green Light. 'Far enough away,' he considered carefully, 'that I could remove the Necklace in privacy, but so close that if anything went wrong, I could rush to the boats and dispose of it.' Besides, Bellaroos had said that payment was required, *after* he had accepted the gift. Glickin was determined that he wouldn't accept *any* gift offered! He was *very* excited about the prospect of seeing the Green Light. What an experience this would be! With heart beating wildly from anticipation, he carefully set the bag on the ground and put on the gloves. He unwrapped the golden Necklace and laid it on the heavy cloth. He sat back for a moment to admire its beauty as it sparkled in the early afternoon sun.

"Now for the tricky part. To see the Green Light, I must *touch* the Necklace," he whispered. He removed a glove and positioned himself as far away as he could. Then reaching, he tapped it, ever so lightly. Green Light erupted from the Necklace as soon as he made contact, swirling upwards and outwards as it formed the image of a woman. A *very* beautiful woman.

She flickered in the sunlight and said, *Hello Glickin. You have called, and I have responded. What is it that you want?*

Chapter 30 - Tainted blood

Back to the present, when Glickin's long reign of terror had ended.

As soon as he was able, Far-fel left the Guild and the dead body of the Silent Reaper, taking with him the loathsome Necklace and its companion green stone. Finn would want to see it. And dispose of it like the other captured artefacts. He found a quiet Inn where he could rest and regain his strength. Even though the Necklace had restored his 'life' the battle with the Reaper had taken its toll.

He had prepared a message to send to Finn, regarding the Mercenaries, the Necklace, and the end of the Silent Reaper. But every time he thought about going to the Communication Guild to send it, he would get distracted and he would forget. Until he saw the message lying on the table beside his bed. Then the cycle continued. He came to realize that he wasn't as free as he thought he was. It terrified him, but not as much as the day he awoke with a desire to head west.

Besides his difficulty with focusing on a task, his instincts, which had always served him well, were unreliable. Decisions were hard to make. And he would become obsessed about something that seemed minor, to the exclusion of things that ought to be more important. For example, his obsession to head west. The desire was very strong, but the reasoning was weak. And when he tried to make sense of it, it was like chasing a fox through bramble bushes. The harder he tried, the further ahead the fox seemed to be.

While travelling, he tried not to think about the dark green stone, but its presence constantly intruded his thoughts. Sometimes he would wake in the middle of the night and see it glowing. He would sit, staring at it, sweating from the effort of resisting its power. But over time, he was coming to realize that for all his effort, he was only delaying the inevitable. His enslavement to the Necklace.

And it had already begun. He had lost something ... or he had changed. Either way, the stone was becoming the Master. Before, when he resisted the Silent Reaper, it was difficult, but possible. Because he felt the full bloom of his Tracker willpower to resist. His grandfather had always said it was the Tracker blood that gave them the advantage. Perhaps his blood was tainted through exposure to the power of the Necklace. It would explain a lot. But unfortunately, it meant he was never going to get out of the mess he was in.

Every morning, as he awoke, the desire to head west was waiting for him. And to meet that demand, he was only allowed to sleep four hours. He felt like a dog sniffing a dark scent.

Occasionally he would ask a traveller on the road, what the name of the next town was. This time, the man said Pechora. He remembered that there was a large Tracking Guild there. But would he dare approach them for help? What would he say? And what could they do anyway? He suddenly laughed darkly, as he realized that his thoughts were insane. He was thinking like a man who still had a will. A passer-by gave him a strange look, reminding him that he must try to resist these fanatical outbursts.

Within a few leagues he found himself on the outskirts of Pechora. Suddenly the fanatical zeal halted. The Necklace was hesitant to move on. Far-fel could feel another force touch him. He listened until he understood the 'thoughts' of the Necklace. Lust and fear swirled together while the Necklace hesitated between retreating or moving forward. He noticed that while the Necklace fought with its own indecision, his willpower increased ... ever so slightly. He bolted forward, determined to take advantage of the situation. As he suspected, every minute he raced towards that 'other' power, gave him an increase in his ability to take control. He was far from being free ... it still took an enormous effort to struggle against the power of the stone.

Standing exhausted in front of the Tracking Guild, the forces within him were churning. The Necklace yearned for the darkness that was somewhere inside this building, but even more, it feared the 'other' power. It fought against Far-fel as it screamed in agony, but the 'other' power was sending a message of encouragement to keep going! Far-fel's face glistened from the sweat of his violent struggle as he walked through the front entrance. The Necklace continued to be the most formidable force against which he had ever fought.

"I need to see ... the Guild Master ... immediately." The effort to speak those few words was enormous. But for the first time since the Necklace enslaved him, he felt a small measure of hope!

The Assistant glanced at the shaking arm that held Far-fel's bag. "Yes, right away. Follow me."

But when the Assistant turned left into an office, Far-fel kept going straight. He was being guided. He came to a locked door. He kicked it in. The two-story chamber was a large storage room with locked cabinets lining the walls. Above him a railing traced a balcony that ran along the two sides and disappeared through doors at the far end.

The 'power' was straight ahead, behind a shallow cabinet attached to the wall. After a few quick strides, his powerful hands tried to open that cabinet. Securely locked, he grabbed his long knife and busted the lock. Opening the cabinet revealed a glowing Crystal Amulet hanging from a silver chain. He could hardly breathe as the power of the Necklace withered, confronted by this Amulet. Instinctively he reached for the imprisoned talisman. He didn't hear the shouts from the doorway nor see the two Archers enter from above as he clutched the glowing gem. Light flashed through him, sweeping the darkness away, purging his blood of the stain that the Green Light had left.

"Walk away from the Amulet," a dangerous voice shouted from above.

Far-fel placed the now lifeless Amulet back in its prison. He looked upward, seeing an Archer on either side ... obvious friends of the Necklace. Leaving his bag on the floor he dashed for the doorway while two arrows sought his death from above.

Chapter 31 - The Future Emperor of Ankoletia

Far-fel's quick glance above told him that the Archers were inexperienced. He would use that to his advantage. He dropped the Amulet into the cabinet and dashed for the door yelling, "Shoot." As expected, they instinctively responded to the command, as he dropped into a perfect slide, dodging the arrows. The Archers never had a second chance as he slid out the door. Unfortunately *without* the Necklace and the Crystal Amulet.

After Far-fel left the premises of the Tracking Guild, the green stone and the Necklace went into hibernation. They would bide their time until they would once again, be far away from the Amulet. The Assistant Guild Master brought the visitor's bag to Bernado's office immediately. "When the Tracker arrived, he was trembling from exertion and drenched in sweat. He insisted on seeing only you. He was carrying this bag when he entered. I led him to your office, but he went straight to the storage room, broke one of the locks, and found the Amulet. It was ... *glowing* when the Archers entered the room from the balcony."

Bernado was intrigued. He thought back to the young man he took it from ... the one who had power over Olleti! 'Now I *know* there are secrets you are keeping to yourself. But with enough persuasion, your secrets will be my secrets,' he menacingly thought. Bernado turned his attention to the Assistant. "I would ask how he managed to escape from inside our heavily armed Guild, but then again, he wouldn't be the first ... would he?" Bernado glared at his Assistant.

"Security has been increased. However, this man was *very* skilled," the Assistant offered in defence.

Bernado dismissed his excuse with a wave of the hand. "Relocate the Amulet to a new hiding place and leave me with the bag," Bernado said, anxious to see what all the fuss was about. After the Assistant left, he carefully laid the Necklace on the table. Golden in appearance, it was graced by six round Medallions, all etched with strange markings that were different from each other. He lifted it to the light. The workmanship was elaborate and very detailed. And there was a cradle in the middle. Probably designed to hold something. He quickly searched the bag. He pulled out a small, very plain, dark green stone. He expected that if he threw it out on the street, people would walk past it without giving it a second thought. Yet, they were together! He was curious to place the stone into the cradle ... but he remembered his experience with the Crystal Amulet. "Best to proceed cautiously," he said quietly to himself, as he returned the two pieces to the bag.

He walked to the window and stared towards the hills, the place the unknown Tracker probably headed to. Bernado quietly let his thoughts find voice. "The man was obviously distressed about something when he arrived with the bag. And how did he know that there was an Amulet hidden away in the storage room?"

He remembered when his Shaksbali Trackers searched the drugged prisoners and found the Crystal Amulet. Curious, they held it up to a wall torch, which in turn attracted the gaze of several of the El-Bhat *guests* who dashed from the unlock cells to snatch it from the surprised Shaksbali jailers. Three El-Bhat dropped to their knees in agony, before they allowed the jailor to take it to Bernado. He later found out that the El-Bhat call it the *glass of death*. He almost lost it to the unknown Tracker. Instead, it appeared that he now had two talismans of power. As for the Golden Necklace, his plan was to take it home that evening for further study. With luck, it might turn out to be more useful, and straightforward, than the unpredictable Crystal Amulet.

Far-fel left Pechora and headed north to the neighbouring foothills, where he could rest until he figured things out. He was not ready to report back to Finn. He had lost the Necklace and discovered another talisman that had healed him of his tainted blood! Sitting in the shade of a small grove of poplars, he began the litany of things that troubled him.

First, he knew that something was terribly amiss at the Pechora Tracking Guild. But was it just a few things ... or many. He never thought that such a situation was possible. But after his experience with the Necklace, he was better prepared to consider possibilities that he might have dismissed before as *impossible*.

In their work, the Specialists would occasionally come across an 'ancient artefact' that was handed down from the time before the

Great War. Clever Devices designed by ancient Storlenians that presented an advantage to the owner. It was what he had anticipated when he took his assignment to track down the Silent Reaper. It was what Finn expected ... a murderer with an advantage.

But the power of the Necklace with its Medallions and a small green stone ... was unbelievable! As far as he knew, there were no record of anything this powerful before the Great War.

'How was such an artefact even possible?' To believe it, one had to be confronted by it, and overcome by it, as he had. When he used the Necklace to restore his life, he unwittingly paid a very high price. Had he known, he would have never allowed this heinous power to invade his body. He probably would have remained a prisoner to its whims, if it had not been for the Crystal Amulet. It also explained why the Necklace reacted as it did when he entered Pechora.

Whatever ancient power created the Necklace, it seemed to Far-fel that its nemesis was the Crystal Amulet. It had the power to overcome the green force and drive it from his body. It was unfortunate that he had to leave them both at the Tracking Guild. Finn would want them both. But if Far-fel had to make a choice, he wanted the Crystal Amulet. Of course, they would have already moved it, making the retrieval almost impossible. 'Unless,' he thought, 'I can still feel it.'

Over the next couple of days, under the camouflage of clothes he'd found drying outside, he took different roads that passed close to the tracking Guild. His suspicion was correct, the closer he got to the Guild, the stronger was the attraction to the Amulet. On his last trip to the Guild, he circled the grounds to test if the pull from the Amulet was clear enough to tell him where it was hidden. The experience confirmed that he would only know for sure once he got inside.

He waited another week before overcast clouds provided the total darkness for which he was hoping. By the time he got through the front door he had easily dispatched three Trackers, further confirmation that the Guild had been compromised, and that the Guardians at the Gates were not Trackers at all. After he entered the building, the rest was easy. With the stealth that was his second nature, he simply followed the pull of the Amulet that guided him directly to its new hiding place.

He slipped the silver chain over his head and tucked the Amulet under his shirt. Under the cover of a black night, he was soon beyond the city limits of Pechora. Although Far-fel had once considered stealing both artefacts, once he slipped the Crystal Amulet around his neck, he knew he never wanted to see the Necklace again. With the knowledge that the Pechora Guild had somehow been turned to the enemy and that he possessed the only power that could defeat the Necklace, he decided to head back to Finn without delay.

Urshen arose from his bed and walked to the iron grate of his cell before he woke up. As consciousness spread over him, he thought about what had just happened. The feelings were clear. It appeared that his Amulet had been taken somewhere else and he was trying to follow it in his sleep!

On the same night that the Amulet left Pechora, Bernado tossed and turned as images of the Necklace invaded his thoughts. Hopelessly unable to fall asleep, he arose and headed to where the artefact was hidden. When he opened the cabinet, the Stone was emitting a soft Green Light. He contemplated picking it up … the desire was so strong.

But artefacts of power could be capricious. He already knew from the Crystal Amulet that they might reject you or embrace you. Harm you or bless you. But … one thing was different this time. The desire to pick it up was not his own. It was coming from the Stone. He was sure of it. He decided to just touch it. Placing his finger on it, the Necklace gave off a soft vibration sound. Suddenly he knew what was happening. The Necklace was excited that he was its new owner. It wanted him to embrace its power! With this encouragement, he clutched the stone, and suddenly he was awash in Green Light and then instructed in the purpose of the six Medallions.

Sometime later, on an evening when the candle was getting low, Bernado pulled out his journal. He wrote,

Today the Necklace introduced me to immortality! It does this by squeezing the life from another and giving it to me. The first person to contribute to my immortality was a Storlenian from

Toobor, a Shaksbali Tracker with a young family working at the Mines of Tenleth. I promised freedom for his family if he would help me investigate the possibilities of a new weapon, designed by the Quorum. He readily accepted.

Initially, I used the first Medallion only briefly, wanting to understand how quickly it would work and the effect on the subject. The experience left him weak and exhausted. After he left, I transferred what the stone took from him to me. It was wonderful!

I requested that he return to my office a week later to continue our testing. When he failed to come, I sent a different set of Guards, wanting to keep my secret. He was not only feeble, but to my astonishment he had aged noticeably! Our second session was our last. Being of no further value, I had a third set of Guards dispose of him. No one must know of my secret power.

The Necklace is truly amazing, but it demands much of the user. I was surprised at how quickly I felt 'spent' after using the second Medallion to extract information from a suspected criminal. The 'Lady' warned me of this, but also reminded me that the first Medallion has the power to make up for all the losses experienced by using any of the other five.

I am beginning to think that with the power of this Necklace, I will one day rule all of Ankoletia ... as Emperor!'

❧ ❧ ❧

Fre-steel had begun to wonder if Bernado had forgotten he was in the waiting room. With the door ajar, he heard the voices of Bernado's many visitors. He was irritated that he was constantly ignored while Bernado attended to yet another 'urgent' piece of business. Finally his anger brought him to his feet. He wanted so much to burst through that door. But he couldn't set aside his need to be subservient. So instead, like a schoolboy, he silently slipped to the crack of the doorway, needing to know who was given preference.

Across the room, Fre-steel saw one of the devoted Shaksbali Trackers tied to a chair, holding a small green stone ... begging Bernado to let him live. 'What is happening,' Fre-steel shuddered. To his horror, he saw the man holding the green stone, age before his eyes, until he slumped dead in the chair.

A wicked chuckle escaped Bernado's lips as he walked over, ripped the stone from the dead man's grasp, and dropped it into the cradle of the Golden Necklace he was wearing! Green Light erupted from the stone and enveloped Bernado. When the light subsided, Bernado was ... younger!

Something snapped inside of Fre-steel as he reeled away from the ghastly sight. Leaning against the wall, he brought his trembling hands to his face, knowing that he had been ... deceived! A hundred images passed before his eyes, casting horror against his commitment to the El-Bhat. In dismay, he relived the moment when Tal-nud kneeled before him at Border Pass, staring up at him in disbelief. Fre-steel heard his own diabolical words, *It would be a pity for Trackers to die ... committed to a lie.*

And then there was the purging of the *unwanted*. 'How can I ever undo my crimes?' he wailed silently. He slumped to the floor as he struggled to set aside the avalanche of dark thoughts, which threatened to send him to the land of the insane. Desperate to find anything that might bring him a small measure of relief, his mind went back to the time when it all started. The day he couldn't wait to submit his report. So he barged into the office of the Head Guild Master ... to discover the unimaginable betrayal. Followed by his permanent transfer to Border Pass, to silence him.

They said it was impossible to break a Tracker. But whoever said that, never considered what he had gone through. Arriving at Border Pass, his mind troubled to the point of unbelievable despair, he was already a broken man. Pahkah must have seen it ... and why he

The Necklace from Harleem

was kept alive when others were murdered. In his desperate state, he needed to believe in something, so he believed what they told him.

Bernado was removing the dead body from the chair! The noise warned Fre-steel that he must slip out the back entrance of the waiting room as quickly as possible. He returned to the privacy of his room and wept.

After a few hours of sleep, Fre-steel felt something he hadn't felt for some time. The strength of his Tracker blood! He had made up his mind. He would wait and watch, for an opportunity to head south. Past the Southland mountains to the Mines of Tenleth. To secure his redemption, he would find a way to release the Storlenian women and children that were being held hostage at the Mines!

Chapter 32 - The Executive Command

Previously. Axion, Head Master of the prestigious Planning and Development Guild at Qar-ana, was surprised to discover that Craslin had already assigned Ranoof to train the new Militia Guard. After interviewing Ranoof, he uncovered an unbelievable story of corruption at the Tracking Guild of Pechora. He asked his Assistant Craslin to follow up. While he investigated another potential concern of his own

Axion invited Aram-Dentee to join him for lunch. He had some things to discuss. That he had immense capabilities was obvious, but the man remained a mystery. Maybe too much of a mystery.

"I am very pleased with your work. Craslin has done well to find such talent so quickly. What work have you done before?"

"I am for hire, so my work varies considerably."

"No doubt you have been blessed with an abundance of natural talent. But your refinement suggests that you came from a specialty Guild," the Guild Master suggested.

"You are correct. I *prefer* specialty. I have been trained as a Butler. It opens doors to exciting and varied assignments ... like this one." He raised his wine glass in gratitude.

"To specialty Guilds," Axion responded, raising his glass ... and purposely drained the goblet. Curious about his other skills, he placed the empty glass too close to the edge of the table. It fell.

Aram-Dentee caught the glass in mid-air, with ease.

"How clumsy of me," Axion apologized, "but your quick reflexes have saved me another embarrassing moment," he praised with a smile. But now he knew something else ... something troubling. Aram-Dentee's training was more 'extensive' than he had thought. Axion had never heard of the Butler Guild, but that was about to change.

As the Assassin placed the glass back on the table, he knew he had been baited! 'A moment of inattention ... and now Axion knows.'

It was early morning when the Aide noticed a small amount of blood on the floor, in front of the window. He stopped to check the area. There was also blood on the heavy drapes. He opened the window and found more on the window ledge that gave access to the river below. He ran to Security. The search was quick and definitive. The concern for the Head Guild Master elevated immediately. For both he and Aram-Dentee were missing!

By the end of the day, Craslin had initiated 'Executive Command' which gave him full power until the Head Guild Master could be reinstated. This temporary condition, which lasted a maximum of one year, would surely be enough time for Craslin to accomplish his designs.

Chapter 33 - The Future Queen of Ankoletia

Previously. Zephra, Yaneek and Benekee, had no idea that the six Trackers, including Urshen, were imprisoned in cells below. Ironically, it was Bernado, the Head Guild Master of the 'trusted' Tracking Guild, that sent them off on a false errand to look for them at Qar-ana

Craslin was looking out the large windows of his new office, watching the crowds below make their way towards the Guild entrance with their petty business. If they had nothing to contribute, they would be turned away. One of his new policies to increase effectiveness. He was about to return to his work when he saw 'her', walking in a small group of three. He was immediately curious. He left his office and hurried to one of the upper balconies, which looked down on the area inside the front entrance. His curiosity was rewarded. She was ... someone he wanted to get to know better. He signalled for an Aide.

"Those three down there, take them directly to the Observation Room." Then he watched while they waited and chatted. He was mostly interested in how she cared for the other two. Things like that created leverage. The Aide returned just in time. "I've seen enough, bring them directly to my office."

Craslin welcomed them. "Please ... take as much time as you need. It will help me understand your problem." The woman with the black hair stepped forward, anxious to start the proceedings.

"We come from Tinker Village in Arborville, where the Tinkers are building superior wagons." Her father would be pleased that she used this unique opportunity to spread the word. "We are looking for a small group of Trackers, seven in total, who left Pechora to come here. It is important that we find them soon and were told they might be here."

It was difficult for Craslin to focus on their trivial request. His imagination was already considering how she would look ... as his wife, in the finest of clothes. Standing beside him as he ruled over all

Storlenia. "I am not aware of their visit ... but not everything crosses my desk."

With Craslin's encouraging comment, Zephra decided to drop a name. "One of the Trackers is called Urshen." She thought maybe his name had been circulated in reports regarding the battle at Border Pass.

Craslin nodded, appreciative of the additional information. "Please allow me to do some checking. In the meantime, my Aide will show you to rooms that we use for visitors from far away." He wrote a signed note and handed it to Zephra. "Use this whenever you want to see me ... they will let you straight through to my office."

Craslin smiled warmly as he said goodbye. She smiled back and thanked him. It was only a courtesy smile, but Craslin knew that he wanted to enjoy that smile for the rest of his life.

The following day Zephra's small group was invited back to visit Craslin. He had sent fresh clothes to all of them and Aides to pour their bath. Their stay in the guest quarters was a welcome change from traveling dusty roads. When they arrived in the Adjoining Hall, Craslin was engaged in a meeting, somewhere else in the Guild. They were asked to wait. Yaneek was busy chatting with Benekee. Wishing to be alone with her thoughts, Zephra left them and went to lean against a pillar. The Storlenian dress made her wish Urshen was there, to see her. The last time she was dressed like this was at the Celebration Dance.

When Craslin walked past a waiting group of escorts, he simply raised his hand and they immediately followed him. He discussed his needs while manoeuvring down various corridors. Each movement and every step bore witness to his new confidence. He was now the most powerful man in all Storlenia.

He approached the Adjoining Hall with eagerness. He was anxious to see how she looked in the clothes he had sent. He stopped three paces back from the large doors, allowing the escorts to open them. Entering the room, his gaze quickly fastened upon the young woman standing by the pillar, the ringlets of her long black hair cascading over one shoulder. Her profile was perfect. Her tanned face glowed as the sunlight streamed upon her from the high windows above. She was deep in thought. He was even more pleased than he thought he would be. His fascination for this Tinker woman soared.

She turned towards him, with a look of strength he hadn't expected. Zephra was truly an unpretentious mixture of beauty and fire. Her look helped him recognize that he was rushing into this like a blind bull! He was reminded of something Axion had said in his early training, "Craslin ... when contemplating a challenging task, or a significant prize, a generous portion of patience is *always* required." He must find common ground. Something that would nurture an irresistible attraction to *him*. But that would take time. So, he turned his attention away from her to the young man and his sister. "I trust you slept well?" He asked, offering a smile of friendship.

"After a week in the wagon, it was most appreciated," Yaneek thanked Craslin. Turning to Zephra she quickly added, "But it *was* the most comfortable wagon I've ever been in," offering an understanding smile to her new friend.

Noting the interaction and remembering that Zephra mentioned that the Tinkers were building superior wagons, he suddenly saw an opportunity that he intended to exploit. "You must tell me more about this wagon," he said as he looked at Zephra, "once we have finished our business. And now if you will join me ..."

They followed him into his office. Once everyone was comfortable, Craslin explained that his investigation to find the seven Trackers was unsuccessful. "However, I have learned that Urshen is a rather remarkable young man. He was given honourable mention for the discovery of the El-Bhat invasion into Storlenia." Craslin was surprised at the lack of response to both the praise ... as well as the dire news of the El-Bhat. "But it appears that you already know about these things?" He asked, allowing a pause for a response.

"I was at Lundeen forest," Zephra said matter-of-factly, not wanting to share the knowledge of her relationship with Urshen.

Craslin remembered something from the Lundeen report as his eyebrows lifted slightly in surprise. "You ... are the woman who killed the El-Bhat Leader," he remarked, looking at Zephra with a whole new appreciation of who was sitting on the other side of his desk.

She was unresponsive ... meaning she truly was!

'Courageous *and* humble. I can hardly believe it!' His admiration sought expression. But he knew he mustn't. The blind bull must be restrained. "As I was saying," he continued, "I appreciate your concern for wanting to find Urshen, and indeed it is fitting that we ensure the safety of a national hero like him. I have sent a message to all the Tracking Guilds requesting information regarding the whereabouts of Urshen. In view of the circumstances, may I offer a continuation of our hospitality and suggest it is best for you to wait until we receive the returned reports." He politely waited for a reply.

The three of them exchanged glances until Yaneek said to everyone, "I think it's our best option ... for now."

Zephra nodded in agreement and stood. "Thank you. Please keep us informed."

Early the next morning, Craslin was knocking at their door. He was delighted when Zephra answered it. "I was serious when I said I would like to learn more about this *superior* Tinker wagon. Perhaps you would be willing to show me its features. I have some free time after lunch," he suggested.

"Thanks ... I'll meet you in the Wagon Yard," she said as she politely closed the door. She supposed it was true that Urshen was some sort of national hero, but still, she was suspicious of all the attention. After all, they were nobody, and this was the Seat of Guild Power in all Storlenia. Why the Acting Guild Master would devote so much of his time and resources to attend to their needs, made her uneasy. It suggested that he wanted something. Maybe something they couldn't give. When she mentioned her concerns to Benekee and Yaneek, Benekee informed them that he had previously met Craslin, and was also very surprised at his generosity. Yaneek suggested that they give it another couple of days. "And if we are still waiting, then let's thank him, and move on."

Zephra had slipped back into her riding gear and was at the wagon early, reviewing the points she intended to cover. Craslin might be flirting, but she was there to sell Tinker Wagons. She smiled, imagining him clinging to the sides of her wagon, as she demonstrated its full capability! But in the middle of her smile, he was there, returning a smile that wasn't intended for him. "Shall we begin?" she suggested, anxious to close the deal.

He nodded.

She started with a brief outline of the Tinker Guild that was organized on land just outside of Arborville. "Our operation includes Blacksmith and Carpentry Shops. When I left, we were finishing a wagon a day," she added with pride. Then she insisted that he personally inspect the new technology. Soon they were on their backs staring at the undercarriage, as she explained the changes.

"I'm not easily impressed," he explained, sliding out from under her wagon, "but what you have shown me appears to be remarkable."

"There's only one way to know for sure." She jumped up into the driver's seat. "Hop aboard."

While they ambled along the crowded streets of Qar-ana's Central District, Craslin admitted that the ride was indeed comfortable, but insisted that his interest was about stability and speed.

"Once we get past this traffic, I will show you what it can do." Then she turned and added, "Unless you're nervous about speed?"

He laughed at the question, while his hand drifted to the railing beside him. After all, this was the lady who had killed an El-Bhat Commander.

Eventually they found themselves on clear roads, perfect for what Zephra had in mind. As soon as she saw a side road, allowing for a high-speed turn, she snapped the reins a couple of times, encouraging the horses onward. Without warning, she pulled the horses into that turn, at a speed that would have upended any other wagon onto its side.

With teeth clenched, Craslin hung on for dear life, expecting the worst. When Zephra pulled out of that perfect turn, he let out a nervous laugh, and eventually shouted, "It certainly corners well, never seen anything like it!" He looked over at Zephra who was grinning mischievously. He decided that she liked the compliment. What he didn't know was that Zephra enjoyed seeing him squirm in fear of his life. He was about to mention her excellent handling abilities when she snapped the reins again. 'The Fates preserve me!' he thought, as if the wagon weren't already travelling at a speed that would cause the frame to fall apart! Strangely enough, the faster the horses pulled the wagon, the smoother the ride became. When she finally slowed the horses to a comfortable trot, Craslin asked, "Do you breed your own horses as well as make your own wagons?"

"Nothing special about these horses, it's the wagon design that allows them to pull harder and faster."

"Impressive ... *very* impressive," Craslin murmured, congratulating both Zephra *and himself*. Since he had assumed the role of Guild Master of the Planning and Development Guild at Qar-ana, his native talents blossomed. Everything he touched prospered. Zephra wanted to sell him Utility Wagons, and indeed the Tinkers had managed to produce a dramatically superior product. 'But if they could do this for a Utility Wagon, imagine the benefits if they applied this technology to War Wagons!' he thought excitedly. 'Mounted with the new killing machine!' he added to his reverie. On the quiet ride back, Craslin thought of a plan that would keep Zephra in Qar-ana for a long time. "This was absolutely splendid!" He exclaimed. "I wish to place a large order immediately."

Zephra gave him a quick look to see if he was serious.

"However, there is a condition. I will need someone with the necessary skills to test each delivered wagon. And considering what you know about these wagons, you are the right person for that job. I will ask them to ship them in batches of ten. That way, you shouldn't have to wait long before the first wagons begin arriving in Qar-ana."

"*How* large?" was all Zephra said.

"One hundred. If you agree, I will have the papers drafted up tomorrow and send messengers with the money for the first ten."

"Agreed," was her simple reply. She smiled at the thought of how excited her father would be. He had sent her off with only a hope that she might sell a wagon or two. If Craslin wasn't sitting there, she would have laughed aloud with glee!

For the remainder of the journey, all Craslin could see was the image of Zephra smiling in appreciation. And it was because of her, that he would soon be in possession of a formidable fleet of War Wagons! Once he removed Urshen from the picture, and she became well acquainted with the power and comforts of his Guild, he had no doubt that she would agree to his proposal of marriage.

When they arrived at the Guild, he suggested, "Perhaps you can send Benekee with the details that I will need to complete the order." She nodded in agreement. He smiled and waved goodbye as he headed for his office. His heart wanted her to come instead of Benekee, but he knew he must continue to restrain that blind bull.

Chapter 34 - Benekee in chains

The Assistant didn't know that three men were already with Craslin. He couldn't have, they always used a secret entrance. He told Benekee, "Go right in, he is expecting you."

Once through the door, Benekee walked right up to his desk and handed him the Wagon order papers from Zephra ... before he saw the three men standing off to the side. He gave them a quick nod as he turned to walk away. But a few steps later he realized that these were the men who had assaulted them on the road and stolen the Machine! Benekee was careful not to show any sign of recognition as he left the office and then calmly closed the door. But that wouldn't matter if *they* had recognized him. He hurried back to Yaneek's room, but as he rushed in, he discovered that both girls were gone.

Craslin's buyers asked for directions to the place where the new wagons were being built. The Tinker decided it was best to send them to Haybin. By now, Haybin had many Tinkers trained in the art of Blacksmithing so he devoted all his time running the Blacksmith shops.

Today, a Tinker suddenly appeared at his side, pointing at the open doorway, shouting a message above the hammering noise. Haybin made his way to the four men. So, it had finally happened. The outside world had started to come to them. With a smile he greeted them. "Good afternoon gentlemen, how can I help you?"

"We are here representing the Planning and Development Guild from Qar-ana. We have seen one of your wagons and would like to place an order, but with certain modifications."

"Actually ... we have a *proven* design. And doubt that you would want to modify it," he stated matter-of-factly, crossing his meaty Blacksmith arms.

"I'm afraid we would have to *insist* on the modifications," the man who led the group countered.

Haybin considered his comment, then suggested, "We could consider modifications, but only if it was for an order of at least ten wagons ... and I would have to agree that the modifications do not detract from our superior design."

"Then there should be no problem," the man replied. "We are here to place an order of one hundred wagons. The modifications we refer to," the man continued, producing a packet of design drawings, "are intended to convert your Utility Wagon design, to War Wagons."

Haybin nodded, while considering an order for one hundred wagons! "Gentleman, if I was placing an order that large, I would want a tour of the facilities," he suggested.

Pleased with the offer, the delegation from Qar-ana, followed on the heels of the Blacksmith-turned-tour-guide.

"Braddock," Haybin announced, his massive body planted at the tent door, "there is an embassy from Qar-ana to see you, about a large order for wagons."

Braddock looked at Wutherstop. They smiled at each other.

"How large?" he asked, turning towards Haybin.

"One hundred ... but not Utility Wagons ... War Wagons."

Braddock's knitted eyebrows reflected his concern.

"No need to be troubled," Haybin reassured, "the men are from Qar-ana and the order is confirmed by the Headmaster's Great Seal."

"Please bring them in." There was no confusion in Braddock's mind as to what this order would do for the growth and establishment of the Tinker Manufacturing Guild.

"It must be your daughter's doing," Wutherstop whispered, before the visitors entered the tent. Braddock quickly gave him a 'no' shake of the head, letting him know that his relationship to Zephra must not be discussed. He stepped forward and warmly welcomed the men. This was a new skill Braddock had developed since setting up their Guild. No longer did he see Storlenians as a problem. Now, they were the solution! When they were finished, Braddock sent them back with Haybin to finish their discussions regarding the technical changes.

"Your daughter is more resourceful than I ever thought possible," Wutherstop mentioned, placing a warm hand on his shoulder. "You must be very proud."

Braddock was shaking his head in surprise, "Never realized what a Tinker's Boon was capable of," he said in response. "At least now we know where they are."

"And something else I think we know," Wutherstop added, "is that Zephra and her friends have not found Urshen and his Trackers. Or else I assume they would've come with these men."

"Yes, it's a bit of a surprise. And as soon as Bru-ell gets back, I'm going to send him on a scouting mission."

Zephra hadn't seen Yaneek all morning. Bored, she strolled out onto one of the marble verandas overlooking the gardens and the field beyond. To her surprise a large group of men dressed in a uniform she had never seen, were in training. Curious, she watched them for a while until her eyes fell upon the person in charge of the training. He was a Tracker. And he looked familiar! She carefully hastened back inside and down the white marble steps to one of the exits. She wanted to get a better look at that Tracker. Casually wandering among the gardens, she drifted towards the training field, until she was close enough to recognize him. He was one of the twelve Trackers that had sworn an oath to safeguard Urshen! The discovery was a mystery. Why was this Tracker not with Urshen? Why was he here, busy training Guards for the Planning Guild? If there was a security issue, why wouldn't the Guild Master bring in more Trackers to patrol the grounds? Or maybe, it meant that Urshen *was* here in Qar-ana! And this Tracker was only doing what Urshen had asked him to do. She would have to pull this Tracker aside at the first opportunity.

The following day late in the afternoon, Zephra sat on one of the garden benches waiting for the Tracker to finish his training. When the field began to clear, she followed him until they were in a private area away from the windows above.

"Urshen ..." she started. He stopped and turned. "... isn't here. Why not?"

"Zephra!" He exclaimed, surprised to see her in Qar-ana. "What brings *you* here?" He said more quietly.

"Looking for Urshen. Something has gone wrong, hasn't it? Unless he sent you here?" She added.

Ranoof placed his hands on his hips as he looked down at her Storlenian boots, tormented by what he must say. "Urshen ... and everyone else in our group, are prisoners. I was the only one to escape."

"Where are they?" She asked as his eyes looked up to meet hers.

"Pechora ... Tracking Guild." The last two words came out quiet. He couldn't believe what he was saying.

She was momentarily stunned into silence, as she considered the irony. "What is your name?"

"Ranoof."

"Ranoof, tell me what you know."

He related how they were drugged ... his meeting Protas ... and his suggestion that Ranoof come to Qar-ana.

She never knew Pechinin, but she *had* met Mitrock ... and now they were probably both dead. She wished Ranoof was still with Protas. She remembered his insane bravado at Lundeen forest. "What will you do?"

"For now, continue training the Militia Guard. Unless I can help the Wielder of the Stone of Fire?"

"My heart tells me to go to Pechora," she responded. "But I suspect that we are here for a reason. I might have some influence with Craslin. But for now, we should keep quiet that we know each other."

She looked around to make sure no one was watching. "I came here with a young man who has an Amulet like Urshen's. And he knows how to use it! What concerns me is that he is young ... impressionable ... and with everything going on, we must be very careful to protect both Amulets. So Urshen will just have to wait." She couldn't believe she had the courage to say that. "Every day when you're training is finished, look for me. I might want to pass on a message ... or something."

The Leader of the three men watched Benekee leave the room and then turned to Craslin, "That's the boy we took the machine and shards from."

Craslin thought a moment. Back to the day the Guild Master from Borit Betoon paid him a visit regarding the glowing shards. With a boy in a Robe. The new clothes, significantly more confident, and like before, overshadowed by the 'other' person in the room, all had worked to conceal the identity of the young man now living in his Guild. Not surprising that Zephra would make everyone else in the room look invisible. "Go the way you came. Leave the boy to me." This was going to complicate his relationship with Zephra, but then he had always felt that the chance was small that she would come to him of her own choice. Yes ... he always knew that he would have to use more 'persuasive' methods if he was going to pluck this jewel from paradise. He sent an order to his personal Guards.

By the evening, Yaneek was becoming concerned as to Benekee's whereabouts, so she went in search of Craslin. But he had already gone home, so she asked one of the Guards.

"He is under house arrest ... don't know why," he added, to address the unspoken question.

As Yaneek contemplated the turn of events, she realized that Benekee had been acting a bit odd lately. He talked less and was noticeably bothered. She had assumed he simply felt uncomfortable being watched by a legion of Guards. She shook her head in dismay.

She nodded hello as she passed another Guard. She planned to visit Craslin first thing in the morning to see what she could do, to get his immediate release. He had been so kind to them. 'There's a good chance,' she thought hopefully, 'that Craslin doesn't even know about Benekee's arrest.'

She went to his office as early as she dared ... then waited.

"You may go in now," the man at the desk instructed.

"Good morning Mister Craslin. I am sorry to trouble you, but my brother has gone missing." She had decided to assume the best conclusion. That he didn't know anything.

He looked up from his papers and studied her as she spoke. He decided that she would probably do anything to protect Benekee. "Yaneek, I have some difficult news. The Borit Betoon Redemption Guild has launched a complaint of theft against your brother. He has been placed in custody until I can complete the investigation." He leaned back and waited for her to speak.

Yaneek was somewhat surprised at the lack of sympathy but she was no longer ignorant of the Shard's power. She decided to proceed with great care or they might discover what was hiding under Benekee's shirt, and then they would all end up dead! "Mister Craslin," she began softly, "this thing he stole, was it broken bits of glass?"

The Necklace from Harleem

His smile was back. "Yaneek, I think we can clear up this entire situation if you tell me what you know."

"Well ... when Benekee returned home from the Redemption Guild, he showed me these broken pieces of glass that he had taken, as a souvenir of his time there. Since they were just bits of glass I didn't think much about it. Until recently. We were riding with Benekee's employer and decided to stop to help a poor traveller whose wagon had broken down. But it was a trap. Men with knives stole Benekee's bits of glass ... and this Device that Mister Wutherstop had been working on. While they were loading it, we managed to escape. We didn't dare go back to Breckenden. Those men might be waiting. So, we kept travelling until we met up with a group of Tinkers who took us in. Mister Craslin, we had no idea that these lost pieces of glass were so valuable. Can you help us?" She pleaded.

"What you have told me will help. But, for the boy's benefit, it wouldn't hurt to leave him there for a couple of days. He needs to understand that what he did was wrong."

"Could I visit Benekee ... with Zephra," she tactfully added.

"I cannot see why that would be a problem. I will send a Guard to take you later this morning."

"When you're ready, just knock," the Guard said officially, leaving them inside the cell. Yaneek and Zephra walked towards Benekee. They heard the clanking of the heavy steel-reinforced door, pulled shut behind them.

"Benekee, are you all right?" a concerned Yaneek pressed.

"Well enough ... how did you know I was here?"

Before Yaneek could answer, Zephra jumped in, "What about him," she nodded her head towards the man lying on the cot, facing the other way.

"Don't worry about him, he sleeps almost all the time. So ... how did you know?" Benekee repeated his question.

"I talked with Craslin. I was hoping to get you released."

"I think I'm going to be here for quite a while," he said morbidly.

Zephra and Yaneek looked at each other, both quite surprised. "Benekee, what happened?" Zephra asked quietly.

Those three men who stole our things," he said as he looked at Yaneek, "They were in Craslin's office when I walked in there yesterday morning."

213

"Oh my," Yaneek added, as she considered everything she had told Craslin.

"Yes, he doesn't seem to be everything he pretends to be," Benekee commented.

"You're probably right but I'm afraid ... it's worse!" she whispered to her brother.

"What's wrong, sis? Did you say something ...?"

"Craslin said you were in here because you took something from the Redemption Guild. I said it was true, but he had no need to worry. They were only 'bits of glass'. But I also mentioned the Device ..." she cringed as she thought about what this might mean.

"Yes, and I think I know who has the Machine," Benekee added bitterly.

"But how could Craslin have known about the Hunting Machine? You and Wutherstop kept that so secret."

"You are right, he shouldn't have known. But it didn't matter, he sent those three men for the Shards!" He whispered louder than he intended.

Zephra looked over at the man on the cot, but he hadn't moved.

Yaneek moved in close and whispered, "So that means ... he thinks he has the Shards?"

Zephra placed her fingers to her lips, encouraging them to be silent. "And he's probably right," she said as she pointed to Benekee's chest. "One thing I learned about Craslin is that he is *very well connected*, and if he says he has the Shards, he probably does," she said while removing the Amulet from Benekee. "Do we need to bring you food?" She asked as the Talisman disappeared under her blouse.

"Some fresh bread would be nice ... if it's allowed," he replied.

Then the girls left.

He looked over at the man lying on the cot. A possible spy for Craslin. The man who now had the Brass Sling. Perhaps Craslin was only doing his job, to keep the Shards and the Machine out of the hands of bad people. But then again, Wutherstop might say something like, 'Benekee, you need to be careful what you say. Better to die alone with your mouth shut, than to open it and lie in a crowded grave.'

After a while, he looked again at the man on the cot. Maybe, like Benekee, he was simply unlucky. Someone who got in the way of Craslin's ambitions. But how could he know? He decided that Zephra was right to be suspicious. Too much was at stake. Eventually the man stirred, groggily sat up and stared at the prison door. To Benekee, the man didn't look like a spy. He yearned for someone to talk to. 'I could always be careful. And if he isn't a spy ... I might even learn something important,' he rationalized. Hesitantly he said, "Have you been here a while?" The man seemed genuinely surprised that he wasn't alone. He turned to look at Benekee with vacant eyes. Benekee was sure he had his answer. Those eyes told him it had been a *very* long time. 'He's definitely not a spy,' he thought. "Do you even know why you are in here?" he asked, suddenly sympathetic to this stranger. But to his surprise, the man ignored his question and returned to his sleeping position ... facing the wall. 'Great! He isn't a spy, but he's lost his mind. 'Now the only thing I have to look forward to, is the next visit from Yaneek and Zephra. 'If there *is* a next visit,' he eventually added, suddenly realizing how difficult his imprisonment was going to be.

Chapter 35 - Ranoof is missing

Wearing both the Shards and White Bauble under her blouse, Zephra walked slowly towards the Gardens behind the Guild. So much depended on what she was about to do. Seeing the men begin to leave the Training Field, she headed for her wagon. She stood up as she re-arranged a few things, making herself very visible. She occasionally glanced towards the trainees, going to their wagons and horses, preparing to leave for the day. Once Ranoof spotted her, she held his gaze until he started to walk with the men in her direction.

"Mind giving me a hand," she asked Ranoof as he walked past her wagon. He quickly hopped up and helped her move a heavy box. While bent over, she handed him the talismans wrapped in a lace hanky, given her by one of Craslin's Aides. Lowering her voice, she said, "Put these Amulets in your pouch, and never return here again. Find a trusted Jeweller and ask him to take the single Amulet to replace the matching shard in the large Amulet. Then give it to Braddock, in charge of the Tinker Manufacturing Guild at Arborville."

"Thanks for your help," she thanked him as she stood.

He had already tucked the hanky into his leather pouch. "Happy to help, ma'am," he replied, jumping down. He left the Guild and hurried towards the stables where the tall black horse with white stockings was waiting.

Once it was dark and the Inn had gone quiet, Ranoof slipped out of his window, mounted his horse, and headed north to Pechora. He travelled all day, wanting others to notice the easily identified horse. The following day, after feeding him, he commanded the well-trained horse, "Go home to your stable," and with a slap on the horse's rump, he sent him towards Pechora. Satisfied that anyone looking for him would continue north, he headed south towards Arborville.

Within a week he was far enough from Qar-ana to begin looking for a Jewellery Shop. He laid the two Amulets on the Jeweller's working bench. The man studied them while Ranoof explained what he needed. "And I need to watch while you do this."

The old man looked up at the Tracker, considering the unusual request, but finally nodded and said, "Okay, but it'll cost more," as he placed the two pieces of jewellery beside his tools. Bending over the single large piece, he examined it until he was confident that he knew which shard to remove from the silver cage. After sliding it out, he laid it on his bench, took the other piece and removed the silver clasp that held the single stone. "Not sure why you would go to the bother," he commented as he held the two pieces up to the sunny window, as they scattered rainbows around the room. "They look pretty much the same to me," the old Jeweller commented as he looked at the Tracker for confirmation to continue.

"Like you, I'm just following orders," Ranoof gave him a little grin.

"Then I shall proceed." He reached for his large tweezers, held the replacement stone just the right way, and proceeded to slide it into the space he had just created by removing the shard. Then holding up his work for the Tracker to see, he remarked "You can see how it's not quite flush with the edges of the other shards. But I'm confident that once I tighten the silver cage, it will be as snug as the other piece was."

Ranoof leaned over his shoulder, watching the skilled hands carefully tighten the silver cage around the shards.

"One last squeeze ought to do it," the old man quietly said. When Zephra's White Bauble made perfect contact with the rest of the shards, the entire Amulet began to glow brighter and brighter. In astonishment, the Jeweller dropped his tweezers. Reaching for a polishing cloth, he instinctively threw it over the silver cage, fearful of the increasing brightness. The cloth had barely covered the Gemstone when a blinding flash of Light brightened the room.

⚜ ⚜ ⚜

For days, while Jalek traveled north to the stable where he would find his horse, he was plagued by doubts that threatened the anticipation of a joyful reunion.

One day, after gathering flowers, he sat on his horse, plucking petals. "He will be there ... he won't be there."

Protas was very sure that the Tracker who took his horse would return him. But ... what if he had decided to keep White Stockings? Could he survive without *Submission*? He didn't think so.

Finally at the stable, and trembling with fear, he pushed open the door ... and there in the stall where he had left him, stood the most beautiful horse in the world.

❦ ❦ ❦

"Ranoof is missing," the Aide reported to Craslin the following morning.

Craslin laid his papers aside. "Give me the details."

The Assistant hesitated, considering how he might share what he knew, without mentioning 'the woman'.

"Well ... there must be something!" Craslin insisted.

The fire of Craslin's impatience helped him make up his mind. He had no choice but to tell him about the girl. "The last person to talk to Ranoof was ... Zephra. Ranoof was helping her move something in her wagon," he hastily added.

"And ..." Craslin prompted him again.

"That's everything ..."

He dismissed the Aide. Craslin always knew that Zephra would eventually spot Ranoof, one of the Trackers she was searching for. He sighed. It was unfortunate, but Ranoof was gone. And it was time to escalate his plans regarding Zephra.

Yaneek followed the Aide to Craslin's office where he left her.

"Yaneek, thanks for coming on short notice. I wanted to let you know that I intend on personally finishing the business with your brother Benekee. The delay in finding those three men that you told me about, has become an embarrassment, so I ..."

"Those three men who stole Benekee's Device were going to kill us," she hastily interjected.

Craslin noted that she gave the *young lad* credit for the design, instead of Mister Wutherstop. This would change everything if it were true. Her reaction also confirmed that Benekee didn't get a good look at the three men who were in his office that morning. "What kind of Device was it?" Craslin pretended to be curious. "Something unique would be relatively easy to find. And return to your brother."

With eyes wet with concern, she looked at Craslin, "You cannot imagine what that would mean, to have my brother released and his Brass Sling returned."

"Brass Sling ... it sounds like a Hunting Device," he queried.

"Yes, you are right," she replied, pausing as tears rolled down her cheek. "I saw him demonstrate it at the Hunting Guild. It's a metal box ... it sits on top of a tripod with a scope ... to help the user fire a brass ball."

He got up and walked around his desk to take her hand. "By tomorrow the paper work will be done and your brother will be released. I will give orders for my men to begin searching for this Device." He gave her a fatherly smile. "And if we find it, I would be most pleased to have Benekee give me a demonstration of how it works. If I'm impressed, I might have a position for him here in our Guild. I am always looking for talented young men with a promising future."

Escorting her to the door, he added, "Thank you for your willingness to discuss this matter with me."

A grateful Yaneek hurried to tell Zephra the news. As soon as she was down the hall, she wiped away her false tears. 'Anything to get Benekee out of that prison cell,' she thought. She didn't know how much of what Craslin said could be believed, but she didn't care. They had *no* options as long as Benekee was in that dark cell. But now ...

Craslin pulled a silk cord that summoned his personal Guards. "I want you to deliver a message to the three men that I use from time to time. Tell them the contract is finished and that I would be pleased if they found work in a faraway place. If they receive your message with ... disdain ... dispose of them in the usual place."

In the middle of the night, Benekee was awakened to the sound of the heavy prison door swinging open on its creaky hinges. He turned towards the three men holding torches, the flickering shadows revealing their identities. Benekee cringed with fear ... it was the men that stole his machine!

"Don't know what you said to turn Craslin against us," one of the men said through clenched teeth, "but those were your last words."

The Leader hit him hard, knocking him to the floor. Dazed, Benekee felt them rush him out of the cell and down the corridor. As his head cleared, he found himself in chains, fastened to a wall, as a large fist hammered into his face. They continued to beat him vigorously, knowing the Guards would return any moment. Benekee wanted to scream against the pain, but the blows left him winded and disoriented. Frantically, forgetting that he didn't have his Shards, he shouted in his mind for their help, 'Strengthen me against my suffering.' Instantly the pain began to slip away like a sound that faded into the distance. The pummelling continued for some time. It seemed that it would never end. 'I should be dead by now,' he thought as his battered head slumped into his chest.

Satisfied that their work was done, they returned Benekee to his cell, throwing him inside for dead. His unconscious body landed hard on the stone floor.

Chapter 36 - The Healers

The next morning Guards found Benekee beaten, unconscious and nearly dead. They rushed to Craslin's office to inform him. Craslin exploded with anger. The Aide outside his office leapt to his feet. Not knowing if he should stay or run. He had never heard Craslin so angry.

As soon as the shouting died down, one of the men in his office offered, "One of the evening Guards saw the three men that you had hired, leave the building last night."

Still fuming, Craslin managed a nod, grateful for the intelligence. But this was a significant blow to his plan. Benekee was his leverage for so many things. Especially expanding the capability of the Brass Sling ... and Zephra. "Obviously ... my message wasn't clear enough," he said angrily. "Find these three men and don't return until you can tell me that they will never be a problem again!"

After they left, Craslin went to the window and looked down upon the training grounds of the Militia Guard that had grown to a force of one thousand. It was an awesome sight to see the men in their new uniforms, moving like a river, well-trained under the command of Nusdek, his Commander-in-Charge, personally chosen by Ranoof.

He pulled the silk tassel to call his Aide. "Tell Nusdek to bring *The Wall* and meet me at Benekee's cell." The Wall was the name Nusdek had given to the Elite Guard that protected Craslin day and night.

Standing in the dimly lit room, he was horrified by what he saw. The boy's face was unrecognizably swollen. Gently prodding him elicited no response.

Nusdek and members of The Wall were already waiting outside the cell. "Nusdek, make haste and return from the Medical Guild with their best. We need to keep him alive!" The men turned and ran.

Craslin stayed for a while, as he considered a future without Benekee. The Head Guild Master at the Mechanical Guild was both impressed and befuddled with the new Device brought to them by Craslin. The Guild was commissioned to manufacture units, copied from the original. But that was the extent of their skill.

"Improvements are beyond us. Unless we can meet the man who designed this," the Guild Master offered as encouragement.

At first, he couldn't believe his good fortune when he found out from Yaneek that her brother was indeed this person. And now, he wasn't sure if the boy would even survive the day. Aside from improving the Brass Sling, there was his love for Zephra. Quickly becoming the most important thing in his life. He knew that she was fiercely loyal to her friends and would hold him responsible for Benekee. If the boy died, their budding relationship might never recover.

Standing alone in the cell, he struggled for some time with that dark thought. Suddenly it occurred to him that there was a way to turn this situation to his advantage! He looked at the swollen face again, while a plan began to form. Starting immediately, he would turn the affairs of administration over to his Assistant. Except for the most critical items, he would spend all of his time with Benekee. He would be at his side providing the best care. If there was a way to keep him alive, he would find it. Then, if the boy survived or died, he would still have Zephra.

He had come to believe that life without her would be empty. He had tried to imagine it. Busy ... responsible ... holding the power to direct the nation. But ... he would sit on that throne of power alone, without love.

Some things were meant to be together. Like a beautiful crystal glass ... filled with fine wine. Someday, Zephra would come to know that she was like an empty crystal glass, elegance with no purpose. And he was the wine, function with no beauty. They were meant to be together!

He looked back at the swollen face. It was important that Benekee survived ... he needed his skills. Together they would modify the Brass Sling to allow the user to fire several brass balls in quick succession.

He would ask the Medical Guild to set up the healing bed in his office. When the time was right, he would invite Zephra to join him in his vigil to restore Benekee to life and health. He imagined them working closely. He would have food brought to his room. They would eat together, he would learn about her, she about him.

Suddenly, he heard running footsteps coming closer. Had he been contemplating his situation for so long? Could the 'Healers' be there already? He turned to the door. It was Yaneek!

She stopped, bringing a trembling hand to her lips as her tears tumbled to the floor.

"Please Yaneek, you shouldn't be here," he implored, as he stepped in front of Benekee to block the view. "I have asked for the 'Healers' to come immediately. I promise you, I will do everything I can to save your brother. But you must not see him now ... and neither should Zephra."

She slumped to the floor, quietly sobbing, wanting to hold Benekee but afraid of what she might see.

"I will stay with your brother ... but you must go to your room," he encouraged.

"Who would do this," she asked between sobs, "he has never hurt anyone."

Craslin walked over to her and helped her to her feet. "You must allow me to take care of Benekee. I will keep you informed of his progress and when you are ready, come to my office. The Healers will be there."

She nodded and left. Broken-hearted she slowly made her way past the Guard that had informed her. "Thank you," she whispered, willing her numb body down the hallway.

※ ※ ※

Tumbling head over foot, Benekee fell downward like a pebble loosened from a hillside. The journey seemed to last forever as he turned and turned, occasionally bumping into a solid surface as he fell through a dark space. Suddenly he felt a hand on his arm, pulling him out of his freefall.

Clumsily he landed on his feet. The person holding his arm was a woman. A very old woman. She looked familiar, but he couldn't remember from where. His head hurt too much.

"Hello Benekee." Her raspy voice sounded like the memory of an old friend. "Once again you surprise me. Quite a feat for someone so young and inexperienced with using an Amulet."

"What did I do?" he questioned, rubbing his temples to help with the pain.

"Look." She turned and pointed to a chasm, a Garden and a young man.

The chasm separated the young man from the Garden. He looked intently and longingly at the Garden. Then he closed his eyes and with slightly bended legs, he fell forward while giving a little push. He floated across the chasm to the other side as a gentle wind carried him until his feet settled on the ground.

With gaping mouth Benekee said, "How... how did he do that?"

"With his belief," she replied, in a matter-of-fact tone.

"You mean he just believes something and it happens?" Benekee asked, surprised that something like that was even possible.

"Amazing, isn't it? But his belief is very strong ... strong enough to pull power from the Garden without needing to touch the Tree of Life."

Interested by her reference to a Tree, his curious eyes wandered across the chasm to the Garden until he saw it. "So that is the Tree of Life," Benekee whispered, his eyes riveted to the sight. The longer he looked, the more he felt the need to touch it.

Like a little child, Benekee lifted his hand upward, reaching toward the bright canopy of leaves ... believing he could touch it despite the space between them. And somehow ... he felt the hard crystal leaf under his finger. In response to the touch, he could no longer feel the pain. He turned back to the young man in the Garden. "Is that me?" he inquired, not certain he understood the message from the Tree.

"Yes ... do you know what this means Benekee?"

"I think I do," he answered with brows creased tightly. "The might of my belief allowed me to use a broken Amulet. If I believe ... I can call to the Shards even though they are far away ... and they will answer."

He turned to the old woman, "Is there no limit to my power?" he asked, quite concerned.

"What did the Tree tell you?" she asked knowing he already knew.

He looked back at the bright image. "The Tree trusts me. I can ask whatever I want ... because I will never ask for something the Tree is not prepared to give."

"Benekee, you have made an old woman very proud." She placed a withered hand to his face and smiled as Benekee collapsed at her feet, unconscious, but free of pain.

※ ※ ※

Zephra was admitted into Craslin's office. She was surprised. It looked more like a Medical Guild. Bathed in the light of large windows, Benekee was lying unconscious, surrounded by Craslin and the Healers. As she quietly walked to his bed, the circle of people parted to allow her to come closer. She lifted her hand to her mouth in disbelief. She knew he must still be alive, but the wall that separated life and death must have been paper thin. Yaneek's brief comment had not prepared her for this.

She thought of how far away her White Bauble would be by now and wondered if she had done the right thing. A single tear glided down her cheek. 'Poor Yaneek. So this is why you wouldn't come ... and couldn't talk about it.'

Craslin took a moment to look up at the visitor. When her gaze met his, he offered, "I know he doesn't look good ... but the Healers have reason to think he is going to make it." She lingered a long time and eventually Craslin asked, "Would you like to join us as we work together to save the young lad?" She nodded in agreement. He turned to the Healers with a look and they responded. Soon she was dressed and working at his side.

Over the next few days, the number of Healers slowly dwindled as Craslin and Zephra took over Benekee's care. On the fifth day, Zephra, wearing the Healer's garb, decided to stay for the lunch that was served on the balcony of Craslin's office. Everyone took turns eating in pairs. She always ate with Craslin.

After working for days at his side, she finally broke the silence during lunch. "This must be very unusual for a Head Guild Master to take such an interest in a young man of no importance," she warily suggested.

Craslin thought about her comment for a moment, then paused from his eating to respond. "As the Trackers would say, *this happened on my watch*, and I still cannot believe it happened. I felt the need to send a message to all who work for me, that things like this should *never* be possible." He continued eating and eventually added, "Hopefully, if they see that I take his recovery serious enough to lay aside my other responsibilities, they will get the message." He shared a thin smile and continued eating, showing no sign that he expected her to respond.

On the following day, while they sat eating, Craslin was the first to break the silence. "As of yesterday, the Tinker Manufacturing Guild is an official, recognized Guild. Thought you would like to know."

She nodded in gratitude. She considered all the work the Tinker Village had contributed to make this happen. She wished she could be there to see her father's face when he read the document ... but she also suspected the hint of a favour.

"Must be the first new Guild in hundreds of years to be accepted ... and so quickly?" she pointed out.

Craslin looked at her suspicious expression, but he was ready with his response. "Some might question the readiness of the Tinkers to be granted this privilege. After all, they have been apart from the Guild society for over a thousand years. But for those who doubt ... I will ask them to take a ride in one of our new wagons, sent from the Tinker Guild."

After a pause he continued. "The Tinkers have done what the Transportation Guild has failed to accomplish in over five centuries. This new design is revolutionary. So, it was appropriate to make room for another Guild ... even if it does compete with existing Guilds. A change from protocol for sure ... but I believe a good change." He returned to eating.

The next morning she was settling into her duties when Craslin pulled her to the side. "I know his recovery has been uncertain," he whispered while nodding towards Benekee, "but the Healers say they expect him to take a turn for the better in a couple of days."

She gave a little smile and said, "Thanks for that," and went to work.

To Craslin, it meant that he had been forgiven. And now his future with Zephra was about to begin.

The moonlight was shining on his face the night he finally awoke. The last thing he remembered was the old woman touching his cheek. Now, he was lying in a bed. The sheets felt new and his pillow smelled fresh. He could feel bandages on his face. He decided it was best not to move. Instead, he explored his memories. He worked back in time, to the night three torches entered his cell.

Now everything was clear. He would have died except for a strong belief in the Shards that he thought were hidden under his shirt. He grinned feebly as he thought about his mistake. Instead of bringing death, those three torches signalled his entrance into the hall of men, experienced in the use of the Crystal Amulet!

His thoughts went to the Tree of Life, the Master of the Crystal Garden, and its enormous power. "The Tree trusts me." The words were almost inaudible, and his lips barely moved. He stared at the ceiling a long time ... before he invoked the healing power. Then he left the Healing Table and walked to the window to stare at the moon.

Chapter 37 - The Black Wind

Previously. Urshen made a welcome discovery as Zephra left the Guild of his imprisonment. Her Talisman had reached out to him ... and the rest of Tal-nud's Circle. Now they were connected as one, giving Urshen hope to face the dark power of the Necklace that his Guide had warned him about, in a dream

Bernado's discovery that Gaeten was actually Urshen was bittersweet. He had been so easily deceived. He felt humiliated. But knowing that Gaeten was really Urshen, the *other* young man the Quorum was looking for, presented a significant opportunity ... one that he needed to handle *carefully*. Before having the Necklace, 'carefully' would have meant letting the young man languish in a poorly lit dungeon. Weeks of disgusting food and miserable confinement had a way of loosening a man's tongue.

But now that he had the Necklace ... there was no need to wait. He was sure his Talisman was more than a match against this clever young man, who could get past Olleti with a mind trick. "Lying to yourself won't help this time." Bernado grinned triumphantly. "I will know why you and the six Trackers came to this Guild. And you will tell me the secrets of the stolen Crystal Amulet."

Everyone was asleep when Urshen was silently removed from his cell and strapped to a chair in Bernado's office. As instructed the Guards left as Bernado entered. No one must ever know the secret of the Necklace.

Urshen wondered if any of the Circle were awake while he watched Bernado carefully remove a golden Necklace from a velvet bag and place it around his neck. He turned towards Urshen, holding a small dark green stone in his hand. He hefted the stone as though he was measuring its weight as he stared at Urshen. The ominous look was one of assured conquest. As though there was no question as to the outcome.

'Anyone there?' Urshen shouted frantically inside his head.

Bernado slowly walked towards him, stopped, and then stared at Urshen's hands. Urshen realized that his hands had been tied facing up and that the stone was about to be placed in one of them. He quickly clenched them shut. But when Bernado retrieved his long knife, he knew he had no choice. He opened them and watched in horror as Bernado curled Urshen's fingers around the stone. As soon as he touched one of the Medallions, the stone flared to life as Green Light circled the room surrounding Urshen with its dark power.

Urshen tumbled into a deep dark place. He landed hard, face down. He arose and looked around at the outlines defined by the Green Light, that cast its nightmarish hue everywhere. He found himself on a path, bound on both sides by barren rockslide. The path led downward but ended abruptly at the edge of a cliff. Beyond, was a dark lake that stretched into the distance as far as he could see.

He felt a wind against his back, a gentle force of persuasion pushing him towards the cliff. The place he knew he wanted to avoid. He turned around and looked up the steep path, but it disappeared into a green mist. A distant memory of that image terrified him, so he stepped off the path onto the rockslide.

Just two steps into the bleak landscape, he fell to his knees from the buffetings of overwhelming emotional turbulence. Love, anger, confusion, frustration, compassion, bitterness, and many other feelings flooded his mind *all at once.* In anguish, he looked towards the path, desperate to return. If he could just place his hand on the path, he would have the anchor to overcome the emotional chaos. Eventually he was back on the path, exhausted. He considered his options as his strength slowly returned. Perhaps he would try the other side of the path. He cautiously placed a hand on a large rock. He didn't think anything could be worse than the emotional whirlwind, but the nothingness he felt from the large rock, threatened to strip him of his entire will. He quickly pulled his hand back.

There was only one option left. He must climb the path upward. He stood, closed his eyes, and pressed into the wind. But the force increased immediately, whipping his clothes against his body. The harder he pushed against the Black Wind, the stronger it became. He clenched his teeth against the stalemate as he considered his impossible situation. He decided to lessen his effort to conserve his strength ... and as expected, the wind subsided.

Then he heard his name ... coming from behind. 'Who knows my name in this place?' he thought. Turning, he saw a woman of indescribable beauty. She beckoned for him to come to her. She stood at the edge of the cliff. He was surrounded by frightening options, except for this pleasant picture. Perhaps she was a friend that had come to help him ... and that idea, put the terrors out of his mind.

I am here to help you, she purred at him.

Words that he wanted to hear. Words that immediately moved his feet in her direction. Suddenly a swirl of Green Light erupted around the woman, an expression of the pleasure she felt for his coming closer. But the swirl of Green Light looked familiar ... in a bad way. He stopped and stared into her eyes ... trying to think ... trying to remember. But there was nothing. Assured that he must be wrong, he resumed his march. Then he remembered! He saw himself tied to a chair, as a green stone was dropped into his hand. And a swirl of Green Light enveloped him, throwing him into this dark place!

He immediately turned to run. But before he had taken three steps, the Black Wind rushed down the path, stronger than ever. So strong it drove him to his knees. It felt like it was going to strip the very flesh from his bones. He lay down, wrapping his arms around his head, trying to protect himself from the Wind. It was no use; he couldn't fight it. The fury of the Wind was so strong it was difficult to breathe. It continued to increase. He knew that within moments, he would be hurled from the path, over the cliff and into the Black Sea beyond.

"Is there no one ... that can help me," he pleaded. But the words were lost to the violence of the Wind. No one could have possibly heard those words. But someone must have. For now the Wind flowed around him, as though a force stood in front. He slowly peeked between his arms. Naked feet and the bottom of a brilliantly white Robe faced him. The Guide formed a windbreak as the dark force blew past Urshen on either side!

He stared at those feet for a while, trying to figure out why the Guide was there. He supposed he could have stopped the Wind, or even sent him back to the chair, but he didn't. He was there because ... he wanted to give Urshen time to remember something. What was it the Guide said before? *Remember the Circle, there is great power there.*

"Tal-nud, can you hear me!" he yelled as loud as he could.

Tal-nud bolted upright in bed. He expected to see Urshen standing right outside his cell. But he wasn't. He was inside his head ... in serious trouble! He grabbed his boots and began banging the cell bars, hoping to wake up the rest of the Circle. As soon as he heard Guards descending the steps with a lantern, he jumped back onto his cot, pretending to be asleep. The signal had worked and soon the Trackers were linked!

A surge of strength filled Urshen when he heard Tal-nud respond, "Urshen I am here!" His breathing became normal, and he was tempted to stand and face the terrible Wind, but he knew he had more friends ... so he waited. Soon four more combined their strength to his, embracing the torture of the nightmare. With the strength of five powerful men assisting him, he stood, faced the Wind, and began to walk up the path, confident that he would make it through the mist and beyond.

But he hadn't gone far when the force became so strong that he placed his hands over his eyes to protect them. And it continued to increase. He braced against the howling anger but then he began to slide backwards ... the sign that ultimately, he could never win.

"Where is Ranoof?" Tal-nud shouted, remembering a different battle, when an extra person made all the difference. "We must find Ranoof!" he encouraged the others. But it was too late. In an instant, Urshen was picked up and hurled over the edge of the cliff.

Ranoof's hand would occasionally drift to the restored Amulet under his shirt. A reminder, that all that stood between losing it or retaining it, was his skill. The brilliant light that had erupted from the talisman the moment the Jeweller added Zephra's shard, was something he had never expected. He was only supposed to be a carrier ... with an assignment to take the completed Amulet to Arborville once the Jeweller had completed his work.

When the Jeweller pulled back the cloth, once the Light faded, Ranoof grabbed the silver cage and ran, knowing that his task might be much more difficult than he had previously thought. Dusk had begun to settle. He wondered where he might stop for the night. Searching beyond the forest trails, he found shelter in a dry ravine.

His sleep was restless. Every time he rolled over, his hand reached for the talisman. In the middle of the night, when the moon was high in the sky, and he was still clutching the Amulet, he heard a chorus of voices shouting his name.

Hurled off the edge of the cliff, Urshen tumbled towards a boiling sea of Black Evil. The churning waves would certainly strip his bones of their flesh as soon as he sank below the surface. Then he would be forced to tell Bernado anything he wanted to know.

"Ranoof, you must join us," Tal-nud shouted in one last desperate attempt, as all eyes locked on the liquid surface that rushed towards Urshen.

Clutching the Amulet, Ranoof sat up, looked towards the voice, and answered, "I am here!" The Shards flared to life, sending a burst of Light like an enormous flash of lightning. The light devoured and banished the sea below in an instant. At that same moment, the Green Light gathered in a swirl and disappeared into the small green stone.

Still grasping the Amulet, Ranoof collapsed, unconscious from the strain of connecting to the Circle, and providing the conduit for the Amulet's power.

Bernado was amused at Urshen's feeble effort to resist placing the stone in his hand. He took one of his Long Knives from his desk, intent to see Urshen's hand remain open, with or without his cooperation. With horror written across his face the young man quickly opened his hand.

"You ought to be afraid," Bernado whispered, curling Urshen's fingers around the stone. He stepped back and with anticipated pleasure, the assured conqueror breathed deeply, savoring the moment. Then he touched the Second Medallion. The stone flared to life. The Green Light circled the room, enveloping Urshen in its dark power as Bernado traced the path into Urshen's mind.

'Why have you and the Trackers come to this Guild? And what is the true extent of the power of the Crystal Amulet?' The words left Bernado's mind like a rushing Wind, determined to strip the information from the young subject's mind.

Bernado waited for the information as the rushing wind ebbed and flowed. Then suddenly without warning, the Black Wind violently recoiled towards Bernado, throwing him out of Urshen's mind with a force that threw him across the room. He slammed into the wall and fell like a limp rag to the floor.

He groaned , turned himself upright, the terror of the Black Wind still flickering at the edge of his mind. 'How ... could Urshen have possibly stood against it?' he questioned.

Bernado was never so relieved when the Wind finally left him. Slowly he pushed himself away from the floor, until he stood again. Gasping and struggling to stay on his feet, he remembered seeing the Green Light disappear into the small green stone.

"Impossible!" Bernado screamed. Angrily he studied the unconscious young man, sweat dripping from his chin. He willed his feet forward until he stood in front of Urshen. He gingerly removed the small stone from his hand. He took the artefacts back to their velvet lair, but before he placed them inside, he thought of the promises of the Green Lady. "Hardly an experience that instils me with confidence! Is this Necklace capable of placing me on an Emperor's throne ... or not!" He muttered angrily. Surprisingly, the Necklace was silent.

He turned to the spent body tied to the chair.

"But then again ... you don't exactly look like the victor in this contest," he reassured himself. "We will do this again," Bernado threated Urshen.

Chapter 38 - The Circle is severed

The Guard was placing the only meal of the day inside the cell when Urshen groggily opened his eyes. He sat up and looked around the dimly lit prison towards the other members of the Circle. Now Urshen knew the purpose of *that* Medallion ... *and* the other five. In an instant, the Light had taught him everything about the insidious Necklace. It was a terrifying and dark enemy. But with a thin victory smile he thought, 'The Circle has grown to include Ranoof ... a Tracker with an Amulet!' He ate, then opened his mind to the others. Urshen was ready to discuss the experience. 'Everyone there?' The response was immediate. Everyone ... except *Ranoof*.

'The recent experience should have brought Ranoof into the Circle,' a confused Tal-nud offered.

'Perhaps he is still asleep?' Urshen suggested to the group. 'The strain of holding the Amulet during the plunge towards the Black Sea must have been terribly demanding.'

'Something isn't right,' Tal-nud offered. 'It's as though he isn't anywhere.'

'What do you mean?' asked one of the Trackers.

'When I want to communicate with someone within the Circle, there is a door that must open. When you are awake, I can hear murmurs on the other side of that door. When you are asleep, like last night, it is silent on the other side of that door. But with Ranoof ... there is no door!'

Urshen was intrigued by Tal-nud's comments. They helped him see a possible explanation. 'When Ranoof connected to us, he was holding an Amulet,' Urshen began. 'I instinctively reached for the Amulet's power as soon as I felt its presence. But ... it wasn't my Amulet.'

'It must have been Zephra's,' Tal-nud offered, remembering their previous experience when they all connected to the Circle, through her talisman.

Hesitantly Urshen answered, 'Yes ... you're sort of right. I mean ... it *was* her White Bauble ... but then again it ... *wasn't*.'

'How is that possible?' another Tracker asked. The group went silent waiting for Urshen to respond.

Eventually, Urshen understood. 'Zephra's White Bauble was never a complete talisman. It was only a *part* of a larger one. Large like mine. The original was shattered by a sword before the Great War, and the largest piece was rescued by a very old woman. This Shard became known as the White Bauble and was passed on from generation to generation. Until Zephra held it. And now ... it appears it has been returned to its proper place with the other pieces!'

'I'm impressed!' added Tal-nud. 'Ranoof has been busy since we last saw him!'

'Yes,' Urshen agreed, 'but there might be a problem. *I* could pull power from this re-assembled Amulet because of the White Bauble. You see ... the time Zephra healed me ... I used my Amulet while she used her White Bauble ... and that experience connected her Amulet to me. Being connected or *accepted* by an Amulet is important if one is to use it. Even though Ranoof had this re-assembled Amulet in his possession, it wasn't *his*. He must have been carrying it to someone. Perhaps to Zephra.'

'You mean, you felt the White Bauble because of the previous connection,' Tal-nud asked, 'and you were able to pull power from it because Ranoof is part of the Circle *and* he was holding it?'

'Something like that,' Urshen responded. 'But ... Ranoof *wasn't* connected to the Amulet and I pulled an enormous amount of power. I'm afraid he has suffered from the experience. I would guess that the link to the Circle has been broken for Ranoof ... and maybe worse.'

There was a pause, until one Tracker brought up something that was on everyone's mind. 'Urshen ... we felt the terror and the black power of the place you fell into ... but what *is* the Black Sea ... and how did you end up there?'

The question reminded Urshen of the price the Circle paid for his rescue. 'First ... thank you ... everyone, for responding to my call. Lesser men could not have accomplished what you did.' Urshen took a deep breath as he prepared to share with them the impossible situation that they now faced. 'When I was dragged back into Bernado's office he wore a golden Necklace with six Medallions, around his neck. Then he put a small green stone in my hand. They work together to allow the wearer of the Necklace to take things from the person holding the stone, depending which Medallion Bernado touches. In my case, he wanted to know why we were here ... and about my Amulet. As the Green Power of the stone was released, my mind created the landscape of path and Sea to help me understand the progression of the Green Power as it invaded my thoughts. Plunging into the Sea was the moment when my mind would have belonged to the Green Power. Like being hypnotized by Toulee.'

'So, what we felt was the power of only *one* Medallion?' one Tracker queried.

'Yes ... there are six in total,' Urshen responded with a groan, 'each designed to perform a different task.'

'How different?' Tal-nud asked hesitantly.

Urshen exhaled as he prepared to share with them the terrible might of the Necklace they would have to face ... without the benefit of the Amulet.

'The first Medallion regenerates the body of the user by taking life from an unsuspecting host. This is the most essential Medallion, because using the other Medallions leaves the User weaker and older than before he used the Necklace.

'The second Medallion loosens the tongue of the victim. Sort of like Olleti. It is the one Bernado tried to use on us.

'The third assists the user to influence the will of the subject.

'The fourth can find anything or anyone the user wishes to find, except a Seer when he is wearing his Amulet.

'The fifth is designed to detect the usage of the Seer Stones. The range is hundreds of leagues.

'The sixth Medallion was designed to bring the people of the Harvested World to Harleem.'

There was more Urshen could have shared but they had heard enough to understand the enormity of the opposing force.

'How do you know so much about the Medallions?' another Tracker asked.

'When the flash of Light touched the Black Sea, I was flooded with the knowledge of the Necklace ... its purpose, and its source of power.'

'The power of this Necklace is terrifying,' Tal-nud commented, remembering the Black Wind and the plunge towards the Black Sea. 'Why have we never heard about this power before ... and why now?'

Urshen lay back on his cot, his arms wrapped around his chest, the fear of the experience still very fresh. He contemplated the similarities between the Amulet and the Necklace, between the Cave and the Waterless Wells. And for the first time he saw the Great War in a different way. He decided he would answer Tal-nud's question.

'The Necklace, like the Amulet,' he began, 'is a talisman of great power. Hidden for us to find ... and to use. The Amulet can never be used for evil. But the Necklace ... can never be used for good. Its power is designed to corrupt and enslave.'

He had barely finished his sentence, when to the surprise of everyone, Urshen closed his mind. He wanted 'off-time' to think about the two powers that came from other planets. Powers that reached down to their simple world, with invitations to embrace one of the competing talismans. Either one could take them to the stars. But if the people of his world chose the Necklace, they would leave their planet as slaves, not as free men. Reflecting back to Border Pass, Urshen understood more clearly than ever, that although wining that battle was important, it was not the event that turned the conflict into a victory, as everyone had supposed. Now there was the Necklace and an entire Tracking Guild that lusted after this dark power! It made him wonder what the future really looked like, because if Bernado used the Necklace again, they could *not* stand against it. Then he would know everything and have no reason to keep them alive! The situation was not reassuring. In fact, the last encouraging moment in his life was the Guide's last instruction.

Be patient in your affliction and remember that the Garden has already touched you with the power of another Key ... now you have your friends who add to your power.

'Friends, like Ranoof and Deema's group,' thought Urshen. 'But we have lost Ranoof, and the other six are not connected through the Circle like we are. And I have no idea where they might be.'

He could hear someone knocking.

'The one that concerns me the most,' Tal-nud began, 'is Medallion number one. Do you know how it works?' he asked, wanting to push back the dark invading cloud that everyone felt.

Urshen searched his recent memory, and there he found the answers ... within that Flash of Light. 'There are sequences of instruction inside us, that our bodies use to direct growth and regeneration. But with time, fragments of the instruction, become lost to us. It is why we grow old. Otherwise, we would live very long lives. The Necklace depends on the energy of Bernado's body to operate the last five Medallions, resulting in fragmentation of the sequences I mentioned. The only way to repair the damage is to capture new, complete strings of instruction from someone younger.'

'Do we all have the same set of instructions?' Tal-nud eventually asked.

'No ...' Urshen offered.

'When the Green Power invades your body looking for a set of instructions,' Tal-nud continued, 'what if it could see all of our instructions at the same time? Wouldn't it be confused and have to leave with nothing?'

'Perhaps. But I have no idea how to do what you suggest,' Urshen acknowledged.

'You managed to defeat Olleti ...' another Tracker offered as encouragement.

Urshen wanted to say 'thanks' but his heart felt sick, so he chose to close his mind. The terror, when he plunged towards the Black Sea, was *not* an experience he wanted to live through again ... ever. And yet, that was exactly what he knew was going to happen as soon as Bernado had his men drag him back to his office. Then, stripped of his secrets, it would be the end of him and his Tracker friends. Zephra would never know what unnamed grave he laid in.

He knew that somehow, he must find a way to cling to hope. The only thing between utter despair and a future with Zephra. Perhaps there was a lily pad or razor somewhere in his immediate future to help him see a way out. Because at the moment, his house of hope was made of straw.

The five Trackers of Deema's group switched between hunting game and providing security detail for Urshen's family. Occasionally Benton visited his favourite plateau, where he had reasonable visibility of Urshen's cabin. If he saw nothing after two days, he would head north, back to the abandoned cabin where his family – as well as the Trackers – had made their home.

It was late afternoon when he pushed open the old wooden door. All five Trackers were leaning against the wall as though they were waiting for him. He dropped his bag, closed the door, and looked to Deema, knowing he would have something to say.

"We uhh ... think Urshen has contacted us," Deema offered hesitantly.

The words sounded like wonderful news, but nobody was smiling. Benton shot a quick glance at Velinti. "Surely this is good news?"

She shrugged her shoulders. She was also confused.

Benton turned to Deema who continued, "Yes and No. It started last night when all five of us were awakened by a bright flash of light."

"What does this have to do with Urshen?" Benton queried. It sounded like something Urshen might be involved in, but a cloud of concern hung over the room.

"The five of us are connected to Urshen through the Circle. Hence, we believe that the flash of Light, *must* have involved Urshen," Deema reviewed the logic.

"The Circle?" Benton looked at Velinti again but got another shrug.

"To understand the Circle, and what happened last night, you need to know what took place on the Plateau at Border Pass," Deema began. "As we explained earlier, Urshen was able to defeat the El-Bhat with his Amulet. But it wasn't that simple because the range of his power is very limited. In the hour of our desperation, he devised a plan that extended that range. But it involved connecting all Twelve of us Trackers, to himself, through our blood. The plan worked … with an unexpected benefit." Deema looked at the other Trackers.

"The same force that extended his power, also bonded us together in a way that we are only beginning to understand. We call it the Circle. At first, that was all we felt … a strong brotherhood bond. Then as the six of us travelled north to find Stek, we were attacked at night by El-Bhat. During the struggle, Peloree died, but before he did, we gained the ability to see through each other's eyes and feel each other's pain. The power of the Circle had expanded."

"Amazing! Does this mean you can contact Urshen through your minds?" Velinti asked hopefully.

Benton was anxiously awaiting the answer but Deema's gaze had sunk to the floor, as though he didn't know how to say what needed to be said.

Benton turned to the Tracker woman, "Well?"

"The flash of Light has broken the Circle … we have lost everything."

Chapter 39 - Biskin hunts Protas

Previously. The Commander, who led the Trackers against the El-Bhat, at Border Pass, placed all plans on hold ... expecting that Pechinin and Mitrock would eventually return from Pechora.

When it was confirmed that Pechinin and Mitrock were dead, The Commander at the Arborville Tracking Guild headed for the Brew-Master to check the supply of Olleti. They would need enough to check every Tracking Guild across Storlenia. The Commander would start with the southern Guilds that stretched eastward like pearls on a string. "How much longer, until we have enough Olleti to cover at least the next three Guilds heading east?"

"Four more weeks should do it."

The Commander knew you couldn't rush Olleti. He nodded, satisfied, and left to find Biskin. "In four weeks, I want you to leave with twenty Trackers. I have prepared letters explaining the unique situation. Your Gift, combined with the Olleti, should ensure success. By the time you get back, the Brew-Master will be ready with another batch. All intruders are to be brought to Arborville."

"Depending on how bad it is ... there might not be enough room in our cells," Biskin suggested.

"I hope to turn most of them to our cause," The Commander replied.

Biskin wasn't convinced. He remembered how hard the spy fought against them, the day they marched him into Pechinin's office. "It might not be so easy. Their families have been forced to work in the Gold Mines of Tenleth and they will be killed if the men ever forsake their vows to the El-Bhat. Makes a man think twice ..."

"You're right, but my plan is to offer them combat training and an opportunity to join us. Eventually, I will submit a report, requesting permission to march into Shaksbah to get their families back."

Biskin was impressed. Already The Commander was thinking like Pechinin.

"I suggest you take six wagons," The Commander continued, "and by the end of the week, give me the list of the men you want."

The infiltration of the three Tracking Guilds was nothing like Arborville. It was now apparent that the El-Bhat plan concentrated on their Guild, with the intent to secure access to the Olleti. The few Shaksbali Trackers planted in the other Guilds, were there only as spies. With their work finished, they added the most recent Shaksbali spy to the Prison Wagon, ready to head back to Arborville.

Biskin was standing by his horse looking off into the distance as the wagons began to pull away. The Second-in-Command walked over, "Something you want to tell me?"

Continuing to stare, Biskin said, "The first and only time I met Protas, I knew our paths would cross again."

"You want to elaborate on that?"

He turned to the Assistant Commander. "At Lundeen forest, my arrows brought down two El-Bhat that were about to kill Protas and Zephra. Ever since then, I have had a persistent feeling ... that I need to protect that young man." The occasion was when he shook Protas's hand, but that begged too many questions, so he left it unexplained. "I can't go back with you." He returned to staring toward the mountains. "Tell The Commander I need to find Protas. He's in trouble and he needs my help."

"The Commander is a man of details ... perhaps you could share a few?" The other Tracker suggested.

"Just tell him ... it comes from my gut. He'll be satisfied with that."

The Second-in-Command nodded acceptance, but in truth he wasn't so sure *that* was going to be enough.

"I'll meet you at the next town heading east when you return," Biskin added.

"The Commander would want to send some men with you," the other Tracker insisted.

"Yes, he probably would. But it feels like I should go myself. If all goes well ... I'll have Protas with me when I meet you next."

"Water boy ... follow me," Ou-Leesen commanded, throwing the staff in the direction of Protas. Arriving at the training area,

Ou-Leesen turned and said, "Let's see what you already know," as he began a simple attack routine. Protas blocked the first strike then trapped the second in the fold of his Robe, followed by his own strike at Ou-Leesen's ribs.

Surprised and impressed, he knew Robe-Man had previous training. "*Someone* has taught you well. Using your Robe as part of your defence was ... clever," he added studying the Robe a little more carefully. "Your training will include the use of your Robe," Ou-Leesen said with finality.

His internal compass led Biskin east and then south. He mused over which force moved the spindle ... his need to find Protas or his natural inclination to 'smell' trouble. Maybe it was both. Either way, he knew he was getting close. The attraction had increased significantly.

From a high ledge, he watched Protas through a telescope, fighting an El-Bhat. But, 'fight' wasn't the right word. He was being ... trained! Biskin turned over on his back, staring at the bright blue sky above as he puzzled over the unusual scene below. He eventually concluded that the situation must be complicated. He needed more information. Biskin continued his vigil.

After the 'training' session, Protas and a young boy spent their time bringing water to the workers that laboured against the strength of the Canyon walls, determined to widen the path into a wagon trail. When the working day was over, and the sun vanished behind Canyon walls, Protas spent his time training the young boy. Things pretty much repeated themselves the next day ... except for one thing! The itch he always felt around 'trouble', grew in intensity!

The Advisor had followed Ou-Leesen around for weeks, answering his questions, often thinking about the words of Shanteef, *When the Pass is finished, Ou-Leesen must return to me ... alive.*

But he was tired of being Ou-Leesen's Advisor. So humiliating to be the pet dog to a fallen warrior. The more he thought about how this El-Bhat had been given this honour of building the Pass, after fleeing the battle at the Border, the harder it was to be his Advisor.

Finally, he decided that he was not willing to wait until the gold was ready to flow. What he wanted, was for Ou-Leesen's *blood* to flow! He only needed a plan.

Everything came into view on the day they wandered into Chitouf. Following up on a report that an injured Storlenian was found and nurtured back to health by the people of the village. The Advisor knew if he were patient, the right situation would present itself, and now it had. Because Ou-Leesen agreed to train Robe Man in the use of the knife, and because he was always there watching, it couldn't be easier! With a knife tied to an arrow, the Advisor would send it towards Ou-Leesen, sinking the knife to the hilt. He would sound the alarm, the Storlenian would flee, and he would quickly remove the arrow from the knife. After the others examined the knife wound, he would send them after the young man.

As the afternoon slipped away, urgency pulled Biskin closer to the valley floor. 'Trouble' was about to happen! He watched Protas engage in the dangerous training of using his knife against the El-Bhat, who pushed him to refine his technique.

He wondered if the green-eyed warrior, was the 'trouble'. So he observed, with bow nearby. Then he noticed that the other El-Bhat that usually watched, had carefully slipped behind a large rock ... where he lashed his own knife to an arrow! Now it was clear. He had found the trouble!

Biskin felt the wind on his wet finger. He considered careful adjustments before he sent his arrow to save Protas. When the man moved out from behind the rock, Biskin stood, allowing the calmness of his training to steady his aim. The distance was agonizingly too far, but the time had come. There was nothing else to do.

He prayed the Fates would guide his shaft. He let loose the arrow and watched, frozen with his bow still in hand.

The Advisor howled in surprise as an arrow landed between his feet.

Protas turned, the sharp sound drawing his attention to the Advisor bringing his bow upwards, trained on Ou-Leesen. Protas quickly stepped in front of Ou-Leesen, while catching the arrow in the fold of his Robe. Immediately, Ou-Leesen sent a hurtling knife into the chest of the Advisor.

Biskin had already dropped out of view when the Advisor fell on his face.

Protas and Ee-lath were busy moving among the workers with the water, when an El-Bhat placed a hand on Protas's shoulder from behind. A jumpy Protas dropped the water ladle.

"Leave it," the El-Bhat ordered when Protas bent to pick it up. "Follow me."

An obedient Protas kept his eyes on the black silk garment in front, as they moved among the workers and eventually climbed to a flat rock where Ou-Leesen often surveyed the activities below. Once they arrived, the El-Bhat Guards were dismissed. A nervous Protas stood, his robe flapping in the wind.

After the death of the Advisor the previous day, Ou-Leesen had angrily dismissed Protas with the words, "Your training is finished." Protas walked away risking a quick glance backward. Ou-Leesen was studying the hill where the arrow had come from, as had Protas, the moment the Advisor had fallen. But whoever had sent the warning arrow, had already disappeared.

"Who sent the arrow?" A stone-faced Ou-Leesen asked, sitting on the flat rock.

"I didn't see him, but I assume he was a Tracker." Protas had laid awake the night before, thinking about what he would say when the expected summons came.

"Assuming he *is* a Tracker, as you suggest, why is he here ... now?"

"Perhaps to rescue me," Protas replied quietly. But the mystery was how anyone could have known Protas was sent south by Bernado. Even if the secret at Pechora had been discovered, Bernado wouldn't say a word ... vows with the El-Bhat were not to be taken lightly. So that left only one other possibility ... Biskin!

On the day he had first met him and shaken his hand, he remembered feeling something odd. At the time, he was so excited for the opportunity to meet the man who had saved their lives, that he had brushed it off as part of the emotional wind that whipped against his thoughts at the time. 'Protector' was the word Protas remembered feeling but had assumed it referred to Lundeen Forest. Now he saw things differently.

"You're that important to the Trackers?" Ou-Leesen asked.

Protas paused, carefully considering what he wanted to say. "Generally, no. But to one man ... I think yes."

"Are you ready to run away Robe Man?"

"It's not that easy. I have Ee-lath to think about."

"Water boy ... you are a puzzle to me. But you have the heart of a warrior." Ou-Leesen's penetrating gaze studied the Storlenian for a long time before he finally asked, "Can I trust you?"

This was certainly another question that required careful words. Protas's eyes drifted downwards. He noticed the knife lying in front of a cross-legged Ou-Leesen. The knife was very ornate, the blade had carvings on it and the pommel was bejewelled. The presence of the ornate Dagger suggested an ominous conclusion to their meeting. But maybe not. So Protas thought of Ee-lath and how he had come to love the boy. "You taught me in the village, that my life belongs to the boy. His people are my people, his ways are my ways."

Ou-Leesen reached forward and placed a rock the size of his hand in front of him. As he set the edge of the knife against it, the dark green stone in the pommel glowed. With a gentle push, the rock split in two, severed as cleanly as if the very rock had divided itself.

Protas shifted nervously on his feet and considered what the knife was capable of.

Ou-Leesen took a deep breath with eyes closed, as if the experience of cutting the rock was taxing. When his eyes re-opened, he began. "When a man is entrusted with this kind of power, he carries a heavy burden. He must be able to trust himself ... and those who serve him," he added with bitterness. "I am convinced that the man who gave me this knife cannot be trusted." He laid the knife down again. "So ... Robe Man, can I trust you?"

"Yes," was Protas's simple reply.

"Good. Then I promote you from water boy to my Advisor."

A stunned Protas simply muttered, "All ... all right." He expected at that moment to be dismissed, and when he wasn't, he decided to ask some questions of his own. "Where does the knife come from?"

Ou-Leesen thought back to his conversation with Shanteef. "Among our people, before the Great War, there existed a tribe called the Sherilin. The Sherilin were the greatest tribe who ever lived south of these mountains. They were skilled in the land, in the use of water, in teaching and learning ... in all the affairs of life. But the greatest of all their skills ... was that they were Warriors of Peace, not Warriors of

Blood. Out on the eastern plains of Shaksbah, they found a stone box at the bottom of a Waterless Well. Inside that box was a Necklace that cradled a green gemstone of enormous power ... and this Dagger."

"The pommel," Protas began, "it glowed green when you used the knife to cut the stone. It reminds me ... of your eyes."

"I recently learned that using this Green Power, leaves its mark. As you suggested, the eyes of the user become brilliant green. And more than this, the color is passed on to the children, until the entire tribe possesses eyes of brilliant green," Ou-Leesen explained.

"May I speak freely?" Protas asked.

Ou-Leesen nodded.

"I have read the ancient history that relates how the Shaksbali buried a Cave of power under tons of rock. That tells me that the Shaksbali are fearful of the Cave's power." Protas cast a glance at the Dagger. "Yet, they are acquainted with power. Why is the Necklace accepted by *our* people but not the Cave?"

"The Cave destroys Shaksbali. The Cave's power must never fall into the hands of the Storlenians, or we will cease to exist as a people."

Protas thought back to the stories that his cousin Ramsey had shared about two different groups who had searched for diamond beds and ended up dead. "I have read tales that tell of a time when the Cave's power killed Storlenians."

Ou-Leesen looked at Protas, surprised.

Protas continued. "But other legends speak of the Cave's power to heal. Are there no legends among the Shaksbali that show that the Cave can be harmless ... perhaps even heal?"

Ou-Leesen's eyes suddenly went narrow. "Robe Man speaks with a blade, and yet he has no Dagger of Truth. You speak of the question that haunts the men who travel with me. Why did the Dark Power pass by *us*, when our brothers fell dead all around? Were we preserved for another time when this evil force hopes to steal our hearts away? What counsel does my *Storlenian* Advisor wish to give me?" Ou-Leesen asked, his words as hard as steel.

Protas decided that it would be wise to steer the conversation away from the Cave. So rather than give an answer, he suggested, "Teach me how to become a Warrior of Peace."

Ou-Leesen was annoyed that his new Advisor had side-stepped his question. But he let it go because he respected what Robe Man was asking. "Very well. But you have already taken the first step in becoming a Warrior of Peace."

He paused, wanting Protas to consider what this meant.

Protas reflected on the words ... *warrior of blood* ... *warrior of peace*. "A Warrior of Blood takes life; a Warrior of Peace saves it," Protas suggested.

"And why do you think this is the first step?" the El-Bhat asked.

Protas crossed his arms as he considered the question. "For others ... I don't know. But for me, it has opened my eyes to another world ... to another people."

Ou-Leesen turned his gaze to the workers below, the villagers of Chitouf who laboured because they had kissed the Dagger of Truth. They were the people who now belonged to Robe Man. This was the *other world and other people* that Protas was beginning to *see*. Protas's desire to become a Warrior of Peace, reminded Ou-Leesen of an experience he had after he left Border Pass. On his journey southward to the Quorum, he felt fully and completely defeated ... stripped of all honour... stripped of any future. A *fallen* Warrior of Peace. But eventually a different truth settled upon him. Because *Something* led his parched soul to the Pool of Sherilin. Where he was given the vision of a desert eagle and the clarity of a mountain stream. His warrior heart was restored. It was an event that he would never forget ... and never completely understand.

Ou-Leesen stood and returned the knife to his scabbard. "I am pleased with your advice, Robe Man." With no further discussion, he left the flat rock and descended towards the valley below.

Chapter 40 - Protas the Advisor

"Training is finished," Ou-Leesen advised his weary Advisor. Protas nodded and started to walk away. "I want to know who he is!" Ou-Leesen ordered, bringing Protas to a stop.

"I'll deal with it right away," Protas responded.

Satisfied, Ou-Leesen left.

Protas picked up a piece of wood and headed up the Valley. Finding a large rock, he climbed to the top of it. He started whittling to help him think about what he wanted to say to the Tracker. It was a difficult situation. A single Tracker, most likely Biskin, had been sent hundreds of leagues to rescue Protas. How Protas was even found, was a mystery. Now he must tell the Tracker to go back home. Because Protas wasn't interested in being rescued.

'If Urshen were here,' he thought, 'and asked me what I intended on doing, I would have to say, *I really don't know. But what I do know is that I have a young boy to take care of and we have been bonded. My loyalties cross race and culture.*' Besides, it felt right ... even if the future seemed helplessly muddled.

The sun disappeared early in the Canyon, but the soft light reflecting off the rock walls allowed Protas to finish his whittling ... and his plan. When he could no longer see to whittle, he stood up on the rock and began to tap it with his rod, like a beacon in the inky black night.

"Protas?" The voice came from somewhere behind him.

He climbed down off the rock and went towards the sound. When he was sure he was close to the Tracker, he began speaking. "I assume that you have come to rescue me?"

"I have to confess. Right now, I'm a bit confused about why I'm here. It seems you'd rather stay ... than go. But my Gift sent me here." Biskin decided that since his Gift wanted him to know about Protas, Protas might as well know about the Gift.

"Sounds like Biskin ... am I right?"

"Yes, and we need to get going soon. That is, if you're willing to go with me?"

"You found me with your ... Gift?" Protas asked, intrigued. Suddenly aware that things were not what he had supposed. It now appeared that the Cave had sent Biskin, but Protas felt like he needed to stay with the boy and Ou-Leesen. And that could only mean one thing! "Biskin, your Gift sent you here for a reason ... that I need to understand. But first, tell me more about your Gift."

"I normally don't talk about my Gift," Biskin offered, wondering how much he really wanted to say.

Protas decided to make it easier for Biskin. "I know about Gifts. I've been around Urshen long enough that nothing surprises me anymore. And I'll tell you something else. I believe that what *you* can do, what a Tinker's Boon can do, and what Urshen can do, is really not so different. Because all these abilities come from the power of the Cave."

Biskin was confused by what Protas was trying to tell him, but he decided to let that sit until another day. Instead he continued, "All right ... my Gift helps me smell trouble. Normally it's that simple, but since I met you, this Gift seems to have expanded. The day we shook hands, I had a strong feeling that I was responsible for your safety. Didn't know what that meant, and I had forgotten about it. Until a couple of weeks ago when heading east from Arborville ... with a supply of Olleti." Biskin paused and listened for a while to make sure they were still alone. Satisfied, he continued. "Suddenly, I knew where you were, and I knew I was supposed to find you. You were in danger. To be honest, I guess I had assumed that I was here to rescue you, but it really wasn't part of the feeling."

"Biskin, what you did, to warn us of the assassination attempt, might be the only reason you are here. If you had not warned us, Ou-Leesen would probably be dead and I would have been accused of his murder and executed." Protas went on to tell Biskin about his experience at Pechora, his walk southward in chains, and his experience with the villagers of Chitouf. "I know it sounds strange, but I think I'm supposed to stay with Ou-Leesen. So, I think you should stay here with me."

There was a pause. "Okay, so what happens next?" Biskin asked.

"Tomorrow morning, we will both walk into the Shaksbali camp. I will share with Ou-Leesen how you are bonded to me through your Gift. I will say that you are prepared to make an oath to stay with me, which will include your promise that you will be no threat to these people or their work. He will probably assign you to serve the water," Protas said, grinning in the dark.

Weeks later, while on patrol, the El-Bhat of Ou-Leesen's Pass spotted another lonely Tracker. They decided it would be best to capture him, instead of killing him. After all, Ou-Leesen had already permitted the Robe Man and a Tracker to accompany them.

The mountain ravine suggested to Stek that he might be looking at the 'pass' where he would find Ou-Leesen. He had travelled in the open to let the El-Bhat know that he wasn't a threat. After hiking along the ravine for a day, he was surrounded by them and stripped of his weapons. He was ready to explain himself, but it didn't seem necessary, they simply asked him to follow them.

When the El-Bhat brought Stek to Ou-Leesen, he was in the middle of training. Ou-Leesen looked at Protas, expecting him to say something about the visitor. But Protas only shrugged, he had never met the man before.

The El-Bhat pushed Stek forward.

"Why are you here," Ou-Leesen demanded of the Tracker.

"I am looking for Ou-Leesen."

"Who gave you this name?"

Ignoring the question, Stek reached into his pouch and pulled out documents. "These are for Ou-Leesen," he said, confident that he had found the man.

Ou-Leesen's eyebrows rose slightly as he read the letter of introduction. When he was finished with the documents he handed them back to Stek. Then dismissed the El-Bhat warriors.

"So ... you have found a Cave?" Ou-Leesen asked, his eyes narrowed.

"Should I leave?" Protas asked. But aside from a brief glance, Ou-Leesen ignored him. Meaning Protas need not have asked the question.

Noting Ou-Leesen's regard for the other Storlenians, Stek continued, "Yes ... I have. My instructions were to find you. Then you would tell me how to find Shanteef, Head of the Quorum. Then I would pass on the location of the Cave to him."

"Your orders have changed. You will stay here ... and you will show me where this Cave is." He nodded towards Protas. "My Advisor will see that you have some food to eat. You will help deliver water to my men." Walking past Protas, Ou-Leesen concluded, "Our lesson is finished!"

After eating, Protas invited Stek to walk together. Protas asked, "Have you really found a Cave?"

Stek studied Protas for a moment, then decided to say, "Yes."

Protas could see that Stek was careful with his information, so he decided to keep his questions direct and brief. "Did you go inside?"

"No."

"Why not, after having found a Cave?"

"One requires a Key to enter. And even if I had the Key, I wouldn't enter the Cave."

"Why?"

"Because the Cave invites you ... you do not presume to invite yourself."

"But you realize that after you tell the El-Bhat where this Cave is, they will destroy it ... or at least bury it under tons of dirt and rock."

"Perhaps."

"So why are you telling them where it is?" A puzzled Protas asked.

"Because I must."

※ ※ ※

Both men were tired and covered in sweat by the end of Protas's training session.

"You are progressing well Robe Man," Ou-Leesen offered, throwing his staff to Protas who nodded in appreciation. Words like these were ... unusual and rationed. Then as though those words were already forgotten, he irritably strode away shouting, "My Advisor will meet me in my tent ... immediately!"

'No dinner tonight,' Protas figured. Ou-Leesen was not only a warrior, but a careful thinker, and their meetings often lasted for hours. Protas ran to fetch Biskin who was busy distributing water as usual. Protas had convinced Ou-Leesen to allow Biskin to join them in their meetings by telling him, *I trust him above any other to keep me alive. He just seems to know when something isn't right.* Ou-Leesen understood that a warrior's skills often included talents that other men didn't appreciate.

Protas sat for quite a while before the El-Bhat finally said, "The Quorum have directed me to travel to Qar-ana, to give gold to Storlenian Leaders in exchange for Guild leadership. It is how we will conquer Storlenia."

The silence returned. Protas considered Ou-Leesen's dour mood. "You feel that this is a job for a diplomat, and not a warrior?" Protas suggested.

"Considering what I know about Guilds and the value of gold to Storlenians, I might as well send Ee-lath to negotiate," he retorted angrily.

Protas had never seen Ou-Leesen this irate. And his lack of knowledge regarding Shaksbali culture made him hesitate ... but he had to say something. "Perhaps the Quorum wishes to bestow this great honour on you ... because of your success with Ou-Leesen Pass?"

The El-Bhat glared back at Protas. "You know nothing, Robe Man," he said in frustration. "The Quorum dishonours me!"

Eventually Protas began to nod, "I see ... it's like placing a warrior at the front of a heated battle ... he cannot survive."

"I have lost confidence in our Quorum," Ou-Leesen snarled. "Warriors of Blood," he muttered to himself. Ou-Leesen reached for his wine skin and drank deeply.

"Is this why you refused Stek's request to deliver his message to the Quorum?"

His only response was a scowl.

"And ... the Quorum assigned your previous Advisor," Protas pressed further.

There was a long pause before Ou-Leesen continued. "Do the Leaders of Storlenia think as you do Robe Man? Would they save a village boy, born of foreign blood?"

"I think ... that Leaders are *born* to lead. But place too much power ... or gold, in their path ... and it becomes a short walk to the war tent where the Warriors of Blood meet. You are frustrated with the Quorum, but I wonder what the great Leaders in Storlenia would do, if they knew how much gold was at Chitouf."

Ou-Leesen was surprised that Protas knew about Chitouf. But he made a hand gesture for him to continue.

Ou-Leesen had mentioned the village boy, so Protas continued with that thought. "One way to keep village boys safe from Mountain Cats would be to feed the Cats butchered lamb every day. But how long before the Cats would tire of scraps and prey on the entire flock."

Ou-Leesen was rubbing the neck of the wine skin back and forth across his lips. His hardened eyes stared at the floor of his tent. Eventually he set aside the wine skin and began, "Ever since Border Pass, my life has been like a wild river ... buffeting my beliefs, challenging my loyalties." He sighed.

"What happened at Border Pass?" Protas asked.

Ou-Leesen brought his eyes upward to stare at Protas as he considered how annoying Robe Man's questions could be. But he wasn't finished so he continued.

"After our infiltration efforts placed Border Pass into our hands, I was assigned to help hold it. It should have been easy ... we also held Seven Oaks." He reached for the wine skin again.

Protas could feel himself lean forward in anticipation of hearing what happened at Seven Oaks and Border Pass ... and he was hearing it from an El-Bhat!

But Ou-Leesen stared at the ground, holding the wine skin, not wanting to continue. Then Protas remembered another occasion when the El-Bhat Leader mentioned the 'Dark Power' that left him and his men alive, while other El-Bhat fell dead around them.

"You're going to tell me that the El-Bhat lost both strongholds. But that's not what is bothering you. Something happened that you can't explain." He thought of Urshen.

Ou-Leesen looked up. Robe Man's insight encouraged him to continue. "We had the catapults ... guarantee of a sure victory. But they had the Wind!" Ou-Leesen turned to watch the tent flap flutter in the evening breeze. "It came from the north side of the Canyon, bringing death to my comrades. They fell where they stood ... caught in the death embrace of that Dark Wind."

"And ... as you said before ... you want to know why this power passed over you and the others that follow you," Protas suggested. He already guessed that Ou-Leesen felt *less* for having survived. A true warrior should have died.

There was no response, but eventually Ou-Leesen added, "There is more. I saw the Storlenian slaves who work the Mines of Tenleth. There are *so many* women and children. The Sherilin would have never allowed such a thing."

Somehow Protas knew Ou-Leesen still wasn't finished, so he stayed quiet.

The El-Bhat reached for his knife and brought it slowly in front of his eyes. He studied the familiar markings and said, "This is the Dagger of Truth. It once belonged to the Sherilin, but it failed the man who first found it," Ou-Leesen said quietly, almost mournfully. "As I told you, it is why our eyes are green."

Protas thought they shone more brightly as Ou-Leesen held the knife.

"But the Dagger's power feels like ... a thirst that can never be quenched," Ou-Leesen finally added.

He set the knife aside and returned his gaze to Protas. "The Pass will be finished soon. But for what purpose Robe Man? Shall I buy the power of the Guilds ... with the gold that was mined by the blood of Storlenian innocents?"

"If I were in your position," Protas finally said, "I would exercise – to the fullest – the latitude that the Quorum has given you."

"Continue," Ou-Leesen said, noting the mischievous look on Protas's face.

"Your orders are to buy Guild Leadership with gold. But how you do it ... that can be *your* choice."

Ou-Leesen grunted ... a sign that their meeting was finished.

Protas rose, but before leaving the tent, he turned and added, "Does not the blood of the Sherilin run through your veins? Let it guide you as you decide."

He went to find Ee-lath, who always looked forward to hearing about his meetings with the El-Bhat Leader. It was a bit surprising to Protas that a young shepherd boy would be so keen to understand the affairs of men.

Ee-lath always began with the words, "Was it a good meeting?"

"Yes ... very good. But he was *very* angry." Protas smiled to let him know there was nothing to be concerned about.

"Robe Man, why was he so angry?"

"Discoveries."

"Discoveries can make someone angry?" The boy asked, wanting to understand.

"Yes, my little brother. Especially when discoveries turn your world upside down." Protas laid a hand on the young boy's skinny shoulder. "Sometimes discoveries are things you don't want to believe ... but know you *must*. This is Ou-Leesen's biggest problem. If he accepts those discoveries, he must make choices that will be very difficult."

"But it's easy to make a choice," Ee-lath reminded Protas.

Protas chuckled. "You are right. But it *seems* hard. Because we know what we will have to do once we make that choice. Do you understand my little brother?"

The young boy thought for a moment then said, "Is it like when you saw the Mountain Cat stalking me? Your choice to save me was hard because you knew you would have to fight the Cat ... and

Storlenians are no match for a Mountain Cat," the boy added with a grin.

"An excellent example," Protas proudly said to his bonded brother, "if I had actually *made* a choice. But lucky for you I acted on instinct. Ee-lath, some choices are just too hard and that's why we *have* instinct."

The two of them sat quietly for a while before Ee-lath resumed his questioning. "Will Ou-Leesen use his instinct to make his choices?"

"I hope so. The Quorum has asked him to do something, and it troubles him."

"Did you give him some good advice?" Ee-lath asked hopefully.

Protas was staring past the valley, far into distant Storlenia when he said, "I reminded him that he has Sherilin blood running through his veins."

The boy joined him staring northward. "Sounds like good advice to me," the young boy added, and placed a hand on Protas's shoulder.

Chapter 41 - Sleepwalking in the enemy camp

Protas's training continued, but it was more like sparring. As though Ou-Leesen needed to fight someone every day to remind himself he was a warrior. Protas insisted they set aside the knives and only use the staffs. Ou-Leesen agreed, but replacing the knife with the staff, seemed to give the El-Bhat permission to fight harder.

One day, Protas approached Ou-Leesen, "The Pass will be finished soon, have you decided how much gold you will take to Qar-ana?"

"What would it take to quench Storlenia's appetite for gold," Ou-Leesen asked.

"Well, what do you hope to receive in return?" Protas countered.

"I have decided I want access to an eastern port and a western port."

Protas grinned. "Now that's a great idea. And … I would take all the bricks from one of the houses at Chitouf. The best Ports for Shaksbali trade are probably Port Airiken on the western coast and Port Aqabah on the eastern coast. How many wagons do you think we will need?"

"Considering the weight, eight. Take twenty of my men and be sure to be back in three days." The stern look suggested that Ou-Leesen had difficulty trusting anyone when it came to the gold.

The bricks were gold bars covered with clay and then baked in the hot Shaksbali sun. When building a house the men of Chitouf stacked the bricks two deep, and then applied a thin layer of plaster which could be easily removed.

It only took a day for Protas and his crew to dismantled the walls and place the bricks carefully in the eight wagons. Ee-lath kept busy carrying the water for the twenty men. Protas told him that the bricks were going to be shipped to the country where he was born. "And as soon as these bricks are delivered," Protas explained, then paused to empty the water ladle, "Shaksbali people everywhere will begin to trade their goods with the people across the mountains."

"This must be Ou-Leesen's idea," Ee-lath suggested.

"Yes," Protas answered as he drank again from the water ladle.

"Then ... his anger has left him, and he knows what to do?" he smiled hopefully at Robe Man.

Protas nodded. "This means that soon ... *we* will be travelling north to take this shipment to Qar-ana, the largest city in Storlenia."

Ee-lath's eyes went wide as he considered the adventure. "I have never left Chitouf before. Will it take a week to come back?"

Protas laughed at his innocence. "Yes ... many more."

Ee-lath, Biskin, and Stek were gathered around the campfire listening to Protas. "... and it looks like we'll be heading to Qar-ana in a couple of days with those *bricks*."

"It will be good to do something other than haul water all day long," Biskin commented.

Protas looked at Stek who rarely said a word, and suddenly decided he would engage Stek in the campfire chatter. "Stek, have you heard about how Ee-lath and I became brothers?"

He shook his head 'no'.

"It all started when I escaped from El-Bhat Guards and headed south at the top of this Pass. Unfortunately, El-Bhat were also roaming these hills, so I thought it best to keep heading south. However, the slim pickings of food became even slimmer when I left the Valley. So, I headed east to find a village where I might steal some food. And while I was looking, I came across Ee-lath, challenging a Mountain Cat to a fight." Ee-lath smiled.

"I thought he could use some help, so I jumped in. But I soon found out that you should leave these fights with Mountain Cats to the villagers!" Ee-lath was laughing.

"What brought you to this Pass in the first place?" Stek asked, showing an unusual display of interest, but still not willing to look Protas in the face.

Protas lowered his voice and corrected, "Not *what* but *who*. Guards from Pechora Tracking Guild."

Stek's head came up and turned to Protas. "You were at the Pechora Tracking Guild?" Stek was suddenly attentive.

"Yes ... twice. The second time wasn't much of a story. I was there only long enough for them to tie me up and send me here between two smelly Guards." Ee-lath was laughing again. "But the first time ... now that was a story with a surprise ... that Biskin missed." Protas turned to Biskin. "Because Mitrock had already sent him ..."

"Mitrock!" Stek interrupted, "that was who I was supposed to see!"

257

"Sorry to tell you, but he's dead," Biskin offered.

Suddenly the countenance of Stek changed from quiet and lost to enthusiastic and in charge as he jumped to his feet, ready to leave. "I'm free!" he exclaimed quietly but with triumph.

"Whoa. Where do you think you're going?" Biskin challenged.

"I don't know," Stek confessed, thinking about what had just happened. "The one thing I do know, I'm no longer confused and no longer divided." His memories were clear about what he had done so far, and his agreed assignment to pass on the location of the Cave. "And that's never going to happen," he said to himself.

"What's never going to happen? And what's opened up *your* tongue?" Biskin asked.

Stek turned to the other Tracker, his face chiselled with concern. "For some time now, there's been a chain around my mind ... but when you mentioned that Mitrock was dead, the chain broke. I don't know why, and I don't know what it's about. But right now, it feels like I've been sleepwalking, and I just woke up in the middle of the enemy camp."

"Well ..." Protas responded to Ou-Leesen's questions about travelling north, "aside from the Trackers, I would only take the twenty men that helped load the wagons. Our story is that we are transporting these bricks to Hilltop Redemption Guild. I am here to supervise the transport and delivery. They will search the wagons for weapons, so I suggest that we only take shepherd staffs. You and your men will need to dress as common labourers. We can pick up clothes and large sun hats at the border town. Wear the hats low. When we stop for inspection, or when we are travelling through a town, look straight ahead and squint hard. That should make it nearly impossible to see your green eyes."

Ou-Leesen nodded, satisfied that the plan would work. The group would be split in two, taking turns sleeping while the others watched over the gold.

"By the way, how much do you know about Ports ... and how they work?"

Ou-Leesen ignored the question ... he was a warrior, not a sailor.

"Yeah me too," Protas responded. "But if we are going to get a fair deal, I suggest that we take the time to visit the Port of Aqabah before we arrive at Qar-ana. We need to know what to negotiate for. For example ... what about custom charges, rights to trade, what would be a great deal on the length of a docking lease? Wouldn't want them to think we are weak ..." Protas added, appealing to Ou-Leesen's warrior pride.

"Aqabah will be our first stop," Ou-Leesen agreed, satisfied with the counsel.

Several leagues north of Ou-Leesen Pass, they came to a Security Gate they would have to get through. Manned by Trackers, these Security Gates were spread across Storlenia. The Tracker at the Gate noticed that two Trackers were among the travellers. He approached Stek and Biskin, wanting to know why they were helping to haul bricks. Biskin told him their names, while Stek took out his knife and twirled it around his fingers. Considering what happened at Arborville, he knew they were looking for Shaksbali Trackers who didn't know the first thing about Tracking. When the Security Guard saw Stek's skill with the knife, he thanked them and moved on to Protas.

"Why so few bricks in every wagon?"

"My Redemption Guild sent me with eight wagons and an order to bring them back full. What you see here is all the bricks I could get my hands on. A week earlier ... and these wagons would have been full," Protas shook his head in disappointment.

"Move on," the Guard ordered and walked towards traffic coming the other way.

After the Security Gate, they continued straight north until they met the eastern road that would take them to Aqabah.

While they travelled the roads towards the eastern coast, Protas was busy educating Ee-lath about the things he was seeing. And answering his endless questions. "We are going to stop at a Shipyard within a day or two and then you will see things you never dreamed of. And you will have more questions than I have answers for!" Protas chuckled.

Late in the afternoon with the sun at their backs, Protas slowly stood up in his wagon, trying to get a better look at the scenery off in the distance ... to the north. He recognized it. But he knew he had never visited this part of Storlenia. And yet there was something *very* familiar. 'Of course ...' he finally realized. 'Urshen described this scenery to me in great detail, after the incident at the river. And beyond those forested hills, where I see the three treeless peaks ... I will find a Cave.' He sat down and thought about what he should do.

He was committed to Ou-Leesen but here was an opportunity to visit a Cave and walk away with an Amulet!

"What's on your mind," asked Stek, his travelling companion.

Protas looked in the back of the wagon, wanting to make sure Ee-lath was still asleep. He turned to Stek, "I need to head north while the rest of you continue on to Aqabah." He grimaced, knowing how difficult it would be to convince Ou-Leesen to let him do exactly that.

Seeing Protas's look of doubt, Stek replied, "You don't think he will let his Advisor leave … and you are right."

Staring down at his boots, Protas knew Stek was right … and he felt miserable just thinking about the lost opportunity.

"Unless … he was convinced that we won't need you at the Port," Stek offered with a grin. "So, what did you have in mind when you talked about leases and customs and all that stuff?"

A hopeful Protas spent the rest of the afternoon training Stek in the skills of negotiating and the right questions to ask at Aqabah. He was impressed with how quickly the Tracker picked up the information. And that meant … he really wasn't needed as much as he thought!

As soon as they pulled off the road, Stek made his way over to Ou-Leesen and asked him if he could share a few thoughts of his own. While the rest set up camp and made supper, Stek explained many things about how Ports operated, what they needed to look for and how they could best get the information. "If you agree, I will take Biskin with me while the rest of you stay out of sight."

"What about Robe Man?" Ou-Leesen suspiciously asked.

"I think he has something else in mind that requires his attention … while we take care of Aqabah."

Chapter 42 - The slaughterhouse dog

With Ou-Leesen's reluctant permission, Protas started his pilgrimage and headed north. When the sound of the wagons became dim, he turned and watched them roll eastward, shrinking out of sight. He thought about Ee-lath and how much he already missed not having him around. He wished he could have brought him ... and maybe sometime in the future that might become a reality ... but not yet. He pushed on, grateful and surprised that Stek's idea had worked out.

The sun was slowly slipping below the horizon when he began feeling something undefined. It pressed upon him as he walked league upon league. Surprisingly, he felt jubilant but equally fearful... as though he should expect serious opposition to his quest. He had hoped to make it to the village nestled at the base of the foothills before dark. But it turned out to be further than he expected and was forced to sleep under a tree. During the night he awakened, soaked from the rain. The irritation reminded him of another miserable experience, shivering on a plateau, under a tree, while searching for Urshen ... and diamonds.

The breaking of dawn as it finally swept the darkness from among the trees, promised relief from the wet and dreary cold. Protas wasted no time resuming his journey.

Grateful for the crackling logs in the hearth and a hearty lunch, he left the Inn and headed for the north end of town. Passing taverns, shops, and houses, he came to a slaughterhouse. He was about to give it a wide berth to avoid the smell when he heard the distressful barking of a dog. He stopped and listened until he had the bearing ... and then ran towards the noise.

He slowed as he approached the containing pen. Protas saw three young men on the other side of a locked gate, throwing rocks at a large dog. They were slowly forcing the animal towards the entry chute which led the pigs to slaughter. He snarled and barked viciously, trying to slip past them, but the flying rocks left him yelping in pain.

Protas scurried over the gate, unlocked it, then whacked at the gate loudly with his staff, letting the dog know that a chance for escape had just been provided. When the hoodlums turned to see what had made the noise, the dog saw his opportunity and dashed past them and out through the open gate.

Annoyed at the intruder, they threw a volley of rocks. But the Man of Redemption swirled his robe to protect himself, letting the harmless rocks fall to the ground. Surprised, but not discouraged, the young men advanced on Protas, intent on teaching him a lesson he would never forget.

Having accomplished his objective to free the dog, Protas turned to leave the pen. But the ruffians were determined to teach the Robed Man a lesson and rushed him. As Protas faced them, he realized how glad he was that they hadn't simply run away. In his mind, dog-abusers ought to be disciplined, and *they* had just extended the invitation.

With staff in hand and the hard training from Ou-Leesen he easily dispatched the three hooligans to the ground. But as they arose, bruised and bleeding, they all drew knives and began to circle the Brother of the Cloth.

'Time to finish this,' Protas thought, and slowly pulled out Jalek's large hunting knife from a hidden fold in his Robe. As the three hesitated, Protas grinned. "My knife has a name. I call it *Hunger*. And you can't imagine how much blood it has seen." With a quick movement, Protas relieved the closest hoodlum of his knife, and left him with a large gash on his arm. Realizing their mistake, the young men backed away slowly then turned and ran away as fast as they could.

Protas knew it was best if he too left as quickly as possible. He knew that eventually the embarrassment of being defeated by a man of the Robe, would push them to do something wickedly vengeful. And next time the playing field might not be as level.

About an hour later, he stopped and listen attentively. Someone was definitely following him, and the noise suggested there was more than one. He hurried along, reluctant to fight in the confinement of a narrow trail. But despite his efforts they were gaining on him. He started looking for another way of escape. Within moments, he saw it. Away from the trail, the forest fell away down a steep incline to a stream below. He hurried towards his new avenue of escape, but half-way down the wooded hill, he tripped and tumbled to the bottom. Bruised and covered in dead leaves, he ran towards the stream, jumped across it, then bounded up to the top of the hill.

The Necklace from Harleem

Breathing heavily while leaning against a large tree, he still heard the advancing group charging up the hill. And now much closer! "Impossible!" he whispered angrily to himself, "they couldn't be that fast!" He knew it was useless to continue running so he pushed himself away from the tree, staff ready to face whoever was about to come over the ridge.

"It's you!" Protas exclaimed. He set his staff aside and extended his arms to the dog. The hound bounded forward, jumped up, paws on his shoulders and began licking his face. Protas wrapped his arms around his neck, and scolded him, "Do you know what you have just put me through? You scared me half to death." He laughed and scratched behind the dog's ears. Protas played with the dog for a while, wishing he could keep his new-found friend. "But unfortunately, you cannot come with me," he finally told the dog. "You must go back ... go back," he repeated firmly, then walked away expecting the dog to return to the town.

Failing to get the expected response, he told him to sit, and stay, then walked away. Luckily the dog stayed. But soon the hound came crashing through the bushes as soon as Protas was completely out of sight. After repeating the process three times, it was obvious to Protas that the dog was determined to stay. It appeared he didn't have a choice, so he placed his hands on his hips and stared at the hound.

"You know, you will probably be the first dog to ever see the inside of a Cave. You must promise me that once inside ... you will behave yourself!"

The dog sat back on his haunches and cocked his head.

"I guess that means we have a deal. But before we continue ... you need a name. I am going to call you ... Sausage! To remind you to stay away from slaughterhouses ... forever!"

Sausage barked.

"Ahh, I guess that means you like your new name." Protas bent down and ruffled his coat. "Come on Sausage, we have to go. There is a Cave out there we need to find."

Standing on the edge of a plateau, Protas panned the valley below and up the other side. He could see where the Cave should be. He crouched down, one arm around the dog, and the other pointing to the spot he was considering, and said, "Sausage ... over there, where I'm pointing, is the Cave we need to find. Once I get the Amulet, I will return you to your village. Are you ready to go?" The dog barked with enthusiasm. Then followed Protas down the steep and treacherous path.

Once in the valley, he looked back several times towards the ridge, comparing that location with the landmarks he had memorized. Eventually he found himself at the base of the hill that housed the Cave. A weary but excited Protas ran up the hill with Sausage at his heels.

But there was no Cave. Confused, he continued to the top, hoping that the higher elevation would help him see his mistake. The summit was fifty paces above the tree line, which gave him a clear line-of-sight of the important landmarks. As far as he could tell, the Cave should have been somewhere below him. He descended in a serpentine fashion, allowing him to cover the entire side of the hill. But still he didn't find it. With the day spent, he returned to a meadow he had passed through earlier, anxious to set up camp.

It was a quiet evening with Sausage as he considered his situation. He had expected that finding the Cave would be straight forward, especially knowing where it was supposed to be. He would just have to try again in the morning.

"It wasn't supposed to be this hard ... makes me wonder if I'm ready," he sighed, petting the dog. He remembered that Urshen waited and *prepared* for years, to find the Cave. And considering the demands that had been placed on Urshen since they met the Tinkers, Protas was convinced that without that preparation, Urshen wouldn't have done so well. With a slow and melancholic voice, he shared his thoughts with Sausage.

"You know ... it's kind of like expecting a knife to be sharp ... without the effort of a sharpening stone."

Sausage lifted his head from where it had rested on his paws. Protas caught the movement and suggested to his friend, "You know Sausage, maybe I can't find it ... because I'm not ready." Disheartened and tired, he used his arm as a pillow and drifted off to sleep, confident that Sausage would watch over them both.

In the morning, he offered some bread and cheese to the hound. While eating the simple breakfast, Protas still remained uncertain regarding his next step. He turned to his friend. He hoped that if he gave voice to his uncertainty, maybe he would realize something, that so far, was not entirely clear.

"My good friend Sausage," he began, noting that the dog responded to the sound of his name. "I'm going to tell you a story about *another* dog ... mostly because you are a good listener." He grinned, then continued.

"When I was quite young, I found a puppy and, like you, he needed a friend. I enthusiastically brought him home, totally expecting that my parents would allow me to keep him. Unfortunately, things turned out quite badly for both of us. My father killed the dog and I became as bitter as anyone could be. This bitterness changed me into someone that only thought of himself. I was so different from the little boy that I used to be. If I had found you back then, I probably would have walked on by, and let those young men do to you whatever they wanted ... not really caring at all."

He sighed. "But lucky for you, three people helped to change my life. First there was Brother Ott ... someone I secretly liked. Of course, I fought his efforts to make something out of me." He smiled as he remembered the many times they duelled over words.

"But sadly, he was killed by someone that slept in the same room as me. His name was Brother Retlin and he is the second person that helped change me. Mostly because he almost killed me. Would have, except for a certain Amulet." By now Sausage had laid his head on his paws, eyes fixed on Protas.

"Having Death knock on your door, can change how a man sees the world around him. But even so ... I needed another shove ... from someone I hated. And I don't think I hated anyone as much as I hated Urshen." Protas paused, picked up a few small rocks and tossed them at the large tree he had slept under.

"He was the third person. And because of him ... I am sitting here, talking to you." Protas looked at the big mutt, remembering the night in Urshen's cabin, as he lay staring at the moonlit ceiling, with tears dripping from his ears and promising himself, *Someday ... I'm going to get a dog.*

"You know ... telling you this story makes me think that meeting you, was more than an interesting coincidence. I wonder ..." Protas got up and immediately the hound was at his side, anxious to continue their trek. But Protas needed to say one more thing. He grabbed the hound's head and looked into his eyes. "I came here to find the Cave ... but I have no idea where to look." Playfully he said, "Do you know where it is?" Immediately the dog barked, pulled away and ran toward the hills. "Okay ... maybe you'll have better luck than me," Protas muttered, amused by the dog's enthusiasm. "Wait up," he shouted as he grabbed his staff.

Running at full tilt, he followed the dog until he caught up. Then the hound dashed off again. It reminded him of his training in FieldBall many years ago ... except he wasn't as fit and was ready to command the dog to stop. Fortunately, when he saw him again, the dog wasn't very far away. Only thirty paces above ... on a ledge.

Protas stopped to wonder at the possibility. 'A ledge?' But the dog started barking. "Alright I'm coming," Protas reassured Sausage.

Standing on the flat outcrop with the dog at his side, he was ... stunned. He was facing a large quartz face, about the size of a large door, very similar to the Cave in the Lithgate Wilderness. It was the very Cave he was looking for. He knew where he would find the Key, but he didn't want to just grab it and walk in. There was a reason *he* couldn't find the Cave, and Sausage could. He reached down and ruffled his fur, "You are such a clever dog," he praised. "And how did you know ..." he added looking at the quartz door.

Protas sat down. He felt the need to think for a while. What was he supposed to learn from this experience. He wrapped his arm around the big mutt and pulled him close. "Sausage, you are *more* than clever. You are special ... and you don't even know it ... because you're a dog." Protas slowly began to scratch behind his ears.

"However, you have helped me see that I was assuming too much. Taking too much for granted. I figured that I was *entitled* ... to just walk up to the Cave and walk away with the Key. But I couldn't even find it," he whispered to himself. "It seems to suggest that I needed to be reminded, that having access to the Cave is a privilege ... and not a right."

He turned the dog's head until he looked straight into his eyes. "But *you* found it straight away. Quite amazing really. So, what does Protas need to learn from that? Sausage can you tell me?" The dog barked softly.

"Perhaps you are trying to tell me, that I need to have faith in someone other than myself ... even if it's a dog." His words trailed off quietly.

They both rested in the sun for a while. Then suddenly the dog jumped up, walked over to the quartz door, and placed his paw against it. "You think it's time?" Protas asked, a bit surprised by the dog's encouragement. "All right," he replied. "You know, the last time I entered a Cave, it was with Urshen." He got up and walked over to Sausage.

"After that experience, I never thought I would see the inside of a Cave again. Certainly not with a dog!" He shook his head in disbelief.

Protas placed his forehead and hands against the cool quartz door and considered what he was about to do. It was one thing to have a conversation with a hound. It was quite another to feel right about entering the Cave ... because he felt invited. His original plan was to leave with only the Key and not enter the Cave. But now that Sausage was with him, he felt that things had changed. Similar to when the Garden had led him and Urshen to the Tinkers, he had this feeling that ...

He pushed away from the rock face. "Sausage ... I've been thinking about why you are here with me." The mutt barked. He seemed to really like his new name. "It was more than just to show me where to find the Cave. I think it's because I will need your help ... keeping the Amulet safe." The dog barked excitedly when the small ledge containing the Key, slid away from the wall. The barking had distracted Protas enough that he missed it ... but Sausage didn't. He trotted over and barked at it.

"I guess that takes care of the invitation," Protas concluded, staring at the Ledge. There, sitting in its host, was the Amulet.

Walking across the threshold for the second time in his life, brought back a flood of memories. Of chimes and Light ... of feeling endorsed and forgiven ... and needed. He turned to say 'sit' but Sausage was already positioned by the door as a sentinel.

Directing his words towards the Tree of Life in the centre of the Garden, Protas began. "I thought with all of the difficulty that we have been having, it would be good to have another Amulet. Urshen told me where all the Caves were. He felt that it would be good for me to know. In case he ever ... but you know that." He looked back at Sausage for inspiration.

"I will need help keeping the Key safe. It's my biggest concern. And I believe you sent me the dog for that very reason." Before he could think of what else to say, the leaves of a Plant, not far down the path, began to glow. He walked closer and touched it as he had done in the Garden before. The small stubby Plant sent a message. He was to invite the dog. Protas called Sausage.

Holding the Key with one hand, while touching the plant with the other, he placed the Amulet against the dog's neck. Instantly, Light coursed from the Plant, then through him to the Amulet. Light as bright as lightening wove a pattern around the dog's neck.

When the Light faded, Sausage was wearing a leather collar that encased the Key, hidden from view. Protas didn't remember letting go of the Amulet, somehow it simply floated away.

He examined the 'leather' collar. The craftsmanship was superb, the design simple and nondescript. Something that wouldn't draw attention. The Plant taught Protas how to extract the Key and return it to the collar. He also learned that the 'leather' was stronger than steel and only he could have access to the Key.

After he let go of the Plant, Sausage looked up at him and barked a couple of times. Protas stared in disbelief. Inside the Cave, he understood what the dog was saying! Sausage knew the purpose of the collar and his duty to Protas.

Outside, Protas followed the instructions and extracted the Key in order to close the door. Then he returned it to the collar. The dog sat still, waiting for Protas to be finished.

"Wait till Urshen sees this … he will be so jealous," Protas declared with a wide grin, while looking into Sausage's eyes.

"Now … we need to hurry back!"

From far away, an El-Bhat observed Robe Man enter the side of the mountain then watched him as he came out. 'Ou-Leesen will be pleased to know the location of another Cave!' the El-Bhat thought. He turned and quickly started his journey back. He had been left behind to recover from 'sickness' while the others headed east to Aqabah. They would pick him up on the return journey and he needed to be there when they arrived. He wouldn't stop running until he was securely inside the Inn.

Chapter 43 - The bargain of a lifetime

Protas was waiting by the side of the road, when the wagons came into view. "Sausage you stay here. It's probably best if they don't know we're together. While we are traveling, I'll keep an eye out for you, and you do the same for me. Okay Sausage?" The dog barked. Protas stood up and turned to add, "Remember the whistle I taught you. When you hear it, come quickly, I will probably need the Amulet. He started walking toward the wagons and the dog headed for the trees.

"How was your experience at Aqaba?" Protas asked Stek, curious to know why there were now only seven wagons.

"We thought since we were already there, we would do a little shopping. We bought six, Silver Sea Shipping Schooners, the best shipping vessels money can buy!"

Protas smiled, he liked the way Stek operated. "Obviously Ou-Leesen didn't complain about my absence?"

"No, he seemed to settle in fine with the idea. He respected your need to make this pilgrimage. You got what you needed?"

"Yeah ... there were a few surprises, but everything worked out."

The wagons headed west, towards the main artery, which would take them north to Qar-ana. The last leg of the western journey offered a short cut that veered northwest, promising to save them a full day. It was a smaller road that went through villages and small towns. And ... seven wagons attracted more attention in these smaller communities. Something that didn't set well with Protas. A mischievous boy determined to steal one brick, would turn their world upside down.

After another long day, they secured the wagons for the night. As the men spread out their bedrolls, Biskin approached Protas. "Something isn't right," he whispered.

"What do you suggest?"

"Whoever it is, they already know there are two Trackers in this company. We will be their target. They will assume little resistance from the labourers, and even less from a man of the Cloth," he grinned at Protas.

"I will discuss this with Ou-Leesen," responded Protas.

In the stillness of the night, a band of twenty men, armed with clubs and knives attacked the Trackers standing Night Guard. Everyone else had their shepherd staffs beside their bedrolls.

Stek and Biskin defended themselves and protected each other's back, knowing they needed to hold off their attackers for only a few moments.

Protas was the first to hit one of the attackers from behind. He was a large man, who turned on him like an angry swarm of hornets. The half-moon provided enough light for the man to see his Robe. "You're gonna regret that really fast," he shouted angrily.

"Maybe," was Protas's quick reply, "but then again..." he added as he easily disarmed the man and flipped him on his back with his staff. He wacked another thief who was close by. By now the first man was on his feet swinging wildly with his fists, determined, with the help of the second man, to bring the man of Cloth to the ground, where he would finish him. But Protas was a surprise to both of them. Ou-Leesen had trained him well!

A short time later, the ground was littered with twenty men, bleeding and beaten. They were told to leave their weapons, remove their clothes, and walk eastward.

"Why did we take their clothes," a curious Ee-lath asked the next day.

"To make sure they don't follow us," Protas explained.

"But as soon as they get more clothes, won't they still come after us?"

"Yup, they probably will, unless they find their clothes hanging out for everyone to see."

As they entered the next town the following day, Protas stopped his wagon beside the Tavern railing, where the customers normally tied up their horses. Instead, he hung the men's gathered clothes. Someone in the Tavern came out to see what Protas was doing. It was quite a sight, a Man of the Cloth, hanging clothes over the horses' railing. Protas looked up and stated, "They lost the fight ... and their clothes. They don't smell good, so I'm leaving them here for them to pick up."

He smiled and jumped up into the wagon. "This just might keep them from following us," he said to Ee-lath. "Now everyone at the Tavern will know who attacked our wagons. It will give them pause." To ensure that there would indeed be no more trouble, the wagons travelled all day and all night, with only short stops to rest the horses. When they finally arrived at the main road, man and beast took a deserved full-days' rest.

On their long trek to the capital city, Ou-Leesen and Protas quizzed the two Trackers what they had learned at Aqabah until they were satisfied that they were ready for the inevitable compromises. Twenty leagues south of Qar-ana, Stek and Biskin were sent on ahead as emissaries to discuss the terms with Craslin.

"Please tell the Guild Master we have a gift from Kel-eetan, capital of Shaksbah," Stek told the Assistant.

Craslin looked down from the observation railing above, surprised to see two Trackers looking up at him. He had doubted the report that came from his Assistant, so he had to see for himself. "Strange," he muttered.

They were stripped of their weapons before they were led into Craslin's office. "I thought you might resist," Craslin mocked them, knowing that protocol insisted that Trackers have complete immunity inside any of the other Guilds.

"We aren't here representing the Tracking Guild, or we would have kept our weapons," Stek said matter-of-factly. "And I prefer if you ask the others to leave."

Craslin paused, as he eyed the two Trackers, trying to make sense of the situation. He failed but found himself dismissing the Guards anyway.

Once the room was cleared, Stek continued, "We are not here representing the government of Kel-eetan as we said, but rather the Quorum of the El-Bhat. They have sent the gift that you requested, and we have a sample with us."

'This must be a trap!' Craslin decided as he considered the unbelievable words spoken by the Tracker! "A Gift from Kel-eetan I can believe ... but not from the El-Bhat," he cautiously offered, struggling to believe their story. He smiled at them. The whole scenario was *too* strange. He was tempted to call his Guards back into the room.

Stek looked at Biskin and nodded. Biskin walked to Craslin's desk, removed his shoulder bag, and laid it on the large oak table where he removed the brick. He set it on the bag, and with his fist he smashed away the brick covering the bar of gold. He returned to stand beside Stek, while the Guild Master hefted the shiny bar.

Craslin contemplated the irony of Trackers delivering the token gift from the Quorum. With his fine steel letter opener, he easily scratched it. 'Pure gold as promised,' he eagerly concluded, dumfounded by how events were unfolding. He looked at the two Trackers, still confused, but willing to adjust to a world, where things were no longer what they used to be. Besides, if things went wrong, it was their word against his. And that was in his favour. "What do they want, and how much gold have you brought?"

"Seven wagons full," Stek said, ignoring the first question. He wanted to see Craslin's reaction before he discussed the demands.

Despite Craslin's ability to shield his emotions, his eyebrows shot upwards in shock.

As Stek figured, Craslin couldn't believe they had brought so much gold. *Now* the Tracker was ready to discuss his demands. "They want an eastern port and a western port, with full rights to trade, no customs charges and a one-hundred-year lease on the docking rights. When you draft the documents, specify that the ports are to be Port Airiken on the western coast, and Port Aqabah on the eastern coast."

Craslin was extremely pleased with the conditions of the trade. But he was never *satisfied* until he understood the complete extent of the trading opportunity. "What about ships and crews to train the Shaksbali ... certainly there is a need?"

Stek nodded. "Good quality gold deserves the best quality merchant ships," he responded, as he removed sketches from Biskin's bag and laid them across Craslin's table. "We have already purchased six Silver Sea Shipping Schooners," Stek clarified, "the best that Storlenian shipyards make. They too were pleased with our gold, and they have advised us that they can have twenty new vessels ... ten from each port ... ready to go within a year. And, we will need the crews to man them. Seasoned sailors to operate twenty six Ships as well as train Shaksbali people as sailors. You get seven wagons of gold. In exchange, we want you to pay for the additional twenty ships and provide the crews. Do we have a deal?"

From the moment, he was given the bar of gold, Craslin had anticipated a robust round of negotiation. But they had offered *so much* gold, he dared not risk insulting the Quorum. Still ... his head was spinning. Nothing was as he had imagined. Trackers as Ambassadors from the Quorum and now an unbelievable amount of gold! He needed to be careful. This had to be a trap! Didn't it? "Tell the

Quorum ... that the crews will be carefully chosen. Men that can integrate well with Shaksbali."

Stek had one last thing to check. "After we deliver the gold, in a few days, we will take the signed Port Contracts with us. But when can we return for the Purchase Contracts of the twenty Schooners, and their crews?"

"Well ... if I knew how soon you could be back?"

"Eight weeks will be soon enough," Stek responded.

Craslin nodded in appreciation of the extra time offered ... and the sure knowledge of how far away the rest of the gold was stored. "All will be ready in eight weeks. And ... when you return in a couple of days with the seven wagons, the Guards at the loading yard will be expecting you and will supply you with fresh horses for your return journey." These dim-witted Trackers would soon lead his spies to the El-Bhat Treasury of gold.

The Trackers offered a nod in appreciation, then turned to leave.

Before they made it to the door, Craslin made an additional offer, "I would hate to see anything happen to *my* gold before it arrived at the loading yard. Allow me to send a group of my Militia Guard to add to the security."

The two Trackers declined with a wave of the hand.

"That was kind of fun," Biskin said cheerily when they descended the large front steps of the Planning and Development Guild.

"Yeah, it felt good to practically give away the El-Bhat's gold." They grinned at each other as they strolled down the paved avenue. To make sure they weren't followed, the Trackers took two days to make their way back to Ou-Leesen.

Craslin sat with the bar of gold on his lap for a long time, contemplating what had just happened. It was all so irregular. Why the Quorum would send two *Trackers* was the first mystery. And with no apparent skill in negotiation. True, it would cost dearly to complete his bargain of securing shipping rights and the crewed ships as requested, but a quick mental calculation suggested that he would still end up with at least three wagon loads of gold ... if not more. They were certainly not a shrewd pair of negotiators. In addition, it was so unusual not to send notice that the shipment was coming. True, there had been secret messages sent back and forth over the last year, but he thought the Quorum had been far from making a commitment. And now suddenly, the gold was on his doorstep!

Craslin carried the gold bar to the veranda overlooking the unloading yard. His thoughts returned to the temptation to send his Militia to spy on them as they returned to their hoard of wealth ... and then simply confiscate the rest of it. However, he was dealing with the Quorum, Leaders of El-Bhat warriors that were at least ten thousand strong. Perhaps their plan was to steal the gold back from him once they had access to the shipping. And leave clues that suggested it was someone other than El-Bhat.

On the other hand, could he be holding the only brick of gold? Was this a strategy of the Tracking Guild to flush out his scheme to kill Axion, and take over the leadership of the Guild? Doubtful ... but he would hide the gold brick until he had the seven wagons as promised.

For now, all he could do was wait ... and alert his Militia to stand ready at the city limits. And ensure the safe arrival of the gold to his loading yard. And if he got that far ... well, he would have seven wagons of gold in his possession and the rest should be easy!

Chapter 44 - The man from Harleem

Previously. In Qar-ana, Craslin was carefully building the scaffolding to his new Empire, with gold bricks, Brass Sling Mounted War Wagons, and his private Militia. His plans included Zephra ruling at his side. Meanwhile, in Pechora, a Golden Necklace will soon envelope Bernado and eventually all Ankoletia in its Green Power

Every evening, in the privacy of his home, Bernado retrieved the Necklace. It had become a ritual ... a time of worship ... an effort to encourage the Necklace to speak to him again. After his failure to use the second Medallion on Urshen, he expressed doubt regarding the power of the Necklace to place him on the throne as Emperor ... and since then, the Necklace remained silent. Carefully he removed it from its safe place and unwrapped the velvet covering. He traced the outline of the medallions with his fingers while he considered what he wanted to say. His aspiration to become Emperor weighed heavily upon his mind. With hopefulness, he began his litany to the golden talisman.

"I remember the day, that the Specialist Tracker delivered you to my Guild ... and how he abandoned you, only caring for his own life. But I ... could never abandon you. I want you to be with me ... always. I have never lost my belief that I will become Emperor of this entire planet," he said softly as he continued tracing the outline of all six Medallions. "And it will be ... because of you. This is my great desire ... my burning ambition. Do you still believe in me? Will you help me reach my ambition?"

Affectionately, Bernado placed both hands on the talisman and waited for a response. As he expected, a Green Light had begun gathering in the room ... but it wasn't coming from the Necklace, it was shining from behind Bernado. He kept one hand in contact with the Talisman and slowly turned around. A man was standing in the middle of his locked room, bathed in the familiar swirls of Green Light. The

Green Light flickered then died. The Visitor gave a slight nod acknowledging Bernado.

The nod of respect was lost on Bernado. He was too terrified by the obvious. The Visitor and the Necklace drew power from the same Green Light! This man must be the true owner of *his* Necklace. He was probably there to collect it ... and *that* he could not allow.

Suspicious, Bernado asked, "Who are you?" as his hands silently opened the desk drawer that held his prized Long Knives.

Everything about the man suggested disinterest ... or power. The Visitor stood motionless, his face devoid of passion, like it was carved from white limestone. Extending his hand towards the talisman, he responded, "I am a servant to the bearer of ... *Goldenrod*." Bernado noticed the gold band on his wrists. Identical in colour to the Necklace. The Visitor didn't seem to notice that Bernado was secretly reaching for his knives. In a blur, the Tracker's hands removed the knives, determined to cut him down.

Long Knives were Bernado's specialty, but he could not touch the man. With only a modest movement of either wrist, this Alien could shift his entire body to a different place. The man's skill was so precise, that his movements were just enough to avoid the blades.

Because of Bernado's unrelenting determination, the Visitor disappeared to the far side of the room. Behind Bernado.

Confident that his opponent had left, the Guild Master turned around to place the knives back in the drawer. He flinched when he spotted him across the room ... staring ... motionless ... waiting for Bernado to speak. Despite his Tracker skills the man was untouchable. He decided to leave the knives where they lay. "Why haven't you tried to kill me? You obviously have the skill."

"It isn't within my power." It was a truth he loathed to share but he needed Bernado to feel safe. And willing to trade anything in this world for his personal ambition. "I am only here to assist you in the use of *Goldenrod*."

"You are not here to take it away? You will let me keep it?" was Bernado's astonished reply. The Visitor said nothing, so Bernado continued. "What is your name?"

"My name is *Kareen-hys-Tebeel-del-Harleem*. You may call me Kareen-del-Harleem."

Bernado thought back to his 'discussion' with the Golden Necklace just before The Strange Visitor appeared. Now it was clear. "You are here to help me become the Emperor of Ankoletia."

He nodded in the affirmative.

The Necklace from Harleem

To Bernado the offer seemed too generous. "What do you want ... in exchange for placing me on the Emperor's throne?"

Kareen-del-Harleem was pleased that Goldenrod's captive thought he could bargain. "I want the man who wore Goldenrod before you. Do you know him?"

"No. He walked in here one day and after a brief skirmish, he departed, leaving behind the Necklace."

"Find him. Then detain him along with the man who resisted the second Medallion. I want them both. Keep these prisoners healthy until I come for them. Do not let them escape."

Bernado was surprised that the Strange Visitor knew that Urshen fought successfully against the power of the Necklace. "How ... do I call you ... if I need you?"

"As soon as you have the two men that I have asked for, speak to Goldenrod ... and I will hear you." Kareen-del-Harleem nodded, indicating that their meeting was over, then disappeared into a mist of green.

Later that night, sitting on the edge of his bed, Bernado was wondering why Kareen-del-Harleem wanted those two men. True they were men of unique abilities ... but the Alien was ... beyond anything he could imagine. So why would a man with such power want Storlenian captives? In fact everything about the Visitor defied logic.

First, why offer the position of Emperor to someone like himself when Kareen-del-Harleem was capable of simply taking what he wanted. "Or is he?" Bernado suddenly whispered into the dark, as he remembered something the Visitor had said ... *It isn't within my power*. Bernado looked in the direction of the Golden Necklace and remembered that it could hear him speak. He would have to be more careful about things he said out loud.

'I am beginning to see,' Bernado thought to himself, 'that everything is not as it appears. Despite his significant skills, Kareen-del-Harleem is ... *limited*.'

Eventually he climbed into bed, knowing that if he ever achieved the status of Emperor, the only way to stay there, was to find out 'how' the Visitor was limited. And he knew that the road to *that* knowledge would be slippery and dangerous!

❦ ❦ ❦

The day before

High above Ankoletia, Kareen-hys-Tebeel-del-Harleem sat in his private control room. Placing his hands on the golden-alloy controls, he ordered, "Show me the man who defeated the Second Medallion."

A three-dimensional hologram was immediately beamed from the panel in front of him ... of a man lying on a cot, in a prison cell. "Scan him and let me see the data." Kareen soon had what he needed to know. Composite Genetics, Mapping Index, and Transference Compatibility were all superior!

Scanning was certainly *broad brush* compared to the data acquired by the Necklace and the Dagger of Truth. But it was good enough to tell him that the genetics of the man on the cot, could be sold for a fortune. Then there was the Tracker whose life force was pulled into The Necklace, allowing their scientists to confirm genetic quality of Class Six! The two specimens were absolutely amazing. But first he needed to smuggle them onto his Ship before the Harvest became official and his ability to skim profits ended.

"Find me the man who wore Goldenrod prior to Bernado," he shouted to his Technicians. Kareen decided to wait for the results while his mind drifted to the wealth that black market genetics could bring.

Thousands of years earlier, when genetic manipulation was in its infancy, the citizens of Harleem embraced the promises ... freedom from disease and extended lifespans. Unfortunately, unexpected complexities followed in the wake of the expanding new science. Infertility and bodies that forgot how to renew themselves. Their race had almost become barren. No fruit ... no future.

But then an important breakthrough was announced. Harleem had discovered the power of Gold-alloys. Almost overnight, their future was restored. With Gold-alloy technology, they were soon hunting the Galaxy for superior unaltered genetic material, more gold, and a continual supply of slaves.

Kareen-del-Harleem was a young man when they planted the Waterless Wells on the planet of Ankoletia centuries ago. And now that those Waterless Wells had sent messages of contact, he was back to coax the process forward.

The conquering armies from Harleem were not free to take

what they wanted. There were rules and they had to be obeyed without a single infraction. Sometimes they won the prize, sometimes they lost to Balhok. And sometimes the planet simply destroyed itself before they could capture the will of the people.

The sound of a muted beep signaled that results, regarding the second man, were coming in. A hologram formed, showing an image of topography that started from Pirtelin. It was the path of the man after he became enslaved by the power of Goldenrod. Once the genetic scent was captured by the Necklace, there was nowhere on the planet he could hide.

The hologram traced the wanderings of the man for hundreds of leagues to Pechora. Then suddenly it switched from a surface view of the planet to the message ... *crystal radiation blackout.*

"Sons of Balhok!" he screamed at the hologram. The man must have found an Amulet. Now Kareen-del-Harleem was blind to his whereabouts. It was time to visit Bernado. He needed to secure his first genetic prize and insist that the man with Goldenrod, find the second. His hands dropped from the Gold-alloy controls. He was finished for today. Things were progressing well. He already had one genetic prize and perhaps with encouragement the future Emperor would still find the second. And ... once Bernado ruled the planet, Kareen would have access to whatever gold could be scoured from the cities of Ankoletia.

He hadn't expected that this planet 279would meet all three objectives ... slaves, gold, and high-quality-unaltered genetic material! It was exhilarating. The bonus he would collect from supervising the conquest of a planet that was this valuable ... well, he would never have to leave Harleem again. He headed for the combat training room. He had a few hours before his first visit with Bernado.

Weeks later

Kareen entered the control room. Everyone was either hovering over a holograph map or watching his movements as he approached the Strategy Bench. "What do you have that couldn't wait?"

There was a tremor of excitement when the Leader of his scientific team placed a finger on the map image. "Here is where they will take it."

"Where is *here* and what is *it?*" he asked irritably.

"A very ... *very* large shipment of gold has begun moving across this planet."

"Are you sure it is gold ... and why have they moved it?" He asked pointedly.

"These questions are exactly why we have waited until now to advise you. At first, we weren't sure it was gold. The signature is distorted and there are only a handful of men involved in moving the supply."

"Curious ... could the gold be shielded?" was Kareen-del-Harleem's abbreviated response.

"Our assumption as well. So, we filtered for typical shielding materials, but nothing matched ... until we tried ... *clay*. It is definitely gold."

Kareen-del-Harleem's gaze went back to the holograph map. "You said you know where they are taking it?"

"The City is called Qar-ana. It is considered the ruling city of the northern hemisphere."

"Well done! Prepare the Transporter for Pechora." It was time to visit Bernado again!

"Oh ... it's you," a surprised Bernado commented as he walked into his study. Bernado hadn't called *him*, so there was only one explanation. 'Something important has happened.' Bernado laid his things on a chair and attentively waited for Kareen-del-Harleem to speak.

"Events are unfolding in a most promising manner. You will soon be Emperor if you follow my instructions with care."

Bernado nodded in agreement to the request.

"The secret warriors that you keep in the lower level, must be sent away. They are not needed." Kareen knew this would complete Bernado's dependence on *Goldenrod*. "There is a man in Qar-ana called Craslin. He will unwittingly help place you on that throne, because of what he has already accomplished. You will need a large and well-organized Militia. In this he has made significant progress. You will need superior weapons to assure the success of this Militia, and this too has been realized by this man. The weapon is called the Brass Sling."

Bernado remembered the skill with which Kareen-del-Harleem used his gold bracelets. He looked at them and said, "But you must have weapons you can give me that would surpass anything Craslin has built?"

"I told you ... there are rules. Even if I could give you a weapon, the *system* must remain in balance and would respond by introducing something of equal power against my weapon. No ... it cannot be done. You have the Necklace ... it is enough. But I can *assist* you ... within limits"

'There it is again,' observed Bernado, 'he talks of his limits.'

"You will need resources ... like gold ... to sustain your rise to Emperor. A very large shipment of gold bars will soon be delivered to Craslin."

A terrifying thought suddenly took hold of Bernado. Craslin, appointed by Executive Order, to the highest office in the land, was far ahead of Bernado in the race to the throne ... according to what the Strange Visitor had just shared. It must have shown on his face because the Visitor had stopped talking. Bernado decided he might as well confront him about his fears. "Why ... why have you chosen to support me when ... someone else," he couldn't make himself say the name, "is in a better position to become Emperor?"

Without elaboration Kareen-del-Harleem simply said, "We have chosen you ... you have chosen us."

Bernado's face relaxed. He unconsciously moved closer to the Necklace as he considered who 'us' might be.

"The gold will be in Qar-ana soon," Kareen continued. "I want you to leave tomorrow. Remember ... send the warriors back to where they came from ... immediately."

As soon as the stranger was gone, Bernado went to Mishri. "I have received notice from the Quorum. You are needed immediately at Ou-Leesen Pass. Choose ten of your warriors to stay behind to guard the Trackers."

Mishri bowed in obedience to Bernado's instructions, but he knew where he must go. He would quickly return to Shanteef, at the Keep. The command for the El-Bhat Band to leave Pechora was ridiculous. Pechora was strategic. The Quorum would never give it up and retreat to the Southland Mountains. Bernado had lied. For now, Mishri would let the matter sit ... until he could discuss this new development with the Quorum Leader. Then they would decide how they would deal with this Storlenian traitor!

Mishri gathered his men and within the hour, his El-Bhat Band had disappeared into the night, heading for a secret pass, west of Border Pass that was so narrow, men could only move through it in single file. Soon he would be in the Keep, discussing the next step in the conquest of Storlenia!

Early in the morning, before leaving, Bernado met with his Assistant. "I will be gone for quite a while." He slipped his hands into black leather gloves. "I see that the El-Bhat are *all* gone ... a problem that I hadn't anticipated. So ... watch the prisoners *closely*. Increase the quality of Urshen's food. When I return, I want him healthy ... and still in his cell."

The Assistant nodded in obedience but that only reminded Bernado of past failures, so he added, "To be sure ... drug their food ... every day!"

The Necklace from Harleem

Chapter 45 - Pheasant and conspiracy

Why? was the question on Bernado's mind, as he headed for Qar-ana, in obedience to Kareen-del-Harleem's instruction. As informed, Bernado knew that Craslin had planned and put in place all the elements that Bernado would need, to feed his ambition to become Emperor of the planet.

But ... *why* would the Head Guild Master of the highest executive governing body in all Storlenia, agree to let him saddle up beside him as his new Assistant? The place he needed to be ... if he was going to take over Craslin's position.

He had two things to think about. First, what could he offer that would convince Craslin beyond all doubt, that he *needed* Bernado at his side? And secondly, how was he going to remove the stigma of being the Head Guild Master of a *Tracking* Guild? After all, the Tracking Guild had always been aloof ... set apart from the other Guilds. By their creed, they *needed* to be set apart *and* they were incorruptible. So why would Craslin believe his proposal.

"Hello, my name is Bernado, Head Guild Master of the Tracking Guild in Pechora and I happen to know that you are planning to conquer the planet and place yourself as undisputed ruler. And by the way, I am here to help." It seemed ridiculous.

The distance between *unbelievable* and *believable* was enormous. Somehow he needed to convince Craslin that he needed Bernado ... to assist him in his climb to the fortress of power above. But how?

Further down the road he suddenly laughed aloud when he realized the solution. His weakness was also his strength! Certainly, one of the biggest hurdles to Craslin's success was the Tracking Guild, dedicated to preventing people like Craslin from ever accomplishing his objective. But Bernado had the power to influence and confuse the Tracking Guilds, long enough until it was too late for them to be effective.

The only thing left ... would be to convince Craslin that Bernado had abandoned his Tracker oath, for ambitions that were in line with his own. As proof, he would tell him about the Trackers held hostage in his prison cells. Fortunately for Bernado, he had sent the three young people to the Planning and Development Guild of Qar-ana, to search for Urshen. There must be a record of their visit to validate his story. Perhaps the Head Guild Master would be interested to know, that among those Trackers was one of the heroes involved in the El-Bhat purge at Border Pass ... Urshen!

He was suddenly very glad that Urshen was still in his cell, instead of being tortured by the Quorum. He laughed again, "Perhaps this will be easier than I thought." He patted the bag that was hanging from his saddle ... carefully hiding the Necklace and the little green stone.

"My my ..." a delighted Craslin said to himself, as he peered over the balcony at the Visitor. "I've been thinking about inviting you and suddenly here you are. The man who holds Urshen prisoner," he whispered to the man below. "And soon you will give me Urshen. The man who stands between me and Zephra," Craslin muttered as he headed for his office.

Inside Craslin's elegant office, the two men of power sat across from each other, exchanging pleasantries. Anxious to begin the serious part of their discussion, Bernado suggested, "I have come here today to offer my services and to pass on intelligence that I believe will be of significant value to the greatest Leader of Storlenia." Bernado had decided to start with a neutral proposal. Something that any Tracking Guild Master would say ... and yet, something that could tease one into thinking that there were hidden implications of great importance. With a tilt of his head, he continued, "Perhaps we can begin our discussions over lunch. This will allow time for me to bathe and change into something acceptable."

Craslin smiled in return, "My Assistant will clear my appointments for the rest of the afternoon. I understand that you are somewhat of a connoisseur when it comes to food and wine. I will alert my staff to prepare a lunch that would be fitting for someone of your taste."

Bernado's eyebrows lifted slightly, surprised that Craslin would know this detail. 'Lunch is certainly going to be interesting,' he thought, and smiled in appreciation.

"I will have my Aide take you to your room. There is a bell rope beside the door. If you need anything, just pull it and one of my experienced Aides will come immediately."

Bernado nodded in gratitude then headed for the door. With his hand on the doorknob, he turned and said, "Perhaps destiny brings us together. See you at lunch."

'Destiny? ... Maybe,' Craslin considered after Bernado had left. But he had always believed that cunning was more important than destiny. It was why he had chosen to have lunch on the terrace overlooking the loading yard. The wagons were due to arrive sometime before lunch and he wanted to have a view when the bricks were unloaded. He also had purposely assigned Bernado to the Diplomatic Guest Room. A room that allowed his spies to hear and see everything.

Soaking in the bath, Bernado considered the comment about him being a specialist on food and wine. He wondered if Craslin was referring to the meal he had served to the seven Trackers. Could he already know about Urshen ... and Ranoof? 'Regardless, this could still work to my advantage,' he decided. Bathed and dressed, he anxiously headed for his rendezvous.

The fresh red flowers provided a pleasant contrast to the white cotton table cloth. Bernado picked up a piece of the silver setting. He admired its heavy feel and ornate finishing. The food hadn't arrived yet ... they were probably waiting for Craslin.

Bernado went to the balcony. The early afternoon sun was shaded by the light blue awning overhead. Not too far away, he saw a crew unloading bricks. A diverse crew. Two Trackers, a man in a Robe and the expected laborers. He was surprised to see a member of the Redemption Guild. Perhaps this was part of his redemption?

'Or perhaps not!' Bernado recognized the *walk*. He remembered the image of Protas leaving his Guild months ago, heading for Ou-Leesen Pass. 'How could you be here ... now?' he thought, as his gaze wandered back to the bricks. 'Protas and bricks ... there is something here that doesn't add up.' Then he remembered Kareen-del-Harleem saying, *A very large shipment of gold bars will soon be delivered to Craslin.*

'Clever ... ordinary bricks delivered by a small crew of manual laborers,' Bernado smiled. The Strange Visitor's prediction was unfolding exactly as he said it would. He turned around when he heard footsteps.

"Do you eat out here often?" Bernado inquired. "It's wonderful. If *I* worked here, I would eat on this balcony every chance I could."

"Not as often as I would like," Craslin responded.

Bernado turned to the view again. "I am very impressed with the expansion of your new Militia Guard. I saw them when I arrived. So many. You see them outside, inside ... they appear to be everywhere," he said waving his hand in the direction of the loading yard. "And their training ... if I didn't know better, I would suspect that you had help from Trackers. But that would be impossible ... wouldn't it?"

'So, he wants to work here as my Assistant and he knows about Ranoof,' Craslin thought, impressed by Bernado's keen intellect.

"All things change," Craslin responded, ignoring Bernado's reference to Ranoof. "Especially things that have outlived their purpose." Ordinarily he wouldn't make the comparison between his new Militia and the outmoded Trackers, to a Head Guild Master. But he suspected that Bernado had ambitions outside the Tracking Guild.

"It appears that your Militia has something that Trackers don't have." Bernado pointed to the Brass Sling Machines mounted on the towers.

"It's called the Brass Sling. I purchased the initial design and the Mechanical Guild is working to expand its capabilities. Perhaps if you stay a few days, I could arrange a demonstration?"

"I am *a man of weapons*. I would love the opportunity."

"Consider it done. Shall we start lunch?"

The conversation drifted to daily life in Qar-ana. Wonderfully prepared dishes were brought, eaten, and removed. With the meal finished, Bernado's eyes lingered a moment too long in the direction of the loading yard.

"Something caught your eye?" Craslin inquired.

"The man in the Robe reminds me of someone who was wanted by the Trackers years ago."

"I will ask the Militia to escort you to the yard, and you can investigate for yourself." Craslin was not concerned about the secret of the gold bricks, because Nusdek was instructed to allow no one, including Bernado, past the locked Gates of the Loading Yard.

"Thank you. It will only take a moment. And if he is who I think he is, I will have your Militia escort him to the local Tracking Guild. Would you mind if we continued our conversation tomorrow?"

Craslin pushed himself away from the table. "I welcome it. My Aide will provide you with the details when you return."

When Bernado left, Craslin returned to the railing. The unloading was going well. They would be finished in another hour. And now that he had seven wagonloads of gold, he could fuel his growing Militia until they were ready to conquer *all* Ankoletia.

Once conquered, Shaksbah would be run like a large labour camp, providing wealth to Storlenia by shipping goods through the ports of Airiken and Aqabah. Thanks to the *shrewd* efforts of the Shaksbali Quorum! Contented, he smiled, left the terrace, and returned to his office.

Chapter 46 - The Regent of Shaksbah

Hours earlier — before Craslin and Bernado met for lunch

The Militia Guard spotted the wagons as soon as they rolled into Qar-ana, heavy with their cargo of bricks. Without a word spoken, the two hundred men formed a security escort to the delivery yard, of the Planning and Development Guild. At first Ee-lath was frightened by the display of armed Militia when they silently positioned themselves amongst the wagons. But the two Trackers in the lead wagon didn't seem bothered at all. Protas nudged him with an elbow and said, with a wide grin, "Almost like a parade." Protas didn't like the attention they were attracting, but an hour later they rolled into their destination and the Guild Gates were locked behind them. The small group began the task of unloading thousands of bricks into a secure holding area.

Under the hot sun, it wasn't long before Ee-lath was scurrying about with his water jug. He kept his eyes on the Guards, especially the ones on top of the towers. When he asked Protas about the strange objects mounted on every tower, he was surprised that Protas knew nothing regarding them. "Best to pretend they are not there," Protas advised. Ee-lath nodded in agreement and took his water to the next thirsty worker.

Later, the boy noticed the important looking Tracker who stood just outside the Gate. He passed the water jug to Protas. "I think he is watching you," Ee-lath whispered.

Casting a cautious glance in his direction, Protas whispered, "I know him. This could be trouble for me. If we get separated … stay with Ou-Leesen and I will find you." The words were barely spoken when he noticed Sausage in front of the locked iron gates. Mid-stride, Sausage turned his head, Protas nodded, and a moment later the dog was gone.

The Necklace from Harleem

Outside the Gates, Bernado watched from the shadows. He took a moment to study the lookout towers that were spaced every fifty paces, all fitted with the Brass Sling. Then, he turned his attention to the two Trackers. He had never seen the one Tracker before ... but was surprised to see Stek! It had been a while since he sent him off to the Quorum with the location of Cradle Mountain Cave. And now here he was, helping to bring the gold to Qar-ana. It confirmed that it must be a gift from the Quorum. 'Once again ... Stek has earned my deepest respect!' Bernado admitted, glad to have the Tracker as an ally.

Occasionally Stek's gaze wandered past the wagons while participating in the monotonous back and forth unloading of the bricks from Shaksbah. He slowed when he spotted the Guild Master standing outside the Gate, resting against the pillar with his eyes fixed on him. There was no other communication extended ... but Stek knew what he had to do. He strolled towards Bernado.

Protas hoped that Stek had his story ready.

Ou-Leesen pretended not to notice, his green eyes following Stek from under the rim of his large sun hat. He knew their lives depended on Stek's quick thinking.

"I take it that one of these labourers is Ou-Leesen?" The Head Guild Master questioned Stek.

"Yes."

Bernado had never met a man with such economy of speech. "Why is Protas here? I thought the Quorum might have dispatched him as soon as they saw him."

"Ask him to remove his Robe ... and I doubt you will have more questions regarding Protas and the Quorum," was all Stek would offer.

Now Bernado understood. The punishments of the Quorum were severe. And to ensure that the message did not go unnoticed among their loyal subjects, they allowed the victims to live ... as scarred slaves. "Protas is wanted by the Tracking Guild ... for murder. Perhaps he doesn't have to die if he is *useful?*" he suggested to Stek.

"He is *very useful*," Stek replied.

Bernado acknowledged Stek's response with a respectful nod. "Are these bricks a gift from the Quorum?"

"More like a payment ... for the rights to two seaports. Port Airiken and Port Aqabah."

"Nicely done," Bernado complemented Stek. Once he ruled all Ankoletia, those boats would transport more than trade. They would also carry slaves. "When the wagons are unloaded, is your assignment finished?"

"We will probably return with more wagons ... loaded with bricks," Stek replied.

The Guild Master was pleased as he contemplated the growing wealth of his future empire. "I look forward to your next visit to Qar-ana. We will have much to talk about," Bernado advised Stek. He had never known anyone like Stek, and he intended to keep him on a leash. Finished, Bernado left the Militia Guards with a message. As soon as the bricks were unloaded, they were to take the man in the Robe to a prison cell in the Planning Guild ... until he could make arrangements for his transfer to the Qar-ana Tracking Guild.

While strolling back to the Guild offices, he admired the manicured gardens and the magnificent architecture of the buildings. It inspired him to make a self-fulfilling prophecy. "Soon, these buildings will also contain a throne room ... from which I will rule my people."

As soon as the unloading was finished, the Gates opened, and the Militia Guards walked straight to Protas to take him into custody.

Biskin shouted, "Stop," in protest. He moved towards them, hand on his knife. A Brass Sling from above fired a warning shot that split open the side oak panel of the wagon nearest Biskin. He turned to look at the Tower, suddenly aware of the dangerous power of the strange weapon. He looked at Stek who shook his head 'no'.

The following day, Craslin stood as Bernado was escorted into his office. He was anxious to see where the conversation would go.

The Tracker opened the discussion. "I watched your Militia practice yesterday afternoon after my business with the man in the Robe was completed. They are trained extremely well. I doubt Trackers could have done better." Bernado was staring into Craslin's emotionless face. "Imagine ... a Militia with the skill and training of Trackers but with allegiance to the Planning and Development Guild."

"Imagine," Craslin replied.

Bernado smiled a knowing smile. "For over a thousand years, the Trackers have provided the military might. As a people, we have come to believe that only Trackers could do this. You have done what no one has considered. I am truly looking forward to seeing the Brass Sling in operation. If it works as well as I think it will, why would you stop with placing it on Towers?"

"Why indeed," Craslin added with a thin smile. "Perhaps that is why you have decided to pay me a visit ... to see the Brass Sling?"

Bernado knew it was time to tell him why he was there.

"Men like us know, that curiosity can never compete with the appeal of vision and competence. *You* are the reason I am here. The rumours do not do justice to what you have accomplished, since Axion ... disappeared. I do not doubt that you will accomplish greater things. But where are the men that will do your bidding, thus allowing you to push your ambitions to even higher heights. Men who have the skill to anticipate problems and provide solutions. Men who know how to deal with the peculiarities of the Tracking Guild. And who know how to provide sufficient smoke to confuse, delay and generally reduce their effectiveness ... until it is too late. I think that such a man would be particularly valuable to yourself ... wouldn't you agree?"

"Tell me about the Trackers you are holding in your prison cells," Craslin carefully responded.

What Bernado omitted to tell Craslin, was after he had left the Militia training grounds, he had wandered the halls of the Guild looking for the Library. There he noticed a young woman with light brown hair. She was one of the threesome who came to Pechora looking for Urshen. And when he sent them off to the Planning and Development Guild he never expected to see them again. Never mind right inside the Guild, as Guests!

The young woman was busy looking for a book. Bernado avoided being seen, as he strolled quietly between the shelves. Eventually he picked a book and sat down in a large chair, hidden in a corner. Soon he heard a young woman's voice ... it sounded like the other *woman. He got up and cautiously peered around the corner. It was her! But with hair adorned and dressed like a lady, she was not easily recognizable. He returned to the corner and listened. Something about 'more wagons arriving ... she would have to miss lunch ...'*

"Sorry Yaneek," she said and left the Library.

Bernado was thinking that it had been weeks since he sent them away. 'And yet these three are still here as Guests of Craslin!'

The black-haired beauty who showed up in Pechora, was definitely a Tinker, and yet now she was wearing Storlenian clothes, expensive Storlenian clothes. Quite interesting,' he concluded.

"Six ... there are six Tracker prisoners in my cells." He smiled a knowing smile and added, "But if you include the young man dressed like a Tracker, that makes *seven*. Yes ... a young man by the name of ... Urshen. I assume that he is the Tracker you wanted to know about?"

Craslin was beginning to think that Bernado had spies among his staff. He had a question of his own he wanted to ask, but instead he simply nodded yes.

Bernado continued, "It seems everyone is searching for Urshen. The El-Bhat Quorum ... Trackers ... and a very concerned young woman who came by my Guild weeks ago. He is apparently quite the trophy. It's a dilemma knowing where to send him. What do you advise I do?"

Craslin was tapping his fingers in staccato on his desk top, as he considered what he was about to say.

"*You* ... would be Regent over all of Shaksbah ... and report to me. *I* will govern all of Ankoletia."

"Splendid," Bernado said with enthusiasm. 'Splendid ... that you will have worked so hard to place me on the Emperor's Throne,' the Tracker thought with delight. Both men rose to shake hands. Then the Tracker left for his room.

As the door closed, Craslin felt a tremor in his confidence. He would need to be careful with this Head Guild Master. On the *bright side*, his rapid rise to power would gain even more momentum, because of Bernado's influence and skill. He would immediately assign him to expand the Militia until it was fifty thousand strong. A Militia of that size, with the advantage of the Brass Sling, was the key to becoming the undisputed Ruler of the world. It would give him the military might to invade and conquer Shaksbah. To take all of their gold. And to disband the Tracking Guild. By then, there would be no Quorum. The El-Bhat would work for him, collecting Shaksbali taxes for the needs of his growing empire.

On the *dark side*, Bernado seemed to have schemes of his own. And if he didn't want to end up like Axion, he couldn't afford to relax his grip on the ambitious Guild Master. He would keep Bernado close, where his spies could watch him every minute of every day.

Knowing he wasn't going back with Stek, Biskin passed him the signed and sealed documents for the Ports. "You will need these ... I have decided to stay here and help Protas."

"You sure this is the best use of your time ... waiting for Protas to get out of prison?" Stek asked as they prepared to part company.

"I still feel the same," Biskin responded. "My Gift tells me I need to protect him. Downside of a Gift ... always being told what to do," he joked. "What about *your* plans? I saw you talking to Bernado. Bet he was surprised to see you here."

"The changes in Qar-ana provoke deep concern," Stek expressed. "I am tempted to stay here until I learn enough to allow the Tracking Guild to press charges. But I think I will be of better use if I stay with Ou-Leesen. Never thought I would say that about an El-Bhat."

"But he's not El-Bhat, is he?" Biskin offered.

"No ... not really. There's a destiny that follows that man around. Guess I want to be part of it. Well, good luck with Protas."

Biskin mounted his horse, waved, and disappeared in the crowd.

As the team of labourers prepared to leave Qar-ana, Ou-Leesen turned to Stek. "Tell me what I should do. I have been inside Storlenia so long I have forgotten how to think."

Stek nodded. "Tonight ... once the horses are fed, bind their hooves with rags. When the moon is high in the sky, leave the wagons behind and head south. Before heading east, exchange the horses for new ones."

Fifty leagues outside the Capital City, Ou-Leesen asked Stek. "What have they done with my Advisor?"

"The man at the Gate was the Guild Master of the Pechora Tracking Guild. He houses El-Bhat as well as select prisoners ... like Protas. He had sent Protas as a gift to the Quorum and now he wants him back."

"He was a good Advisor. What will become of him?"

"Don't know, but Biskin will protect him the best he can."

"I will need an Advisor ..." Ou-Leesen stared at Stek.

"For how long?"

"As long as it takes to remove the Quorum."

Stek nodded slowly as he considered the offer. "Okay. Never been an Advisor before, but I guess you already know that."

Later, in the shade of a large tree, Ou-Leesen shared, "Things that I don't understand with my mind, but yet see with my eyes, trouble me."

"Perhaps I can help," Stek offered.

Staring into the distance Ou-Leesen began, "My mind tells me that you and Biskin are enemy Trackers. But Biskin saved my life when my El-Bhat Advisor was intent on ending it. And together, you traded away valuable Storlenian shipping rights for Shaksbali gold. How is this possible? And how is it that a Tracker, can be an Advisor to a Leader of a small band of El-Bhat?"

"Education," Stek replied thoughtfully. "Perhaps I too have a question. How is it that an El-Bhat warrior with the blood of Sherilin – Protas told me – would even consider asking a Tracker to be his Advisor?"

Ou-Leesen nodded in agreement. "The future is not clear to me. But this I believe. Old things must pass away to make way for the new. In this new future, a man will be measured differently. Where he lives will no longer be important. The ways of the Sherilin will return. I am sure of it."

"By *old things* I guess you include the Quorum. Do your men see things as you do? Or will we be left alone as two men, to accomplish what two men cannot?"

"Our trip to Qar-ana," answered Ou-Leesen, "helped me to become a free man. If I am alone ... I am alone. But I think not."

Chapter 47 - Escape to the Crestal Mountains

Months earlier when Craslin was still the Assistant Guild Master, Axion had invited Aram-Dentee for lunch. By the time the meal was finished, Axion knew that the Butler was an Assassin and Craslin could no longer be trusted

After Axion had thrown the bleeding chicken out the window, he jumped and drifted downstream, until he spotted the lantern. When Axion reached the shore, Jokta pulled him out and led him to a safe place where he changed into dry clothes. They headed east.

Searching for information on Aram-Dentee, led Axion to the Communication Guild where the thread of secrecy began, and he learned that the title *Butler* was synonymous with Assassin.

He was convinced that Craslin was behind the mystery, and considered approaching the Trackers, but knew he would be dead before they walked through the front door. His only course was to fake his death and escape to a faraway place ... immediately. This would also force the hand of Aram-Dentee, who would disappear with his payment, just as soon as Axion was presumed dead. That should end the threat ... if everyone believed it.

Both he and Jokta were dressed as common labourers, looking for work. His plan was to travel to the only place he would find men he could trust completely.

By the third day, Jokta decided it was time to get down to business. He asked, "How far are we going?"

"To the Crestal Mountains ... I need to find Special Assignment Trackers."

Jokta was aware that Special Assignment Trackers existed. "Didn't know they had Headquarters."

"They don't. Before I left, I used the Great Seal to prepare a few letters of introduction. It should help us in our search for the people I need to find."

"Why do we need to go so far to find help?"

"First, Craslin needs to believe I'm dead. But probably more important ... our nation is in a whole lot of trouble. Not long ago, I received reports that battles were fought with El-Bhat at Lundeen Forest and Border Pass."

Surprised, Jokta turned and stared at Axion.

"Yeah, it was kept very quiet," Axion explained. "The Trackers in charge even delayed the reports a couple of weeks. Wanted to know everything from everybody before they sent in reports they knew would raise more than a few eyebrows."

"I assume that we won the skirmish and continue to hold Border Pass?" Jokta asked.

"Actually, we had already lost Border Pass ... and we didn't even know it!"

Jokta gave a low whistle. "This just gets better by the minute, and now you're going to tell me that a group of El-Bhat were hiding in Lundeen Forest waiting for orders?"

"No, I wish it were that simple. The El-Bhat that we fought in Lundeen, came from Seven Oaks Redemption Guild, where they had taken over the facility. When an entire Tinker Train showed up at their doorstep to challenge them, they chased them with War Wagons all the way to Lundeen Forest. Luckily, we knew they were coming. And – praise the Fates above – the second El-Bhat Band, hiding close by, didn't engage in the conflict!"

"Seems ... impossible!" Jokta exclaimed. "War Wagons carrying a Band of El-Bhat inside Storlenia ... all the way to Lundeen where another Band was waiting?" Jokta was shaking his head. "How do you intend to get your Guild back?"

"First, I'm afraid it's going to get worse before it gets better.

"What do you mean worse?"

"Craslin is busy assembling a Militia for his own ambitions," he said dryly. "Jokta, I don't know if I ever will get my position back. It's not the reason I asked you to help me. My biggest concern is that our country could be facing another Great War. And this time I intend to involve the assistance of the Crestal Mountain people *before* we get to that point."

Jokta replied, "All right. When we reach the next town, I'm going to send a message to my wife. She thinks I'm gone for a week."

At the end of the fifth day, while leaving the tavern, Jokta's keen eyesight caught the movement of a man down the street as he ducked into a doorway. "This Aram-Dentee ... does he dress a bit unusual?"

The two men stared at each other considering what to do next. "We need to leave right away," Axion finally said. "I'll go back to the hotel, pay for three nights, and then leave through the back door. You head for the stables and trade our wagon for fast horses. I'll meet you there as soon as I can."

It was unfortunate that he was spotted, but now he knew that Axion had help. A Tracker. It explained a lot. He stayed in the doorway for a long time. He was in no hurry, he was sure he knew where they were going. It was a special ability that never let him down ... and always guaranteed a successful kill.

Jokta, a retired Tracker, knew they needed to change how they journeyed if they were to keep ahead of the Assassin. They travelled at night through the hill country, constantly changed horses, avoided Inns, slept in forests instead. When possible they avoided roads and followed wilderness trails. They stopped often to ask instructions to places they had no intention of going to. If it rained they pressed on, knowing their tracks would disappear. Once, during a two-day downpour, Jokta left the trail and went in search of a farm. They stayed a week, working in exchange for food and a place to sleep.

When an exhausted Axion finally arrived at the foothills of the Crestal Mountains, he asked his friend to continue without him.

"Here are the letters, signed with the Great Seal. Find the Gatherer. He leads the Unit of Special Trackers. Bring him to me."

Jokta carefully folded the letters and placed them in his waterproof pouch. "Take care not to leave this Inn. I will ask someone to leave your food outside your door, because you are very sick."

"You fear that Aram-Dentee is close behind?"

"I don't know where he is and I don't need to know. It is enough to know he is a Butler."

Axion knew that his friend would be gone awhile, giving him lots of time to plan.

The Necklace from Harleem

Jokta had used his last letter of appeal at a hilltop village, deep in the Crestal Mountains. It was more difficult to find the Gatherer than he had anticipated. He was lying on his bed when a knock came to his door. He was hopeful that his search was over ... but instead a ragged villager with sad eyes stood before him, an obvious request for his assistance.

"My children need medical help. Could you spare a few shekels? I have already approached the villagers, so I'm left to beg from travellers."

Jokta went to fetch his pouch. "How many of your children need this help?"

"Two," the villager said quietly. The Tracker grabbed some shekels, paused, and asked, "How far do you need to travel to find medical assistance?"

"Qar-ana," was his hesitant reply. The Tracker decided he needed to give more, so he went back to his pouch. "This is all I can spare, but I have a friend that I left a few day's journey from here. He could probably afford a lot more. I leave tomorrow, if you care to tag along?"

The villager gratefully took the shekels and nodded in the affirmative. "See you tomorrow," he quietly added.

When the old Tracker left in the early hours of the morning, the same villager was waiting outside. Jokta threw his traveling bag over his shoulder. "I see you travel light," Jokta said, noticing that the villager only carried a very small bag. The villager offered a weak smile but said nothing.

"My name's Jokta. What's yours?"

"Finn," was the quiet reply.

"Well we best be off," Jokta said, and headed south. They travelled until the sun was high in the sky before stopping to eat. Dropping his bag on the forest floor, he leaned down and removed the lunch that the innkeeper had provided. They both rested against a tree trunk, but Jokta was the only one eating. He stopped. "Did you not bring any food?" He asked his traveling companion.

Finn looked timidly at the food. "Perhaps you can spare a bit of your own?"

"Of course," Jokta said reassuringly. "I've had better," he passed half a portion, "but I'm guessing you're not that fussy." He smiled at the traveller.

Days later, the sun had set by the time Jokta knocked on Axion's door. The ex-Guild Master looked past his friend's shoulder in anticipation. But once they both walked into the lighted room, it was obvious that Jokta had failed to bring the Gatherer.

"Axion, this is Finn. A villager I bumped into. He could use some financial help to get his sick kids to Qar-ana. But first, how about you buy us dinner? It's been a long day! Then we will talk about his kids."

"Sorry to hear that your kids are so sick," Axion started the conversation when they began eating.

Finn nodded, feeling a bit uncomfortable.

Jokta decided to jump in. He would do the begging. "It's not often that a great opportunity like this comes along. I mean to help kids who are sick enough they need to travel to Qar-ana."

"How much more do you need?" Axion asked.

"About a hundred ... I guess," Finn suggested, while looking down at his food.

"Consider it done," was Axion's generous reply. "I'll have the shekels ready in the morning before you leave. And I'll see about getting you a room for tonight."

Back in the room, Axion was anxious to hear Jokta's report.

"Not much to say. The people are friendly, but nobody knows who the Gatherer is. They said they would check around, so I left one of your letters of introduction at every village as I travelled deeper into the Crestal Mountains. I told them it was very important that I meet the Gatherer and would return to check on progress. I only met Finn on my way back."

Axion considered Jokta's report for a while then explained, "The Special Trackers are a cautious lot. I'm not surprised that you found nothing. I guess we will just have to sit tight and wait."

"Any sign of Aram-Dentee?" Jokta asked.

"No, but then I haven't left my room until tonight."

Jokta got up and headed for his bed. "It was nice of you to offer so much to Finn," he praised Axion as he slipped under the covers.

"Like you said, these chances don't come around often. Especially sitting in Qar-ana. I wonder what the names of the children are." But Jokta was already asleep.

Axion cashed in a gold coin the next morning and set aside a hundred shekels for Finn. They found him outside, ready to leave. They shook hands and Axion handed him the bag of shekels. "Pleased we could help. What are the names of your children?"

Finn took the bag and hefted it a bit. "I haven't held so much money in a long time." He smiled gratefully and looked at his two benefactors. "Their names? Well that would be ... Axion and Jokta."

Aram-Dentee observed from the shadows as they gave coins to a beggar. Soon the threesome headed for the eastern forests. The Butler Guild had the best maps of anyone, and those maps informed him that his prey would have to exit the same way they entered. He would wait ... and then it would be over.

Chapter 48 - The misfits

Axion and Jokta glanced at each other as if to say, 'So this is the Gatherer?' Then they looked at Finn. "Thanks for answering our summons. I suppose this was your way of getting to know who we are," Axion inferred.

"We hear of troubling things. One cannot be too careful. But then you must already know that, if you've come all the way from Qar-ana to find me," Finn said quietly. "Guild Master, we mustn't talk out here in the street. Meet me back up the road, just after the bridge. Enter the forest on the left side." Finn turned to go and then shouted back, "Thank you for your kindness good Sirs."

Once in the forest, they spotted Finn ... waiting. He beckoned for them to follow him. They barely kept him in their sight as they raced through forest and across valleys to keep up with him for the next ten leagues. Finally, he stopped in a meadow that backed onto rising foothills.

"This is *your* country," Axion commented, after he caught his breath. "I'm surprised you need to take such extreme caution in your homeland."

"It's how we stay alive. The nature of the assignments we take demands it."

Jokta, a retired Tracker himself, had questions of his own. He had heard about the *Specialists* but it was mostly legends discussed around the fire pit to pass evenings away. "How long have the Special Assignment Trackers been in operation," Jokta asked Finn, amazed that he had met the Gatherer.

"The Group has been around for hundreds of years."

"I've often wondered why the Group was formed. After all, what intrigue could the Tracking Guild not handle by itself?"

"It wasn't that at all," Finn smiled. "Our Group began because of a misfit."

"A misfit?" Jokta said, curious to hear the rest of the story.

"Yes ... a misfit. He was a Tracker that had skills, stamina, and intellect far above everyone else. He was continually restless, never content with the everyday activity of peaceful times. So, on his own, he began investigating what only he saw as suspicious behaviour.

Turns out, he was very good at what he did, and he brought in a continuous stream of criminals ... before they stopped him."

"Stopped him?" Axion questioned.

"They had to ... temporarily. They couldn't have a Tracker accountable only to himself. From the beginning, the other Guilds have allowed the Tracking Guild to be autonomous, but only on conditions that we govern our own. The first step was to find a Gatherer, because if there was one misfit, there was sure to be more. And there were."

"How many misfits do you manage?" Axion asked.

"Twenty. Assuming Far-fel makes it back."

"A particularly dangerous assignment?" Jokta guessed.

"There were many reports of people gone missing. And rumours that occasionally they would show up dead ... as old corpses. People started to refer to the killer as the *Silent Reaper*. And I've lost three good men just trying to find him. He is the most notorious criminal our Group has ever come across."

"How easy would it be for you to gather your men together?" Axion asked, ready to talk about why he was there.

"It would take some time. And in my lifetime ... it has never happened. So why don't you tell me why you have come for our help."

"I am here for two reasons. First, because our nation is in trouble, and secondly, because I was forced to flee from a hired Assassin."

"Tell me about the Assassin."

"He is a Butler, hired by my Assistant."

"You are lucky to be alive," Finn said grimly. "Tell me about our national troubles."

"I have recently received reports that were hard to believe. El-Bhat forces had taken over the Seven Oaks Redemption Guild *and* Border Pass. The Trackers eventually defeated them, but only after the El-Bhat got as far north as Lundeen Forest. And they had War Wagons! Besides this, there was an off-the-record discussion about Shaksbali infiltration into our Guilds. Storlenians, who migrated to Shaksbah centuries ago, are being pressed into helping the El-Bhat. Many were found inside the Tracking Guild at Arborville and now they are busy scouring the other Tracking Guilds looking for Shaksbali spies." Axion paused, considering his next words. "I am afraid that the magnitude of this problem confirms that there are unspoken conspiracies in our country, that we know nothing about!" Axion's agitated voice slipped into a whisper as he glanced at Jokta, who was anxiously scanning the meadow below them.

Finn studied the two men for a while before he said, "I have read in our history that the Specialists have gathered before. But our law demands that the need be national, that the *matter of concern* cannot be dispatched by the local Tracking Guild and finally that the source of the request be unquestionable. Like the Qar-ana Head Guild Master of Planning. So ... it would appear, that I need to gather my men. I know where all of them are ... except for Far-fel. And we must wait for him." It was not Far-fel's skill that Finn needed. He wanted to know what was behind the success of the Silent Reaper. If he were going to gather his men to face a national crisis, he needed to understand how one man could kill three Specialists! "So now we go to the Place of Waiting," Finn announced. "It's a small cabin, in an isolated region of the Crestal Mountains." He stood up and led them into the forest.

The last day of their journey was spent cutting their way through trail-less brush and forest. They finally descended into a ravine where they came across the cabin, nestled among a small grove of trees.

"Two of my men will be here within a few days. In the meantime, make no fires and leave the cabin only when required. The rest of my men will trickle in over the next three weeks."

As the door closed, the exhausted Tracker and Guild Master headed for a bed, not expecting to rise before the first Specialist arrived. Outside the cabin, Finn disappeared up the ravine like a ghost.

Having retrieved the Amulet from the Tracking Guild, Far-fel headed east, to find Finn

Far-fel was anxious to return to Finn with his findings. His discovery of the Necklace and the subverted Tracking Guild at Pechora made the death of the Silent Reaper almost irrelevant. And now, the Pechora Tracking Guild possessed the Necklace, an evil Device nobody had ever heard of before. The intelligence must be passed on to Finn! And if that wasn't enough, there was his healing experience with the Crystal Amulet. On his eastward journey to the Crestal Mountains where he would find Finn, he thought often of the Amulet and marvelled at his fortune to be brought to the very place where it was hidden away. It was a remarkable coincidence that begged many questions like, *Why was this Amulet in Pechora? Where did it come from? What was the power behind the crystal stone?*

But it was hard to think about the Amulet without remembering his experience with the Necklace. They were giant powers in opposition to each other. And he supposed that he had only scratched the surface of understanding them. When he accepted his assignment, Finn had been clear that his target was the Silent Reaper. But now Far-fel knew better. It was the Necklace!

Whenever he stopped to check if he was being followed, he cautiously took out the Amulet and held it. The cool touch reminded him that the nightmares were truly over.

He was still a couple of days from Finn when he started to feel that something was pulling him. Like an iron filing is pulled to a magnet. Initially he ignored it. His priority was to get back to Finn as quickly as possible! But later in the day when he felt that tug again, he took out the Amulet. As he suspected, the feeling was stronger when he held it. In fact, by holding it, he knew in what direction he must travel. But he didn't know how far it would be. Or for how long he would have to hold the Amulet. He took out his knife, cut off a strip of cloth from his shirt and bound the hand holding the Crystal. He was going to run until the Amulet told him he was there. He would only stop to drink.

When the sun set, he was still running. The coolness of the night caressed him while he ran through the dark, and when the shadows fled from the breaking dawn, he was still running.

By mid-morning he stood at the base of a mountain range, depleted. He sank to his knees, his sweaty clothes clinging to his body. His exhausted eyes stared at the cloth-bound hand holding the Amulet. He couldn't go on, but he must. "Please ... I need help, if I am to do your bidding."

This was the first time in his life that Far-fel had asked for help. It was humbling, but he had no choice. He waited ... and then added, "You saved me from slavery to the Green Power. I am ready to serve your power, but I need ..."

He gasped when a glowing Light seeped out between the cracks of his fingers, brighter than the daylight around him. He felt that Light enter his body and infuse him with energy. As soon as the light faded, he jumped to his feet and raced up the mountain, following the Amulet's direction. Later he was taken down into a valley that led to an upwards-climbing ravine. Within a few hours he was standing in front of a slab of quartz. 'This must be a door,' he thought as he searched for a way in. He found a hole in the shape of the Amulet and a moment later he was standing inside a Cave. He took precautions to close the door behind him.

Standing at the threshold, he absorbed the wonder of the sight before him. Being a man of the forest, the crystal forms of flowers, bushes, and the Tree, left him breathless. In front of him was a path that curved gently towards the centre of the Cave where he saw the top of that Tree. He did not assume the right to walk any further into this place of power. He thought for a while then finally said, "Why have you brought me here? Is it because I rescued the Amulet?"

In answer to his question, a wide crack appeared in the path. Then a Green Light began to pour out of the opening, swirling upward until it became an image of the Silent Reaper sitting on his chair and wearing the Necklace. Gripped by the returning nightmare, Far-fel unconsciously took a step backwards, confused, and fearful as to why the Green Light would be inside this Cave. A moment later, a thick green mist seeped from the Necklace, tumbled to the floor, and wound its way towards Far-fel like a snake. He backed up until he was stopped by the quartz door. Terrified and bewildered by the green mist, which continued to wind its way toward him, he wrenched his eyes from the abomination and looked towards the centre of the Cave where the Tree stood in majesty, and shouted in desperation, "Help me!"

In the blink of an eye the mist was gone, and the path was restored. Far-fel wiped the sweat from his forehead. He believed that he understood. The Necklace and its power did not belong inside this Cave, but it was meant to be an answer to his question. "You brought me here because I have experienced the evil of the Necklace ... not because I rescued the Amulet." Then added, "And because I loathe it and fear it."

Suddenly the Tree in the middle of the Cave began to shake its leaves, creating a sound of chimes and tinkling crystal, which increased until it filled the interior of the Cave, wrapping Far-fel in a joy that he never thought possible. On impulse, he slowly stepped down the path towards the Tree, hardly aware that he was moving. As he came to the Tree he dropped to his knees for the second time in his life.

The music stopped. The only sound he heard was his own breathing. His eyes drifted from the Tree to the floor before him. Suddenly it vanished, revealing an image of stars, a window to the night sky. But it wasn't the night sky of Ankoletia.

'Where am I?' he wondered. As if in answer to his question, he was pulled through that window, the stars fleeing behind him as he sped forward through space. To Far-fel the distances were unfathomable. He headed directly to a bright star in the middle of his vision. The heavens slipping behind him, faster and faster. Surprisingly, the Cave was not taking him to the star, but to a planet that circled it.

He descended through pink clouds until he found himself inside a building. A man came rushing forward to the person on a throne, with a message. First, he kissed a circle of gold on the floor then prostrated himself. "Most Holy One, we have another report – from the planet called Ankoletia."

"You may rise," the Harleem General commanded.

The man didn't move, but said with trembling lips, "I prefer submission ... the report is not in our favour. One of their kind was able to resist *Goldenrod*."

"Give me the details."

"After losing much of his *life* to the First Medallion, he successfully resisted the Second. In his depleted state, he managed to kill the bearer of the Golden Gift. But luckily, he used *Goldenrod* to restore his genetic life-patterns."

"Wonderful! Now we can study this unique specimen!"

"That should have happened ... except that he managed to completely break the link, shortly after we acquired his genetic signature. This has never been done before on this planet ... your Holiness."

"Could there have been *interference?*"

"Nothing from Balhok. We believe however, that he had access to ... *crystal power*." The man stopped to kiss the Gold Disc again, hoping to purify himself from the words he had spoken. "But ... if he possessed an Amulet, we could not have subjected him to the Necklace in the first place. We are confused and concerned ... your Holiness. Perhaps this race is stronger than we had anticipated."

"A threat, perhaps ..." the General considered the thought. "But more likely ... the genetic material we are always looking for. Is there anything else?"

"Yes," he said with enthusiasm.

"You may rise."

"Recently, one of our Daggers was in proximity to vast quantities of refined gold."

"How vast?" the General asked excitedly.

"The gold was partially shielded but our estimate is impressive ... your Holiness."

The Harleem Commander brushed his fingers across his gold-alloy Command Panel, allowing the anticipation of victory to wash over him. "You must keep me informed of any changes! Vast quantities of gold and excellent genetic material. I don't need to remind you how important these are to our race."

"No ... your Holiness." Again, the messenger prostrated himself and kissed the Gold Disc before leaving.

Far-fel moved closer to get a better look at the Gold Disc, surrounded by pink marble. The outline of the Necklace was carved in its centre. 'So, this is the origin of the Necklace and its power.' Far-fel had no sooner had that thought when he found himself back in the Cave kneeling, staring through the floor at a starry sky.

Before entering the Cave, Far-fel had decided to wear the Amulet. Still kneeling, he glanced at the stone hanging from his neck, and wondered where *this* talisman had come from. As soon as the thought formed, the image of stars changed again, as it swept him across the galaxy in a different direction.

The Necklace from Harleem

Chapter 49 - The gathering

Far-fel descended to the valley floor. Occasionally he looked back at the secluded spot that housed the Cave. Now things were clear. Clearer than he ever thought possible. During his life, he had always been valued and readily chosen for difficult assignments. His exceptional skills rendered him indispensable. But that had all changed after his experience with the Necklace and its nemesis, the Crystal Amulet. Now he was more ... and yet he was less.

More, because he had gained knowledge from bitter experience, regarding the seductive dark power of the Necklace and its enormous threat to the people of Ankoletia. Less, because he realized so clearly, that his success and that of the people, depended on the power of the Cave, not his own skill. He had much to think about as he resumed his journey to find Finn.

For two days, nineteen Specialist Trackers, including Axion and Jokta, discussed the desperate situation of their nation, in a large one-room cabin. In all their history, since the Great War, there had never been a time like the present. Society was unravelling, and they could only guess at the true extent of the threat ... within and without.

With Far-fel, they would be twenty. But only twenty Specialists in the face of a maelstrom of deceit and ambition did not seem enough. The El-Bhat were well-organized and had many allies. The Head of Storlenian government was compromised and even Axion was unsure of the alliances Craslin might already have in place.

On the positive side, the Trackers still held Arborville and access to Olleti. This was important to the support of the cleansing effort, but how secure was Arborville? The Head Guild Master and his Assistant had died together only recently, ambushed by El-Bhat.

Border Pass was retaken, another positive sign, and there were rumours of the formation of a new Tinker's Guild, headed by those who fought side by side with Trackers at Border Pass. Tinkers had always been a scourge to the El-Bhat but had remained aloof and uncooperative to mainstream society. Maybe that was about to change. This new Guild held out the promise of uniting all Tinkers in a combined front, against their common enemies. And surprisingly, they had brought to market, a superior wagon fitted with advanced technology ... that mystified everyone!

"In summary," Finn offered, "the Fates have not abandoned us, but the task is formidable. We must be careful. We cannot afford a misstep."

"Well said," boomed a voice from the open door. All turned to behold Far-fel, his frame filling the doorway.

"Glad to see you're still alive," Finn gave the usual greeting.

Far-fel scanned the room. It was obvious that all the Specialists were gathered, including the unusual addition of two outsiders.

"Finn my brother, why have you gathered us? And why do these two men sit among us," he added, glancing towards Axion and Jokta.

"Our nation is at a crisis, and we must decide how best to move forward." Finn nodded towards Axion. "This is the Head Guild Master of Planning and Development at Qar-ana. He has provided us with invaluable information and insight as to the breadth and depth of the situation. He has had to flee the Assassin's plot put forward by his own trusted Assistant. Beside him is Jokta, a retired Tracker who has brought Axion safely to us despite the continued efforts of an Assassin ... a Butler."

One of the Specialists that knew Far-fel best, spoke up. "Does your return mean we can stop sending more Specialists to die at the hand of the Silent Reaper?" He was grinning from ear to ear. He had been confident that Far-fel would succeed where three Specialists had failed. Far-fel returned a tired grin to his friend.

"Tell us about the Silent Reaper," Finn suggested. He was convinced that Far-fel might share surprises that would help explain their national dilemma. "I would invite you in to sit, to pamper your weary body, but as you can see, there is no room." The men chuckled.

Far-fel parried, "I'm fine ... running from Pechora to here in less than two weeks has only limbered me up!" The men roared in approval.

When the noise died down, Far-fel began.

"His name was Glickin, Head Guild Master of the Financing Guild in the town of Pirtelin. Finn, you were right about him, he indeed did have an ancient artefact that gave him an enormous advantage. He is now dead." Words of recognition for a job well done echoed briefly around the cabin.

The Necklace from Harleem

"If you throw me that artefact, I will bury it in the usual place." Finn extended his hand for the catch, but Far-fel did not open his bag.

"It's complicated," Far-fel said.

"Then why don't you un-complicate it for us," Finn suggested, concerned that such a powerful talisman was still 'at-large'.

"As you have probably guessed, the real target wasn't the Silent Reaper, it was the artefact. *The Necklace* has the power to take life from an unsuspecting victim and transfer it to the holder of this strange Device, thereby restoring him to a youthful state every time he uses it."

"It makes you wonder how old the Silent Reaper actually was," Finn added thoughtfully.

Far-fel let the question remain unanswered and continued. "The Necklace was made of a gold-like material with six Medallions, each with different powers. In the middle of the Necklace was a cradle that held a dark green stone when not in use. The *owner* of the Necklace tricks his victim into holding the stone and depending on which Medallion he touches, a part of the victim would flow to the Silent Reaper. Could be his youth, or what he knows, and so on."

Finn was puzzled. His men were adept at defending themselves against such schemes. "So, he just threw you this green stone and you caught it?" an unbelieving Finn asked.

Far-fel paused before responding. "You have to experience the power of this Necklace to understand how easily it can seduce even a Specialist." What Far-fel said made sense. Everyone remembered the three Specialists who never returned from the same assignment.

"Truly unfortunate that you don't have it with you," Finn declared, inviting Far-fel to explain why he didn't, since he obviously defeated the Silent Reaper.

"The Silent Reaper had already *transferred* much of my life to the green stone, before I managed to kill him. I needed to use the Necklace to get my life back ... or I wouldn't be here."

"Between a fence and a fox," one of the Specialists offered.

"Yes ... sounds like an impossible situation," Finn added, surprised that Far-fel was there to tell the story.

"You're right, I shouldn't be here," Far-fel agreed. "Without the Necklace, I knew I was a dead man. Staying alive meant I needed to use it. And that was my fatal mistake. Because living with the Necklace is worse than death! I had assumed that it was only an instrument. But it is much more than that. It behaves like ... it's alive!

Once I used the Necklace, I was trapped. It carefully ... and slowly ... made me a slave to its power."

Around the room, the light-heartedness had been replaced with sober reflection.

"As soon as I had my life back, I felt the urge to head west. Without realizing it, the Necklace was leading me to its lair in Pechora. Specifically, to the Tracking Guild!" Far-fel added, his words laced with venom. Hushed murmurs went around the room.

"How ... did you manage to escape?" Finn quietly asked, hardly believing that anyone could have walked out of the situation that Far-fel described.

Far-fel removed the chain from around his neck and held the twirling Amulet to the side. The sunlight streaming through the door caught the crystal Talisman and sent rainbows of shattered light into the room. The men stared, anxious to hear the rest of the story.

"When I arrived in Pechora, my beleaguered spirit, destitute and almost in ruin from the demands of the Necklace, became aware of another power. I was attracted to this beacon ... but the demon within me was repulsed. It fought me every step of the way. But the closer I got to this *other* power, the stronger my own will became."

"So why would the Necklace take you to Pechora in the first place?" Finn interjected.

"It was looking for a new home, where darkness could cast a blanket of secrecy over its black works. I believe that it would have *never* taken me there, if it knew that this Amulet hung behind locked doors."

"Any idea why the Amulet was there or where it came from?" Finn probed.

Far-fel hesitated. He was willing to talk about the Amulet but not the Cave. He looked at the spinning stone. "Not exactly. But this power ... is above the Necklace, and fortunately, it can never be used for evil purposes. The fact that it was locked away, instead of hanging from someone's neck, suggests that someone found, or stole this Talisman ... and then quickly realized that its response is selective. It must have become a threat and its power secured away."

"Perhaps it was the goal of this Necklace to find a particular individual," Finn offered. "Why do you assume that the entire Tracking Guild is under suspicion?"

"When I entered the Guild, the Assistant led me to the Guild Master's office. Right away I felt the power of the Crystal pulling me towards a locked room. When I found it, my first impulse was to take it in my hand, and as soon as I did, it purged me in an instant, of the dark power that had held me bound. In the very moment I was healed, men appeared on the balconies above the room with bows drawn ... ready to kill me. At most, my behaviour was only a breach of protocol."

"Yes ... their reaction tells us they wanted to keep that Crystal hidden," Finn conceded. "Can you tell us anything else about this Amulet?"

Far-fel looked around the room, "As far as I can tell, I have been invited to use its power."

A few surprised murmurs travelled around the room.

As soon as it was quiet again, Finn continued. "The enemy is vast ... and there are but few of us. Perhaps finding the Crystal is not a coincidence?"

"You are right. This is no coincidence. In fact, *both* instruments have been waiting for us ... to respond," Far-fel confirmed.

"By *waiting*, you mean since the time before the Great War, when these artefacts were more common?" Axion suggested.

"No," Far-fel advised the group. "This power is beyond anything our race has ever developed."

A silent hush returned as the significance of Far-fel's declaration was considered.

"You mean *both* talismans," Axion continued, "must be ... from somewhere else."

Far-fel was nodding yes, then added, "Once you have understood this, it helps you realize how high the stakes are in this conflict."

"If you have access to this power," Axion was curious, "does it tell you what we ought to do? Is there some sort of plan?"

Everyone in the room leaned forward, ever so slightly, anxious to hear how Far-fel's words would address the concerns they had carefully discussed the past two days.

"The Tinkers have begun to unite. This is no coincidence. They were the ones who first helped rebuild our society after the Great War. They have set up a Guild at Arborville. We need to go there."

Far-fel looked at Finn. Was he willing to accept the guidance of the Amulet?

Finn's response was immediate. "As always, we will travel separately. We meet in Arborville. Far-fel, you will come with me. We will assist Jokta in keeping the Butler away from the Guild Master. The wagon is to be packed with weapons ... including armour."

313

The Specialists regarded one another. Armour was only used when facing a formidable enemy.

After everyone was gone, Finn asked Far-fel, "You're absolutely sure we can trust this artefact of yours?"

"If you had seen and experienced what I have ... you wouldn't ask the question."

"Humour me."

"The Amulet took me to a Cave that was filled with treasures from another world. Yes, I am sure. As sure as I know I am alive."

Finn slung his bag over his shoulder. "Alright, let's get going."

Chapter 50 - The three-day death

Axion and Jokta rode in the wagon, while Finn and Far-fel ran ahead through the woods, checking for signs of the Butler. By mid-morning, the two Specialists stopped for a short rest in a clearing. "Can the Amulet tell you if there's danger about?" Finn asked after drinking from his water skin.

"Do you mean ... why do we bother to check the forest, when all I have to do is ask?"

Finn liked how Far-Fel answered his question with one that answered it. "I guess if this Amulet is as smart as you say it is," Finn began, "it wouldn't want to spoil us at the very time it's trying to build us into something better."

Finn's insightful comment made Far-fel think of something he hadn't considered. "Finn ... it feels strange wearing it ... when it ought to be you. If something should ever happen to me ..."

"Far-fel. I wouldn't know what to do with it. Best plan for me is to keep you alive!"

Entering the sleepy town of Qolton, the foursome reunited and stopped at the stable yards to feed the horses and buy some supplies. Axion remembered a question that had intrigued him. "Why did you insist that your Group travel separately? It would seem to me that force in numbers would serve us better?"

"In some circumstances, this is true. But what you are not considering is the risk of losing a significant number of the Specialist Group at once. It's also human nature to relax one's guard when someone is watching your back."

They were sitting at dinner waiting for their meals when Axion quietly asked, "Do you think the Butler will continue to pursue me with so many Specialists protecting me?"

"Last time we were called in to protect someone from a Butler, I had to send three of my men to track him down. It was the only way we could stop him. And *him* turned out to be *her*." Finn gave a knowing look at his companion. "Far-fel was the Specialist that took her down."

Axion spotted the serving maid coming towards him. "I'm looking forward to this meal. First decent one in many days," he added as she laid the plate in front of him.

Finn watched the serving maid carefully while she set their bowls of stew on the table. He caught her eye and she smiled at him, then at Far-fel, but she wouldn't look at Axion. "Put your spoon down," Finn said quietly after the maid had left their table.

Far-fel understood immediately and said to Axion, "Trade me bowls." He slid his hand under the bottom of Axion's bowl to check for the expected signature. Something sticky held it to the bottom. "If Axion had collapsed, the Butler would have us know that he was the one responsible," Far-fel stated as he removed the silver calling card and discreetly passed it to Finn.

"He can't be far," Finn exclaimed in hushed tones. "You need to settle this now," he said, as he passed the card back to Far-fel.

"This will take me right to him," Far-fel announced. He arose holding the silver calling card in one hand and the hidden Amulet in the other. He allowed the words *I need to find this man*, pass across his mind. With eyes closed, he clearly saw where the Butler was. With eyes open, he headed for the kitchen, with a grin of triumph. Far-fel paused at the kitchen door window and motioned for Finn to join him. The disguise was perfect ... but wasted. The Butler was about to die. "He's the cook in the kitchen," he whispered. "Guard this door. I will bar the back door." Entering the room, Far-fel watched the staff from the corner of his eye as he headed quickly for the back door. By the time the door was secure, all the staff, except for the cook, were staring at Far-fel. "All of you need to leave now," he said firmly.

The cook didn't even look in his direction ... until the others had left. "How did you know I was in the kitchen?" The curious Butler asked.

Far-fel took a few steps closer. "You have a gift for disguises," he said in admiration as he withdrew his knife.

The Butler cocked his head to the side, "You didn't answer my question. I would like to know before I kill you."

Suddenly the kitchen door opened, and another Tracker came in.

"This just isn't my day," the Butler exclaimed and then he threw a meat cleaver and a knife, in the direction of Far-fel.

Far-fel dodged the cleaver and deflected the knife.

The Assassin grabbed two large knives, pushed the preparation table towards Far-fel, and rushed Finn. The blades became a blur. The Butler and Finn attacked each other ferociously. They moved back and forth as the clinking of metal resounded off kitchen walls, each warrior trying to gain an advantage.

Far-fel could do little more than watch. The intensity of the conflict demanded that he stay out of it.

Serving trays and smaller tables went flying as the two men requisitioned space around themselves, to avoid losing a path of retreat.

Finn was the first to draw blood. But Far-fel admitted it was meaningless, considering the boundless energy and skill of both men. He should've noticed the warmth of the Amulet beneath his shirt, but he didn't. Far-fel was too busy watching the fight. Suddenly Light burst forth with such power that his shirt glowed. He quickly retrieved the gem and held it in his hand. He knew the response from the Amulet was about the Butler! He shouted "Stop!" to the two men.

They responded with a quick glance ... then paused as they stared at Far-fel, holding the Amulet. Its Light exploding into the room between the cracks of his fingers!

Finn was ready to reengage, but the Butler was mesmerized ... and puzzled to see that such a power even existed. He forgot all about Finn.

Far-fel took advantage of the Butler's hesitation and said, "You don't need to die today. The power of the Crystal is extending an invitation to you. You are *needed* to assist us, in a conflict that threatens to destroy our world."

"What is this power you hold?" The Butler asked, ignoring Far-fel's invitation. "You must tell me ... I can feel it as I stand here!"

Far-fel extended the Amulet towards the Assassin, like a torch of freedom. "What is it you don't understand," he asked. "You are being invited by the greatest power in this world to change your life and join us. If you do not, we will kill you. Is that clear?"

"Words are only words," the Butler retorted, frustrated that he wouldn't answer his questions. "If I agree, how do you know I won't kill you in your sleep?" He asked, pushing Far-fel to answer his questions.

The Light of the Amulet began to fade, increasing Far-fel's concern for the Assassin. "You only need to give us your word," he replied anxiously. "The Amulet will know if you lie. And if you lie, it will kill you. What else do you need to know?"

"Can anyone use this Amulet?"

"No. If you were to try ... it would be very unpleasant! *Will you join us?*" An impatient Far-fell shouted.

"It's that simple? All I have to say is *yes?*" The Butler laid his knife on the counter.

Far-fel walked slowly towards the Butler. Then he extended his arm, and ordered, "place your hand over mine, and say you will join us. If it's a lie, the power of the Amulet will kill you on the spot. But if you speak the truth, it will ... *prepare you* for this assignment."

After an agonizingly long pause, the Butler took the step that closed the space between them and grabbed Far-fel's hand. The Amulet, immediately flared back to life when the Assassin's hand covered Far-fel's.

A cry of pain was heard by everyone in the Inn. The Butler sank to his knees. Far-fel used his free hand to secure the Assassin's grip. He knew the Butler mustn't let go until the *preparation* was over. Light coursed through the Butler's quivering body. Moments later, as the pain increased to intolerable levels, the Butler tried to withdraw his hand as his body thrashed about. But Far-fel dropped and pinned their joined hands to the floor, leaning his full weight and strength against the Butler's struggle.

The cries of agony continued so long, Finn doubted the Butler would still be alive at the end of it. Worried that concerned travellers might want to enter the kitchen, Finn quickly placed himself on the other side of the door.

Eventually the Assassin succumbed to the endless pain, lying lifeless on the floor. Finn, who had occasionally looked through the circular window, saw the collapsed Butler. He entered. "Is he dead?" He fully expected that he was.

"No. He has entered the last and longest stage of his preparation. I need to stay here. Why don't you take Axion up to the room, once the guests are all gone."

In the morning, Finn found them still on the floor, Far-fel looking remarkably refreshed. "Still at it?" He asked, completely surprised.

Far-fel looked down at the Butler who hadn't moved all night. "We are ready to go. He can spend the rest of his preparation in the back of our wagon." Far-fel threw him over his shoulder and walked out of the Inn.

For three days, they kept the body under a blanket in the back of the wagon. The body lay there as if it were dead. It never moved.

At the end of the third day, while they sat at the campfire eating a hot meal, they heard a voice from behind.

"You cannot imagine how good that smells. I am so hungry!"

They all turned to see the Butler walking towards them. Far-fel greeted him with a large grin, "You assume that there's some left! We didn't save any ... thought you were dead!" The other two laughed.

"There must be something I can eat," the Butler pleaded. "Potato peels ... or anything you don't want to finish?"

Finn pointed at the pot, "You'll find lots in there."

They grinned at one another, amused at the Butler's changed attitude.

The Butler didn't say a word until he had licked the pot clean. Once done he looked up at Far-fel and said, "I don't remember a thing after I grabbed your hand. What happened?"

"Perhaps you know that better than any one of us," Far-fel suggested.

The Butler frowned and thought for a while. "Nope. I really cannot remember a thing." He looked at the other two, hoping that someone could tell him more than Far-fel had.

"You don't feel any different?" Finn asked, "because you thrashed in pain in that kitchen for a long time. For the last three days you haven't moved, as you lay in the back of that wagon."

"I guess that's why I feel hungry as a bear ... that just woke from a winters' sleep."

Far-fel looked steadily at the Butler. It was time he understood the change.

"Butler, now that you're rested and fed ... I have an assignment for you. I need you to kill someone for us."

Aram-Dentee sat there and stared back at Far-fel for a long time, and finally said, "Yes, you're right, I do feel different. I will have to refuse your request."

"Thought you might say that," Far-fel replied with approval.

"But ... I have a question," the Butler said with furrowed brows. "Before the glowing stone in the kitchen ... I knew who I was, but now ... who am I?"

Far-fel noticed that Axion was deep in thought. "Why don't *you* answer that one," he suggested to the Guild Master.

It felt strange to Axion that he was asked to help the Assassin. Someone who wanted to kill him. Eventually he looked over at the Butler. "Perhaps it's easier to comment on who you are not," the Guild Master offered. "For one thing, you aren't an Assassin anymore."

Axion watched while the Butler considered his remark. "And as far as who you are," Axion continued, "I guess with your old life left behind, you can choose to be anyone you want to be. How about my new Assistant?"

Aram-Dentee laughed, "A true twist of fate! I'm about to replace the man who hired me."

"What's so funny?" Axion asked.

"Butler's have only two rules. Never get caught ... and *never* take the position of the man who hired you."

"Looks like it's official. You're expelled from the Butler Guild!" Jokta laughed.

The ex-Assassin nodded solemnly towards the Guild master. "From Assassin ... to Assistant of the most powerful man in Storlenia. Not something I deserve."

"Looks like the Fates think otherwise," Jokta observed, thinking that this was probably the first time a Butler had changed profession.

Looking at the others, the Butler introduced himself, "My name is Aram-Dentee. What are your names?"

"Finn."

"Far-fel."

"Jokta."

After the introductions, his eyes locked on Far-fel. "I need to say something." He caught a glimpse of the chain that he was sure held the Stone hidden under his shirt. "I Don't know who you are, or how you came to have that Stone ... but ... I'm grateful for what you did."

"I think you've forgotten that I was ready to kill you," Far-fel grunted.

The Butler grinned, knowing it wouldn't have been so easy for *anyone* to kill him. "Tell me about the Stone. Tell me how you use its power."

"You can't use the talisman like you would a weapon ... or a tool. Because it's intelligent."

"I see. Is that why you said it selected me?" He remembered Far-fel saying, *You are needed to assist us in a conflict that threatens to destroy our world.*

"I have no idea why you were chosen. I suppose others would say that you have talents it wanted to recruit, and maybe that's right. Either way, the Stone knows ... everything," Far-fel clarified.

Aram-Dentee suddenly realized how they knew he was in the kitchen. "The Stone told you I was in the kitchen."

"Well ... I asked," Far-fel volunteered.

"You only have to ask?" The ex-Butler said in amazement.

"Well ... if I ask for something that it *can* honour, then ... the next thing I know, I am walking into a kitchen."

Aram-Dentee nodded that he understood. "How long have you had this Amulet?"

"For a week ... but it's been a *long* week."

"And it's been a long day. See you in the morning," Finn declared, as he strolled to his bedroll.

The next morning, while they gathered their equipment, Aram-Dentee noticed Jokta leaving. "Where is he going?" he asked Axion.

"He will be our ears and eyes for what happens in Qar-ana. I am sure Craslin is *very* busy."

The ex-Butler turned to Far-fel. "Our little force is obviously heading somewhere ... as part of our assignment to save the world. Do we have a plan? Besides using the Stone to force our enemies to join us ... one at a time ... like me."

Far-fel smiled. "We are heading for Arborville to join up with Tinkers."

Surprised, Aram-Dentee paused and asked, "You think they're ready to integrate?"

The Tracker shook his head once. "I know it sounds strange. But that's where we are supposed to go. Something unusual has been happening among the Tinkers. They have even started their own Guild."

Aram-Dentee jumped up into the wagon beside Axion, while Finn and Far-fel headed down the road on foot. "Of course, the Stone must be right," the Assistant commented, "but still, it's strange to me that Tinkers were chosen!"

"Welcome to a changing world," Axion responded, flicking the reins.

Chapter 51 - The Stones meet

Passing by the clothing shops of Arborville, Aram-Dentee lamented, "I miss my clothes!"

"Do you wish to return to dressing like a Butler?" Axion asked, not convinced that the image would settle well, with being his new Assistant.

"No ... but the Butler Guild bred me to appreciate the finer things of life."

"Yes, I suppose we can't have you dressed like a cook either. What do you have in mind?"

"I would prefer to be *dressed* prior to our meeting with the Tinkers." He cast a hopeful glance at Axion.

Axion was bemused. How different the new Aram-Dentee was from either his old self ... or Craslin! "Perhaps we ought to give you a new name," he said changing the subject.

"But why?" protested Aram-Dentee.

"It feels strange to call you by your *old* name, it ..."

"I know ... it conjures up memories of barely escaping with your life. But I like my name. Beside my taste for finer things, it's the only part of my old life I cherish."

"Okay," reflected Axion, "how about Aram-Dentee II?"

The ex-butler smiled. "That's perfect, and I think I've just spotted the clothing shop I want to visit."

When the Specialists first arrived, they were not certain they had found the Tinker Guild, but they were assured by people on the street, that it was. Far-fel had told them that the Tinkers had *started* a Guild. And everyone expected to see the usual itinerant wagons and tents. Instead, there were houses, administration buildings, blacksmith shops, and yards for manufacturing wagons. They were taken from the front gates to the head office, where they met Braddock. Only Finn and Far-fel entered. Braddock was advised that there were another eighteen Trackers waiting outside. After the exchange of names, Finn got right down to business.

"We have come from the Crestal Mountain area. We are few, but we all have Specialist training. We are here because we were recently visited by Axion, the Head Guild Master of the Planning and Development Guild at Qar-ana."

Braddock wore an expression of surprise but waited for Finn to finish.

"His Assistant paid a Butler to assassinate him. And he has advised us of the El-Bhat infiltration that has successfully moved all the way north to Pechora. In fact, inside the Pechora *Tracking* Guild," Finn paused for affect.

Braddock slowly walked from behind his desk. He faced the Leader of the Specialists and with eyes locked onto his, he quietly asked, "Are you saying that the Pechora Tracking Guild, has been compromised similar to Arborville?"

"Worse. We have reason to believe that the entire Guild is run by the Quorum."

Braddock's thoughts went to the people that had travelled to the Pechora Tracking Guild in good faith. Pechinin, Mitrock, Protas, Bru-ell his trusted Assistant, and Urshen's family, were all on that list. Then there was his future son-in-law Urshen and his small group of Tracker bodyguards. Finally, he had watched as Zephra, Benekee, and his sister headed there to find Urshen. Fortunately he knew *they* were in Qar-ana. But what about everyone else? The information helped to explain the delays that he had tried to justify. He wanted to rush out, find Coustin, and organize a contingent of Tinkers to head north to find Zephra and Urshen. Instead he asked, "Where's Axion?"

"The Head Guild Master and his new Assistant are not far behind. They will be here shortly. We came ahead because the men were anxious to see the new Tinker Guild."

"Why have you come to me? Is it about the wagons I sent to Qar-ana?" But he knew it wasn't. 'No,' he thought, 'anything that involves Urshen and Zephra, is going to be a tale of trouble.'

"The group of Trackers waiting outside are ... *different* than conventional Trackers," Finn began. "We specialize in taking on difficult and oftentimes extremely dangerous assignments. We refer to ourselves as *Specialists*." Finn turned to Far-fel, inviting him to continue.

"Recently I was assigned to track down a criminal that we referred to as the Silent Reaper. I was preceded by three Specialists who died trying to bring him to justice. This is *extremely* uncommon because of our training ... and abilities. We had concluded for some time that he must have some special advantage. Perhaps an ancient artefact. This was partly true. The artefact turned out to be a gold-like Necklace, and it is extremely powerful. He used it to extend his life ... among other things."

Far-fel paused, allowing Braddock to comment.

The reference to a talisman of evil was not a total surprise to Braddock. Unwelcome news for sure, but the world was changing. Perhaps it was part of the Legend of Balance. He simply nodded for the Tracker to continue.

"I successfully killed the Reaper, but I lost my life to the Necklace." Far-fel looked at Finn, seeking confirmation for what he was about to say. Finn nodded as he knew he would.

"I wouldn't be here except for a Crystal Amulet. It gave me back my life. And it told me to seek your help. This Amulet has the power to defeat the Necklace and ..."

"I am no stranger to Amulets with power," Braddock interrupted. "Since the Great War, such an Amulet has been passed down for generations amongst the Tinkers. It is currently worn by my daughter."

Far-fel was immediately interested. "Is your daughter here? Can I talk to her about her Amulet?"

"Unfortunately ..." Braddock's gaze went to the maps on the top of his desk, "she left for ... Pechora. But is now in Qar-ana." He couldn't think of Zephra right then, so he asked, "Is the Amulet with you?"

Far-fel was surprised at the direction the conversation had taken, but he knew they needed to recruit the Tinkers, so he slowly reached for the chain.

Braddock stared at the crystal stone attached to an intricate and beautiful silver clasp, and exclaimed, "It's ... *exactly* like Urshen's Amulet! Where did you get it?"

Far-fel was watching it spin the sunlight around the room. "It was locked up in the storage room at the Pechora Tracking Guild." He looked back at Braddock. "Who is Urshen?" he asked, anxious to know more about the previous owner of the Stone.

Suddenly creaky hinges announced another visitor. All eyes turned to see who had just entered.

"That's *not* the question we should be asking right now," Ranoof said, standing in the doorway. Ranoof walked rapidly towards Braddock ... while holding a *glowing* Amulet, with outstretched arm.

With relief, he set the talisman on Braddock's table. "We *should* be asking ... why is this Amulet glowing with the fierceness of the sun! Zephra asked me to bring this to you," he explained, glad to be finished his task.

Far-fel could feel the warmth of his own Amulet, glowing in his hand. He knew it was responding to the glowing Amulet brought by the Tracker. And he knew what to do.

He picked it up with his free hand, closed his eyes ... and collapsed to the floor.

Chapter 52 - Benekee's plan

Previously. At the time the Specialist group headed west to Arborville, and Ranoof began his journey to deliver the re-assembled Amulet to Braddock, Benekee used the power of the distant Amulet carried by Ranoof, to protect himself from the beating that left him close to dead.

After healing himself on the inside, Benekee walked to the window and stared up at the moon. He had never paid much attention before to its battered surface. His face probably resembled the white orb in the night sky.

Sometime earlier

Before he invoked the power of the Tree of Life to heal his body, Benekee knew he must think carefully about his situation. Someone was obviously trying to save his life. But to his surprise he found himself in Craslin's office. It was all very odd. Why would Craslin make such a fuss over Benekee?

Only a short while ago, he had sent him to a Guild Prison cell. Especially odd, was the fact that the three men who stole the Brass Sling, whom he saw in the Guild Master's office, *were the ones who tried to beat him to death.* From the first time Benekee visited Qarana, along with his Redemption Guild Master, he had known that Craslin was a man who seized opportunities, with no regard as to how this might affect others. If his office had been rearranged to save Benekee's life, then Craslin must need something from Benekee. Something *exceptionally* valuable. Perhaps it had something to do with his interest in Zephra ... or the Brass Sling ... or both. Or maybe this was all more complicated than Benekee would ever understand. Regardless, he needed to know what to do. And he preferred to ask the Amulet.

"Benekee ... Benekee" the old woman called softly while shaking him.

Benekee opened his eyes. The first thing he saw was the night sky above, and an old woman standing beside him. "Oh, it's you," he exclaimed, pleased that she was there. "Why have you come?"

"Because you know something," she replied with an eager smile.

Benekee tried to imagine what that might have been. Puzzled he said, "I'm afraid you will have to help me with that one."

"You know ... that when all else fails ... you can ask, and I will come." She took his hand gently in hers and looked deeply into his eyes. Immediately he tumbled into another time and place.

His head jerked towards a door that burst open, hanging shattered on its hinges. Men with drawn swords entered. They slowly approached an old woman with white hair so long, it almost touched the floor. She was holding a talisman. "We have orders to leave with your Amulet and throw it into the East Sea."

'They have come for her Amulet!' a panic stricken Benekee thought. "You mustn't give them the Amulet," he screamed at her, but nobody paid him any attention. He watched in horror when she agreed to give them what they wanted. He moved closer to the old woman, knowing that he needed to somehow stop her from making this huge mistake! "You have the power of the Amulet ... you can stop these men," he insisted. Again, she paid him no attention. It was now clear. He was powerless to say or do anything. He was not part of this world. Stunned, he watched the bright sword come crashing down on the Amulet, shattering it into several pieces. He wanted to look away. It was unbearable to watch her gather up the shards. But he felt responsible to see it through. Until the broken Amulet was finally taken away. He wrung his hands while her quick movements gathered the broken pieces into a leather pouch ... except one! Did he see what he thought he saw! Was the largest piece safely tucked away in her billowing sleeve?

She handed The Commander the pouch.

As soon as they were gone, she allowed herself a little smile.

Like waking from a dream, Benekee was back on the Medical Guild table with an insight to the question ... *what should he do?*

The white-haired woman could have sent the soldiers to their early graves ... but she didn't. She could have confused their minds, believing they were leaving with the talisman ... but she didn't. Because ... either of those actions, and many other possibilities, would have only brought more soldiers back to hunt her down. And eventually the Talisman would have been lost ... and many men, who were only following orders, would have died.

What she did do ... was to use her imagination to produce a plan, which would be acceptable to the Tree of Life.

He stared at the ceiling a long time before he knew what he wanted to do. He invoked the healing power to heal himself on the inside, but not on the outside. This way, everyone would think he was recovering because of their expert care. And because he was whole again on the inside, he was free to determine when he would leave the confines of the Healing Table. And, most important of all, there would be no risk of exposing his Gift. To access the power of the Tree of Life ... no matter where he was and without the need to hold the Amulet!

Finished with his healing, he sat up, walked to the window, and stared at the battered moon with his one good eye.

Chapter 53 - The apple of his eye

Zephra finished the last page. She leaned back with a sigh of satisfaction and turned over the book to read the title again, *The economics of community living.*

She smiled. She had never imagined herself reading beyond the four designated Tinker books, that all young Tinkers were to read as part of their *right to passage.* Her attention was suddenly diverted when she heard soft footsteps approaching. It was Yaneek, all smiles.

"Craslin has sent me. He was wondering if you wanted to be there when they remove the bandages?"

Zephra returned the smile, quietly rushed to Yaneek, and threw her arms around her. "I'm so happy for you and Benekee," she whispered. "And of course I want to be there," she added as she pushed away, wanting to study Yaneek's happy face. The gloominess of Benekee's brush with death, and his slow recovery, had hovered over the daily activities inside the Guild for far too long. Zephra cupped Yaneek's face in her hands. "I am so glad this day has finally come." Her smile faded as she stared into those beautiful green eyes. "Have you considered what you might see under the bandages? Maybe it's better to hear my report before ..."

Yaneek interrupted. "I have always wanted to be more like you. So ... I will be there when the bandages come off."

When they entered the room, Craslin was standing beside Benekee's right shoulder. He turned and motioned for the two women to come and stand on the opposite side of the Healing Table. "Our efforts have been rewarded. Benekee has asked that we remove the bandages. He is ready for the final stage of his Healing."

The two women looked at each other. Yaneek slid a hand into Zephra's.

Craslin nodded towards the Healer who had been standing off to the side. He approached and with expert care removed the mask that had concealed, for many weeks, the gruesome result of Benekee's beating. Everyone held their breath as the Healer moved away to allow everyone to see.

Benekee surveyed the room with his one good eye. He was pleased to finally see his sister.

Yaneek squeezed Zephra's hand tight to remind herself that she wanted to be strong ... like her. She smiled at Benekee but wanted to run away in tears. It was still much worse than she had imagined.

Craslin laid a hand on Benekee's arm. "We are all pleased that you have recovered so well." Hoping to allay the awkwardness of the moment, he said to the group, "I have some business to attend to." He turned to Zephra. "Please stay as long you wish." He wanted the two women to feel free to express themselves in private. Zephra gave him a smile of appreciation and then he left.

Benekee could see that both women struggled to look at his damaged eye. He turned to the Healer. "Do you have something that could help assist the healing of my eye?"

The Healer nodded and left the room to retrieve the drops.

"I guess I don't look so good," Benekee said, with a twisted smile, noticing Yaneek's teary eyes. "You wait sis, those drops will work just fine. Soon this one-eyed bandit will be free to leave this bed ... and be as good as new!"

And to everyone's surprise, within a few weeks, Benekee *was* as good as new ... almost. He could even see out of his damaged, badly scarred eye. Surprising even the Healers.

At least he was able to leave the Healing Table. Although they were reluctant to let him walk without a cane. So, he gladly accepted it, knowing it would help avoid suspicion from an abnormal sudden recovery.

Craslin looked on as the Healer examined Benekee one last time, before signing the release papers. 'It's a shame that his face will remain so scarred,' he thought. 'He was such a nice looking young lad.'

As soon as the Healer was gone, Craslin invited Benekee to his desk. After a long pause, Craslin started. "I have to confess, I am glad that the ordeal of watching over you is finally over. Not just to see you alive and well, but I have been itching to get back to work for some time." He smiled at Benekee ... for the first time ever.

During his recovery, Benekee was more awake than anyone ever knew and was able to observe the Guild Master, especially when Craslin was caring for him late into the night. Lying on the Healing Bed, he was the perfect spy. Always there but ignored as though he was invisible.

He knew about Bernado, and Craslin's instructions to have him expand the Guild Militia to fifty thousand strong. He knew about the intrigue and suspicions that took place between them, at least from Craslin's viewpoint. He also knew of the plan to expand the capabilities of the Brass Sling ... once Benekee was restored to health. And how this would ensure a complete conquest of the El-Bhat and the Shaksbah government.

Benekee knew so much about Craslin! 'If you knew what I know ... I would not live another day,' Benekee thought as he looked at a smiling Craslin.

"Perhaps you feel the same way I do ... anxious to do something?" Craslin suggested. "It's been a long time since we carried your battered body from my prison cell," he smiled again as though it was all a mistake.

It was interesting to Benekee that Craslin never took any credit for his involvement as one of the Carers. While he was still in his pretended coma, Benekee saw a part of Craslin that was hidden to others. The part where he was genuinely interested in his recovery. Of course, it was critical for expanding the effectiveness of the Brass Sling. But it was more than that. Every night when the Guild business was done, and everyone was long gone, he would visit Benekee ... to arrange the sheets and fluff his pillow. So strange for someone like Craslin.

"Yes ... you are right." Benekee used his cane to shift his position in the chair, ever careful to showcase his apparent injuries. "I am most anxious to do anything."

The cane reminded Craslin, that Zephra would watch him to make sure he wasn't demanding too much of Benekee, while he continued to mend. He would have to find a balance between getting the new Brass Sling design finished and giving the young man adequate time to finish healing. "Your sister confided that you were the one who produced the brilliant design for the Brass Sling. I am most anxious to discuss possible improvements as soon as you are well enough."

Benekee had already decided that when this conversation came up, he would neither accept it nor refuse it. He would let Craslin bear all the responsibility for the new design. "I am concerned about what this Device is capable of in the wrong hands," Benekee admitted, "but I will do what you ask me to do."

Craslin had expected more resistance. 'Perhaps the time on the Healing Table matured the boy,' he thought. "However," Craslin clarified, "I want you to finish healing. For now, your assignment is light cleaning and dusting of the artefacts in the Gallery Room."

'Duties I'm familiar with.' Benekee thought of his time at the Redemption Guild.

"... and while you dust ... I suggest you think about the Brass Sling improvements. When you are ready, we will begin our discussions in earnest."

Benekee turned to leave his office with only one regret. He would no longer be able to spy on Craslin.

Yaneek was on her way to join Benekee in the Gallery Room when she saw two Guards escorting someone wearing a hooded Robe. It looked so much like her brother when he wore his Robe, that her mind saw Benekee ... once again a captive! 'Now where are they taking Benekee?' she wondered, as she stood frozen with fear. Seeing that Robe disappear down the hallway, sent shivers down her spine. She was fearful that somehow events had changed again, against her brother!

"Benekee," she called. "Benekee," she repeated as she rushed after them.

Everyone stopped and turned towards the anxious shouts.

Eyes wide with surprise, she said, "You're not Benekee."

On his way to a dark prison cell, Protas was glad for the intrusion. Especially from the girl standing before him. With a suppressed grin he responded, "No, I'm not ... should I be?"

"Well ... I don't know," she managed to say, as she stared at the handsome face, hiding inside the hood. "It's just that you're wearing ... a Redemption Guild Robe."

"It makes for an interesting story," Protas found himself saying. "Perhaps you would like to hear it?" he added as the Guards pulled him away.

"Yes ... I would," she replied loudly and watched as they continued down the hallway. Eventually they disappeared ... but not before the man in the Robe sent her a little smile as he went around the corner.

She stood there for a while longer, not able to forget the words, "... should I be?" And how could she not notice the playful grin that danced at the corners of his mouth as he said it. She didn't know what to think. A stranger ... probably a criminal ... and yet she remained standing as the footsteps went quiet. When the Guards returned she was still there ... but she had made up her mind. She locked her eyes on the Guard with the more agreeable face, and when he got close, she opened her mouth to speak, but he was quicker. "Tomorrow ... come tomorrow," he quietly told her as they strolled past.

It felt strange ... acting like a schoolgirl swooning over a cute face. But there was *something* she couldn't explain. She remembered Benekee's Shards ... a power that could intervene ... make you do things you normally wouldn't. Eventually she willed herself to the Gallery Room, her original destination.

She tried to visit Benekee every day ... hoping to help. Since his recovery he was more withdrawn. Not the cheerful younger brother she knew before he was thrown into the prison cell.

Zephra told her that his behaviour was normal, considering his terrifying experiences. But she felt there was something else. It was like he was carrying a terrific weight on his shoulders. But where would it come from? She took her usual deep breath before entering. Then chatted with Benekee about his work for a few minutes and smiled goodbye as she prepared to leave.

Before she could walk away, he exclaimed, "Craslin wants me to improve the design of the Brass Sling. He wants me to begin next week. The safety of all three of us probably depends on my cooperation," he added quietly.

She placed a light hand on his shoulder. She sadly remembered the day she told Craslin that it was her brother that designed the Brass Sling. "What are you going to do?"

"Whatever he asks me to do. Well ... I should get back to work." But he didn't go. Instead he smiled and added, "Yaneek, I have a feeling everything is going to work out all right. You need to worry about me less ... and thanks for coming."

For all his thoughtful kindness she smiled and told him that she would try to worry less. She left, not believing a word he had said. Of course, he was trying to comfort her. But to her it was clear. He had been thrown into a dark prison cell, forced to give up the talisman, beaten until he was unrecognizable, and now worried about their safety. Because he no longer had the Shards to help him complete Craslin's request! For now, she wanted to think about something more pleasant. Of course, that something was really ... *someone*. She laughed softly and hurried along the corridor. She found herself thinking of his face, the colour of his eyes and the playful grin that were all carefully etched into her memory. Surprisingly, she *knew* that he was attracted to her as much as she was to him! She couldn't wait!

333

But first she must tell someone, before she exploded from the excitement. She would tell Zephra. "How was *your* day? Wagons all check out?" Yaneek began, trying to show interest in her friend's activities. Desperate to tell her about *The Mystery Man*.

"Wagons were faultless." She gave Yaneek a quick smile, thinking about what she needed to tell her. "As you know, Craslin has encouraged me to read books in his Library. I spent the afternoon reading about Tinkers."

"Tinkers?" Yaneek smiled as she thought about all the things she could've read about.

"Yes, I know. It was Craslin's idea. He's very clever you know ... I expect to learn a lot from him during the remainder of our stay. How was your day?"

"Normal stuff." She decided not to tell her about *him*. She was disturbed about Zephra's attitude towards Craslin. "Just be careful," was all she said, thinking about the time Zephra had spent in Craslin's office ... working at his side.

"Careful about Craslin? Don't worry, he means well," Zephra countered. Then she got up to retrieve her book. "I really should take you to the Library. You can learn so much from books. Look at this for example. Turn to the bookmark."

Yaneek took the book and sat down for a little read. She turned to the bookmarked page. There was a note scribbled on the bookmark.

We are being watched. I am convinced that there are spies everywhere that report back to Craslin. We can use this to our advantage if we are careful. Leave the note, I'll destroy it later. Zephra

She kept reading for a while, then responded, "You're right ... it's very interesting. Let me know next time you go to the Library for a book." She smiled in gratitude as she gave the book back. As she left, Yaneek decided that when she met the Mystery Man again, she would have to let him know about the spies.

Protas had been thinking about Ee-lath, when he heard iron grinding on iron, announcing a visitor. Yaneek stepped into the open doorway, more confident than the day before. She paused momentarily, staring at Protas. He sat up, his hood was down. He seemed less playful. She supposed that a day in prison could do that. But that didn't matter ... she knew why *she* had come ... and with assurance she nodded to the Guard to close the door.

"I'm glad you came," Protas greeted Yaneek. Although he had hoped she would come, he didn't expect it. Most people wouldn't have accepted an invitation from an unknown prisoner.

"Me too. I know how lonely it can be in here. Nearly drove Benekee insane."

"Who's Benekee?" Protas suddenly needed to know.

She walked over to Protas, sat close to him on the cot, and whispered into his ear. "Benekee is my younger brother."

Pleased with the answer, he leaned towards her and whispered, "It was kind of you to visit him. But why are we whispering?"

"Spies everywhere," she whispered back. "I suggest that we continue whispering."

He liked the idea. Whispering was fun. It reminded him of the time Zephra had wrapped her arm around his neck, leaned her head into his shoulder, and murmured, *Where would I be without you Protas?* But this time, the lady wasn't his best friend's girlfriend. Their cheeks brushed as he placed his lips close to her ear. He continued, "How do you know there are spies *everywhere?*" He teased.

"I don't ... but my friend is sure of it."

He was tempted to ask her who the friend was, but he decided to wait until another day, when he felt less ... threatened. 'Hmm, haven't experienced *that* emotion for a long time,' he thought. "Want to hear my story?"

"That's why I came," she reminded him.

Her warm breath on his neck was like rain to flowers. "Before I start ... do you like dogs?"

She paused a moment, then without whispering she said, "If you have a dog who needs to be fed while you're in here, I'll be happy to do it." She was suddenly very serious, like he should've mentioned this before.

He responded to her with a whisper, mostly because he enjoyed it so much. "No ulterior motive, just wanted to know if you like dogs." But he had hardly finished his sentence when he felt a reminder. He was a Seer, and Truth was his forward path. Quickly he amended, "Correction. I do have a motive. I have a dog ... and *we* want to know."

He seemed intent on whispering, even about trivial things, so she followed his lead. "I ... *love* ... dogs," she responded.

Grinning from ear to ear, not knowing if she was teasing him or not ... and not really caring, he looked at her for a while. Leaning into her ear again, he began, "To understand my story about the Robe, you need to understand why I went to the Redemption Guild in the first place. It was for the food."

She let out a soft moan just thinking about Benekee's meals. "Benekee is such a good cook!" she exclaimed.

"But it wasn't just the food ... It was the *archives!*" Protas explained with a mischievous grin.

She burst out laughing at his humour. "You know, I don't even know your name," she told him, "and before you continue, you must tell me."

"You first," he insisted, looking into her beautiful green eyes, trying to imagine what her name might be.

As she leaned forward, his eyes drifted to those tempting lips as they whispered, "Yaneek."

The way she said it ... it sounded to Protas like the most interesting name he'd ever heard.

"Well?" She reminded him of the agreement.

"Protas. And now I must tell you about Brother Ott."

Ten minutes later he decided to bring the conversation to an end. "That's all for today."

"That can't be the whole story," she complained quietly.

"It's not, but it's the only way I can be sure you'll come back."

"Keep your stories interesting ... and I'll keep coming back," she whispered alluringly as she got up and left.

The following day, Yaneek searched for the same Guard without success. She found out that he wouldn't be on duty until the end of the week. It was hard to wait. But she didn't want to lose her right to visit ... and she didn't know how the other Guards would respond.

At the end of the week, filled with anticipation, she went to the prison after breakfast. The Guard recognized her right away. She smiled and said, "Thank you for helping me with the last visit." Like before he was sympathetic to her interest in the handsome face, but his news was grim. He was gone.

"Do you have ... any idea where he might be?" She tried not to sound desperate.

"Against policy. Sorry ma'am."

She had started to leave, then turned around with a hopeful question. "Who took him away?"

"Now there is a question I *can* answer ... Trackers. But still, you didn't hear it from me."

She hurried towards the exit where she would find Transport Wagons. But at the last moment she had an idea, that sent her back to her room.

'Seems like *everything* in Qar-ana is large and elegant,' she thought while climbing the wide steps of the Tracking Guild. At the front reception she confidently walked up to the old Tracker who sat there. "Hello ... my name is Yaneek. My brother Protas was brought here recently. I have some papers that he needs to sign. Will you tell him I'm here to see him?"

When she entered the cell, Protas arose and kissed her on the cheek. "My dear sister Yaneek ... so kind of you to come."

The kiss was unexpected, but she decided that if Protas could take advantage of a situation, so could she. She immediately threw her arms around him and exclaimed, "Protas, we miss you terribly. You must promise to write every day." There was a pause. "Mother sends her love," and then she kissed *him* on the cheek. "Mother asked about the dog. She wants to be sure ... he is all right." She added the last part quietly, wanting him to know that she was worried about Protas.

"Tell mother Sausage is fine." He gently pushed away his sister. "Before you know it ... we will be together again," he replied, mimicking her quiet finish.

"She will be pleased to hear the news," Yaneek smiled.

"Speaking of the dog, can you whistle?"

"You mean the kind of whistle that one uses to call a dog?"

"Exactly! If you ever need him, you only need to whistle – like I do – and he will come. He is very devoted to me, so why don't I teach you this whistle?"

For the next few minutes, the Tracker outside the cell patiently listened while Protas struggled to teach her how to whistle just right. Finally, his emptied patience told him he must intercede. He walked into the cell and spoke directly to Yaneek, "No ma'am, more like this," he explained, as he placed fingers carefully between his teeth.

337

It wasn't long before she had perfected the whistle, so he walked out with a reminder, "Don't forget to get those papers signed."

After Yaneek left, she spotted an available Transport Carriage at the end of the street. She hurried, hoping to catch it before he left. But halfway there, she saw a dog watching her from across the street. She stopped and for a while, watched him watching her ... thinking of Protas and ... his dog. 'Hmm,' she wondered.

She brought her fingers to her lips and whistled. The dog hesitated as though he expected someone else, so she whistled again. Slowly he began to cross the street, but when she smiled, he hurried to where she stood. "Are you Sausage?" she asked, feeling a bit embarrassed to be talking to a dog, as he circled and sniffed. Hearing his name, he immediately barked and jumped up placing his paws on her shoulders. "You can smell Protas on me, can't you?" she said while scratching behind his ears.

He gave a little bark as though he was answering. Her eye caught the collar. Nothing fancy, but there was something about it. She moved as if to touch it, but he immediately sat down before she could, and then looked up at her as though waiting for instructions.

She thought back to her visit. Protas had insisted on her whistling just right. At the time, she thought they were just having fun ... getting to know each other. But he was in prison and couldn't talk freely. Anything that was said could have been a message that she was supposed to interpret. She certainly noticed that he liked her. But the dog ... she wasn't even certain there was a dog ... until now.

"Protas said you would watch over me. Like you watch over him." She turned to see if the Transport Carriage was still there. "I need to get going, but I'll be back to see Protas." She gave him a last scratch behind the ear, then ran to catch her ride back to the Guild. As soon as she was on her way, her thoughts went back to Protas's dog. What an unexpected addition to their budding relationship. In a way, the dog was just as much a surprise as Protas. The dog was certainly intelligent. Responding to his name right away. But the most remarkable thing was the way he appeared to be *listening*. As though ...

Curious, she turned and looked out the carriage window. She half expected to see him, and indeed there he was. Following from a respectable distance. She watched him for a long time but eventually he abandoned her and diverted into a back alley. "Silly girl, to think he was watching after you," she chided herself, "after all, he's a dog."

But her mind wouldn't let go of the image of the animal rushing into the alley. Then she realized. "He's taking a short cut! He knows where I live!"

As soon as Yaneek left, Protas stretched out on his cot, hands behind his head, as he considered recent events. He was surprised at his sudden interest in Yaneek and pleased that she apparently felt the same way. But of all the places to meet a girl ... in prison. And probably on his way to another prison far away. He supposed that Bernado wanted him back in Pechora. Probably curious as a cat to know what had happened to him. He never expected to be spotted by Bernado. Especially while unloading bricks in a storage yard. At Qar-ana. What were the chances! What ever happened to the luck that followed him around his whole life? 'Maybe you can't have both. Guess it wouldn't be fair to have luck *and* the Amulet.'

He thought he heard a whistle, which meant she had contacted Sausage. The dog would have smelled him on her clothes. Probably understood that he was to *watch* her. But what would the dog do if Protas was sent away? Would he stay with her ... or follow him to Pechora? Once in Pechora, would he find Urshen still there? And if he did, what would he say about Zephra?

While leaving the Planning and Development Guild a few days ago, between two Guards, he had glanced up. And there was Zephra watching from a balcony. Dressed in fine clothes, watching him, as though he was a distant memory. That no longer belonged in her life.

Chapter 54 - Where in the world is Chitouf ?

Before Ou-Leesen left for Qar-ana, he had sent the villagers to their homes and left instructions with his men to watch for his return. "I will look for a reflection off the blade of your knives before I re-enter the Pass." But there was no signal! Ou-Leesen reigned in his horse. The Pass stood before them, seemingly welcoming the returning warriors. But he didn't feel welcome. The sharply climbing hills that formed the entrance smelled of death.

Stek rode up beside him. "Change in plans?"

"My warriors are not here. We must leave this place immediately, or we will not live to see tomorrow. Advisor lead the way!" The galloping horses left behind a trail of dust as they retreated.

Assured that they were not being followed, they gathered around and ate a simple meal. "What will you do?" asked Stek. Ee-lath's head came up, curious to hear the reply.

"Return the boy to his family ... find my men ... then deal with the Quorum."

"Simple plans are best," Stek agreed. "What do you think happened at Ou-Leesen Pass?"

"The Quorum commissioned me to build the Pass. And to assist me in this great task, they sent an Advisor to work with me. But he was no Advisor. He was their Assassin. Fortunately, Biskin saw what I could not. The Assassin was probably sending them regular messages and when they stopped, the Quorum must've sent men to investigate. While we were gone with the gold."

"Why would the Quorum want to kill you when the Pass was finished?" Stek queried.

"Because of this," Ou-Leesen responded as he held up the Dagger of Truth.

The Tracker studied the knife for a moment. "It's a fine piece of work. I bet there's a story behind that knife."

"We call it the Dagger of Truth. Until recently I thought it was lost with the now extinct tribe of Sherilin. But the Quorum had been using it for generations to achieve their dark purposes." Ou-Leesen scowled. Just holding the evil talisman made him angry. He quickly returned it to the scabbard.

"Well ... we still need to make it through the Pass. But at least it will be on our terms," Stek added with optimism.

"Advisor do you have a plan?"

Expecting that question, Stek had been preparing an answer since their retreat. "They probably spotted us. I suggest we wait a week to let them think we are searching for another Pass. Leave the horses at the town closest to the Pass. Travel by night, climb the hills up to the ridge, head south till we reach the end of the mountain range. Then down to Chitouf."

Days later they found themselves at the southern end of the Pass. Progress was slow as they worked their way down from the Ridge, swinging wide to avoid the Guards who watched the Canyon. Eventually the mountains were behind them as they hurried towards Chitouf. On a crest of the foothills that lay close to their destination, they all gathered, staring south to where Chitouf should be.

But it was gone! The houses ... the villagers ... the gold.

Protas heard the lock of the outer door click open. He sat up, ran his hand through his unkempt hair, suddenly conscious of his appearance. But when the door opened it wasn't Yaneek ... it was Bernado.

"Perhaps you were expecting someone else?" the Guild Master questioned.

In an instant, Protas's expression morphed to a blank stare. There was no fear, no anger, nothing to suggest to Bernado that there was leverage to explore. 'He mustn't know about Yaneek!' Protas reminded himself. "You'll do," was Protas's bland reply.

"I have to confess, when I sent you to the Quorum, I never expected to see you again. To meet again in such unusual circumstances suggests ... careful consideration ... wouldn't you agree?"

"I suppose," Protas replied cautiously.

"Some would say I have a duty to take you back to Pechora, where you would face your crime of murder. But Stek tells me you have skills. People with skills can be useful."

"I would *prefer* to stay in Qar-ana," Protas said slowly, "where I can be useful."

"I want the same thing," Bernado reassured him. "I will notify the Guild Master here in Qar-ana regarding our arrangement. Then I will return from Pechora within a few days to clarify your *usefulness.*"

Bernado turned to go ... then changed his mind. "I was told by someone I trust that the Quorum enjoyed your visit. But I prefer to see the evidence. Remove your Robe."

With an icy stare, Protas reluctantly stood and dropped the Robe to the floor. He slowly turned in a full circle, allowing Bernado to see every scar that embellished his naked body. Stek must have inferred that the Quorum had inflicted them.

"I'm surprised you survived." Seeing those scars, Bernado knew he could guarantee Protas's loyalty. Anyone who had descended into that black pit of pain ... could never forget.

Protas re-tied the Robe in silence; obviously unwilling to discuss the torture.

"I will have you transferred to my quarters just as soon as I find residence in Qar-ana."

Protas gave him a respectful nod. It was more than he expected. At least he would be close to Yaneek.

Bernado was pleased with his second recruit. Not really a surprise considering that Stek had thought he was useful. And Protas was more agreeable than before. Bernado had no delusions that Qar-ana would be anything but a den of deceit and conspiracy. If he were to stay alive, it would be important to surround himself with clever and useful men that were loyal to him ... in any circumstance. And the Necklace would guarantee that they would *remain* loyal.

Bernado was soon in his wagon, on his way to retrieve Urshen. First, because Kareen had entrusted him to his care. And secondly, someone like Urshen would be extremely useful to him. And, he now believed that Urshen would help him to understand the Stranger's *limits.* The most important thing of all.

It was hard to believe that someone like this Alien, who could disappear at will, harness the Green Power with bracelets, and know when and where gold would arrive in Qar-ana, could be constrained by limits! And yet ... there were things this Visitor couldn't do!

Limits! Like why Kareen couldn't just take Urshen? Like why Kareen needed to give Bernado his power to find and capture the Specialist Tracker?

Bernado had tried to find the Specialist Tracker by using the Necklace. The Green Lady had told him that the fourth Medallion could find anything or anyone the user wished to find. But he had failed. He had assumed that it was his lack of experience with the Green Power. 'But maybe not ... if Kareen himself could not find this man,' the Guild Master concluded. He looked up at the sky above and asked the most important question of all. 'How does one defeat a Colossus?' Smiling, Bernado knew the answer as he flicked the reins. 'By knowing his secrets!'

Days later in Qar-ana

The drugs had mostly worn off. But Urshen was still feeling dazed as he struggled to open his eyes. The ceiling told him he was no longer in his Pechora prison cell, but rather in someone's house. He seemed to remember being moved ... in and out of a wagon. He sat up, surveyed the room, noticed the bars on the windows and assumed the door was locked from the outside.

"Welcome to my world," a voice said from a barred doorway.

Urshen was never so happy to see a familiar face. "Protas!" he exclaimed. He tried to stand, staggered, and sat back down.

"You don't look so good," Protas observed. "But you're alive."

Urshen nodded slowly. Rubbed the drowsiness from his eyes and then turned to Protas. "You were more correct about the infiltration than I ever suspected. The tracking Guild at Pechora belongs to the El-Bhat." His eyes went to the floor as he considered his next words. "The enemy has a talisman of immense dark power," he whispered, eyes returning to the robed figure. "And ... they have my Amulet," Urshen confessed. He expected more of a reaction. At least more than a blank stare ... that eventually turned into Protas's familiar mischievous grin. Urshen rubbed his eyes again, but he saw Protas still grinning. "What are you so cheery about?" Urshen protested.

"They should have never put us together in the same place ... it will be their ruin."

Rick AW Smith hopes that you enjoyed the experience of reading
The Necklace from harleem.

To find out more about
The Caves from Balhok
Book 3 of *Seeds of Balhok,*
visit *Amazon and search Rick AW Smith*

ABOUT THE AUTHOR

Rick AW Smith, a fan of fantasy, decided it was time to contribute, while working in the cold dark reaches of northern Russia. After returning to Canada, he finished the trilogy *Seeds of Balhok*.

His ambition to write began many years ago when he was asked to stand in front of his literature class to read a couple of short stories that he had written. But like many youthful ambitions, this one needed to incubate for decades.

He always enjoyed heroes that were as mortal as anyone, but not overly reluctant. Adventure with a bit of romance that kept him turning pages well after midnight, and an ending that not only left him begging for the next book but explained the mysteries that were carefully woven through the plot.

Manufactured by Amazon.ca
Bolton, ON